Old Treacle Press

Our Man in Estepona

ISBN 978-1-913218-99-7

First published 2020 by Old Treacle Press

www.oldtreaclepartnership.com

OUR MAN IN ESTEPONA

David Spear and Debbie Glynn

Edited by Raechel Turner Murch

Old Treacle Press

2020

Dedication

Unlike most works of fiction, many of the peripheral characters in this thriller are real and reside in either Estepona or Brighton/Hove. It is not in my nature to embarrass them, nor paint them in a disagreeable light, but as friends. Had they not been there, my Estepona life would be all the poorer.

I will leave the reader to distinguish who they believe are real or a figment of my imagination. Thank you all for giving Debbie and I the inspiration to write this novel.

Chapter 1

7.14am. Monday 10th August 2015. Estepona. Spain.

One more restless night mercifully grinds to a halt. My problem with sleep deprivation has nothing to do with insomnia or the kid crying from the apartment next door, no, it's caused by the bloody object hovering just below the horizon, champing at the bit to release yet another dose of its ferocious power into yet another clear blue sky. It's futile believing lost shut-eye can be recaptured, when mercury speeds past the 90 Fahrenheit mark heading north in stagnant air; an atmosphere totally governed by the silent, aggressive culprit striving to poke its circular, bald scalp above the skyline.

Wholly unrelated, I simulate this gigantic angry ball's trajectory with my own disgruntled head. Raising it from a shaped dent it's made in the pillow triggers warning signs of an impending hangover and a sudden craving for coffee. Slurred reactions kick in, motivating my lethargic body to slide out of bed and welcome the coolness of stone tiles beneath my feet. I look back to where I lay. The impression on the bottom sheet is distinct, but unlike the pillow, this one is moulded by a pint of my sweat. All of a sudden, I can believe in the story behind the *Turin Shroud*. If this entangled mess of cotton fabric I'm looking at, through slits of glued-up eyelids, can be misconstrued by the *Tate Modern* to be art, then my creation is every bit as good as that *Tracey Emin* woman's and should be earning me millions. A fuzzy brain conjures weird messages as it continues to do me no favours when directing my naked, aching torso through open terrace doors to accept the day's first sunbeams. Not escaping my newly found art critic-like eye, my linen curtains hang depressingly limp. If there is a wisp of air circulating around the town, my position perched way above the surrounding rooftops guarantees I get at least a portion of it. But this homespun meteorological forecasting system is nothing special when it suggests the same as usual, yet another oppressive, intolerable endurance test; a warning as to what is about to descend upon this part of the world within the next hour.

Oblivious to the state of my scant attire, I stand peering out onto the vast expanse of the Mediterranean before me, its waters a visual flat calm, pre-empting the beast before it cascades its blinding mirror-like reflection into the eyes of those daring to look at its shape through a negative photo of my Aunt Jessie riding a pig. If only I could remember my thoughts when sober, it's times like these when I know I could give *Keats or Kipling* a run for their money. Shit, I'm badly hungover and probably still stoned. I need nicotine and coffee. On my wrist, my watch implies it's twenty to eight, not long now. Ominously, the small magnifying panel on its glass face obliterates the number three on the dial, but indicates the date. Showing the tenth of August, it's four months to the day since it last rained, but worryingly coincides with the start of what is turning into a ridiculous period of prolonged heat. And when I say heat, I mean hot, sweaty, humid, nigh intolerable heat. Not once dropping so much as a few degrees during daylight and bequeathing nothing in the form of relief when dark, the peoples of this tight community in southern Spain wonder when it will end. Don't get me wrong, this is precisely the reason why I moved to these parts with its blue skies and sea, the sandy beach, cheap beer, cigarettes and honey bronzed females, but even for me, a self-proclaimed sun lover, the situation is becoming an unbearable monotony.

Unlike my fake *Rolex*, bought for twenty Euros a few years back from a West African beach peddler, the locals' reaction to this, sauna-like, phenomena is real enough with the elderly dropping like flies, if the English version of the journal *Sur* can be believed. Unlike my situation, whereby I can find relief by just hopping on a plane, they lack the means to escape. In the bars and shops, the weather is the sole topic on everyone's lips; rattled off discussions in a high octane Andalusian dialect. I understand very little of their garbled debates, but deciphering their hand gestures and the occasional nods of heads, endorsed with the odd *'Si'* and *'Claro',* the general consensus of opinion seemingly reassures them it can't last and, by September, cooler air will filter through from the Atlantic. Being a sceptic more than a linguist, I am not too sure of the facts supporting their weather reporting abilities.

Living in a sixth floor apartment, I squint in the direction of the cause of this discomfort, my timepiece ticking down the minutes until I feel the full blast of its power. From where I stand, my eyes settle on the tattered, blue European Union flag, hanging limply on a pole on the esplanade displaying exaggerated flaccidity. Similar characteristics to my linen curtains. But nobody put a gun to my head, I chose to live here, deciding to uproot and distance myself from the life I left behind in Brighton, well, Hove actually. As though I'd usurped the magical qualities of the *Tardis,* I'd escaped the drudgery of mundane Britain with its lethargic, politically correct brigade of do-gooders, not to mention its policy to allow every Tom, Dick and Harry into an already crowded country, whilst taking its eye off its own internal problems. But for me, what put the cherry on the cake at leaving its shores, was the daily dose of the *BBC News* confirming all my worst fears at the direction the country was heading. It became quickly evident the powers of law and order were being handcuffed instead of restraining the criminals they were designed to shackle. But the one thing I loathed most of all was the British weather. Yes, retreating here was definitely turning out to be one of my better ideas.

I landed on these shores, care of *easyJet*, some four years back, evading the stuff hitting the fan after getting wind that my sector of employment was to be dissolved, especially my office. One might think this a cowardly decision not to stay and fight with my workmates, strike and create turmoil instigated by union bosses who themselves hypocritically earn more than the Prime Minister, but in my line of work, which bore the same insincerity at high management level as to that of all public sector workers, regardless of the state of the nation, we couldn't strike, not that I would have bothered anyway. You see, I was a copper, a detective chief inspector to be precise within the auspices of the fabled New Scotland Yard. The premises might sound grand, but in the end I was becoming an expert at shuffling paper into its correct pile before handing it on up the ladder for some other poor soul with a higher rank to do likewise. A school leaver of sixteen could have done my job and probably made a better fist of it than me.

Born in the year of England's greatest international football achievement, I'm surprised I wasn't burdened with the handle of one of the victorious players, something like Bobby, Nobby, Geoff or one of the other eight names my father insisted on, but, thank God, he bowed and relented to mother's conventional wishes. School years went oh so slowly and I couldn't wait to leave with a handful of 'O levels' and an 'A level' in art to my name; sufficient credentials to head in the direction of my father's profession, the police force. Utilising his station sergeant's prerogative at Brighton, though, proved not such a good idea. Where was my first posting? Well, of course, Brighton, East Sussex. I remember it well. On my first day, I accompanied another 'bobby' on the beat along the seafront, my chest expanded whilst attired in a white helmet, short-sleeved white shirt and boots you could've seen your face reflected in. Today, if you're fortunate to see one in the first place, the vision of a copper is one of a black-knight, attired in body armour sporting an *ArmaLite M-15, semi-auto rifle* strapped over his shoulder.

Ironically, under his ever watchful eye, I couldn't wait to leave and put in for a transfer. Thereafter, I endured twenty three years of service, many of them when seconded within the *Metropolitan Police.* Faces came and went during those years, some individuals stayed, attempting to fulfil a dream, some left after their penchant for a uniform faded, but my conscience was clear, I'd overstayed my welcome. My patience commuting up to the capital every day from the south-coast was fast wearing thin and the advent of governmental cuts to the policing budget, suggesting longer hours for less pay, steered me to take only one possible course.

Early retirement when offered no longer tempted, it positively screamed at me to remove my arse and live on a very nice little inducement to get out early, together with a pension designed by some faceless civil servant philanthropist, who obviously based his figures on his own high living standards. Who was I to argue? At forty five years old and with an array of acrimonious, childless partnerships behind me, it was time...me...Clive Grainger, tasted the finer things on offer, where nobody knew my past or were even interested to enquire. The place I chose to kick-start my new life? Why, Estepona on the Costa del Sol in southern Spain of course. The town's name translated from old Spanish into English describes its qualities perfectly...'It is beautiful'.

~0~

During those years in the force, I learnt many important lessons, but one sticks out from the rest and that is, there are a hell of a lot more nasty bastards outside jail than banged up and I include some of my ex-colleagues in that equation. Bitter? No. Just a fact.

CHAPTER 2

7.25am. Monday 10th August 2015. Estepona.

As darkness dribbles away into daylight, I become aware my lone, naked torso might be misconstrued by those hurrying to work below as a weird exhibitionist, something to shield your children's eyes away from, that is, should they care to look up. Wisely, I retreat to the bathroom, diverting on my way to the kitchen to switch on the kettle. A shower can wait for the time being and, instead, I just douse my face under cold water. Reaching for my black silk robe, hanging on the back of the door, is a daily reminder of its significance, a Christmas gift from my ex-partner in better times, but now faded to grey, an ironic testimony to our failed time together. I should throw it and rid myself of past gremlins, but in some way it acts as a reminder of a time when I enjoyed her company. No, it'll stay for a while longer until the cigarette burn holes become too obvious.

Retracing my way back to the terrace, coffee-cup in one hand, a packet of '*Superkings*' in the other, I lean back on a wicker sofa, crossing my legs, knowing at this level I'm invisible and needn't have bothered covering my torso as sweat already dribbles south from my chest and armpits. Why I didn't take a shower a few minutes earlier, I don't know, but it will have to wait. My first cigarette of the day tastes as good as it always does but never seems to repeat the satisfaction when it comes to the second or subsequent inhalations, which is a good enough reason to quit, but I know I'll always crave that first hit of nicotine. On the other hand, good strong coffee is my life blood, a rejuvenator to kick-start my brain. Heaven knows how many thousands of cups I've consumed sitting in a lifeless office, surrounded by mundane creatures, usually unwashed, whose efforts were mostly taken up with counting the minutes on the clock to when they could disappear without fear of retribution.

I glance at my watch once again, feeling the heat building from a transparent sky. It tells me I have just over an hour before meeting Andy, a local bar keeper, on the first tee at *Estepona Golf* and knowing my luck, I'll need to stop off at a cash machine just in case my game's not up to scratch and Andy's is. Nice bloke, but constantly moans about his lack of the folding stuff and takes great delight when he relieves me of some of mine. I might just give Laurence and Teresa a bell to see if they fancy a late lunch down at the port after my exertions around eighteen holes. My mind drifts.

The theme from *The Great Escape* blasts from my mobile as it precariously throbs closer to the edge of my bedside cabinet, snapping me out of my trance while figuring out how I'll negotiate the tenth hole.

Confirming the caller, I answer.

"Morning Fred, what's so important at this time of day? Run out of *Jägermeister* have we and you want me to collect a few bottles from *Costa?"* I flippantly enquire.
Another British bar keeper, but this one has the honour of my custom on more than a few occasions a week. Not to be confused with the more salubrious Singapore version of the *Raffles* bar, his establishment of the same name is, shall we say, homely, more the size of a bungalow sitting room than the spacious surrounds of the afore mentioned hotel. Endeavouring to replicate the bar's distant cousin, a sole fan covering most of the ceiling area (a danger to anyone over six foot six) looks convincing but does nothing to alleviate the temperature.
"Listen, you arsehole." Fred possesses a turn of phrase that might put off a more discerning customer. "Jessica has been murdered. The police found her body floating in her swimming pool in the early hours of this morning. Neighbours reported hearing gunfire. What the fuck is happening"?
Fred is a joker, but even he wouldn't stoop so low to get a laugh.
My idyllic life at this moment collapses. Memories of similar announcements in the 'Office' hit me like a blow to the solar-plexus even if I didn't know the victim, but this is different. This just couldn't happen here. I'm retired from all the misery of dealing with death and going after the scum bags who instigate it. I want to play golf and drink and socialise with friends, not wake up to learn a close friend has been brutally wiped out and for what possible motive?

A pause of considerable seconds pass before my voice returns. "If this is a wind-up, Fred, I'll come round there and reconstruct your face."
"Don't be so fucking mad. It's true, she's been bumped off."
I hear his voice quiver, whether through fear or sorrow, I can't tell.
"Where are you Fred? I'm coming over. I need to know what you know. Give me fifteen minutes to shower and dress."
I know if anyone, Fred or *The Estepona Bugle,* a title fondly bestowed on him to describe his sponge-like ability to soak up gossip, would glean as much information as there was available outside a police station.

~O~

Green shorts, a tee shirt advertising *Theakston* brewery and wrap-around sandals are probably not the appropriate attire when learning of the death of a close friend, but the heat is building to its accustomed level, even though it is just after nine. More body covering would be plainly suicidal.
From my apartment I walk down *Avenida Juan Carlos* at a pace I haven't replicated for years, as there's been no need in the past to get anywhere in such a rush. Turning left into *Calle Real,* I come face to face with a tsunami of people, holiday makers just mooching before the temperature soars, necessitating their retreat to the shade of an umbrella or under the shadow of a beer glass, but they get in my way. Oblivious to their vocal disapproval in an assortment

of languages to my efforts to clear a path, I realise, too late, the seafront might have been less crowded than where shops do business. The familiar feel of sweat infests my body and I know, without checking, *Theakston's* good name is soaking it up, much as their bar towels absorb spilt beer.

Two unassuming *Police Locale* officers saunter in the shade, wearing false *Ray Bans* and 'hi-viz' designer shirts, at the junction of *Calle Terraza*; their appearance is a reassuring deterrent in this day and age of terrorism, but if push came to shove, I wonder if they are trained for such an occurrence. A car stops at the crossing, probably to avoid attracting stares from the law, allowing my uninterrupted progress.

At this end of town, shops are few, but bars and restaurants fill the spaces and with most not bothering to open at this hour, few pedestrian obstacles get in my way. Maintaining my pace, three minutes later I enter *Plaza Ortiz* and immediately stop. I feel quite buoyant feeling my heart-rate hasn't gone through the roof considering my exertions. In a town housing hundreds of bars, my memory for their names disintegrates, but I think I know where Fred suggested to meet. Over the heads of an assortment of wandering souls, attired much the same as me, I spot him sitting in full sunlight at a table not thirty yards away, his head jerking from side to side, attempting to witness my arrival.

I've known Fred for four years and using my policeman's nose, during those days in the Met, I instinctively built a personal profile and noted characteristics of an individual, but from where I'm positioned, he displays none I've seen before. He is nervous, sitting on the edge of his chair, fiddling with a beer mat, his eyes alert, seemingly intent to unload a burden or even a secret. Visually, his confidence has deserted him.

From my concealed position, I approach him from his blind side.

“Good to see you, Fred.”

He jumps from a sitting position onto his feet causing his half-drunk cup of coffee to spill across the table.

“Fuck me, Clive. Don’t do that. You scared the shit out of me.”

My instincts are not wrong. This is one scared hombre.

“Take it easy, mate. Sit down.” Reassuring, I place a hand on his shoulder. “I think you need more than just a coffee and I’ll join you.”

Witnessing the mess Fred caused with his physical antics towards a cup and saucer, a waiter approaches armed with a damp kitchen towel in hand.

“*Ah, camarero. Dos brandys Españoles y dos cafes expresso y hacer que los grandes brandys. Gracias.*”

My Spanish isn’t as good as it should be, but the waiter gets my drift I want two large brandy’s and strong coffee. He then spoils my illusion of being able to get by speaking his lingo by repeating my order back in perfect English. Why do I bother trying to learn the language? My day is not going well.

~O~

“Right Fred, what do you know?”

Mimicking too many films he'd seen, he glances surreptitiously over both shoulders, obviously thinking there might be unwanted ears in close proximity.
"I know Jessica was shot three times, all in the head. That's for starters." Fred whispers. "And from what I hear, it was a professional job. Not some burglar getting caught on the job and just shooting his way out. I took a drive by her house this morning and the place is crawling with the law. Every car and wagon displays it's being dealt with the *'Guardia Civil'* or anti-terrorist brigade. This isn't any normal murder, Clive. This is big."
Ignoring the coffee, Fred sinks his brandy in one, much the same as I'd seen him demolish a *Jägermeister.*
"Oh, that was clever. An Englishman driving past her place in a conspicuous blue *Porsche,* hours after an English woman has been murdered on the same site. No, they're not going to find that strange, are they, you prat. I think it's most likely you'll get a visit from the boys in the flat fronted, black, patent leather hats quite soon."
Fred's face resembles one that has just swallowed a clove of garlic.
"Oh, fuck it. What have I just let myself into?"
"Don't worry mate. If it happens, just tell the truth. You got nothing to worry about."
My words of solace are not having their desired effect. If anything, his trembling goes up a notch.
"Is there something else you want to unload, Fred?" Before, his eyes wouldn't leave mine, they now look anywhere but. "You're not leaving anything out, are you?"

Fred stays muted, but gives me a chance to digest what he reported. It wasn't a lot, but sufficient for me to ask myself where he'd picked up these fragments of information. He'd mentioned three shots delivered by a professional executioner. Who told him?

"Fred, look at me. Where did you get this evidence from?"

The effects of a large brandy at this hour in the morning, appear to be working. His demeanour relaxes, his eyes focus on his fingers still fiddling with a beer mat. I'd witnessed suspects over the years in interview rooms display similar characteristics when withholding the truth and the moment when it finally dawns on them it's useless to continue with the charade. This is one of those moments.

"Come on Fred. It's better to get it off your chest now, than wait to be interrogated by the old good cop, bad cop routine, facing a lone spotlight shining in your eyes." I didn't intentionally scare him, but I certainly struck a chord.

"I've been seeing Maria, Jessica's housekeeper, for about six months. She...Maria told me."

"Woo...slow down a tad. You mean to say you have been knocking off the person who found Jessica? And then she tells you all this? When did you talk, because I'm surprised she's not in some police station right now being heavily questioned?" I wait for Fred's brain to figure out in what order I'd eventually get to the truth.

"Maria went to work as usual early this morning. She prefers to get her work done before sunrise, which is understandable in this heat, and this she does three days a week and today was one of those days. It was just after six when she let herself in and, though the lights were on, she couldn't find Jessica anywhere in the house. Though it's still dark outside, she looks through the window but there's no sign of her. She said this made her feel uneasy, as this is the first time Jessica hasn't been at home when she arrived. In the past, Maria said Jessica would always tell her if she was away during one of her working days. So, she goes upstairs and searches the bedrooms and still nothing. It's then she looks outside again from the first floor and sees Jessica floating in the illuminated pool, surrounded by diluted blood. Maria said she screamed and rushed down to the poolside. Not knowing what to do, she phones me. I tell her to phone the police." Fred annoyingly stops, alerting a passing waiter to order refills.

"But how do you know there were three shots, presumably fired from a professional hitman's gun?" I attempt to keep Fred's mind focused.

"It was sometime after the police arrived, when the plain clothes boys were talking and Maria overheard them. She asked if she could phone her family and they agreed. She phoned me instead."

I can't believe the police are so lax. The first person on the scene of a brutal crime is allowed to make a phone call before being fully interrogated. "Tell me about Maria. Who is she? How did you meet? How old is she? That sort of thing."

Fred waits for the approaching waiter to replenish our goblets, this time without the accompanying coffee.

"I first met Maria down at the port, or should I say, she saw me first. I was in my car just cruising past and

she must have recognised me from the bar. The next thing I know, she's brought her boyfriend in and has a drink. She speaks English okay and we exchange a few words. As her boyfriend doesn't speak a word of it, she lets me know she's interested and the rest is history." His first smile of the morning uneasily creases his lips.
"How old is she?"
Fred doesn't reply immediately, probably knowing what my reaction will be, as he is probably a few years older than myself. He might even be in his early sixties.
"Twenty-four."
"Oh...fuck me. I can see it all now. Here's this young woman who's immediately smitten by a *Porsche* owner, who just happens to own a bar and lives in a nice little penthouse on the seafront. I take it you've entertained her in your gaff so, not to state the obvious...she wasn't attracted by your good looks, you randy bastard, but what she thought she saw...money." Even with the seriousness of the matter, I can't help but smile. "I suppose this'll stop you putting your leg over her ever again." It's impossible, I just laugh.
"Oh, I'm glad you think it's funny. What am I going to do?" Fred doesn't appreciate my humour.
"Look, old friend. If the fuzz do catch up with you, just tell it as you told me. Nothing will happen to you, believe me."
What Fred says next rocks me back into my chair, nearly toppling me over. "Is that the advice from a friend or a copper?"
I haven't said a word to anyone down here about my past and sure don't know anyone here from the past who knew me back in the UK.

"What makes you think I was a policeman?" I try to deliver the question without a trace of annoyance, now my secret doesn't appear to be as watertight as I first thought.

"Oh, I've known for a few years. When was it? Summer before last, a bloke comes into my bar one afternoon and we get talking. He's down here for a week playing some golf while his misses gets herself tanned on the beach. He just sort of stumbled into my joint. We talked about the ex-pats living down here and I just mentioned you and some of the others. When I mentioned you, he said he knew someone of the same name who'd just retired from where he worked. He described you perfectly and I knew you were the same person he knew. He then gives me his business card, or that's what I thought it was, but printed in bold print is the *Metropolitan Police* logo above his title and name. I've still got it somewhere back at the bar."

"Can you remember his name?"

"No, not off hand, but if you come round later, I'll fish it out."

"What about his rank?"

"Yep. That's one thing I do recall. Detective Chief Superintendent. He's a big fish, isn't he?"

"Yes, you could say that. Is this the reason you called me, because I'm an ex-copper?"

"Yes Clive. I knew you'd know what to do."

"Well Fred, I would be obliged if this conversation doesn't get broadcast and my past remains our secret. It's funny how people you thought you once knew, change when they learn you are a copper. So keep it shtum. Cheers."

Fred nods, accepting my suggestion. "But what can you do? I mean Jessica has just been murdered. Surely with your background and connections, you can find out more and a possible reason why."
I finish my brandy, contemplating what Fred just said. "I can't do anything until it's become common knowledge. Once the press have written about it, who knows? We'll wait until then. And Fred, remember, not a word of this goes any further than between the two of us."

CHAPTER 3

9.30am. Monday 10th August 2015. Estepona.

Thankfully, it appears Fred believes I'm immediately on the case and prepares to leave, sinking the remnants of what is left in his brandy glass. On the other hand, I'm just relieved a third brandy wasn't ordered. Two large ones before ten in the morning isn't the wisest way to start the day, especially as I'm expected to focus on a golf ball. I phone Andy and tell him I'm running late, then tell myself whatever I do next, and contrary to what Fred might think, I'm retired and mustn't get involved in this murder, though it has all the hallmarks of a case that would have whetted my appetite and most certainly the file would have landed on my desk, that is if I was still in the job.

I change my mind and phone Andy again to tell him I can't make it, before he unleashes a tirade of abuse in my ear concerning my reliability. I smile knowing he's just pissed off, having had his chance to relieve me of some of my cash whipped away until another day. I walk back to *Calle Terraza,* but slower this time, and buy a *Daily Mail* from a kiosk. Continuing on my way, but along the seafront this time, I flick through the pages and stumble upon an article concerning the forthcoming battle for the leadership of the *Labour Party.* My eyes read about an unlikely character, who started the campaign as the rank outsider, but my brain refuses to register the significance that he's now become the frontrunner for the job. Instead, what little Fred told me rings alarm bells.

Murders of this calibre just don't happen by accident. Three head shots are not random and why three when one would have done the job. Fred was right when he said this wasn't a burglary gone wrong. This was planned, but why? I might have understood if this happened in Marbella or Porto Banus, where drug traffickers of various nationalities relieve their grievances by means of administering similar doses of lead poisoning in the same manner, but here in Estepona...killing an old lady in her seventies for no apparent reason...no way. There has to be a motive. But then I ask myself the most important question that I should have asked immediately. Just who was Jessica?

~O~

Giving Andy's bar a wide berth, for obvious reasons, I slink into *Paco's Chiringito,* a place sitting on the beach where the staff know me and rustle up a good imitation of an English breakfast. Not surprisingly, even at this early hour, an assortment of sun-worshippers have bagged the best located loungers and are busily basting their white bodies in readiness to be cooked. Taking advantage of an umbrella, I sit at a table in the shade. My tan, after four years, has mellowed into a shade of mahogany, unlike my neighbours stretched out in close proximity who might have just a week to prove they've been abroad.

I light a cigarette, my third of the day, and look out at folk enjoying being by the seaside, mulling over in my mind the thought that one or more could have been responsible for Jessica's death, but that doesn't happen in real life. No, whoever is responsible is miles away and might even be out of the country. My hidden mobile pulsates against my thigh, muffling the sound of the war-film theme tune.

"Fred...what is it?"

"I don't suppose you're anywhere near a television." His speech is fast and staccato-like.

"No, Fred, you're correct. I'm nowhere near one, why?"

"I'm back at my flat and just turned it on in time for the news. They are reporting her murder. How did they know so quickly, for God's sake?"

"Take it easy, Fred. *Reuters* act fast and this is a big story. One I should think the Spanish are not too happy about, happening on the Costa del Sol in the height of their tourist season. Okay, I thought it might take a little longer, but now it's out in the open, I can ask a few questions. But like I said, keep your mouth shut, Fred, and keep it between us."

"If it helps, I'll dig out that business card I told you about. Are you coming in later?"

"Yeah, I'm interested who's been snooping around and yes, I'll be there."

My egg, bacon and the works arrive as I ring off. The question is; where do I start unravelling some of these questions? I left the 'factory' some four years ago and there'd been no reason to keep in touch with any of its employees. Good riddance, I thought at the time of my departure, but in retrospect, I might have been a little hasty in my condemnation. I need to get back to my apartment and go through my belongings from a past life. I must have kept notebooks, something to give me a helping hand to get started.

CHAPTER 4

11.14pm. Monday 10th August 2015. Estepona.

I stand between the door jams of my spare bedroom, staring at an assortment of cardboard boxes of all shapes and sizes, that have stood unopened for years, but nothing indicates what they contain. I must have had a system four years ago or a piece of paper replicating a filing procedure, which might explain why I'd scrawled a motif on each carton when I got here. Maybe this was the reason I escaped in the first place...too much paper work.

I count eight boxes in number, so begin my search with the closest. Winter clothes are not what I hope to find in the first, so move on. By the fourth, I'm just about to retreat to the refrigerator and hunt down a beer, when I spot what I hope I hadn't binned. Inside a plastic covered portfolio is my book of numbers, mostly informers whereabouts and their contacts, but the one I need is where I hope to find it, under the initial of her Christian name...Debbie.

Debbie Glynn, a woman somewhere in her middle years, was my eyes and ears. Not employed as a policewoman, but a civilian, who after twenty years of being my office bound assistant, became my confidante, friend, a person of high morals, but who never questioned my style or methods to solve a case.

Totally loyal, I didn't require a sidekick of a lower ranked officer, Debbie's brain and discretion superseded anyone who might have started their career in a uniform. In fact, had she joined the force, she'd probably be a Commander by now. There was nobody within the *'Yard'* who knew procedure better than she.
"Oh dear." I mutter to myself as, flicking through the pages, a plastic coated object falls to the floor. I smile, knowing I should have handed it in when retiring, but it was a memento and I'm relieved I didn't follow protocol. The passport sized photo, taken eight years before, shows signs my hair was then starting to grey, but accounting for the time passed, it is me alright, though possibly ten pounds lighter.
Chief Inspector Clive Grainger, it reads under the insignia of the *Metropolitan Police*, a piece of kit to open most doors and put the fear of the devil into anybody it was flashed in the face of. My warrant card. Armed with sufficient ammunition, I don't have the faintest idea where this will lead, but it's a start. I'll phone Debbie

CHAPTER FIVE

7.29am. Monday. 10th August 2015. London

Monday morning, slightly hungover after a 7 hour 'Sunday lunch' with the girls, I endure the drudgery of the 7.29 Brighton to Victoria, a journey famously hitting the headlines last year as being, punctually, the worst service in the UK - not arriving once on time in 2014. In my seat of choice, I politely nod to the usual carriage dwellers, hoping to God no day trippers will board and talk incessantly loud all the way up, with no regard for us poor souls that have to do this every day, when all I want is a nap after reading the *Metro*. Thankfully, the line appears to be clear this morning – but, hold on a minute, it's delayed again, naturally, due to points failure somewhere completely unrelated to my line (tweet my frustration to *Southern Rail* as we all do on a regular basis to no avail). I arrive 15 minutes late at the office, builders tea and bacon roll in hand - (Monday is never going to be a muesli and yoghurt day) just in time for the toe-curling, awful, ritualistic huddle around the whiteboard, hosted by Baldrick, to share and discuss with the team our tasks and mood for the day.

I abhor this daily, happy-clappy, let's all energise together...bollocks.

Baldrick…"Debs can you reach out to the Super with the final cut of next year's section budget?" REACH OUT!! For fuck's sake. Unless you're an actual member of the *Four Tops*, this corporate psychobabble has no place in normal conversation in my world.

I finally saunter to my desk, fire up the laptop, drink my now lukewarm tea, eat my bacon roll, then I notice my voice-mail indicator winking at me.

No caller ID displayed, looks an international number. I punch the plethora of codes to listen to the message.

"Debs…it's Clive, need a huge favour, please call me back ASAP from outside"

Clive and I worked together here in the bowels of *New Scotland Yard* and at Brighton nick for twenty years, he as an Inspector, me his admin assistant or, as I would prefer to label myself - Clive's Bitch!!!

Not a glamorous role by anyone's standard, managing his dubious expenses, trying to ensure we adhered to the minimum of regulatory compliance - not an easy task when most of the time he could be found in any number of drinking hostelries or bookies surrounding the building in a 'meeting'.

Over the years we became good friends, saw each other through various crises, both professional (for him mainly) and personal. On a daily basis I would have to put up with his incessant ramblings on the state of the country's borders, the madness of public sector cut backs, 12 year old bureaucrats running the department, horse trainers and jockeys who have been paid more to lose than win (especially when he's had money on one of them) and any other subject matter that would have just irked him on the day, of which, there would always be plenty.

At times, just to completely tip him over the edge and for my own amusement, I would pop my head over the monitor and chip in with how I thought political correctness and mass immigration was the way forward, just to light the blue touch paper and watch him almost combust into a fizzing rage. Made me smile, whilst adding 'only kidding'.

We complimented each other and were both of the old school JFDI philosophy of achieving results (Just F****** Do It). I would get him out of all sorts of administrative scrapes, turn a blind eye to his sometimes-outrageous methods of getting an arrest.

Not a man who embraced technology, I include the mobile phone, which was indeed a challenge, to say the least, and months of indecipherable text messages as he refused to accept predictive text. Don't even start me on the *Blackberry* or the ever-multiplying operational systems, that would drive him potty, to the degree it was quicker for me to log on as him and complete all the reporting myself. Wasn't difficult, as the main body of his password never changed... 'Wankers', followed by a number. Think we got up to 72. Online compliance training was one of his particular favourites, especially when Andy the odious 'Continuous Improvement Officer' (unbelievably in this day and age of cut backs, this role actually exists. I would swap the 'O' in the first word for a 'U' when referring to him!!) would send Clive snotty email reminders, which, in turn, he would forward to me saying, 'There's a bottle of *Pinot Grigio* in it for you if make this shit go away'.

The photocopier was about all he would muster to attempt at a push, if I wasn't around. The coffee machine positively terrified him and he flatly refused to go near the thing.

I do owe him where I am today, though. As he rose through the ranks, it was always on the proviso that I went with him as his assistant, a decision senior management warmly embraced, as I'm sure they secretly thought no other schmuck would put up with him for more than a week. Since taking early retirement four years ago, I have to admit the office is a much duller place and most of what he smugly predicted would happen, actually has.

I am now called an Operations Manager, which basically means shovelling crap and wiping the backside of this entire CID team comprising of two cocky, chavvy upstart sergeants - Sam and Keavo, three inspectors - Baldrick (Steve), Ian and Jason, two chief inspectors - Bronzey and Naomi, then a dotted line up to the superintendent – Ingrid, an expert in all budgetary, compliance and regulatory tick boxing nonsense.

Managing Clive was so much simpler than this lot. It's like herding cats in a dog's home on a daily basis. I'm amazed that, so far, I've dodged the cut back bullet. I think after twenty-four years, I'm the only one who knows how everything works and the bureaucratic shortcuts. If there's something I don't know, I'll know who does, and having kept my ear to the ground for all those years, there are many skeletons in cupboards that I've stored in my reservoir of 'things never to forget' brain. As in all walks of life, especially as I no longer have someone watching my back, other people's secrets offer a good starting point when leverage requires applying.

I've visited Estepona many times over the years, as I have a variety of friends who live or have apartments there, some in the port and some in the old town. It's like Costa del Hove - cheap holiday!

I actually bumped into Clive over there a couple of years ago. I was walking round to Lorraine & Paul's barbeque in *Calle San Miguel*, from the seafront via the tiny cut through road of *Calle Teatro*, and there outside Fred's bar was his unmistakable stance, having a smoke. What did blind side me, was his colour - the likes of which I have never encountered on any other Caucasian human being. I could only assume where normal people applied factor 20+ on the beach, he smothered himself with gravy granules!

He ushered me round the corner to *Javier's Bar Tipico*, ordered a wine for us both, and explained no one in Estepona knew his police background and that's how he wants it to stay, so as far as the good folk of Estepona are concerned, we just know each other from Hove. Fine by me, as I would always respect his privacy.

We had a good catch-up chat about the goings on back at the shop, who's left, who's been promoted, who's shagging who, all the usual stuff and agreed no such conversation should be repeated anywhere near the man cave, that is Fred's place, as he (Fred) is the most incorrigible gossip.

We arranged to meet for a beach flop and late lunch the next day at *Paco's*.
After a very late wine-fuelled barbeque, I wasn't feeling the greatest the next day. Spotted him immediately, lounging on a sun bed with the paper. Funny how you work with someone for twenty years, share all sorts of things in the office or over a glass of wine and yet the vision of them in pair of trunks (thank God not Speedo's) is weird to say the least, when all you've known is them in a crumpled suit. After the initial awkwardness of the whole 'I'm in a bikini and you're in shorts scenario' ended, he told me about his life in Estepona and, bizarrely, how many mutual friends we knew there, mainly through Fred's bar. Amazingly, we'd not bumped into each other before.
Estepona certainly suits him. What's not to suit? The weather, the unspoilt vista, the bars, the people, the lifestyle...he certainly was enjoying his life.
That was the last time I saw him as I didn't holiday in Spain last year and, unfortunately, lost his contact details when I changed my mobile number.
Why do I get this sinking feeling in my stomach that he's dragged his charcoal skinned body off the sun lounger and stuck his big copper nose into something he shouldn't touch with a barge pole!!
No good can come out of this call, I'm almost positive.
I'll creep out for a ciggy break when the nicotine police aren't looking and find out.

Outside, the smoking den, being a doorway to an empty office block round the corner and gratefully uninhabited, I extract a piece of paper on which I'd written the number down and call him.

"Hi Clive, it's Debs, how are you doing? What's the favour?"
"Cheers, Debs, for calling back, are you still stepping out with married Nick the archivist and still pally with that woman in HR?"
"Stepping out." Who uses that terminology anymore? I'm so not liking the way this conversation is going. "WHAT? Well...of sorts and incidentally, Nick's soon to be separated - not that it's any of your business. Come on Clive, what do you want to know that for?"
"I need you to look up and get any information or file in existence, on a woman called Jessica McGill. I know you don't have clearance to the archive rooms and database, but Nick does if I remember rightly. I need you to get anything you can. Really can't discuss this over the phone. Look, I know this is a big ask and I can only imagine the names you're calling me right now. This is important Debs."
"Who the hell is Jessica McGill, Clive?"
"She was a retired, seventy something expat, enjoying the trappings of Estepona until murdered, that part is in the public domain."
"And you're getting involved with this because...?"
"She was a friend and may have had dealings with the Yard. I heard whispers down here that she might have done."
I'm beyond speechless. Has he gone effing mad? So, I'm to casually, over a drink, ask Nick for his security code, no suspicion there then! That's just archived files, personnel data is another ball game altogether.

"Big ask doesn't even begin to cover this, Clive, how the hell do you expect me to pull this off under the radar?

If she did have any dealings, it will be classified information. As you rightly pointed out, my authority level stretches to the giddy heights of *Office Depot* for stationary!!"

"You'll think of something, you always do, just use your charm with hapless Nick, if you need to. I wouldn't ask you if I didn't think you could do it. Come on...JFDI...and it goes without saying this is between you and me."

"Oh, so now I'm literally taking one for the team. Jesus, Clive, I can't believe you're asking me to do this. IF, and that's a massive IF, I manage to get anything without being fired or jailed, you owe me large and we're not talking a couple of *Tinto Verano's* at *Paco's*. Alright, I'll see what I can do. You just go and bloody sun yourself on the beach, leave the security breaching to me." This is turning out to be my Monday from hell. I've even briefly forgotten about my hangover.

I finish my cig and head back into to the office. Okay, think.

I stare at the usual paraphernalia adorning my desk, particularly at my 'twenty year in the making rubber band ball' for inspiration.

First thing, *Google* Jessica McGill, - sure enough an article appears on how yesterday morning her housekeeper discovered her body floating in her pool in the old part of Estepona town, with apparent gunshot wounds to her head - *Guardia Civil* appealing for any witnesses to come forward, locals in shock blah blah blah - why do they always say 'apparent' gunshot wounds? Either it is or it isn't. I've never known a

gunshot wound pretending not to be one jumping up and shouting...Ha!..fooled you all.
I call my mate Lesley in the Brighton nick, she heads the research team.
"Les, can you do me a favour and look up Jessica McGill on the MEPO database and email me the results."
"Stay on the phone as I'm logged in anyway."
I can hear her tapping away.
"Debs - there is a record outlining the dates between 7/6/1972 to 1/5/91, but it's all blank and marked highly classified - please refer to CO (commissioner's office). Just who is this Jessica woman?"
Shit, this doesn't look as though it's going to be easy.
"Don't know, Les, that's why I'm asking you. Thanks anyway for looking, never mind. I'll get you a wine in *The Albion* on Friday. Cheers mate."
Hmm, nothing there then, but why is a classification attached to all her files? Worryingly, this will get Clive even more suspicious.
I need a strong coffee and some sort of plan!
Ambling to the kitchen area, I toss over in my mind alternative strategies, when I interrupt the usual morning gathering around the ever oppressive coffee/tea machine. Sam and Keavo stare at the 'clear overflow' digital message display beaming back at them.
Sam..."Nan, thank God. Can you fix this bloody thing? We're gasping...oh and how was your weekend?"

"For fuck's sake Sam - watch and learn - take tray out, empty the ground coffee into bin, put tray back - can it be that difficult? How did you ever get through

Hendon? And the next time you call me 'Nan', I swear to God, I'll lamp you. It would be worth seeing you in pain and the subsequent disciplinary. Now, get out of my way as I'm getting my coffee first. Thank you, I had a great weekend - not being in here."

I take my oversized, very politically incorrect, inappropriate and sexist cup of brown muck purporting to be coffee, (yes, one of those dreadful bronzed, ripped male-in-trunks images that changes to full blown nudity with the application of boiling water, a typical secret Santa gift from one of the boys) back to my desk.

Luckily, most of the budget work has already been done. Just have to make the numbers look pretty and presentable, but essentially the message is loud and clear, less funding, less resource, more work load, shouldn't take me long, then back on the Jessica trail.

An hour later I emerge from Ingrid's office, (She that has to be obeyed and she who behaves in the office like a cross between *Jane Tennyson* of *Prime Suspect* fame and *Margot Ledbetter* of the 70's sit com, *The Good Life*, at home). Having received a verbal lashing on how are we supposed to operate with these figures, I politely point out it was she who advised me of the high level numbers. All I do is put the beans into different pots. However you dice and slice, it's the same amount of beans! She then reminds me of yet another annual barbeque she and the long suffering Steve, the husband, are hosting at their country pile at the weekend. Well, I think it's this weekend. Will I be bringing anyone? I'd rather douse myself in petrol whilst reaching for matches, than inflict on a potential suitor such a soiree. I always, for reasons unknown, end up babysitting her brats whilst she wafts around swilling gin and tonics, but to not attend could be a career damaging clanger.

Can't think about that right now.

My next call is going to be about as tricky as it gets. Any detailed information on our Jessica will certainly be contained in her Personnel file and this means getting past Julia in HR (Human Resources department or Human Remains, as I like to call it).

Julia is a large imposing, single woman of a certain age, who at her level of Senior Administrator can be spectacularly indiscreet about anyone after a bottle or two of Cab Sav and completely by the book when sober. I wouldn't trust her as far as I could throw her, but have to keep her on side. To this end, we would often go for drinks after work and about a year ago, during a particularly heavy session, she confessed to having a full blown affair with the Deputy Commissioner - Phil. Both Ingrid (who Julia also blurted to) and I had suspected this for a long while. Both agreed, we didn't think he could be so stupid as to risk his marriage and position for a fling (still going on incidentally) with a woman who, at best, is a bunny boiler in any relationship, but hey...he's a man with a dick...say no more! This little nugget of knowledge could now prove to be very useful.

"Hi Julia, how's it going? What'd you get up to at the weekend? Hear from Phil?" I ask down the mouthpiece of the internal phone system, a sarcastic smile creasing my face.

"No, I didn't, not even a bloody text. Sent him quite a stroppy one Saturday night, though."

I can just picture the scene, she alone in her lounge demolishing a bottle of red, he on holiday in the sun with the wife and kids.

"He's on holiday, so can hardly slip out and call you or spend all day sending texts. You know the golden rule, never send any Tourette's strewn communication when pissed."

"Yeah, yeah, I know you're right. What can I do for you anyway?"

'This is a bit of an odd request and I appreciate that I can't actually view personnel files, but I need to gather some information on one Jessica McGill. I'm not interested in personal stuff like salary or sickness records, just if there's anything else."

"Debs, come on, you know I can't give you any details from someone else's file. Why are you thinking of even asking me? This conversation is over."

Here goes the tricky bit.

"Hang on Julia, I get that, but this is a real favour and it's important. You just have to go and have a look, call me on my mobile with any relevant details which, may or may not even exist. Nothing would come back on you; you look at these files all the time."

"Which part of No don't you understand? I'm not doing it, don't you understand, Debs?"

She isn't expecting what she hears next. Hope she's wearing protective knickers. In barely an audible whisper.

"Listen Julia, I'm simply asking a favour here. I'll tell you what I do understand - loud and clear and that's, if word were to leak somehow of your shenanigans with Phil to the higher echelons of this place...need I say anymore?"

"Are you fucking blackmailing me??"

"No, just think of it as an assurance, you need me to keep my mouth shut and I need some information - Simple! I'll leave that one with you to work out."

I hang up. I do feel quite bad and have really put her on the spot - hey ho, I have no doubt she'd do exactly the same to me.

I spend the next half hour sifting through various emails, when my *iPhone* goes off. It's Julia.

"Sorry, Debs, there's absolutely nothing I can tell you I'm afraid." The tone of her voice indicating, if there was anything of note, she's not going to tell me anyway.

"Thanks Julia, sorry for putting you in that position. I really do appreciate it, incidentally I wouldn't have said anything about Phil anyway. Pot's and kettles, eh, re Nick."

Thankfully, she did laugh at that and suggested we catch up for a wine after work sometime this week.

It started eight years ago at the Christmas party - flirtatious conversation after copious volumes of wine turned into a walk back to my hotel, followed by several night caps at the bar, as we clearly hadn't had enough to drink! Inevitably, we stumbled up to my room. The joy of the alarm trilling, four hours later, with the mother of all hangovers then finding your colleague naked next to you, held no bounds.

His wife was away in France, which she would do on a regular basis without him, so wouldn't know he hadn't been home. It was he who had to do the walk of shame, unshaven via *M&S* for a change of shirt, socks and pants to the office.

Drunk and discretion really don't make for good bedfellows. Raised eyebrows as soon as I got to my desk. Yes, we'd both been spotted heading for the hotel and yes, we'd been spotted walking towards *M&S* – hmm, why would that be?

Clive gave me one of those 'you've let yourself and the team down' looks, then burst out laughing.

So it was out. Oh well.

We would both go out for lunch almost daily, drinks after work, the odd day off together, not making any secret of it, best way in an office environment. He'd call every night after his wife went to bed, usually by 8.30, wanting to know where I was. Was I in the pub and who with?

It got to a point where he was becoming a bit too jealous and possessive, which was rich considering he is married, albeit a marriage appearing to be a mutually loveless convenience with no children.

I put a stop to that nonsense after about two years. He was very hurt at first, but eventually got over it and we remarkably remain close friends. Still go out for drinks without any of the previous intensity and, yes, I can wrap him around my little finger.

The potential separation - his wife wants to move back to France, he does not - is a slight cause for concern as I wouldn't want him to think I'll pick up where wifey left off, as they say - I'll burn that bridge when I get to it!!

Although Nick would have been a pushover, as Clive annoyingly predicted, particularly after three glasses of

Sancerre, I elect not to mention my need to gain access to Jessica's file. What was the point? I don't know what I'm looking for anyway.

We just chat generally and about Ingrid's barbeque coming up, who was going, was he taking his wife?

"No she's away, so I could be your plus one." He said with that glint in his eye.

Spot Bronzey and Naomi in a corner table sharing what appeared to be bottle of *Merlot* number two - they must be having a bad day. They just wave as if it's perfectly normal that we are all in *Balls Brothers* drinking on a Monday.

We saunter back at 3.45.

Bronzey shouts out - "Where've you been. Ingrid was looking for you, something about numbers - enjoy your lunch?'

"More's the question...did you enjoy yours? And the two bottles of *Merlot* will be put down as what on your expense return?"

I go back to my desk and start sifting through the piles of receipts Bronzey has already, so kindly, deposited for me to scan into the CONCUR expense system.

That done, I take my oversized, inappropriate mug back to the kitchen. Heaven forbid the cleaners would actually perform such an arduous task. Power down the laptop - home time.

So that's that - All I've managed to glean is that our Jessica was a civil servant and had retired, end of.

I stroll round to Victoria for the daily scrum on platform 17 to get the spot where the 5.46 to Littlehampton doors will open. When and if it arrives, everyone jostles for the same coveted position, vying to get a seat. If you're not in place you run the risk of having to stand at least to Haywards Heath. A situation I can't bear, being the lofty height of 5ft 2in, I nearly always find myself under the armpit of some sweaty bloke attempting to read my *Evening Standard.*

The train slowly pulls in, I brace myself for the commuter shuffle, not knowing exactly when the train will stop and where the doors open. So we all do the little to the left and a little to the right time-warp-style jig, hoping among hope, when it eventually grinds to a halt, you're right in front of the green flashing orb to open the doors. Allow other folk out, then bolt for the comfy 'Billy big boy' seats with arms on. Ideally, by a window.

Huge success, got my favourite seat. Settle down to read the paper and nod off just past East Croydon.

Hove Station arrives, thankfully while I'm still awake. I always leave in the morning from Brighton and return to Hove, my flat being smack in the middle of the two, affording me a choice as to which local hostelry I'll pop into when I get home, be it the *Seafield* or *The Albion* in Church Road. This is my time, time to unwind with a couple of glasses of wine with friends before heading back to an enticing bed.

The *Seafield* is one of those pubs that, if it were a small child, only a mother could love it. Tiny with dated decor, dodgy seating and flooring, the toilets resemble port-a-loos you could only find at a music festival. It boasts a Mediterranean sun terrace at the rear, which, in reality, is some poorly laid decking going into a neglected patio garden, but it's sheltered and where I can have a fag out of the rain.

The landlord, Robbo, is a man who's had the pub for twenty odd years. I've known him for at least twenty-five. Now in his early sixties, he's a large, rotund chap with a walrus style moustache and can always be found standing at the end of the bar doing the crossword. If you're lucky, he might grunt an acknowledgement if you walk in. During the day, horseracing is on all four TV's, with the regular boys enjoying a gamble. In the evenings, he changes channels to receive *Grand Designs*. Quite hilarious. Avidly watching these programmes, he applies none of what he's learnt to improve the state of his own premises.

To his credit, the *Seafield*, despite its veneer, is a welcoming and friendly place to go, particularly as a single woman. Over the years, all we regulars have become good friends.

It is a shithole, but it's our shithole!!!

Ironically, Robbo also has a house in Estepona and is particularly good friends with Fred.

I walk down from the station and chose the *Seafield*.

Before my shoes get a chance to stick to the carpet, Robbo and my friend Jane beckon me over, both in quite an animated state.

"Debs - heard about the murder in Estepona? Jessica found shot in her pool. You knew her didn't you? She lived just up the road from my place?"

I feign surprise and reply that, no, I hadn't heard and no, I didn't know her.

"*Google* it, Debs"

I go through the Google process, ordering the least acidic glass of wine I can think of at the same time.

"God that's awful. Must be a shocker down there. How did you find out? Actually I can guess - Fred?"

"Yeah, he called me this morning. He's quite shaken up by it. Reckons it's a professional hit."

"Oh come on Robbo, even with Fred's tendency to exaggerate the facts- a professional hit!!! How would he possibly know?"

Robbo did the annoying 'tapping on the side of his nose' thing, like it's a big secret and not fit for my ears.

"Whatever Robbo. Here's the *Standard*."

I throw the paper on the bar. "Did she have any family over there? They must be devastated."

"Fred says she had a daughter in England, thinks she's flying out there tomorrow."

I take my wine and go and have a chat with Jane.

Three wines later, I leave and head to the bus stop across the road. I could walk back to my flat but I can't be arsed.

I get into my one bed ground floor garden flat- the spoils of divorce!! Immediately change out of my suit into slobby pyjama bottoms and tee shirt.

8.30 here so 9.30 in Spain. I pour myself a decent glass of wine and call Clive.

He takes an age to pick up, either he's going deaf or in a bar, the latter I suspect.

"Hi Clive, firstly I'd like to thank you so much for brightening up my otherwise dull day." I sarcastically say.

"Sorry Debs. Did you manage to dig anything up?"

"No, not really. I asked my mate Lesley in research, on the QT, to search the MEPO database and the only information she was able to view were her dates of employment being 7th June 1972 to 1st May 1991. Any other data is marked highly classified and would need to be referred to the Commissioner's office, which obviously I'm in no position to do. I then tried Julia in HR. Again she confirmed only the dates, not even any ranking, although I detected in her voice that she was holding something back. Just a hunch. Sorry Clive, that's all I can tell you for now. I didn't even bother to ask Nick, there's no point if I don't have a scooby of what I'm looking for - by the way, I popped into my local on the way home and I don't know if you've heard of him, but Robbo the landlord is a good pal of Fred's and has a house down there. Interestingly, he received a call from Fred this morning spewing the same details I already knew from Google, but then he came out with the speculation of a professional hit. Please tell me that's a load of bollocks, Clive?"

"Debs - there are a lot of unanswered questions."

"Great. Oh and another thing, did you know she has a daughter here in the UK, who is apparently flying out there in a day or so?"

CHAPTER 6

9.38pm. Monday 10th August 2015. Estepona.

I anticipated Debbie might have unearthed more than just proof that Jessica actually existed. But the mere fact there was so little in her file struck me as strange. I could have asked Debbie to extract a file on any one of the United Kingdom's sixty odd million population and get back more information than the few typed words relating to dear old Jessica. Something isn't right, which only whets my appetite, or if I was still in the force, make my 'coppers nose' twitch. Similar to my endeavours, keeping my past life history safely locked away from prying eyes, I'm beginning to wonder if Jessica did the same. But, for what reason?
I end my contact with Debbie and replace my mobile in my pocket with her last words ringing in my ear.
"I suppose this is not the last I'm going to hear about this Jessica woman. Is it?"
And she's probably correct with her assumption.
I need a clear head for what I propose to undertake tomorrow, but the need for a drink supersedes rational thinking and I think better with alcohol in my system anyway.

Fred's place has a few recognisable customers, who I amiably acknowledge, but before I rest my backside on

a stool by the bar, the proprietor is at my side, ushering me outside.
"What have you found out?" Fred whispers, appearing to be fearful of even his own shadow.
"Give me a break, Fred. She's been dead less than twenty four hours and you expect me to come up with answers. Have you forgotten; I've been retired for four years?" I whisper back, disengaging his hand from my elbow.
"I know all about that, but don't you coppers say the first forty eight hours is the most important time to catch a criminal?" My interrogator is becoming annoying.
"I've done some spade work with a call back to London, but there's nothing there to go on. Are you sure you know nothing about Jessica's past, or what she did for a living, as it seems ridiculous for me to understand why an old lady...okay she might have been a tad overweight...should be gunned down in such a way." There's humour in my voice, as by mentioning the size of the lady might be a factor into why she was killed.
Fred looks at me open-mouthed at my callous phraseology and is just about to voice his admonishment, when he realises I'm taking the piss out of him. Thank God he smiles, casting his gremlins away and returning humour back into the place I call my 'local'.
"Oh, very funny. Come on in and let me buy you a drink. I've managed to find that card I told you about. What an apt name for a copper....Detective Chief Superintendent Jack Gordon. Shame he's not a full

blown Commissioner. With a name like that, he could get a part in a *Batman* film.
It was Fred's turn to laugh, but I knew the name all right and didn't like the fact he knew where I'd escaped to.
"Before we go in, Fred, is it correct what I've heard about Jessica having a daughter?" It's my turn to grab his elbow.
"Yes, she has, or should say had. By what I hear, she's coming over tomorrow to organise the funeral."
I look at Fred and he immediately senses I'm annoyed.
"What's wrong with you, Fred? You ask me to find out why she is murdered and then, after I ask for everything you know about the woman, you conveniently forget to tell me she has a daughter. Do me a favour and ask Margaret if she knows when the daughter is coming over." I know if anyone knows anything about Jessica, it'll be Margaret, her best friend. But whether Margaret knows anything about Jessica's secret past, I doubt. If Jessica was the woman I think she was, like me, she kept her cards close to her ample bosom. "Don't tell me next the daughter's been in your bar and you actually know her quite well."
Fred responds by looking away, a similar mannerism he'd shown before when knowing he'd withheld information. I'd not noticed this trait before, but in future, I'll be looking out for it.
"Well...yes. Shelly has been in the bar. Quite a few times."
My facial contours give away my frustrations on hearing this snippet of news. My eyes narrow.

"Oh...fucking hell, Fred. I've asked people back in the UK for favours I wouldn't normally ask, as it could get them in serious shit if they were found out. And then you just casually slip in the conversation, Jessica's daughter comes into your place and you know her by name, Shelly. You've wasted me a whole day, when all I needed to do was to wait for her to arrive. She'll know everything I want to know about her mother...thanks Fred...yeah, I'll take you up on that drink, but not just the one. You owe me."

CHAPTER 7

8.13am. Tuesday 11th August 2015. Estepona.

Ground Hog day number one hundred and twenty arrives, accompanied by yet another hangover and another clear blue sky to accompany the usual oppressive heat. I look at my watch and it reminds me there have been just twenty four hours since Fred phoned declaring the fate of Jessica. I slip out of bed to start my usual daily ritual of robe, kitchen, coffee and fags, my curtains again replicating the EU flag on the seafront by hanging limply, as I lower myself out of view of the public below onto my wicker sofa on the terrace.

My heart-rate quickens hearing the first chords of my ring-tone blast out. No, I've been through this same scenario yesterday. I stop myself from answering straight away to break the sequence, purposely taking a mouthful of coffee before lighting a '*Superking*'. It's Fred.

"Yep." I answer, letting the caller know I'm not too happy, and sure enough, Fred's first words attempt to appease me.

"Hello, Clive. I'm sure you're not too happy with me, but I didn't do it on purpose. Sorry...look...after you left last night, I got Shelly's number off Margaret and phoned her. She's landing on the eleven o'clock flight into Gibraltar this morning and I'm picking her up. She's distraught, of course, but we spoke for a while. She doesn't know you, but wants a meet."

I cut in, anticipating what I didn't want to hear next. "You didn't tell her I'm an ex-copper. Please tell me you didn't."

There is an audible silence on the line.

"Oh, fuck me, Fred, you did."

"No, no, it's not like that."

A blustering kerfuffle of excuses pour into my ear. It finally ends with the word...sorry. It's become an all too common word.

"I needed to convince her of who you were and if we are going to get reasons why this happened, you are the only person equipped with the experience to get the job done. She's promised to keep your identity a secret and I believe her."

"Oh, it's so kind of you to say you believe her. It's down to me, you arsehole, if I believe her." The line goes quiet until I respond, losing the aggression from my previous rant. "Okay, Fred. Good work." I praise, probably totally confusing him. "We'll strike early, so on the way back up here from the airport, recommend somewhere for us to meet before you take her back to Jessica's place. Once inside her mum's house, with reminders scattered all over the place, she might just collapse into a shell of remorse and clam up. Don't need that. When you've thought of a place, phone me. You know this town better than me, so chose somewhere quiet, where we can talk without some overzealous waiter hanging around."

~O~

Shelly McGill, that is if she is still using her mother's surname, isn't the vision I expect to see when she follows Fred into *Paulo's Chiringito,* a beach bar half way between Du Quesa and Estepona. The old fallacy of 'if you want to know what your future wife will look like in thirty years' time, just look at her mother' would be entirely incorrect in this case. I guess her age to be in her early forties and from where I get to my feet, resembles not a trace of her parent. Six inches over five feet, or thereabouts, her height is extenuated by three inch heels. I like tall women. Her shoulder length, brunette hair appears natural and bounces off the straps of a summer dress, quite conservative in design, but on her, stunning.

I ignore Fred and don't even respond to his gracious introduction of his companion when pulling a chair out from under the table, offering a place for Shelly to sit. She smiles, not sheepishly, but as a confident woman, her make-up sparse in its application, but sufficient to highlight deep blue eyes. Now seated, she crosses her legs confirming the entire package has been well looked after.

"Hello. It's Shelly, isn't it? I'm Clive." Oblivious to Fred's summary of names, I repeat the roll call. "I'm so sorry we have to meet under these circumstances. I knew your mother and I'm shocked this could've happened. With your help, Shelly, I might be able to unravel this mess, but I need to ask you some questions. Some questions you might feel you can't answer, but I hope you do to the best of your ability. You understand?"

Shelly nods, but still hasn't spoken.
"Shall we have something to drink?" I enquire, knowing if Fred's mouth is as dry as mine, he'd readily accept a dampener.
I turn, getting a waiter's attention, which isn't hard, as apart from a couple outside on the beach, we are his sole customers. I turn back when Shelly utters her first words.
"It's a bit early, but a gin and tonic would be nice."
Her voice is devoid of an accent, apart from it being educated. Fred pipes in with his need for a lager.
"I've seen the TV weather and news reports back home, but it's not until you feel it for yourself that you can understand the intensity of this heat. It would drive me crazy."
Reaching down to her handbag, she extracts a *Kleenex* and skilfully dabs her neck, not intentionally sexual, but I see Fred's eyes following her hand. "I suppose you get used to it after a while living down here."
She visually contradicts herself, as she appears to be as cool as a cucumber.
Maybe it's the state of grief Shelly is feeling, that explains why she chooses to comment on the weather rather than the reason why she is here. I'm not sure, so there is no point fluffing around the subject or making small talk, as all three of us know precisely why we're here and it isn't to criticise the heat or indulge ourselves with a liquid lunch.
"If I appear insensitive, Shelly, I apologise, but, as Fred has probably primed you, I need some answers concerning your mother. I believe you can save me a lot of unnecessary leg work with what you know."

She smiles at nothing in particular and certainly not at Fred or me. To be certain of not being interrupted once I start interrogating Shelly, no, interrogate might be the wrong word, I wait for the waiter to bring over the drinks. Fred chose well to meet here, as the closest ears are sprawled out under an umbrella, quite a considerable distance away.
"I must start by asking, when did your mother retire?" It was an easy question to start the proceedings, asked on purpose to try and put Shelly at ease, but she stalled with her reply. This is not going to be as easy as I first thought.
"I'll have to get back to you with that. I'm not sure." Her manner isn't brusque, but I feel she isn't being as forthcoming as I need her to be.
"Okay...then how long has she been living down here in Estepona? Approximately will do."
"She's had a house here for ages. She sold up and moved out of London, using the proceeds to buy the house down here. I used to spend my summer holidays with her every year, but that stopped for some reason." Ah, we're getting somewhere close to answering my first question. "Can you remember when that was?" I need Shelly to relax.
"Yes, I do remember." It is as if she has struck a 'eureka' moment. "The millennium. The year two thousand."
"Are you sure, because through my preliminaries, I believed she retired in nineteen ninety one." This is interesting.
"No, I'm certain it was that year. The year she reached sixty. Yes I'm sure."

I scratch down notes as I talk.

"Now I'm going to ask probably the most important question." I stall before asking. "Just what did Jessica do for a living?" I wait, looking at Shelly's face for any twitch or nervous reaction. There is neither. She is as calm as when I first set eyes on her.

"I don't believe I can answer your question."

Before she continues with probably a well-rehearsed monologue, I interrupt. "Look, Shelly. If you want to find out why your mother was murdered, you need to trust me and Fred. If my career taught me anything, I believe there is more to this than meets the eye. If I am correct with my assumptions and I have very little to go on, unless you're frank with me, this action against your mother will be judged as just another insignificant murder. The culprit will never be found and the case will forever be filed as unsolved. I promise, I shall do my level best to hunt down the culprits."

"But you are also retired. What can you do?" At last Shelly shows signs of emotion.

"Correct and you know what that means...my hands aren't tied by correct procedure."

Shelly remains silent. I see she is unsure whether to allow me the nugget I need to proceed. "I was a very good copper, Shelly, and know how to reach very important people." I wait and take a mouthful of lager. Fred mimics my action, his presence unnecessary, but does no harm.

"Okay Clive, but what I'm about to tell you might be contravening the official secrets act."

Now we are getting somewhere and I had an inkling it might go along such lines, what with all the secrecy Debbie stumbled upon.
"This must go no further than you two and I must ask for your complete discretion. If, at some later date, I am questioned about this, I shall deny everything. Do I have your word on this?"
Fred and I nod in unison, but knowing his reputation, I wonder just how long he'll be able to stop himself leaking it out as one of his special morsels. I'll need to have a word with Fred later.
"After leaving university, my mother was approached by someone, I can't mention names, but he was of high standing within the civil service. She was simply asked if she would care to join his team at *The Treasury*. I believe she agreed, as the money was quite good, but didn't believe the position to be any more than a stop-gap in her career. You see, she studied law and achieved a first, believing one day she'd enter chambers as a junior and climb as far up the ladder as she could. Maybe a barrister or reaching the heady heights of 'silk'."
Watching her recall her mother's early life, much of it a correct account, I can't help but see Shelly adding her own version of how she saw her mother's aspirations.
"Excuse me." Her head drops and her voice descends to a whisper.
It takes time, but I see a heart emerging from under her armour. Justifiably so. Would I pour my feelings out to a person I'd only met minutes before? But maybe Shelly did it too quick.

After a short pause, she raises her head with confidence restored. “As I was saying, my mother had been in the same office for about eighteen months when an interview at a completely different department was offered. So, I believe my mother jumped at the offer and accepted. This was with *MI6.*”

Fred nearly chokes on his lager, but I suspected something of this kind.

“You don’t look surprised that my dear old mum became a high ranking officer within that organisation, Clive.” She threw me a look to see my reaction.

Before answering, I wait for Fred to regroup, wiping spilt lager from the front of his t-shirt with a napkin.

“As I said, Shelly, I was a very good copper and not shocked easily. Thank you for taking us into your confidence. I now have more than enough to start digging for answers, but there are just a few more questions I must ask and I believe one or two might be the hardest for you to answer.”

If it’s possible, Fred’s curiosity increases, whilst Shelly looks quizzically at me, attempting to pre-empt what I might ask.

“What is your date of birth?”

Without hesitation she relays the date. “The second of June, nineteen seventy-four. Why do you ask?”

“This might be the hardest part to answer. Can you tell me your father’s name?” I quickly reply, wanting to take her off guard.

Shelly’s eyes widen for a second before returning to their beautiful, normal state.

“I’m sorry, Clive. As you guessed, I cannot answer you.”

"Why is that, Shelly?" I persist, listening to Debbie's long lost words ringing in my ears when criticising my Rottweiler-like methods. Not everyone you interview, she would say, is guilty, so cut them some slack. I would reply to her over a glass of red in *The Albion*, 'let them prove their innocence before I turn into a poodle'. Again, with a few choice words, I have pierced her defences. For some, strange reason, Shelly has retreated, becoming economical with the truth.

"Is it because you don't want to tell me or is it you just don't know?"

"You bastard, Clive. You're so bloody clever, why don't you tell me?" For the first time since we sat, Shelly turns her head and gazes out, in this case across the Mediterranean, a trait I'd learnt long ago when an interviewee is attempting to summon up any old bullshit to get them out of a scrape.

"Shelly, you're not on trial here, but if we are to work this all out, I need the truth and not some garbled version of it. I believe you do not know your father's name (I'm guessing) and that your mother has never married (guessing again)."

Shelly turns her eyes onto mine. Hers are beginning to moisten.

"I don't know where you have got your information from, but you are correct." Her back straightens to lift her G&T off the table and sink the entire contents in one go. "You're very good at your job, Clive. I would hate to get on the wrong side of you. Were you ever married? Poor bitch, if you were."

I'm beginning to like this woman a lot. A feisty sort and one who could give me a run for my money if I so chose.

But calling me a bastard? That's strong, coming from the lips of one.
"Do be careful, Clive. I don't believe you understand how devious and cunning these people can be. If they get wind you're sniffing around, they can make your life very uncomfortable, even dangerous." Is she warning me or advising caution?
"As we've come so far, it would be a wasted opportunity not to ask just one further question before we take lunch and forget all about this for an hour or two. If that's alright with you, Shelly? What do you do for a living?" Immediately, I see I've struck another chord.
"I can tell this worries you, so allow me to answer for you." The drama is beginning to be too much for Fred. He's visibly hanging on to my next words. "You are also connected to MI6, am I correct."
Shelly smiles and looks into my eyes. She re-crosses her legs from the position she was sitting before and leans down to her handbag on the floor. Reaching inside, she pulls out a packet of *Marlboro,* flips open the carton and extracts a cigarette. Placing it between her red lips, she lights the tobacco and sucks the smoke deep, not once blinking or removing her piercing stare. Oh, you are good, I evaluate, wondering if her mother might have taught her all these little tricks. She didn't have to answer because she knew I already knew, but perhaps to appease Fred's curiosity, Shelly obliged.
"Yes Clive, you are correct and I see it doesn't surprise you."
"No it doesn't, Shelly. Like mother, like daughter."

CHAPTER 8

8.21am. Wednesday 12th August, 2015. Estepona.

This morning arrives, much like all the other previous mornings. I've forgotten what clouds and rain look like, but on this morning, my usual garb, which usually consists of shorts, vest and flip-flops, are not suitable. Turning up to a funeral wearing such items, I believe, would not be appreciated by mourning folk and make me stick out like a sore thumb, which is precisely the opposite of what I want to achieve. Jessica was a popular old girl and I believe many will wish to pay their last respects. I expect a crowd containing a few who do not live in Spain. These are the targets I want to identify as they should be easy to spot with their London grey faces, but they are also the ones I need to keep well clear of, but at the same time, surreptitiously get their image on my mobile. On the face of it, not an easy exercise to execute, as assuming some will be from the agency, keeping a low profile will be high on their agenda. If it wasn't such a macabre occasion, I'd enjoy pitching my art of being incognito against theirs, a bread and butter exercise requisite when working at the *Yard.* But apart from all this subterfuge, I'm amazed at the speed of things happening regarding Jessica's funeral, especially in a country where the word *Mañana* is a clue when to expect a modicum of action. Died on Sunday, autopsy Tuesday, cremated Wednesday. It would never happen in the UK, especially when the corpse has been murdered.

Opening my wardrobe, I fish out one of five suits which have been hanging there, untouched, since arriving on these shores four years ago. My choice is charcoal grey, the nearest I own to black, but who's going object? I wager my dress code will be more respectful than many who attend, but a black tie is beyond the scope of my accessories. Navy blue will have to do. I shower and shave, don a clean white shirt, followed by the suit which miraculously contains straight creases running down the front of each trouser leg. A long forgotten feeling interrupts the third inhalation on my second cigarette. A feeling of going to work.

From below my terrace I hear a car's horn blast out three rapid honks, a signal Fred has arrived to give me a lift.

"Hello mate." I say greeting Fred, crunching my frame to squeeze into his *Porsche's* passenger seat. "I bet you weren't expecting to hear what Shelly said yesterday."

"No, you're right. Who would have thought dear old Jessica worked for that lot, eh, and not just a bead counter. Looks as if she was one of the top bitches." Fred laughs and I'm pleased to see he's back to his old, irreverent self.

"And what about Shelly? Talk about keeping it in the family. It's going to be interesting to see if any of her old work mates turn up and we'll know who they are by their interest in the daughter."

Fred drives out of town, under the motorway onto a road heading for the mountains. A mile further on we approach a stucco, whitewashed building standing alone, where, although we are early, a crowd predominately dressed in black, has already gathered. I tell Fred to drive past and park up the road away from the prying eyes of those who might be doing exactly what we hope to achieve by taking a record of those attending who might be unrecognisable.

Utilising Fred's knowledge of the area, we slink in through a back gate, entering the open halls of remembrance, a conclave of roofless high walls in which the ashes of the deceased are held in symmetrical holes, well, that's what I call them, but they must have a proper name. I'm not at all religious and can see the reason to cremate, but this honeycombed construction leaves me cold with very little feeling. It doesn't matter what I think, but I couldn't leave a deceased loved-one in this heat, festering in an urn, squeezed into a hole in a wall. Mind you, on a brighter side, it takes up less space than a hole in the ground and doesn't require tending. We appear to be alone, away from the other sheep-like mourners congregating at the front of the crematorium. An ideal opportunity to light up and get used to the layout of the place.

"You don't suppose there's anybody from MI6 here, do you Clive?" Fred poses a question.

"I bloody hope so, Fred. That's the whole point of this charade. I want to see faces and recognise their profiles if I see them again. Then I'll know who they are before they know who I am."

To retain our sanity, it's essential we escape this brick fenced cauldron preventing heat to escape. I see beads of sweat dribbling down Fred's face and can only imagine what's going on under his shirt, if what's happening under mine is anything to go by. Eerily, the sound of an out-of-view, muttering crowd descends to silence.

"The funeral cortège must be getting close." Fred whispers, mimicking the reverence of the unseen mourners. "What do we do?"

"We wait until the coffin is carried inside, then join the rear of the crowd, so nobody witnesses our arrival. Hopefully, everyone will be facing one way, following the coffin towards the chapel of rest, if that's what it's called out here."

Stealthily, we integrate, joining the back of the crowd where a hearse is parked in front of the building's main doors, its tail-gate swung upright, allowing eight pall bearers to slide out the white casket. True to my prediction, everybody is reverently watching the action. Nobody notices our arrival.

There must be over a hundred people squeezing into a space catering for only sixty, when Fred and I are the last to enter. From unseen hands, the large doors close behind us, their unforgiving solidness pressing against our backs, leaving not the thickness of a cigarette paper between those standing. If this isn't a recipe for people to drop like flies, I don't know a better one. It must be a hundred and ten in here, at least and getting hotter. Where are the 'Health and Safety' brigade when you need them. I can just imagine Debbie giggling, waiting for something to happen.

The service begins, fronted by a white gowned, bespectacled, balding middle-aged man whose Spanish dedication hasn't ventured too far into his monologue, when true to form, as I envisaged, the first of what I expect to be many, passes out. This is definitely not what I want at my funeral. Fortunately, it's someone seated, a black veiled Spanish woman who's found the occasion and temperature all too much. Thankfully she's near the front and is carried out aboard her chair to a side door. Even when it opens, there is no respite to the inside temperature.

The service continues with true grit, but delivered in Andalusian, an accent indecipherable to an outsider's ears, especially those attached to a British head. If it were at all possible to comprehend her sense of humour, Jessica probably chose the language it would be delivered in just to piss off those she probably didn't want to attend her funeral in the first place. Yes, Jessica could be irritating if you didn't know her, but can't we all?

I look to my left, avoiding the stares of an elderly gent squeezed up against me and see Fred loosening his tie so as to unbutton his shirt with sweat visibly dripping down his face. I take his lead, but remove my tie completely, stuffing it into my jacket pocket, much to the annoyance of my Siamese twin welded against me, his tilted face staring up at me from my chest level.

"Got a problem, ol' son?"

He doesn't reply.

Fred looks at me, winks and smiles. Somehow he's managed to extract his mobile and lifts it above his head, slowing moving it from left to right, obviously videoing. I can do nothing, but wish he could just take photos. I take his cue and retrieve mine whilst agitating my 'friend', who knows better this time not to show irritation. Lifting my hand, I pretend to lean against a white, stone pillar, but in actual fact, find it the perfect disguise to cover the entire populated floor with a zoomed lens. Whilst the white gowned fellow prattles off to the congregation in his obscure lingo, I sweep the area taking God knows how many stills.

A second body succumbs and slumps to the floor, landing softly due to the surrounding 'human cushions'. Obviously triggered by events, our gowned Master of Ceremonies brings this folly to an abrupt end after just fourteen minutes into the ceremony. By pressing a button, he 'brings the curtain down' over the raised coffin, signalling with outstretched arms and in broken English, 'That's that'. To the entire gatherings relief, the doors swing open, allowing bodies to tumble out, the first being Fred and me. But the scramble from the interior serves as the perfect shield. It isn't 'women and children first' stuff, but beautifully orchestrated to mask our presence. Intent to save their own sanity, nobody cares who we are. They are just relieved to escape the oven, and I don't mean Jessica's final fate.

It should be a solemn occasion, but to an innocent observer, the sight of a crowd of men hurriedly removing ties and jackets and the women raising the hems of their dresses as high as to remain decent, they might be forgiven for believing they are witnessing the beginnings of a mass orgy. The crematorium's courtyard is in total disarray. Perfect camouflage to make our getaway.

~O~

Jackets discarded and thrown onto the *Porsche's* back parcel shelf, Fred and I try to regain composure with wound down windows doing sweet FA to offer relief.
"Well Clive, I don't know about you, but it doesn't feel like I've been to a funeral. What a fucking fiasco." Fred eloquently phrases his view of the ritual and I don't think I could have put it any better.
"No mate, you're right."
From our covert, seated position, we have a perfect view of the continuing mayhem.
"Do you know where the wake is being held?" I ask, but have no intentions of going.
"Yeah...it's at *Kempinski's.* Must have a bit of money in the bank, if she can afford that place for sixty odd people. Shelly did ask me if I'd do it. I told her she must be joking. All that lot descending on me...can you imagine? Ten inside and the rest scattered around the street outside. It would've been worse than the crematorium. Are we going?" I see Fred is eager to indulge in the grand spread *Kempinski's* would undoubtedly layout.
"No Fred, not me. I've got all I want. If you could text over to my mobile all the videos you took, that would be great. It wouldn't be clever to get involved in small talk with faces I don't know, who might be, at a later stage, found to be connected to all this. No...I'm going to keep well away. I'd appreciate a lift home though, Fred. Cheers."

~O~

My body temperature must be nearing the passing-out point and I'm exasperated by a frantic attempt to rip off my clothes and dive under a cold shower. The shock of opposite sensations give my neighbour's an audible message that I've arrived back home, but oh...the luxury of something so simple.

I grab my robe and via the fridge, I fondle an iced beer bottle on the way to my terrace. The sun is as high as it'll get today and beats down, drying my skin in seconds, only for sweat to take its place within minutes. My thoughts are private and I shouldn't say this, but Jessica's death has made me feel alive again, dispelling the slow decent into pretending I love doing nothing. What I can do and how far I can take this is out of my control, but I'm going to enjoying finding out if I'm as good as I think I am.

Bringing up the photo library on my mobile, I realise I must have taken over sixty shots, far too many, and decide to store all those with a milk-bottle appearance and delete those who obviously live here. I recognise most of these, even know some of their names, so can safely discard them as being 'innocent'. I hope I'm not being too hasty, but witnessing Margaret's distraught image amongst the many who became her friends, none of them could be connected to Jessica's murder.

I allow my robe to open, believing the message my misinformed brain tells me that the sun's heat will dry the sweat covering my torso, but of course, it does the complete opposite. It's unnerving to believe only ten minutes have passed since a soothing encounter under a cold shower stabilised my body temperature, but I feel similar action is soon to be warranted. God, it's so hot.

Thankfully, the contents inside the chilled beer bottle relieve my parched throat with just one gulp, but before a second can be savoured, my Samsung emits four, just audible, notes from a pocket, signalling an incoming text. True to his word, Fred's message arrives with an attachment of two three minute videos. It reads *"Hope these help. You should be here. Great party if everyone wasn't so sad. Whoops, shouldn't say that."* His humour is not everybody's cup of tea, but it's what endears me to the bugger.

Viewing his handy work, they're good and precise, showing the height of individuals. Whether they can be utilised is another matter.

What I'm about to do next, I know will not be well received. I phone Debbie, warning her there's a text on its way containing a gallery of mug-shots and videos of people I need names to and if convenient, their place of employment. As sure as the Pope is a Catholic, she'll not be happy, but if anybody can achieve a result, Debbie can, by identifying each image with a brief history. She's not going to like me asking.

CHAPTER 9

11.14am. Wednesday 12th August 2015. Gibraltar International Airport.

Julia's view from her window onboard Gibraltar bound flight EZY8901 from London Gatwick, seemingly encompasses the entire, sun kissed Mediterranean below, until the pilot begins his decent and circles into the wind to begin his approach. Not quite believing her eyes, it isn't the size of the 'rock' she stares at, but where the hell is this thing going to land. Unprepared, and more used to international airports where the nose of her *Boeing* should be landing on acres of concrete, this one is scarily different. There is sea at one end and sea at the other of a very short, narrow runway, some might liken it to a section of a Spanish motorway - unfinished.

For all her doubt, the plane, of course, lands and grinds to a halt. Within ten minutes she finds herself outside the newly built terminal, her sole piece of hand-luggage being a wheelie case containing nothing more for a two day break than a swimsuit, sari and shorts, linen trousers, tops, evening dress and her best "*Victoria's Secret*" underwear sets. Julia wasn't given much notice, twenty-four hours to be precise and isn't prepared for the heat smacking her in the face when exiting the plane. Garbed in a roll-neck cotton sweater, black jacket and trousers, surely she'd read about the heat down here in Spain, but no, I forgot, she's 'Human Resources', how stupid of me.

Things happened yesterday for Julia, which came completely out of the blue. Firstly, Phil's email arrived, stating, he'd been ordered to attend a funeral in an 'Official' capacity in a place called Estepona. He had cut short his family vacation further up the coast in Alicante. Secondly, it was the bit about 'Could you join me for two nights of fun at the *'H10 Estepona Palace Hotel?'* which excited her.

His instructions were simple. When you land, grab a cab to the hotel and check in. A reservation is in your name for a single room. Enjoy the spoils of an infinity pool, spa and bar and wait for me to turn up post funeral, post wake. Julia salivated at the chance of a bit of sun and two nights with her man.

Passing through the Spanish border on foot, a group of taxi drivers notice her approach and without fear of her understanding a word of their garbled lingo, discuss what this over-made-up and dressed totally wrong cougar, might be taken for. Having agreed a price, well not really agreed, more she points at her email with the hotel address and the driver states a price. Whilst neither understands each other, Julia barters, the driver smiles, but the price doesn't budge...ninety euros. Thirty over the normal fare. Oh well, 'Human Resources'. Resources being the optimum word in her case, as all she will do is get a receipt and charge it. And if she is really resourceful, might add a cheeky number one in front of the ninety.

It doesn't matter how much is charged, she would've willingly paid double just to get out of the sun and get relief from air-conditioning whilst sitting back in plastic-coated rear seats, marvelling at the beautiful and picturesque coastline from the cab window. All too soon her journey comes to an end, arriving at the hotel. Handing over the fare, *sin* tip, Julia enters the foyer, somewhat impressed with the luxurious surroundings. Yes, she is going to enjoy the next couple of days.

No more than twenty minutes pass when, refreshed in suitable attire and under a floppy hat, bought from the hotel souvenir shop, Julia is faced with the dilemma of which sun-lounger to flop on. Each heavy duty, plastic bed is adorned with a monogrammed hotel towel, the size of which would swamp a family of six, but regrettably too large to fit in her overnight luggage. Pity, she smiles, sauntering to her choice, garbed in a see-through linen sari, her modesty protected by a polka-dot swimsuit underneath. Another definite plus is apparent. No screaming kids or overweight northerners parading their loyalty to *Manchester United.* But it soon becomes clear and all too obvious, high temperatures aren't fun, testament to sweat and eye-shadow dribbling down her face.

Conditions dictate she finds solace, so abandons her quest to go a shade darker than *Michael Jackson,* by retreating to the comforts of her air-conditioned room. How typical, she thinks, now stripped naked, peeking out from behind the protection of a convenient curtain upon the sun-kissed panorama. Back home I crave for sunshine, then when I get into it, I can't bear it.

Further relief from a tepid shower precedes donning a little floral number, elegantly camouflaging the purple lacy bra and knicker set underneath. Phil's last Christmas gift is perfect for these conditions, but possibly too young for London. Preened and inspected, her reflection bounces back from a mirrored wall. A waft of *Jo Malone* creates the finished article. Yes, she is good to go.

Unwilling to parade too early in the bar, fearing her sole presence might be misconstrued, Julia waits, seated bolt upright for fear of creasing anything, waiting for a word from her lover.

Her mobile throbs, sending a quaint electric shock of anticipation through her body if it's Phil's text. It is, informing he is on his way and to meet in the bar in ten minutes. Unintentionally swinging her hips, Julia enters only to find she is the sole occupant, apart from the barman, in a room opening up to a vast patio resembling a designer's idea of what postmodernism resembles when clashing with Spanish tradition. Okay, she thinks, it's only six o'clock and still light. I'll order a wine and find a nice secluded table, after all, there's the whole place to find the ideal spot.

A white wine is delivered along with olives, how civilized she thinks, but ten minutes come and go with no sign of Phil. Unconsciously, her fingers rhythmically begin tapping the glass top table, seriously encouraging chipped nail-varnish. The smile she's practiced earlier slides from her lips after twenty minutes and is replaced by one she keeps for work. Shit...won't he ever appear on time? A rat-tat-tat fierce drum beat, reminiscent of *Ginger Baker* at his finest, punctures the air.

Right on cue, as Julia seriously thinks of abandoning her plans, Phil appears and calls out his order for a beer, how anal she thinks whilst melting at the vision of him approaching. A man of fifty six, six feet odd tall with steely blue eyes, topped with close cropped salt and pepper hair, he is, as usual, impeccably turned out in navy chinos, pale blue linen shirt and loafers. The perfect colour scheme to exaggerate a deep tan.

Rising to her feet, her practiced smile returns, Julia accepts a peck on her cheek. A waft of *Hugo Boss* stings her nostrils. They sit, not too close, but sufficient for Julia to drop a hand beneath the table top in search of his. Flattering, as ever, Phil comments on her appearance, only for the small talk to be interrupted by the barman. Obviously parched, Phil empties half the glass as Julia prattles on about her day, concluding with, 'whose funeral was it that was so important to cut your vacation short?'

Raising a finger towards the bar, the steward acknowledges Phil's requirement for another beer, but not for Julia. He's witnessed her behavioral changes before, caused by drinking too early in the evening. Fully aware of this problem, she begrudgingly accepts his ungallant posturing, but is troubled by his vague response to her question.

"A retired ex-pat who worked in some department decides to drop dead, so as I was already over here in Spain, it's decided, that as DC, I represent the firm as a mark of respect at her funeral."

"Did you know her?" Julia enquires.

"No." Giving Julia the look, Phil clearly indicates there would be no further chit-chat about the funeral. Knowing better than pursue the drift of this conversation, Julia is happy to enjoy the precious snatched time together without talking shop.

~O~

Much later, after being wined, dined and brandied at *La Pampa*, a restaurant on the edge of the old town, they retire to Phil's sumptuous double extravaganza. It's far from the first time Phil has bedded her in a hotel room, but Julia is excited, tingling at the thought of what will follow, whilst stripping, leaving Phil to waddle off, slightly under the influence, to the bathroom.

It was then, Julia notices it, a crumpled order of service pamphlet left on his bedside cabinet, in memory of Jessica McGill.

The name staring up at her produces a shiver. The same woman Debs wanted a file check on two days ago. Surely, this has to be one of those bizarre coincidences. There just can't be any connection between the two events.

Should she mention Debs' enquiry to Phil?

Phil emerges naked from the bathroom, one look and she knows her answer - an emphatic NO. Not for now at least.

CHAPTER 10

7.15am. Wednesday 12th August 2015. Brighton Railway Station.

For some reason, I absolutely loathe Wednesday's. Monday's you just have to claw your way through the day, laying low normally as a result from the excesses of the weekend. Tuesday's, you feel somewhat rejuvenated from a sluggish Monday, but Wednesday's are just dull. It's a common fact, people are most productive on a Tuesday. By Wednesday you're bored and weary of all the damn bullshit.

Today, being Wednesday, is no exception. This morning at 7.15 a.m., I stroll up platform 4 at Brighton station, *Metro* freebie newspaper in hand and am already depressed. Job demands I have to commute to London on what has been forecast to be a beautiful and sunny day and here am I leaving the seaside to travel up to the smoke. My first annoyance of the day occurs when my favourite seat is taken, or should I say, in the seventh carriage, the fourth one down on the left next to a window and out of sunlight, is not mine. I know it's petty, as a seat is just a seat, but only those of us who commute can understand what I'm talking about - end of.

I sit, instead, in the one behind. On-time leaving, but what has departure time got anything to do with it? It's when the bugger arrives. How extremely kind of an enormous, lardy-arsed, fat bloke to decide to squeeze his sweaty-self next to me at Preston Park. My joy being here in the first place explodes into emphatic euphoria when he not only takes out his lap-top, but also a *Tupperware* container filled with muesli and a carton of yoghurt. I tense in readiness as this throwback from *Fred Flintstone,* prepares to begin noisily tapping away at the keyboard whilst demolishing, open mouthed, his daintily formulated dietary breakfast...I'd wet myself with laughter if I wasn't already depressed. My joy reaches new heights as we close in on Haywards Heath. The quality of his screeching down a *Blackberry* to some poor cow at the other end, allows everyone in the carriage the privilege to be informed we are running late and to reschedule all his morning meetings. Clearly this idiot is on the wrong train...what a pretentious knob.

I'm now in such a stroppy mood, even before we arrive in Victoria a mere twenty nine minutes late, only to be greeted by an automated announcement by 'Southern'. "Due to overheated signal boxes between East Croydon and Clapham Junction we are delayed by 29 minutes. We apologise for any delay and inconvenience we may have caused to your journey"

I fume, 'May have caused to your journey'. We're all bloody late for work. I'm positive *Southern Rail* do this deliberately to infuriate the poor hapless commuter as you can only claim "delay" refunds, if the train is thirty minutes late or later - bastards!

In a muggy, morning city heat, I make the fifteen minute walk to the office in trainers and suit. Never a good look, but why wreck your good shoes. Late again. No time today for a decent coffee stop at Nero's. I go through the daily ritual of "Morning Alan (he's security at the front of the building), Morning Deb's" courteous greeting, then demands I show my ID pass despite he's known me for 10 years. He's lovely, but an absolute job's worth and takes great pleasure in giving the 'none shall pass' hand gesture, insisting I rifle through my handbag to fish out my pass to show him, a process repeated down the line to facilitate access through more security barriers to get to lifts. I don't begrudge him still working, but at well passed his sell-by date, in the event of an actual attack, he'd be as effective as a fart in a tornado—no offence Alan.

I make my way through more security pass swipes to my desk, just in time for the daily huddle. Deep joy, Baldrick presides over an ever-annoying whiteboard, where the troops update on cases they're working on. Bronzey has a good result in nailing a big shot eastern European women trafficker and who is now singing like a canary to the vice squad. Sam and Keavo are still trailing a big time cocaine dealer in north London. Brightening the day, I pipe up, endorsing the splendour and glamour of my role to insist they all complete their online fraud compliance module by close of play today. This is received, obviously, with rapturous enthusiasm! In absolute Clive style, I wonder how many lunch offers I'll receive in the next hour or so, to do it for them.

I change from trainers to appropriate office heels and head to the beast that is the coffee/tea machine.

It appears to be working, thank God for that. I get my usual cup and join in with the general discussion surrounding Ingrid, the 'Super's', dreaded barbeque on Saturday.
Am I going? Who with? How's everyone getting there, what should we take...blah blah blah. Yeah, like you lot are going to knock up a cheesecake or bannoffie pie! I bemoan that I'm on coleslaw duty.
I wander back to my desk, fire up the laptop to view today's delights.
Unsurprisingly, the upcoming deadline of the online compliance module has spurred my colleagues into a frenzy of emails, prefixed with the words "could you just..., here's my log in," followed by, "let's go to *Ball's Brothers* on me." - so bloody predictable from the mob, but it suits me. Rack up a few lunches...so that's to be my dull day.
Email from Ingrid, "*Could you also do some BBQ ribs as they were soooooo good last year. That would be great. Thanks, and do you know if Julia is coming? Just emailed her and got her out of office message saying she's not back in the office till Monday. Has she gone away? X*"
For fucks sake! I'm a humble administrator not a bloody caterer. Why doesn't she just order all the food from *Waitrose*, as she normally does?
I email back - yes I'll do some ribs and no, have no idea where Julia is or whether she's attending - slightly annoyed at myself for being slightly sycophantic, but hey, it's only a few ribs and sauce.
The rest of the morning till lunch is dealing with Sam, Keavo and Naomi's on line compliance modules. Out

of the blue, Bronzey suggests we go for a bite to eat and a glass - fine by me.

Over lunch Bronzey, a man in his fifties who's been with the force in his position for ten of those years, resembles a rotund, seventies porn star who, whilst complimenting this vision with a moustache and slightly too long wavy hair, asks me to do him a massive favour. The vice bust he just nailed saw him going into some seriously dubious places on a regular basis. Having to pay with a personal credit card, he needs to claim it back. Only problem is, all the receipts are charged to "*The Kitten Club.*"

Okay, I say. I can do some scanning wizardry. Copy and paste say a *Ball's Brothers* logo address and VAT code on the top of the receipt and if we get it into CONCUR, Ingrid should sign it off. Get it done by tomorrow, as she's too preoccupied with her bloody barbeque to notice. And Bronzey, you owe me massively.

A chink of a wineglass seals the deal.

Well-fed and wined, I return to the office and embark on another round of compliance modules. By four o'clock, all the troops are compliant and owe me large, leaving time to browse Amazon for new books when my phone rings.

Bloody marvellous. It's Clive. This can't be good. I get up and swiftly move into the little windowless room housing the beast of the photocopier.

"Hi Clive"

"Debs, need a favour. I'm texting some stills and videos I've taken at Jessica's funeral. Can you run them

through that face recognition database thing to see what you can find?"
"Whoa there, what happened to...How's the weather? How's your day been? Pleasant chit-chat...and where's the 'PLEASE'? Clive, not being funny mate, but whatever mad cap theories you may or may not have down there, it seems a complete closed shop over here on your Jessica, and you know dammed well I don't have access to the NEOFACE database."
"Debs, come on, you know what I'm like, I'm intrigued by this murder and I want to find out as much as I can."
"All very laudable I'm sure Clive, but my hands are reasonably tied, you bloody know that by now. Why don't you just let this go and enjoy beach life retirement?"
"Debs – I'm absolutely banking on a helping hand. Regrettably, I do understand, but will you still try to do it?"
"Clive you are an absolute cock."
"Undisputed, but will you do it please?"
Clive, really irritatingly, is normally right and he might be on to something, but I wish he would duck me out of this one.
"Oh, for fuck's sake, okay, I'll see what I can do. The boys have access to it and one in particular owes me a massive favour, but these favours have got to stop, Clive, before someone starts wondering what the hell I'm up to by poking around. You know what it's like here with everyone busying themselves with what everyone else is doing. Jesus, I should know being one the worst offenders. Are you listening to me? After

this, no more Miss Helpful, you got that? Oh, and don't text the files, they'll be too big and I don't think you can anyway from Spain to the UK. Email them to me using my personal address, I'll text it to you now."

"Yeah, yeah, yeah, Debs, I hear you. Last favour I promise, seriously though – cheers."

"You promise? Yeah, whatever - I've heard that bollocks before, Clive. Bye-bye for now then."

I go back to my desk, my iPhone pings denoting I have received an email. I'm just about to power down and leave the office, shall I look, oh well why not? Whatever Clive sent won't go through until tomorrow. I'll get Bronzey's login.

I quickly scroll through some of the stills, images of the backs of mourner's heads, then with side shots, presumably from an angle. The photographer (assume Clive) was tucked-up at the side of the pews. Might be able to get something from those. The NEOFACE system, designed by the Japanese giant *NEC*, is pretty sophisticated when using all its cloud based jiggery-pokery. Facilitating searches from its worldwide agency and border databases, If you've so much as booked a day trip to France, your passport details and photo will appear, all too "Big Brother" for me.

I fear backs of heads will prove useless, however. Even with such advanced technology, NEOFACE hasn't quite mastered the art of deducing who your hairdresser is.

I mutter under my breath. "There's a bloody clue in the name NEOFACE, Clive!"

There are two video files attached. I click the arrow to play the first, a 15 second shaky frame (*George Lucas* production this is not!) of more backs of heads. Once more, not a lot to go on. Whoever was taking this must have been 'Mister and Misses Popularity' at a funeral. The second video, a twenty second frame, is much the same, but at thirteen seconds, a tall guy in a grey suit briefly looks back at the film maker, clearly irked at their inappropriate behaviour in a place of remembrance.

The pit in my stomach lurches, in that 'What the fuck have I just seen?' way.

I stop the video, scanning around to ensure I'm not overlooked. The boys are animatedly discussing tonight's football match between *Tottenham Hotspur* and *Chelsea*, a big London Derby clash. The younger ones deciding (less well off) which pub they'll go to watch it at.

Just as I'm about to replay the video, Mister cocky-arse Sam yells down the office. "Nan, we're going to the '*Elephant*' to watch the match, want to join us?"

"Sam, I'd rather stick needles in my eyes but thanks all the same for the very kind offer."

They excitedly bundle out of the office. Baldrick has already left. Naomi looks as though she's on a date, if her appearance is anything to go by, emerging from the ladies loo. Too much lippy I'd say, but hey, far be it for me to say.

All quiet on the western front.

I tap the play icon on the video again, stop it at 13 seconds and stare at the screen. There, looking directly into the lens, is the unmistakable image of Phil Blunt, the DC. My head spins with so many questions, but I still just carry on staring at it. What is he doing there? He's supposed to be on holiday with his family.

What's his connection to our Jessica?
Why the brick wall and classified secrecy surrounding any search results?
Could it be pure coincidence that Julia is out of the office until Monday?
No, I'm not liking this at all. This is beginning to smell not too fragrant to me.
I power down the laptop, pop it into its bag, change back into my trainers and head off to catch the dreaded 5.46 to Littlehampton.
After the jostling to perform the platform to door shuffle, I secure a window seat with a copy of the *Evening Standard.*
From an observer, I'm scanning the front page, but am way too preoccupied to care about the Mayor of London candidate hopefuls' race.
I do nothing but stare out of the window all the way down to Hove, wondering what the fuck I've stumbled across. There could be a very simple explanation, of course. Phil just happens to leave the family holiday to be in sunny Estepona to join the locals paying their respects to a popular old lady, whose history just happens to be highly classified and only accessible through his office.
And, furthermore, Julia just happens to be out of the office...where?
Yeah right - simple case of pure coincidence - NOT!!
Nothing more to be done than text Julia.
"Ingrid wants to know if you're going to the BBQ on Saturday. Be warned. She's got her 'everyone bring a dish' head on."
Ten minutes later I get a return text.

"Yes, will be going. Sitting in a bar in a fab hotel in a place called Estepona. Waiting for Phil!! Yes, all very last minute. Will fill you in. Back Friday afternoon." Text ends with three smiley faces.

Okay, so we now throw the bunny boiler into the mix. The same bunny boiler who knows I asked about our Jessica and whose married shag was at the funeral.

This is getting worse!

It's alright for sodding Clive, barking his orders from his fucking sun bed, it's me that could get into serious trouble here if during the throes of passion, she tells him I was asking questions.

No, stop panicking - they wouldn't talk shop, surely, they'd have better things to do?

The train stops at Hove, I hadn't even noticed it is approaching.

I get off and outside the station immediately light up a cigarette, God I need this.

I call Clive.

It rings onto his voice-mail. Oh great.

"Clive, its Debs. Call me back as soon as you get this message."

There is one synonymous thing I notice living here by the sea, as soon as you get off the train the air is so much fresher, cleaner, particularly in the summer, so speaks me dragging on a cigarette!

Taking my usual route from the station to the *Seafield,* I am just about to cross the luxurious threshold, when my phone rings – Clive.

"Hey, Debs, what's up? Surely you haven't got a report back so quickly from whatever that system is?"

"No." I gabble. "I haven't run anything through yet. I may try Friday when Bronzey is back in with the stills passing as usable, or, there again, I may not. I had a quick look at the videos and recognised the bloke turning round to the camera. Clive, its Phil Blunt, the bloody Deputy Commissioner, who is supposed to be on holiday in Alicante with his family and is having an affair with my mate Julia in HR, who, quite suspiciously, also appears to be in Estepona for two days. And, get this, who also knows I asked for Jessica's details on Monday."

"Debs, calm down. Slowly repeat what you just said."

"Clive, I will not fucking calm down and don't give me that slowly repeat shit. If Phil is anyway involved in whatever nonsense is going on down there and finds out I've been fishing around on your bloody behalf, I'm toast - at best I'll be fired, which part of that don't you understand?"

"Look, you don't know if he's involved. It's interesting though, don't you think, that he's here and attending the funeral? We need to dig deeper into this."

"Clive you're so not listening to me are you? There'll be no 'We' in the digging. Phil is a big cheese who will not take kindly to a small bean counter looking into his activities."

"He's having an affair with your mate, Debs, there's leverage there I'd say. We need to find out why he is here and in what capacity. Can you not just get Julia drunk and see what she knows"

"No..no..no. Not a chance - I'm not getting involved any more than I already have done, Clive."

"Sure you will Debs, you can't help yourself. I know you too well, don't forget. Just see what comes out the face recognition gismo tomorrow, we'll take it from there, okay. Talk to you soon – cheers."
He hangs up - the fucker!!
I need a large wine. What is royally pissing me off right now is that, yes, I am intrigued by all of this, and the bastard knows full well I would be.

CHAPTER 11

8.22am. Thursday 13th August 2015. Estepona.

I might have been a bit pissed the night before, but if my memory hasn't deserted me, Debs recognised one of the faces, a certain Phil Blunt, a Deputy Commissioner. I don't know of him, but it's interesting someone of his rank would attend Jessica's funeral. What doesn't make sense, though, is why a high ranking *New Scotland Yard* officer would pay his last respects to an *MI5* operator. I can understand it if Jessica was attached to *MI5*, as the *Yard* is closely connected to that department in joint homeland security protection, but I was definitely told the contrary to this by Shelly. Is someone telling 'porky pies'? Was I purposely led astray to dissuade me not to get involved, as attempting to delve into the background of an officer from *MI6*, the international side of state security, could seriously create big problems, especially for Debs. Maybe that's what she wanted. I need confirmation of which bloody department Jessica worked for, or else I'll be going on a wild goose chase. Maybe that's the point. I need to speak to Shelly again before she returns to the UK.

"Morning Fred." I purposely sound chirpy, knowing he probably drank more than I last night and might just

have a worse head than mine. “Need you to do me a favour, old chap.”
“Morning Clive, what’s this you want me to do this time.” Fred’s voice betrays he’s suffering.
“I’ve got to meet Shelly again. I believe she might not have been telling us the truth the other day concerning her mother. It’s only a hunch, but if I’m right, could make my job a lot easier to get to the bottom of all this. Could you phone her and ask for a meet? Sooner rather than later would be handy.”
“I’ll see what I can do. I’ll phone you back.”
The line goes dead. Yes, Fred is suffering.
I venture out onto the terrace, my obligatory third cup of coffee in one hand, my third cigarette of the morning in the other. Encompassing the view, nothing has changed since yesterday, the heat, the limp EU flag, the pedestrians below attempting to find relief under sprawling orange trees. No, everything is exactly the same except I’m a day older.
The thirteenth of August is registered on my lookalike *Rolex,* three days after Jessica’s body was found and I am beginning to doubt whether I’m getting anywhere close to getting answers to the simplest of questions. Maybe I should listen to Debbie and leave all this to people still employed who search out murderers and stick them behind bars. If *MI6*, or for that matter, *MI5* are somehow involved, who am I to think I can break down their masonic-like secrecy and get to the truth? I’ve been retired four years and during those one thousand, four hundred and sixty odd days, I never once regretted my decision to escape down here, but it’s taken the death of a dear old friend to shake me out

of my ever increasing, pointless way of life to confirm one thing...I'm bored.
Loathed to admit it, but I miss the puzzle of clues, the chase and satisfaction of knowing some nasty bastard is finally paying the ultimate price, having their freedom taken away from them for a lot of years. No, I'll do this properly, not necessarily by the book, but by using all my well-honed senses to get justice for an old lady. To the best of my ability, I won't allow this tragedy to be pushed under the carpet, to be placed into a folder stamped 'Case Unsolved'.
The vision of *Steve McQueen* racing across the Austrian Tyrol on a motorbike pursued by Germans, snatches me away from reality. My mobile indicates it's Fred at the end of the line.
"Hi mate, what have you found out?"
"Well Clive, Shelly isn't staying at her mother's place. She says there's too many memories there, so decided to stay at *Kempinski's*. Must have a few more quid than I first thought, if she can afford to pay for a wake and now book a room there. Just the sort of woman I'm looking for." Fred laughs down the line, affording me time to ask myself another question of how he knows she's single.
"I asked if we could come over because you want to just tie up a few loose ends and she's okay about it, though, at first, she didn't seem to be too pleased. She said to pop over at twelve. I won't open-up the bar until after I get back, as there's sweet fuck-all business to do at that time of day anyway. August is always a crappy month. I'll pick you up in half an hour...okay?"

Languishing under the shower, the force of tepid water bouncing off my head does wonders to rejuvenate a tired brain, regurgitating the question of why I didn't know Shelly's personal status. Was she married with children, divorced or seeing someone? I didn't know and I should do, after all, she is a good looker and if there's a chance of a 'liaison', it'll be me fluffing-up her cushions and not Fred. That is, of course, if she comes over kosher with the truth.

~O~

Fred parks his *Porsche* in the forecourt of the expensive, terracotta coloured hotel, bordering the beach, before we enter the large expanse of the *Kempinski's* reception hall. A mass of marble flooring, towering ceilings and sparse furnishings allow the eye to detect human life, especially the one we're looking for, but not only isn't she here, no one else is either. And why should she or anyone else be? Think, you stupid idiot. This is a Spanish hotel and not the *Regency* back in England. Everyone will be outside, in the sun, especially if you have just one day left to get a colour.

Standing on the upper level patio outside, we scan the poolside and lawns below, me in *Ray Bans*, Fred squinting against intense sunlight. There must be a hundred or more people, mostly all prone on their backs or getting relief submerged in the pool.

"Why don't we ask at reception if they know where she is?" Pipes up Fred, the palm of his hand shielding his eyes.

"Shut up. If she's with someone, I want to see who it is without advertising we're here. We're early, so might just see something we are not supposed to."

But my hopes are dashed when I pick her out, under an umbrella, way off on the lawn near the beach. No sun-lounger for her. She's sitting at a table with two spare chairs, a bottle in a cooler, smoking a cigarette. She's prepared.

"Hi Shelly." Fred gushes, a smile on his face giving away his secret intentions.

"Hello Fred. Hi Clive. Take a seat. Would you like a glass of wine? It's a very good white *Rioja.*"

"Thank you. That's a nice choice." I answer before Fred.

I sit directly opposite Shelly, in the shade and remove my sunglasses. Fred takes up a position in the sun. It would be good if I can see her eyes, but they are hidden behind a pair of *Polaroids* and probably will remain so, shame.

"It's good of you to see me again, Shelly. With all the commotion going on at your mother's funeral, I didn't think it was a good time."

"No, that's thoughtful, but I didn't see you there. Did you come?"

Her lips are ruby red, contrasting majestically against her perfect white teeth as her words spill out from her mouth. If I wasn't here on anything more than a chat, I'd be like Fred...drooling.

"Yes, we were both there, but at the back. It's a shame the whole thing resulted in a bit of a fiasco, as Jessica deserved better, but knowing her, she would've had a bloody good laugh at how it turned out."

Shelly smiles and lowers her head and for the first time removes her sunglasses. She definitely is beautiful.
"Yes, it didn't go off very well, did it?" She looks at me and I see her eyes for a second before she replaces her bins.
"I was wondering, Shelly. Are you married?" Strike when they least expect it, has always been my motto.
"Why do you ask?" Shelly throws her head back as a sign it's such a frivolous question.
"Well, I knew your mother, but know nothing about you. If you are hitched, at least it'll stop Fred from thinking he has a chance with you."
Shelly laughs, but Fred is left opened mouthed at my audacity.
"Maybe, Clive, that's the way I like it...you knowing nothing about me." Shelly's lips smile, but her cheeks don't move.
"I apologise, but being a beautiful woman," Nothing like a bit of flattery. "I would have expected a number of suitors in your life." Her lips are not curving anymore, but before she answers, I continue. "There is something else bothering me. When you told me both your mother and you have connections with *MI6*, you weren't really telling me the actual truth, were you?"
I see I've struck a chord. Re-crossing her legs, a good sign of nerves, even if they are long and shapely, Shelly reaches for a cigarette. Composure returns after a deep inhalation.
"The truth, Clive. What do you mean by that?"
"Well, Shelly, it's like this. I ask myself why Phil Blunt should attend your mother's funeral. As you know, he's attached to the *Yard*. By this afternoon I'll know

the names of others who attended and I would like to bet, none are connected to *MI6*. Which begs the question…" Before I can continue, Shelly cuts me off.
"You're correct. I tried to prevent you from making a fool of yourself by telling you we both worked for *MI6*. I believe no good will come from you nosing about. It's a nasty world out there and by yourself, you can do nothing. So please, Clive, forget about it and go and play golf or whatever you do in your spare time."
I've got to her and she knows it. Whether she's been primed for this meet, I'm not sure, but her rhetoric is not from a grieving daughter, more of a warning-me-off. Briefed by whom? Phil Blunt, no doubt.
A claustrophobic silence indicates Shelly is not in the mood for small talk. As I don't want to be seen as the culprit for ruining her day, I glance through the wine menu, stupidly believing another bottle of wine might heal the division I've just created. Matching the bottle she ordered, I run my finger down and find the majestic little number alongside its price. Fuck that! Ninety euros for a plonk of a wine I can pick up from *Carrefour* for less than five. No chance.
"We won't take up anymore of your time, Shelly. Hope you have a pleasant journey home and you never know; we might meet again sometime in the future."

I rise to my feet, beckoning Fred to do the same. I smile, but it's not reciprocated and it's a shame I feel I've outlived my welcome. In different circumstances I would have loved to stay. Who wouldn't want to be seen in the presence of a beautiful, bikini clad woman. The thought of getting to know her, enticing, the prize of unleashing her bikini-top to see if they're real, even more so.

~O~

"Well, that was a fat lot of use." Fred utters the first words since we sidled out the hotel and sit stationary in his car.

"Wrong, Fred. She told me a lot by what she didn't say. They definitely worked for *MI5*, which cuts the odds down for me as to which direction to start digging."

"You heard what she said...telling you to drop it."

"Exactly, Fred. She couldn't have made me more determined. That red bikini she wore not only begged to be torn off, but flashed at me like a red rag to a bull. She knows a hell of a lot more than she's telling me. I've got a horrible feeling she's protecting something or somebody."

"Does this mean you're carrying on?"

"Too bloody right I am."

I need an update from Debs, but I'll wait until tomorrow morning, Friday.

CHAPTER 12

7.29am. Friday 14th August 2015. Brighton Railway Station.

Thank God it's Friday, poets day (piss off early, tomorrow's Saturday), yet another glorious morning to trudge up to London on the 7.29. I get my usual seat and settle down to a stress free commute with a newspaper, but my tranquillity is shattered at Hassocks when Mummy, Daddy and little Johnny descend from hell to my table, jabbering loudly about their planned day trip to London. Even adorned with headphones, I still hear them yapping. I hate school holidays and there should be laws against day trippers allowed to travel on any train before 9 am. Failing to comply should be punishable with castration for the father. Even my death stare and deep sighing isn't working on this lot. I could, of course, move, but there are no available window seats left in the carriage, plus that would mean conceding defeat.
The morning redeems itself slightly, as I have time to pick up a decent bucket of foaming coffee before heading to the office or as we often refer to it - the *"Death Star"* a la *Star Wars*.

The main topic of today's 'love in' at the whiteboard is a three line whip by Baldrick to ensure that the department is fully represented at Ingrid's barbeque. All to behave appropriately despite free flowing booze, etc, etc. Honestly, anyone would think we are all teenagers going to the end of term school disco.

Note to self - must remember to go to *Tesco's* on the way home and buy the ribs, cabbage, carrots, onion, lemons before heading to the *Albion* for the usual Friday night gathering.

Marinade for the ribs is already done, not by me I hasten to add. Luckily, I have a good friend, whose company, *Jethro's*, kindly makes marinades with all the necessary ingredients and bottles it. Cheating? No, just sensible. Naturally will pass it off as my own creation, boasting it's the molasses and chilli that do the trick.

First priority, check emails. Nothing too onerous that can't wait. Ingrid sending out directions quoting the fun starts at 2pm - too hideous for words.

Just as I'm about to call Nick to confirm what time he's picking me up at East Croydon, Bronzey pulls up a chair by my desk clutching a pile of *"Kitten Club"* receipts.

Three hours later, after much copying, pasting and scanning, his £2,349 expense breakdown is ready to be submitted. I congratulate myself on a fine piece of artwork. Just need Ingrid to sign it off. I certainly don't want to know the finer details of what he really spent the corporate coffer's on.

"Fancy lunch, Debs" He says. "As it's a nice day we could sit outside *Corney and Barrow."*

"Okay, give me 15 minutes. Actually, I've got a favour to ask. We can discuss it then."

I call Nick. “You still okay to pick me up at the station tomorrow?”
“Yes of course 12.30, and my reward for this selfless act of gallantry is what?”
“My scintillating company for the duration of the journey is reward enough, plus you get first dibs of the ribs.” I say.
“Ooh...you are such the tease, what are you doing for lunch? Fancy a walk?”
“Sorry can’t do - out with Bronzey. He owes me. I’ll see you tomorrow, Hun.”
Bronzey and I search for a table and find one in the sun. Despite the weather it’s actually quite depressing knowing you have to go back to the office when you could quite happily stay out all afternoon. We order wine and sandwiches.
“So what’s the favour Debs?” He says.
“Okay, I want you to run some photos through NEOFACE for me and see what it throws up. There’s not much to go on I’m afraid, at best they’re side shots.”
“Debs, this really is an odd request coming from you. What’s the background?”
Shit, didn’t really think this one through. Stupid, stupid!
“Well, it’s a bit of a long story that I won’t bore you with. The upshot is a friend of mine attended a funeral in Hove and she thought she recognised an old flame from way back when. She surreptitiously took some shots and was going to approach him after the service, but didn’t see him again. I said I’d try to help and didn't want to go through the crime analysis boys as it’s not police business in any shape, way or form. I told her

it's very much a long shot to see if we can get a name. You see, she couldn't remember it for the life of her. If it works then she can trawl *Facebook* to see if it's the same guy"

"Good grief the lengths you women go through to find out about a bloke. Yes of course I'll do it. Email them over and I'll do it this afternoon as it'll be quiet back at camp."

"Aww...thanks Bronzey. It will be my personal email address and obviously keep this to yourself as we don't want the powers that be to know we're using official software as a potential dating platform."

"Ha ha. Now that would be funny."

We polish off the bottle of *Pinot Grigio* and have a cheeky extra glass each, belly laughing at the potentially disastrous scenario's that could descend tomorrow's shindig into a disaster. For example, no one turns up with their assigned dishes, the barbeque won't light and the Pavlova melts. Sam & Keavo get absolutely hammered on sneaked in *Jaeger*-bombs and throw up in the plunge pool, whilst Julia chucks her red wine all over Ingrid's chic summer dress. Naomi, having consumed her body weight in *Pimms*, attempts to lure senior management into doing the "*Macarena*", and Baldrick, bless him, attempts to remain the responsible adult when all around him is going tits up. Sadly, we agree the 'Carry On Corporate Barbeque' scene wouldn't happen and head back to the office.

I email Bronzey, apologising for the quality of the photos, having removed the video showing Phil. Half an hour later he beckons me to the coffee machine.

In hushed tones he whispers. "There's only one name that came up. The photos really are shit quality, Debs, in terms of the facial angles and your mate must be pretty tall for a woman by the way - I'll email the result."

Bronzey raises his left eyebrow slightly and continues. "Another tiny little detail I discovered. NEOFACE also determines the location of where the photo was taken via the GPS on the smartphone used. These were taken in a place called Estepona, Costa del Sol, not Hove. Are you sure your 'friend'," He does the two finger quote sign. "is telling you the truth here, or indeed, I must ask, are you?"

I can feel myself reddening, floundering for a response. "Bronzey, that's all I know, seriously, I'm just as perplexed as you are about them being taken in Spain. I'll have words with her tonight. Thanks mate for this."

I hurry back to my desk, get my iPhone and look at the email.

The attachment shows a picture of a balding white man, overweight judging by the face with short white hair and blue eyes.

Name: Martin O'Connell

Born: 01/07/1948

Nationality: British / Irish

Status: Married

Occupation status: Retired Civil Servant - member of the Anglo Irish advisory board.

Residence: Belfast.

Bronzey then adds - "No criminal file - was known back in the late 70's and 80's as a person of interest to the intelligence agency as an IRA sympathiser - nothing else on him, Debs. He doesn't really look the type to be a hot date for your "mate!!!!"

He also doesn't appear to be the type to attend our Jessica's funeral either, I thought.

Something's afoot here, methinks, but this is Clive's baby not mine. It can wait.

I've got a train to catch and shopping to do and I'm more worried about what Julia knows. Did Phil tell her whose funeral he attended? Did she tell him I was enquiring?

I'm going to be walking on egg shells tomorrow.

I bid everyone goodnight "See you children at the party." Power the laptop down and head off for the Hove train, allowing time to stop at the *Whistlestop* store at the station to pick up my end-of-the-week-commuting-treat of two plastic glasses of wine, complete with the foil lid and a bag of bacon flavour crisps. Always a classy look!

The train pulls in on time, doors open right where I want them to, all good so far - then the blast of heat whacks me in the face from inside. They've fucking well done it again and have had the heat on instead of air con. An hour and a half in a sweat box, fan-bloody-tastic!!!

Julia texts. *"I'm back and will see you tomorrow at the do. Can't wait to tell you about the trip."* More smiley faces and no clues as to what she might be talking about.

I drink my wine and eat my crisps a bit too quickly before the stifling heat gets to them and read the paper.

The relief of finally getting off at Hove to sea air is immense.

The world and his wife are clearly having a barbeque of their own this weekend, if the crowds in *Tesco* are anything to go by. Where racks, housing pre-packed hamburgers by their hundreds, once stood, empty shelves now glare back at customers, their faces spelling out their dilemma of 'what shall we do?' Makes me smile. Why don't they just buy mince on the adjacent shelf and make their own.

Luckily, I scoop the last four packs of ribs before they're swallowed up by the marauding rabble, much like a kid grabbing the last sweetie.

Ribs - tick, coleslaw fodder - tick, now I can go to the pub. Not the *Seafield*, but the *Albion* just along the road, a bigger traditional boozer, famed for having the grumpiest landlord in East Sussex – Jeff - who's been there since he kept a dinosaur as a pet. Yippee, a live band on tonight, but probably much the same as other past Fridays, featuring old farts regurgitating hits from a bygone age. The place is crowded though, just in case one week they turn out to be quite good.

I immediately spot Les at the bar with Pippa, Jane, Ash and Mick. Becky too has just got off the London Bridge train. We commiserate, as commuting comrades do with each other, about our respective trips home.

As promised, I get Les a large wine whilst she indicates she's going outside to the smoking area. Odd, because she doesn't smoke.

Once there, I light up.

"Debs did you get anything on that search on Jessica McGill?"

"No, I drew a big fat blank, why do you ask?"

"Well." She said. "I just thought I would give it another go yesterday to see if I was missing something in the criteria selection and absolutely nothing this time came up, not even to confirm her name or that she existed. It's almost as if someone, it would need to have been a higher ranking officer, has completely deleted the record."

"Really? Surely that can't be done, wipe a record?"

"That's what I thought, really odd. I haven't mentioned it to anyone, just wanted to check with you first."

"Thanks Les. I'd appreciate it if you don't say anything to anyone. I have no idea what this means, if anything at all, but I'll try and look into it. Come on, let's sink some wine and please don't let me stagger home without my shopping."

"Oh God, you've got your Super's barbeque tomorrow."

"Yep, a good reason to get pissed tonight."

We head back in. What she just told me doesn't make any sense at all. This is getting curiouser and curiouser - again Clive's problem. The sooner I extricate myself from whatever is going on within the sun lounger lizard's head, the better.

CHAPTER 13

8.17am. Saturday 15th August 2015. Estepona.

I impatiently wait until ten before phoning, believing nine o'clock back in the UK isn't too early to arouse my little mate. Familiar with her routine on a Friday night, she probably won't expect my call this morning, let alone appreciate it, but I'm eager to know if her gizmo face recognition machine has thrown up any new info. The length of time her mobile buzzes is not a good sign and I fully expect to be leaving a message on her voice-mail, after all, I'd do the same and not pick up if I saw my name flashing, the perpetrator of the incoming call. But she finally picks up.

"Morning Debs." I immediately feel my voice isn't the most welcoming sound she's craving to hear.

"Seriously Clive, what fucking time do you call this? Whoever or whatever you're chasing, I'm not in the mood right now. I haven't even had a cup of tea or cigarette yet."

I am right with my assumption, but I'm buggered if I'm about to apologise. I've been 'sorrying' too many times in the past week.

"Did you have any joy with face recognition?"

"Clive, you probably know already, but you're the most inconsiderate bastard I've ever had the displeasure to meet. My head feels like it has a monkey inside, hammering on my skull with a hippo bone, trying to get out. There's five pounds of spare ribs waiting in the kitchen to be marinated, a cabbage and carrot combo to be knocked up so it resembles coleslaw, then I've got to transport the lot to Ingrid's fucking barbeque in Hertfordshire. Oh...deep joy and its Saturday, my day of bloody rest. What sort of relaxing day have you planned for yourself? The beach possibly, or a saunter round a golf course, followed by a spot of lunch in *Paco's*. You arsehole."

"Glad to hear you're in good spirits, Debs. But apart from all that, have you dug up anything interesting?"

"You're one incorrigible shit, Clive, do you know that? And to answer your question, other than me identifying Phil Blunt as anybody remotely connected to the firm, only one other face was identified from your rubbish photos, a chap called Martin O'Connell - I'll email you the details. Strange though, your face was recognised, and do you know what it said? You can't guess, can you? Well, it said you were retired. Shall I spell that out for you? R-E-T-I-R-E-D with a post script added saying you are an arsehole. Incidentally, and you probably couldn't care a shit, I made up some bollocks as to why I wanted these pictures scanned and have spectacularly shot myself in the foot because you had your location data on your bloody mobile switched on. Bronzey knew straight away they were taken in Spain not Hove and whilst I can trust him, I know he doesn't entirely believe my story. I respectfully request for the future, you ask a 5 year old child how to turn location data off. Now, piss off and let me get on. By the way, something else turned up that is strange, Jessica's

records appear to have been completely deleted according to my mate Les, nothing, nada, zilch on the database! I'll phone when I get back from the Ingrid's soiree, even if there is nothing new to report, depending when I get home. Don't you dare call me again at silly o'clock tomorrow morning. I'll call you - you have a good day now."
The line goes dead. Does my copper nose detect she's not happy with me?

~O~

Saturday morning, the fifth day after hearing of Jessica's murder and what have I found out? Not a lot, but sufficient to know it was a planned job, not some burglary that went terribly wrong. Also she worked in some high position within the auspices of *MI5*, as does her daughter, who took up her mantle when she retired. I say I know these things, but they aren't confirmed, only a supposition. I need to take this a step further and find someone who has no connection to any of these agencies and isn't shackled by the secrecy act. If the 'someone' I'm looking for lives here in Estepona, then I'll probably have to come clean and tell them of my past employment to be taken seriously. Might be the worst thing I can do, but I need their confidence. Now, who would this person be? She's been in the back of my mind as someone to talk to, someone who probably knew Jessica better than anyone else down here. It is time we spoke. I'll phone Fred to see if he knows her mobile number. Of course he'll know Margaret's number, how stupid of me.

~O~

It was a clever suggestion of Fred's to arrange a meeting with Margaret at *Surs,* a favourite restaurant and bar both she and Jessica frequented in happier times. But it could have a down side whereby it brings back memories, which could be too traumatic. It is a gamble and I'm pleased Fred took it, but I think he didn't consider the consequences.

Though just after five in the afternoon, the oppressive heat continues, if the flashing sign outside the pharmacist in Calle Real advertising its volume can be believed. I hope Margaret is sheltering in the shade, as it registers thirty nine degrees. I enter *Plazoleta Ortiz,* where the bar sits on the opposite side and immediately see she's done as I hoped.

Margaret spots me approaching and smiles, a greeting of warmth or one of uncertainty, I'm unclear.

"Hi Margaret. It's good of you to meet me. What's that you're drinking?"

I could sit opposite her, but choose to get close. No matter what time of day or heat, she is a woman who takes pride in her appearance and is immaculately turned out and for someone whose best years are behind her, she does justice to the words of looking good. Donning an off white, summer, cotton dress, a couple of thousand quid's worth of gold must be wrapped around her wrist in the form of bangles and bracelets.

"Hello Clive. It's just a house wine." Her eyes are masked by extra-large sun blockers, glasses which saw their day in the eighties, but suit her down to the ground. Very *Sophia Lorenesque.*

I get a nod from a waiter; he understands I'll have the same.
"I'm pleased you decided to meet me, Margaret. Believe me, I understand what you must have gone through this last week and the last thing I want to do is make matters worse. I don't know how much you know about me and my past, whether Fred told you, but if you're good to talk about Jessica, I believe it will be invaluable for me, and for you, to try and get some answers."
Putting her glass to her lips, she takes a refreshing sip. I know she's fond of the odd cigarette, but a packet with a lighter sitting on top is a fresh habit.
"Fred didn't have to say anything about you, I already knew. Jessica told me years ago, when you first arrived, that you'd just retired from the *Met.*"
Why didn't this come as surprise?
"Jessica really liked you and would say you were just one of a few she could talk to down here as an equal. She was a terrible snob, you know, when it came to intelligence. It's probably why she never told a soul of her past. As she would say 'I'm not here to discuss the reasoning of going to war over the Falklands with some ignorant, jingoistic, beer swilling *Chelsea* fan.' In fact, without you knowing it, when you two got together, she enjoyed your points of view, especially about the government." She laughs, a good sign.
"Am I to take it, the whole bloody town knows I was a copper?"
"No, not at all. Just like Jessica's privacy, your secret was and is safe with me." Relieving a cigarette from its confines, she delicately puts it between her lips. How

very feminine. "She said you could be trusted and for this reason I'm sure Jessica would wish me to be as helpful as I can be. I know bits and pieces about her, so start asking some questions and let's see how much I knew about my dear old friend."

I'd possibly underestimated Margaret as just being Jessica's convenient side-kick.

"Thank you for those kind words. Yeah...I liked the old girl as well." I'm not used to flattery and when it comes from such an unexpected region, I wish I'd given Jessica more time. I imitate her action but take a less feminine approach when sinking half of what's in my glass.

"I've spoken to Shelly, but never got a positive answer from her. She had a good teacher, in the shape of her mother, when it came to steering clear of anything contentious, much like an MP does. But it doesn't help me. I don't know how well you know her, but if anything, she appears to be trying to knock me off the scent." I look at Margaret for any visible betrayals that she'd be the same, but thankfully, nothing. "Am I right in believing Jessica worked for *MI5*?" I start with the easy ones first.

"Yes, she did, but has been retired for years."

"Did Shelly join the same organisation?"

"Correct."

"Was Jessica ever married?"

"If she was I didn't know."

"Do you know who Shelly's father is?" I expect a pause, but Margaret doesn't falter.

"Jessica did talk about him, but never mentioned a name. I believe he was the love of her life when much younger, she never found anyone one else, although the chances of finding someone were enormous as her work meant she was surrounded by men."

"That's what I want to get round to talking about...her work, because that's where, I believe, I'll find answers. I have dates of her tenure working within the service, but they differ from the ones given by Shelly. From my source of information, I'm led to believe Jessica left the force in May, 1991, but from what I gleaned from Shelly, she is positive it was in the millennium year."

Margaret doesn't stall, but goes into thinking mode. Takes an exaggerated sip of wine and retrieves another cigarette from its hiding place.

"Well...let me see. I've been here for twenty six years and if my memory isn't playing tricks, Jessica came about the same time. I remember she bought her house, but commuted back to work for a year or two after. No, your information is correct...Shelly is wrong." Not hiding her enthusiasm, Margaret is on the ball and definitely on my side.

"I guess Jessica was about seventy five, so on that premise, she would have been about fifty or there about when she retired. A bit early, even by today's standards, I would say." I give Margaret a clue in which direction I'm going.

"She did work for them for something like twenty odd years, you know."

"I know Margaret, but what age were you when they pensioned you off to the funny farm?" I try humour and it usually works.

"You cheeky bugger...but yes, I get your point."

"Do you know why?"

We have obviously come to an impasse, unless Margaret throws some light on the reason. The rationality for Jessica's early retirement must be relevant. Margaret remains relaxed, a half smoked cigarette between her fingers of her right hand, the other fiddling with the base of a wine glass. I allow an interval to pass whilst she is in this mode of deep thought and order dos mas vinos blanco con hielo. I believe she is enjoying this moment and if anything, the cloud of mourning she's been under since Jessica's death, has been removed, even if it is only for a few hours.

"Do you know, Clive, you're right and I never thought about it."

As if she's just put her fingers into an electric socket, she sits bolt upright, her cigarette falling from her hand when grabbing the arms of the chair supporting her. "Oh...fuck."

My reaction to this phraseology is simple. I jettison a mouthful of wine, spraying it in a fine but robust cloud to the amusement of those sitting in close proximity, but Margaret isn't contributing to the humour. It is one of those precious 'Eureka' moments.

"Oh, Clive, I've just remembered. Many years ago, Jessica put on a little party for a few of her friends, all girls, and I must say Jessica did like a drop of wine when in the mood. Something came up whilst we chatted and, as I wasn't as pissed as she was, Jessica asked if I could go to her bedroom and get a book. An autobiography by some MP she'd had dealings with and knew it was a load of fiction. I remember her laughing and saying it was tosh. Yes, it's all coming back to me.

She said it was in the left-hand side drawer of her dressing table. So off I went and by the time I got to her room, I'd forgotten which side drawer she said it was in. I opened the right one by mistake and fumbled around. Under knick-knacks and one thing or another, I stumbled upon an out-of-date passport. Obviously nosey, I looked inside just to see how old she was...it's a stupid thing we girlie's like to know about each other. The photo is definitely of her, but the name was completely different."

Margaret looks at me wide eyed knowing this can be important, emphasized unconsciously by her left hand grabbing mine.

"Can you remember the name?" I push her memory.

"Oh, Clive, I wish I could, but it was so long ago."

"Did you mention you found a passport belonging to her?" It is beginning to feel I'm back in the bowels of the *Yard*, interrogating an informer, a buzz of excitement tingling my nerve ends.

"No, I never said a word, not to her or anyone else. It was probably something she wouldn't have wanted me to know, anyway, otherwise she would've told me herself since that time."

Relieving my hand from hers, she lights a third cigarette, the same amount of tobacco she probably gets through in a whole day rather than just the twenty minutes we've been sitting together.

"I've got to know her name, Margaret." Silence prevails for what seems to be an age, but probably only seconds. "I need to get into Jessica's house and find that passport, if it's still there. I wonder if it is still considered a crime scene and cordoned off. Shelly is

at *Kempinski's*, so won't be a problem and I'd prefer she didn't know of our conversation." I am about to voice other thoughts when Margaret cuts in.
"I have a set of keys."

~O~

The cause of this stifling heat has long retreated back to its hiding place under the horizon, at least for another ten hours, when I cut the headlights and engine of my battered Honda Civic, about a quarter of a mile from where Jessica lived. Apart from a series of sparsely spaced street-lights, emitting various strengths of low illumination, the place is virtually blackened out with only a far-off barking dog sporadically breaking the silence. Careful not to add to the soundtrack, I ease the driver's door shut, look around and only then when I'm satisfied my arrival has gone unnoticed, I tread as though on thin glass in the direction of Jessica's house.
My Caucasian ancestry seeming no longer evident, I choose a pair of *Levi's* instead of shorts and a black tee-shirt as camouflage. Keeping to the shadows, I melt into the background. Finding Jessica's place doesn't present problems, but to be safe, I wait for certain privacy. In my pocket is a pen-like torch, keys, some cash, a pair of latex gloves and a packet of cigarettes, but much as I crave for one, it would be senseless to walk around with a red beacon dangling from my mouth, attracting anyone who has nothing better to do than gaze into the night. Nervousness cohabits extremely well with adrenalin, but does nothing to keep a thin film of sweat forming on each

palm. I haven't done anything as stupid as this for years, but strangely, I'm beginning to enjoy it. Head high bushes surrounding the property afford additional cover to confirm my loneliness as I fumble to don a pair of latex gloves, picked up free from a filling station in town. Each step in darkness is an adventure until I stumble across a gap in the foliage, in daylight a formality to find, but now a positive result.

My vision slowly acclimatises to the conditions and if this place is still considered to be a crime scene, there's no proof of it. All good, so far. Speeding up, I make my way to the back of the house where Margaret said her keys will fit the lock on the patio doors. I'm banking on no burglar alarm, but even with confirmation there is no such thing, I'm cautious. Slowly, the key turns and answering my prayer, the well-oiled contraption unlocks.

Closing the door silently behind me and following a picture of Margaret's instructions, I find where the bottom of the stairs should be and begin to climb, keeping my feet close to the wall to avoid any creaking floorboards. Estimating each riser to be nine inches high and the ceiling to be the same in feet, there should be twelve or possibly thirteen steps to reach the landing. If I'm correct and don't find myself in a sprawling mess, there will be no need for the torch just yet. Keeping to the guidelines appears to be working as I find and open the second door on my right.

Now, if this murder happened in the UK, all relevant material appertaining to Jessica would have long been gone, stacked up in evidence bags, waiting to be sorted back at headquarters, but this is Spain and I'm hoping the boys down here are not so pernickety. I find the suggested drawer in the dressing table and slide it open without the aid of a light. There's lots of bits-and-bobs but nothing remotely the shape of a passport. Fuck it. I try other drawers, but like the first, nothing. Away from the window, in an even darker side of the room, the shape of a floor to ceiling wardrobe attracts my attention. Scaring me out of my wits for a brief second, a ghostly dark image of myself bounces back from mirrored doors, rocketing my heart rate even higher.

Though I can hardly wait to get out of this place, I try to regain my composure before continuing with the hunt for what I came for. Easing the door open, I encounter Jessica's clothes, hanging all neatly separated, unlike mine back in my apartment. Footwear is spaced evenly on the floor accompanied by an unemployed umbrella standing in a corner, but nothing else to suggest it held what I am after. Lifting my eyes, five shoe boxes above my head attract my attention. They're too high to reach and knowing Jessica with her portly proportions, she probably had a set of steps somewhere, but I haven't time to search. Lugging a rickety chair over as a substitute is not the wisest option, but it'll do the job.

I open the lid of the first; nothing but handkerchiefs and scarves. The second and third boast even less. Why do people keep so much junk? But the fourth bequeaths its treasure. Bingo. One out-of-date passport and a black one to boot, dating back years. All is forgiven, Jessica. How relieved I am, that you were one of those hoarders I'd just castigated. Just holding it sends electric pulses running through my veins. In a narrow, oblong shape indention on its cover, a name should be printed, but is impossible to decipher in this light. I open it, but again see nothing. Stuffing the magical prize in my back pocket, escape is my foremost priority, as confirming this little jewel of information with torchlight might just be taking a minute or two too long to guarantee being undetected. Retracing my earlier footsteps, my arrival back to the safety of my car doesn't arouse suspicion from neighbours' or a nosey cat that might find my legs a temptation to rub against. Diligently, keeping my speed down when the devil on my shoulder is screaming to speed away, my arrival back at my apartment coincides with my craving to scream and have a drink.

I consider my terrace as my haven, a place of complete privacy and where I do my best thinking. Six floors up and far from the madding crowd below, the object in my back pocket dents the denim and has taken on the shape of my backside as I withdraw it. Handling it like a present my mother used to tell me not to open until Father Christmas gives the go-ahead, prolongs the excitement until, with a beer in hand, I finally succumb to opening my 'Pandora's box', accompanied by a broad smile.

Through wear and tear and age, the panel on the front page is totally illegible, which only extenuates my curiosity to what little jewel I'll find inside. There is a picture of Jessica and as Margaret said, it's definitely her. Running from the top of the page to the bottom are all the necessary facts, including the most important one...the name Jessica was born with...Jane Constance Brewer. Got you!

But why the need to change it? Even Shelly, it appears, followed suit, but was her identity altered before she knew too much about why it required changing? Was she still a kid at the time? Jessica's profession must be the catalyst for why it was necessary. Would this drastic action be tantamount to survival if Jessica was say, a hairdresser or mechanic? Yes, it might be, if the hairdresser witnessed something terrible enough to put her life in danger. That's it, the only logical conclusion, considering her profession, was that she was under a witness protection order and uprooting her life to Spain makes perfect sense, including the early retirement. It also explains why Jessica's HR record and MEPO database was empty and later totally removed. In essence, the hierarchy of her department effectively killed her off with the aid of a paper shredder. No, her job had to be the reason.

I sink half the beer. If I had some marijuana I'd roll a joint. A good day's work. Thanks Margaret. I stop myself phoning Debs. She's probably had enough for the day at the dreaded barbeque. It can wait until tomorrow.

CHAPTER 14

9am. Saturday 15th August 2015. Hove, East Sussex.

Saturday morning and the last thing I need at 9 am is to be rudely awakened by Clive calling. Feel a little bad as I'd ripped his head off by the end of his call, but my forgiving nature doesn't last long, he should bloody well know better than to poke the 'hungover bear' before a cup of tea and a cigarette at the weekend.
I forward Bronzey's email to Clive - job done - over to him now.
10.30 am, still in dressing gown and 3 cups of tea and 2 paracetamol later - ribs marinating in sealed bags - check, not the most beautiful coleslaw I've ever seen but all fresh in a big *Tupperware* bowl - check, cool bag to transport with one of those odd blue blocks kept in the freezer, tucked inside - check.
Need to be on the 11.49 train to East Croydon. It's a sunny day, so I'll go for cropped jeans, loafers and white linen shirt with some arty-farty beads...that should do it. The casual barbeque look.
I shower and feel slightly better for it. Leave home with sun glasses in hand and cool bag over shoulder at 11.30.
The last thing I want to do right now on a sunny Saturday by the sea is get the train to Croydon.

Really odd being in casual clothes on the train and not in commuter mode and how remarkable, they run absolutely to time. Why can't they do this during the week?

It's impossible not to spot Nick immediately as I exit the station, laden down like a Tibetan pack animal, towards the car-pick-up bays. Sticking out like a pickled gherkin from the crowd, his six feet two frame is shrouded in the most garish, Hawaiian-type shirt I think I've ever seen. It appears as if the *Pantone*-colour-palette-monster has vomited all over him in hues of orange, lime green and turquoise. To compliment this couture atrocity is a pair of khaki shorts - what happens to a man's wardrobe brain when sun and barbeque are combined in the same sentence? He's waving at me frantically like some do to steer clear of a disaster, but doesn't he realise he's attracted, not just me, but the entire crowd who have just disembarked. Idiot.

Disregarding my attempt to stifle giggles, he plugs Ingrid's post code into the sat-nav and we're off, in his little ford *"Ka."*

"Nick, what the fuck are you wearing?"

"I only have one barbeque outfit and this is it. You're only jealous you don't have a shirt like this and I think it's rather fetching. Can't see what your problem is? I'm doing the driving, so you can just shut up for a change."

Okay, understood. Have been put in my place and stay schtum, but jeez, Ingrid will freak out.

We move swiftly on from the subject of his attire and while away the journey discussing the appropriate time we can politely beg our leave.

Just after 2pm, the 'lady of the sat-nav' announces we have arrived at our destination.

A sweeping gravel driveway fronting a detached pile directs us to a parking area, a space resembling a Park Lane luxury car showroom, but without salesmen. Poor old Nick's car looks decidedly out of place among the *Mercedes', Jaguar's* and *BMW's,* parked ceremoniously in a straight line. Thank God we aren't the first to arrive.

Pushing the doorbell, Ingrid's youngest daughter, Ella, aged I reckon about 12 years old, opens the door and ushers us through the vast hallway into the kitchen area.

This refurb from last year's kitchen is probably the size of my entire flat. Lots of tasteful Italian marble, stainless steel appliances, all matching of course, a cooking range and the obligatory *Aga.* Just how many ovens does one woman want for God's sake? All very county set. Probably has been photographed for *House and Home* magazine.

I approach the mirror-reflective counter top island and breakfast bar in the middle of the room, wondering whether I should put my rather shabby cool bag on such splendour, when Ingrid sashays through the patio doors wearing a floaty, 70's style kaftan-looking ensemble. Gin and tonic in hand - yes, as expected, all very *Margo Ledbetter* from *The Good Life.*

She approaches Nick and me with outstretched arms, slapping an exaggerated 'mwah-mwah' non-existent kiss that doesn't touch cheeks, as a greeting. I stop myself from recoiling in horror - she's my boss. We so don't do air kissing!

I suppress a smile when she turns to Nick, her eyes spelling out what she's thinking - 'I hope the neighbours don't think he's anything to do with me.'

"Ingrid, I can't believe what you've done to the kitchen. It's fabulous." I schmooze. "Where do you want the ribs and coleslaw?"

"Just leave them on the island, Steve will sort it all out. Come on through to the patio and get yourselves a drink."

Now we're talking!

We go straight out to the patio area. 'Patio?' This looks more like a terrace you find at the back of a four-star country hotel favoured for wedding receptions. The garden has been extensively landscaped since last year, manicured lawn, water features, a pagoda, architectural plants in tasteful pots dotted everywhere and even the splash pool at the bottom of the garden appears to have had a makeover.

We weave our way through people we don't recognise, (probably due to the guest list including Steve's colleagues, friends and neighbours) through the rattan tables and chairs, liberally spread out, proffering such delicacies as crisps, dips, peanuts, olives, to find a free table right at the end - perfect - far enough away to have a sneaky cigarette when we want and a vantage point to people watch - one of my favourite pastimes. The only disadvantage to establishing camp here is the drinks and food gazebo/marquee is at the other end.

I dispatch Nick off to get a large glass of *Prosecco* while I go and say hello to Steve, who's firing up a barbeque that wouldn't look out of place in an Argentinian steak house.

Back at the table, nibbling on crisps with my drink, the music plays through surrounding speakers, some Latin summer collection making us think we're by the Med and not in Hertfordshire. I spot Julia coming through the patio doors desperately looking around for a familiar face. I stand and wave her over.

"Hey Julia, nice dress. Looks a bit Spanish, sooooo, come on tell me all."

Reading signs of forthcoming girly talk, Nick flees the scene to chat to some geeks from the IT dept.

"Well, Phil emailed from his work phone last week, asking if I could get a last minute flight and join him for two days in Estepona, as he had some urgent business to attend to there, a funeral actually. So obviously, I jumped at the chance and was lucky to get a seat. Oh Debs, what a lovely place, the hotel was fantastic, the port, the old town - it's just adorable. We ate in the hotel the first night then spent the next day exploring the place, having lunch on the beach-front, walking along the promenade, looking at the shops, enjoying tapas in this lovely square whose name escapes me. You've been there haven't you?"

"Yes, last time was a couple of years ago. I've got mates from home who have places down there. Yes, it's fab and the square is *Plaza del Flores,* I think, lots of orange trees."

"Yes, yes, yes that's the one, anyway we had a great time, albeit far too brief and flew back yesterday."

"So where was the fragrant Misses Blunt whilst Phil was enjoying the trappings of this diplomatic emergency?"
"She's still in Alicante, back tomorrow apparently"
"Is Phil coming today?"
"Yes, but he's going to be a bit late for some reason"
Judging by the conversation, so far I'm thinking she hasn't a clue whose funeral it was. What a relief. She gets up.
"I'm going to get us a refill, then there's something I want to chat to you about."
Oh shit, I might have read that all completely wrong? I formulated a rather weak explanation for my enquiry on our Jessica in preparation for this line of questioning just in case, in my head.
Returning, Julia places two more glasses of fizz on our exclusive table.
"Debs, on Wednesday night, while Phil was in the shower, I saw a copy of the order of service."
Oh God, here we go. Clive once told me that he could tell suspects were lying by watching their eyes, if they danced a bit to the left they were telling porkies. I put my sunglasses on just in case.
"The funeral he attended was for one Jessica McGill, hmm, would this be the same Jessica McGill you asked me to give you information on last Monday?"
Eyes forward and earnest. "Okay, yes, look Julia, my trying to find any information is quite simple – I didn't actually know her, but a friend of a friend who knew her down there wanted to say a few words about her life at the wake. She apparently was a bit of a dark horse about her career history. They had a hunch she

could have been a civil servant or something of that ilk, so I was asked if I could do them a huge favour and see if I could shine any light into her working background. That was it."

I carry on a bit riskily "So why was Phil there? What's that connection?"

"I tried asking Phil about whose funeral it was over dinner, but he wouldn't say, so I left it. Wasn't really that interested anyway, just couldn't wait to take him to bed."

"Whoa, way too much information mate."

Julia continued. "I didn't say anything to Phil, as we only had one day left in paradise and I didn't want to spoil it. I thought I'd mention it to you first and now you've explained, I see no reason why I should tell Phil, but you do need to be careful doing people favours. I know you probably just wanted to help, because that's you, you're forever covering the team's arses, sometimes slightly bending the rules by poking around potentially sensitive data. For whatever innocent reason, your good nature could land you in a spot of trouble if the 'Grande-Fromage' floor ever found out."

Yeah, fucking Grainger - hear that? I thought.

"Yes, you're right I know. Thanks. Changing the subject, what dish did you get lumbered with by the way? I'm sure Ingrid thinks it's some team building exercise, getting us girls in our respective kitchen's to rustle up some exotic tit-bit, but when you look at her kitchen, don't you think it's taking the piss?"

"Yes, they could easily afford to get caterers in. I got the Caesar's salad gig, sod it, just went out and bought it ready made and put the lot in a big bowl. What's with Nick's shirt? Did he get dressed in the dark or did he do it deliberately to piss Ingrid off?" She laughs.

A few more of our bunch arrive and head straight for the bar.

Julia puts her sunglasses on, trying to be subtle, and searches the growing crowd, clearly for Phil. Better watch how much drink she puts away.

Sam and one of his numerous female companions approach. "Jane." He introduces me. "This is Debs, or how we all like to call her, Nan. Nan this is Jane." I shoot him a savage look and apologise on the cretin's behalf to the hapless Jane, who must be wondering what on earth she's doing here.

Keavo joins without a girlfriend in tow. She went shopping, sensible girl and Naomi arrives without a date. I ask her how it went the other night, knowing the answer already.

I see Bronzey and Baldrick with Steve, clearly admiring the sprawling Argentinian style barbeque, by pointing and lifting lids for inspection. Definitely a man thing. There's also, a massive table with what looks like a huge haul of assorted road kill piled high in various trays, including my ribs. Happy days. Appearing to be in his element, Steve begins the ritual everyman has inherited from doting mothers by believing they know what they are doing. How hard is it to slap a side of beef on a grill and wait until it's burnt to a cinder? I'm starving.

My turn to do the bar run and check out the food. Saving trudging backwards and forwards to the impromptu bar, I see if I can't sneak a couple of bottles away with an ice bucket. Julia got a lift, so not driving and Jane is also apparently on the fizz. The boys can sort themselves out.

Two empty bottles down later and nicely feeling the effects, I walk over to the food area. My God, how much does Ingrid think we can all eat? The spread would easily cater for a four day music festival. No one will go hungry, that's for sure.

Bypassing the abattoir products, the bar beckons. I spy a whole fridge full of wine and troughs of iced water containing beers and *Prosecco*. Excellent.

Surreptitiously grabbing two more bottles, I turn to head back to camp. As I do so, I literally smack straight into Phil.

"Hey Debs, you thirsty??" He smiles.

"It's not all for me...honest. Nice tan, Phil. Did you have a good holiday?"

"Yes it was very relaxing thanks and obviously good weather. Here Debs, let me introduce you to Mark."

He waves Mark over.

"Mark, this is Debs. She looks after all the administration and compliance for one of my CID units. Been with the firm for...oh, what is it now, twenty-three years?"

"Twenty-four actually, and counting." I stumble.

Prattling on like some museum curator, he continues. "Debs is what we refer to in the firm as a national treasure, so if you need anything, she'll steer you in the right direction."

He turns to his obvious protégé. "Mark, here, is assisting me on a project for a few months, so you'll be seeing him around, Debs. Thanks by the way for all the work you put in on the budget. Ingrid was singing your praises to me; I know she wouldn't tell you herself."

"Hi Debs, pleased to meet you." Mark finally has his turn to speak, in a Northern Irish lilt. "I'd shake hands but yours appear to be full." He chuckles. "Look forward to catching up with you." And with that they go and get themselves a beer.

I just stand for a second, my head almost physically hurting "M A R K" ???? If I'm not mistaken, and I know I'm not, the man I will be 'Ooh so helpful to, if required', is the same man Bronzey unearthed calling himself MARTIN O'Connell, spotted at Jessica's funeral - what the fuck is going on here??

I go back to the table, trying to disguise the greedy two bottles from Ingrid, as she wafts around playing hostess with the mostess.

I open the first bottle and pour myself a large glass, gulping far too quickly to mask a raucous belch, how gracious. "Have you seen Phil yet?" Julia asks.

"Yes actually, just bumped into him and had a quick chat in the drinks tent. He introduced me to an Irish bloke called Mark. Have you come across him? Apparently helping Phil with some project or other."

"No, I haven't heard of him and no one's asked me or the team to set anyone up lately as a temporary or contracting staff member that I know of, maybe he's been seconded from another division, that happens quite a lot. Why, do you fancy him or something?"

"NO I do NOT! I just wondered who he was, that's all."

We down a few more glasses in unison with the mood of the barbeque, now well and truly underway. Agreeing we need substance to soak up alcohol, we head off for some food, positioning ourselves in the salad queue. Trying to make sense of these coincidences, I can't. I'm not a bloody detective, but my gut tells me something's really not right and I don't like it one bit. I rue the moment I ever picked up that bloody phone call from Clive.

By the time we return to our table with our mini banquet, Phil and Mark/Martin are standing nearby awkwardly balancing plates and filled glasses, another man thing at barbecue's. My observations, over the years, are that men never sit down. Almost as though, if a plate of food is eaten off a table, it's taking up a place reserved for a lady. Idiots!!

Nick, clearly reaching for his feminine side, joins us.

When we finish eating Julie excuses herself to find the toilet

"Nick, who's the bloke with Phil?"

"Mark somebody-or-other. Phil bought him in and introduced him to me about a week or so ago. He was very interested to see how my archive operation works. I've got his card on my desk - why'd you ask?"

"I just got introduced to him and just wondered what he's doing with us."

Phil and Mark/Martin are now joined by a very attractive, sophisticated looking brunette, unlike us lot! Jesus, I hope Julia doesn't throw a green-eyed wobbler when she returns.

What I need to do, I think, is to try and get a photo of Phil with Mark/Martin to send to Clive. See what he makes of it.

"Nick, come on, we need to do a barbeque selfie."

"Debs, fuck off. You know I hate that sort of thing."

"Aww...come on, just one, for me. I can frame it and put it on my bedside table."
"Debs, you're full of shit, alright just one and no putting it on bloody *Facebook*, okay?"
Positioning ourselves, drinks in hand, so we're in line with Phil's table and with *iPhone* held aloft, we both smile, and I click away.
"Let's have a look." He says - I look at the photo and it's a good one, the brunettes in it but that doesn't matter, I quickly save it in my secret photo app.
"Bollocks, I'll have to do it again. I didn't have the phone in selfie mode - come on quickly."
We pose again, this time doing a proper selfie.
Phil laughs and shouts over "aren't you two a bit old for doing selfies?"
"You've got to get down with the kids Phil." I shout back.
The music volume increases - mercifully no one yet is tempted or seriously drunk enough to throw a few moves on the lawn to *La Bamba.*
Julia returns and predictably stares at the brunette, hissing to me "Who's THAT with Phil?"
"I have absolutely no idea, she just joined them a while ago. Wind your neck in and have another glass."
Making no bones to cover his action, Nick looks at his watch. A flamboyant object, probably bought from some market stall, ideally matching his shirt. It's 6.30. I can tell he wants to make a move soon, rightly so, as he's only had one beer and is gasping.
"Shall we start to make tracks, Debs?" He says.

"Suits me." It'll be another twenty minutes getting away after all the "bye, see you all Monday" and "thank you for a wonderful barbeque" syndrome.

I tell Julia we're off and that we'll go for a drink next week.

Just as we're about to open the front door to exit this extravaganza, Bronzey calls me from down the hall. Do I detect irritation in his voice? I tell Nick to go ahead and I'll be two ticks.

"You have not been entirely truthful with me, have you, Debs? That little job you asked me to do concerning face recognition, remember? I might be office bound, but I've still got a copper's nose. Why are three people I put names to in your photo, here at the barbeque? Monday lunchtime, you and I are going out and you're going to tell me the truth, Debs."

I feel the colour drain from my cheeks.

"Okay Bronzey." He turns and goes back in the direction he came.

In the meantime, Nick has pulled the car round to the front. I stand, with a cigarette in hand, wondering what level of shite Clive has spectacularly got me into.

We're little more than ten minutes into the journey when Nick breaks the silence.

"You've gone very quiet, you okay?"

"Yeah, I'm fine hun. It's just been a long day."

I put a disc on to break the silence up.

Nick drops me off at East Croydon Station. We hug, kiss good night and I promise to take him out next week as a thank you for driving.

There's a fast Brighton train in ten minutes on platform 2. As if I hadn't had enough already, I have time to get a glass of plastic wine.

I do the 'staring out of the window without really looking' thing. The wine tastes crap - what the hell am I going to say to Bronzey on Monday? Clive is seriously going to have to guide me on this one, but he's the last person I want to have to admit that 'I don't know what the fuck to do'.

I get home at 9.20pm, and tempted to go to the *Seafield*, but I'd only get battered and I need to unload what I've witnessed earlier to Clive, whilst it's still fresh (albeit *Prosecco* tainted) in my mind.

That said, I go against all my previous good intentions and pour myself a large glass - open the back door to the garden and have a cigarette before I make the call.

I dial his number - 10.45 his time.

"Debs, how'd it go today? Did you manage to drop something lethal into the punchbowl and choke someone to death on one of your rib bones?" He sounds a bit pissed, but hey, who am I to talk?

"No, it went much worse than me killing somebody, you cheeky fucker and you know what, I would love to shove the heads of the prats who represent my firm up your arse. And then, you'll be near enough to them to ask for your own fucking favours. You have no idea how you've dropped me in it from a great height."

In a Tourette's peppered dialogue from my end, I recount the conversation with Julia, being introduced by Phil to Mark/Martin and finally the Bronzey meeting on Monday.

"So Einstein, how am I going to play Monday's little tête-à-tête, then?"
"Debs, I don't know. I need time to think about it. What you've come up with so far is intriguing."
"Fuck your intrigue, Clive, you have till tomorrow to come up with how I handle Bronzey." After the threats, I hear no breathing and wonder if he is still on the line. "By the way I got a photo of Phil and Mark/Martin, I'll send it to you. There's a woman standing with them, no idea who she is. She had a quick drink with them and happened to be in the photo. You need to focus on the men by using your head and not on her using your dick. She looks to be right up your strasse."
I go on in the hope I'm not talking on a dead line. "Clive, this whole crusade is getting as smelly as the biggest dung heap in smelly-land and it's following me right into the office. Enough. Whatever YOU'RE determined to get into, leave ME well and truly out of it. Do you hear me...Clive." I shout down the line.
A pause of maybe five seconds elapses before I get life beaming from Spain into my mobile.
"I know Debs, but..."
I've had enough and really can't be bothered to speak to him anymore, it's always all about bloody him.
I hang up and disappear into the garden, a large fishbowl of wine in one hand, a nicely rolled spliff in the other.

CHAPTER 15

9.32 am. Sunday 16th August 2015. Estepona.

Sunday morning supposedly, as I've been told, is the beginning of a day of rest for most hard working and sincere people, but as I represent neither, my head feels like it does every other day of the week. Hangovered and in desperate need of coffee.

I bend, attempting to locate my sunglasses, but a shooting pain in my head straightens my back. The shock seemingly gives me five seconds of unblemished memory. "Oh shit." I say to myself, remembering Debs phone call from the night before and how I didn't have a sober ability to attempt to give her a cover story. If I am to get anywhere near solving this mystery, I need to cut down on booze and when I say, cut down, I mean nigh absolution from the devils potion.

I won't get back to Debs till lunchtime, it would probably break the last straw gluing our friendship together if I aroused her out of sleep before midday. But I must have thought about doing just that, as I have my mobile in my right hand. I put life into it, only to see if any poor bugger decided to text me out of their boredom, before I settle down on the terrace. Bless her...Debs has sent me a snap she took on her mobile at the barbeque. At first glance I see three figures, one I recognise as Phil Blunt and the other I'm sure was at the funeral. I study his face wondering if it's the same one Debs put a name to, a certain Michael O'Connell. For a moment or two I'm distracted by the two faces standing in front of the third, but then the brunette blasts her features to the fore. Shelly. Well, this is cosy, but what does it mean? Am I going down the wrong track by putting too much credence into believing these three, especially Shelly, have something more sinister to hide, or is there another slant I haven't yet even considered. I need to delve deeper into Jessica's background. After all, what was the reason to murder, in a ritualistic fashion, a retired old lady other than it was something she did or was responsible for in the past. There are facts staring me in the face, but I can't see them apart from knowing she was shot three times in the head. Who or what faction of a disillusioned sect could administer such an assassination?

My coffee remains untouched. I've forgotten it's sitting there getting cold on the table alongside a shrivelling cigarette in an ashtray. My mind abruptly jerks back to an earlier thought. 'A faction of a disillusioned sect'. Come on, Clive, now you're getting somewhere thinking along these lines. Stop earmarking those three in the picture, though I'm sure they know more than they are letting on. They are not the guilty ones. No, it's something more sinister. Something Jessica was responsible for many years ago, and she knew there might be reprisals.

Why else change her name at about the same time she had a child. Who was the father? Where was he when this all started to erupt? Her records show nothing.

They have been totally wiped of any proof she actually existed and then she escapes down here sporting a new identity. The clue to all this is when this transition began. I guess, from the snippets I've unearthed, it might have been in the early seventies. What was happening in that decade that warranted such drastic action? I have a theory, but I need confirmation and I'm not going to get it sitting on the beach, my arse cradled in a sunbed on the sands of Estepona.

~O~

Pre-retirement, when still in my office at the *Yard*, I'd have readily at hand all the gizmos and updated files appertaining to the case, not to mention a team of astute detectives who wouldn't need wet-nursing when it came to working these fancy machines. We'd meet each morning and I would listen to suggestions, theories and the progress we'd made, before deciding which direction we'd concentrate on, by allocating officers to specific areas of the case, thereby not necessarily proving guilt, but to eliminate the innocent. It would very much be a team effort. But all that has gone. I only have Debs as my eyes and ears and by the way our friendship is progressing, I doubt I'll have her services for too much longer.

Retrieving my cigarettes from my bathrobe pocket, my fingers brush against another object. Placing both items on the table, I first light a cigarette, then pick-up my note book. How it got there in the first place, I can't remember. Flicking through the pages brings on a twang of remembrance; names and numbers, memos to myself and thoughts at the time of certain scrotes, who were free but needed banging up. It brings a smile to my face as I thumb through memory lane.

Finally, I come to the last page, specially reserved for names and numbers of people of the public and police officers I could trust. I focus my eyes on my finger as it runs down the page, each name I ponder on for a few seconds, then move south to the next name and so on. Half way down, my pointing digit stops under the identity of a police officer who I grew to respect enormously when I was seconded to Brighton in my early days. He's older than me and retired way before I did, but he was genuine, fair and refused to take bullshit, reasons why he declined promotion and remained a detective constable for his entire career. I once asked him why he didn't go for it and all he said was 'I like being a copper'. We became friends, he taking me under his wing before I accepted promotion, meaning our union was severed when I had to commute to the 'Smoke'.

Unlike him, I accepted the bullshit and insincerity that initially goes hand in hand with an upgrade in rank. Persuaded by the inducement of a hefty sweetener in my wage packet, it convinced me the daily grind up to London was worth the trouble. Don't blame me, after all, I was still only in my twenties, still too young to work out the ramifications of what promotion meant when invited to be entombed in a *Masonic*-type organisation.

My memory also hasn't deserted me when remembering this individual was transferred to *New Scotland Yard* for a while, after his involvement with the Brighton, *Grand Hotel* bombing. From rumours flying round the factory, I had heard Jack also spent a while with *MI5*, probably because he was the first copper on the scene after the building collapsed, the intention being to take the government's inner cabinet with it. It's a tenuous link, I know, but worth at least a call.

Donning *Ray Bans*, my tempered gaze from my terrace out to the Mediterranean beyond is at least bearable, I wonder if his telephone number is still valid or at worse, disconnected. In a time before mobiles, it's a landline number I dial. Surely he must have moved on since those days, but it's worth a gamble. It's 9.30am here, so 8.30am back there. I'll give it a try. Hope he's still not in bed nursing my type of hangover, or worse still, he might be dead.

Miraculously, I hear a ringtone in my ear. At least the line is connected, but who'll answer?

It burbles on half a dozen times before the receiver is picked up.

"Hello, Jack Wakeling."

Bingo!

"Hi, Jack, it's Clive Grainger. Sorry to interrupt you so early in the morning. Do you remember me from the Brighton nick?"

There's silence, probably wondering who the hell I am, then a gushing reply.

"Clive...Clive Grainger...fuck me. Now there's a name from the past. What the hell are you phoning me for after all this time? I'm amazed you still have my number."

"I'm amazed you still live at the same place." I butt in.

"No, I've moved a few times but took the number with me. Why this call after so many years?"
Purposely bypassing his last question, I begin by giving him the low-down on where I am in life, skipping over the Jessica affair for the time being. He in turn gives me a resume on where he's standing.
"Look Clive, it's great speaking to you again, but why are you calling me, especially from Spain?"
You can retire from the police force, but the copper's nose is always stuck firmly between your eyes. He's more than curious.
"It's awkward, Jack, and don't really know where to start. I thought you might be able to give me a lead."
For ten minutes I talk, without interruption, about my friendship with Jessica, her murder and everything relating to what Debs and I have uncovered. The possibility Jessica might have been under a witness protection program. Her daughter. The lot.
"Interesting Clive, but I don't see where I come in for any advice." Jack's turn to speak finally responds through my mobile.
"Look Jack, weren't you seconded to the *Yard,* back in the eighties for a while after the Grand bombing? This all happened long before I joined the force, but I remember when I arrived you were a bit of a folk hero amongst the lads. They couldn't understand how the Chief Constable got all the plaudits and you were hardly mentioned. It was my lucky day when I became your partner to replace Jim. Every copper in the squad wanted to take my place. I might have risen to Chief Inspector, but you were, by far, a better copper than

me. I need your help, Jack, anything you've got that I might have overlooked."
Only silence prevails, not what I expected to be an answer.
"Clive, it was a long time ago and you know only too well I shouldn't be talking to you about that episode."
"Come on Jack, we're both retired. What the hell difference would it make? There's nothing happening over here with nobody appearing to give a hoot as to why she was knocked off. And as far as I can make out, the police back home couldn't give a fuck either. Well, that's not good enough. Jessica was shot three times in the temple, which says to me it was an assassination, not some fly by night murder. I need some answers to why it happened and find out who the bastards were that pulled the fucking trigger." Anger in my voice is evident.
Silence repeats itself. I wait.
"Okay, Clive, but what I have to say can't be relayed down a telephone line. You'll have to come over."

~O~

1.30 pm. Monday 17th August 2015. Approaching Gatwick Airport
My *easyJet* flight into Gatwick at lunchtime is uneventful, though it cost me a fortune, but hey, I'm not what one would call skint. Taking Jack's advice, I take a cab down to Brighton and hopefully we'll coincide our timing to meet in *The Queensbury Arms,* a pub nestling behind the *Metropole Hotel,* just off the seafront. He said it was a place where we could talk

without danger of being recognised by the locals. I have this faint suspicion he doesn't want this meeting to happen.

I enter and am immediately confronted by faces turning to inspect my arrival. My first reaction is to pick out Jack, but its twenty five odd years since we last met. Nobody here I recognise, but then, from behind the bar, I spot another accessible room down a few steps. Apologising, as I interrupt a few locals in my quest to make it to the salon in the back, I realise, much to my amusement, it's a gay pub. Good cover, Jack, I think. Unused to being in such surroundings, I smile. What else am I supposed to do? I spot Jack sitting at a circular table, a pint of what I really miss in Spain, perched in front of him.

"Jack, good to see you." I gush, much to the amusement of our fellow drinkers who might be thinking of other devious, solicitous reasons why two men should be meeting in such a place.

He stands, holding out his hand. We shake. He appears to be pleased to see me. Our onlookers disappointed we don't hug.

"Fuck me, Clive, look at the colour of you. Looks like you're having a really hard time down there in Spain. What can I get you?"

"A pint of *Harveys* will do just fine." I respond, my lips smacking at the thought of tasting real ale after such a long break.

It's not entirely private, but with just a couple sitting in the far corner not five yards away, it'll do. Jack is first to talk, albeit in a lower voice.

"What I have to say must be important to you if you're prepared to travel so far."

He's aged, but haven't all of us. Must be in his late sixties, but his hair is in one piece though a few pounds have stretched his belt. All told, he's standing up to the rigours of retirement and ageing quite well.

"It is, Jack. I've got this theory, but it means fuck all if I can't put the pieces together. So tell me, what the fuck went on all that time ago?"

Looking over his shoulder, Jack confirms no one appears interested with what he's about to recall. Beckoning me forward, our heads are no more than eighteen inches apart.

"What I'm about to tell you is strictly between us. Don't ever quote me...shit will hit the fan if it ever got into the public domain. I might be retired, but they can still hurt me in the same way as they can hurt you if it ever got out. So watch your step. It's difficult to know where to start though...memory, you know...not what it used to be. It all began on October 12th 1984 in the early hours during the Conservative party conference. Jim and I, that's Jim Moran my sidekick, were back at John Street nick when all hell breaks loose. The *Grand Hotel* where *Maggie Thatcher* and half the cabinet are staying has been bombed, with half the place collapsing. We race round before any of the other services arrive and are confronted by sheer bedlam. There's no way through the front door, the whole place had collapsed into the foyer. It didn't need an expert to see this wasn't some amateurish job, this was very serious and there were only the two of us to do anything about it. For all I knew, there might have been a secondary device, but we had to do something instead of just looking up at this fucking great hole in the front of the building with our pricks in our hands. So we scoot around the back and find a fire escape with people tumbling down in pyjamas and nighties. We climb up, opening doors on each floor to check, but it's only when we get to the sixth floor where there's total chaos. You can hardly see a thing; the air is pea-soup thick with dust and smoke. People are just screaming and stumbling about. I grab a bloke, still dressed in a suit and scream at him 'where are the secret services', you know, the boys who are supposed to deal with these type of emergencies. He knocks me to one side and runs off. Jim's having trouble keeping up, but we find a room where the door is open and low and behold, its Maggie standing there. She's as calm as a cucumber, dressed in some dressing gown, attempting to calm others. I must admit, she's one tough cookie. I tell her who I am and ask where her boys are, the ones detailed to protect. She hunches her shoulders and blurts out she hasn't a clue. Do you know, Dennis was in the other room, pissed as a newt, sprawled out comatose under the covers. You wouldn't believe it if you read about it in some novel. So I take the decision to take control, not because I wanted to, but there was nobody else. Then this woman appears and hugs Maggie. She's crying. What do I do? From outside I hear sirens, hundreds of the bloody things. I tell Maggie to dress and do what she can for Dennis, the old soak, but this other woman is still hanging about. I must admit Maggie got a wiggle on as within five minutes they were all standing fully dressed. Maggie wanted to go and care for the others, but I said I wouldn't allow that, as I was taking charge and to follow me. She held my arm and Jim had Dennis' around his shoulders and bugger it, the other woman was following. I didn't know until later, she was Maggie's best friend, but for the life of me, I can't remember her name. We get back to the fire escape where a few others are now fully dressed and are getting the hell out. Outside the hotel, the place is covered with fire engines and ambulances and would you believe, a couple of our boys have turned up and are wandering around like spare pricks at a wedding. Jim and I finally get Maggie and Dennis into the back of our car with her mate in the front. I jump behind the wheel and tell Jim to get a lift back in a squad car." Jack pauses to take a mouthful of ale, his manner quite different to when he started, upbeat as though he's enjoying the recollection. "I drive to John Street and go straight for the back door leading to the cells. Maggie's fine but the other two need supporting. What a mess. Here am I, a DC in charge of the whole shooting match. Sorry." A wide smile creases his lips. "That might be the wrong phrase to use, but what a fucking laugh, Charlie, the station sergeant is there to open the door. When he recognises Maggie, you should have seen his face. The only safe place I could think of putting her was in a cell, but I take my hat off to her, she didn't question anything. A PC led Dennis and this other woman to an adjacent cell leaving me alone with the Prime Minister. I remember thinking, 'Oh fuck, what do I do next'. So I ask her if there is something I can get her. She pipes up in that authoritarian way of hers, she would like a telephone. Well, that was easier said than done. Before mobiles, you know."

Again, a pause for refreshment. "I get out of there and run up to the sergeant's office, where phones are ringing off their hooks and he's in a right mess. She wants a phone, I tell him. Well, fucking give her one, he replies. Thanks, I say and start raiding his cupboards. There's wires and leads of every description plus a few telephones of different colours. I grab a red one, quite appropriate I thought at the time."

Now Jack is definitely in the mood. Whether he's embellishing the story, I can't tell.

"Someone in a black suit arrives at the front desk, covered in dust and demands he sees Thatcher. His credentials are checked and he's shown down to her cell. Turns out he's someone from the security, which branch I never found out.

When I arrive back with a fifty odd yard extension lead and phone, he's whispering in her ear. I couldn't hear what he said, but fitted the thing up and placed it on the bunk-bed next to her. He orders me to leave, but I refuse, telling this pompous little shit I was in charge and where was he when needed. Maggie, bless her, tells him instead to go and to leave me guarding her. I stand by the door whilst she tests the line. Without introducing herself she talks into the mouthpiece to some faceless person on the other end of the line. Of course I'm listening. Without so much as a raising of her voice, I hear her order the assassination of three high ranking *IRA* activists in Belfast."

Jack stops abruptly and looks at me. What he sees is my mouth gaping open and a look of total disbelief on my face.
"You have got to be joking." I manage, at last, to remember the art of talking.
"No mate. It's the truth. Our Maggie ordered someone she obviously knew, to rub out three blokes, just like that. It wasn't until later that I learnt what this bloke had whispered in her ear. He told her three of her own were dead in the hotel and there was a good chance they'd be others. What a girl...eh?"
I thought for a while, admiring Jack's choice of beer, before taking up where he left off.
"Do you happen to know who she spoke to that night?"
"Yeah, when I was ordered up to the *Yard* for debriefing, all the events and statements from those involved that night were scrutinized by the top brass. I was then ordered over to *MI5* to be interrogated again, but this time by some nasty little bastards. To cap it all, it took me a further week to read the entire brief, in case something was missed out. That's who she phoned and they did the dirty work."
Oh fuck, the pieces are starting to come together. I wonder, no it couldn't be, if Jessica was on the other end of the line to Thatcher. No, couldn't be; pure fantasy.
"Can you recall any of their names?" I hastily quiz Jack, hoping he can.
"No mate, none of them used even a Christian name in my presence and if they did, I can't remember. There were three men in the room and a woman. We all sat round a table with them firing questions at me. Come

Friday, I was knackered and allowed home. Big fucking deal, but they finally got the bastard who planted it. Arrested in Glasgow, or some other place up there, if I'm not mistaken. Do you know, if Maggie could have had her way, she would have done what she ordered to be done to the other three, stuck the bastard up against a brick wall and shot him. Instead, he was allowed out after only a few years as part of the *Good Friday Agreement.* What a joke...eh?"

It's hard to digest Jack's recollection of what happened on that night in Brighton and I wished I'd brought along a tape recorder, but probably, he would have schtummed up if he saw one.

Our glasses are empty, so I re-order at the bar. Looking back over to him, he's deep in thought, probably reliving the horror of it all. I need a smoke, so gesticulate to him I'm going outside. In return he gives me a thumbs-up and follows. Accepting one of mine, he mumbles on about something to do with the price of tobacco, but I'm not really listening as my mind is set upon précising what I heard into sound bites I can remember.

"Have you any idea who those four were questioning you round a table at *MI5*?" My question needs asking, but I didn't expect an answer.

"No...as I said, they never mentioned names."

"The woman present. Describe her to me." Persisting to try and unlock his memory, I endeavour to do it without it appearing to be an interrogation.

"Well...she was probably in her forties. About five feet four or five. Light wavy hair and a tad overweight. Nothing peculiar about her, nothing standing out. Just an everyday woman who you'd see behind the till at *Tesco."*

It could have been Jessica, but the description also fits millions of other women walking the planet. It may be August, but I'm getting cold standing on the pavement in the shadow of the *Metropole Hotel.* I need to get back inside to the warmth and make inroads into my second pint.

CHAPTER 16

7.47am. Monday 17th August. 2015. Somewhere Outside Guildford.

Monday morning doesn't begin well for Deputy Assistant Commissioner Lewis Bowen, the great grandson of one of the founders of the homeland securities concept during the back end of World War I, so the story goes. Having travelled no more than a couple of miles after kissing his wife goodbye, on the steps of his expensive pile of bricks and mortar situated in a half acre plot of land outside of Guildford, his chauffeur driven car punctures its front offside tyre in the middle of the town's giro-system, during rush-hour.

"What's the problem, Harrison?" An enquiry, he knows only too well what the answer will be.

"Looks like we have a flat tyre, Sir."

"Well, have you got a spare?" Irritation is evident.

"Hope so, Sir, but don't know until I look in the boot. Only picked up this car this morning."

Behind, other drivers grow impatient, a chorus of horns discharge at irregular intervals giving a clue to their annoyance.

"Pull over onto the pavement, then get out and have a look, man."

Harrison does exactly as ordered and disappears under the boot's bonnet. If matters couldn't get worse, Bowen rolls his eyes skyward as a constable approaches, his demeanour suggesting he's not too pleased. Bypassing the driver's window, he taps on the smoked glass concealing the identity of the passenger, requesting it be lowered. Once the black uniform, lapels emblazoned with a pip over a commander's badge become evident, the constable knows his day hasn't got off to a good start. Standing bolt upright, his right-hand fumbling to exchange his radio to his left, a laboured salute acknowledges the superior officer.
"Morning, Sir. Can I be of any help?" The PC offers half a smile, camouflaged by stiff lips.
"Yes you can, officer. Get on your radio and get me a taxi."

~O~

Brushing his way through security on his arrival at *New Scotland Yard*, a twenty story edifice in Broadway, Victoria, Bowen boards a lift to the nineteenth floor, ten minutes late for a meeting with his direct superior, Assistant Commissioner Andrew Brooks. There isn't even time for a coffee. He knocks and enters knowing full well it's not a done thing to keep higher ranking officers waiting.
"Morning Lewis. Had a spot of bother with a tyre, so I hear. Get yourself a coffee whilst I talk. It appears from an internal email from Thompson at Thames House (*MI5*) that someone here in the department and at Brighton nick has been looking into one of their

retired associates, namely one Jessica McGill. Last week, on two separate occasions, their internal intelligence database flagged up warnings of unauthorized searches for her file. Now Lewis, fill me in again with what we know about Jessica McGill?"

With cup in hand, Bowen returns to the Assistant Commissioner's desk and sits opposite.

"You'll remember, Sir, she was the English woman who was murdered down in Spain a week ago. When we got wind of it only an hour after it happened, Thames House was onto us in a flash, suggesting a joint operation to put a lid on it. You see, McGill was a Deputy Director General within their organisation and the death of such a high profile operative is throwing up dangerous conclusions on who might be responsible. What with the resurgence of killings in Belfast this summer, all pointing to *IRA* involvement, we must seriously consider if they are responsible for the murder of Jessica...and personally, I believe they are. Taking this into consideration, it makes my meeting with an officer of the *Guardia Civil* in half an hour all the more delicate...during our talks over the phone last week, they suggested that three shots into her temple pointed to an assassination, rather than just murder. I attempted to pour...not cold water on their assumptions, but shall we say...lukewarm. They understand where I'm coming from, but they require her file and anything else that might throw up reasons why she was targeted. How would you like me to proceed?"

During his meteoric rise within the *Metropolitan Police*, Bowen played the safe game of never taking a decision, always passing the buck upwards to a more senior level. By taking this course, when judgements went wrong, his name never appeared on file as a culprit. These small, but some might say cowardly characteristics, were becoming evident and noted by his superiors.

"How do you believe we should proceed, Lewis? Have you tracked down those responsible for these indiscretions concerning the unauthorised use of the international data base? If you haven't, then I suggest you do so before you meet with our Spanish counterparts. Put off your meeting until this afternoon. It'll give you time to question those who tried to bring up McGill's file. Get a grasp on what's happening in our own back yard and then consider the consequences accordingly. Once done, then we advise the *Guardia Civil* on which way we think they should proceed." Brooks threw the gauntlet back, catching Bowen unprepared.

"Well, Sir...isn't that the job of a detective chief inspector? I'm sure they are more qualified than me in this instance." His reply isn't accepted.

"Listen here, Bowen...when I order something to be done, I don't expect it to be passed down the ranks. It might not have sounded like an order, but it was. I expect a report on my desk by no later than two o'clock today. Now, I believe you have work to do and so do I." The meeting ends abruptly.

~O~

"I don't care what you're doing, I want the names of anyone poking around in the database for Jessica McGill's files. Get onto Thames House and ask where the terminals were sited and whose names they are registered under. DO IT NOW...do you hear me?" Bowen screams down the internal phone to an unsuspecting DCI.

~O~

The door firmly closed, Bowen sits in his office, fingers unconsciously strumming his desktop whilst his eyes dart back and forth to his clock, a promotional present given by his 'workmates'. Ignorant of the subtlety of giving such an object, it wasn't out of their respect; they knew of his clock-watching antics, when the time was safe to leave the office without fear of recrimination.

A long awaited knock rattles his door.

"Come."

"Morning, Sir." DCI Hitchens acknowledges his superior with a smile, but quickly deduces it's not a time for niceties. "I have the information you asked for."

"Good, sit down whilst I go through it." Bowen points to a chair and opens the file, flicking from page to page. Hitchens remains standing. "I want this woman brought up to my office immediately and whilst you're at it, phone Brighton and get someone down there to interrogate this...Leslie Bonnerly. When they have answers, get them to me immediately. And while you're at it, it might be a good idea if I also spoke to Bonnerly's superior. He should know what his subordinates are up to and if he doesn't, he should do. Do I make myself understood?"

Looking down at his superior from the opposite side of the desk, Hitchens' eyes have a guarded, disdainful stare, one which needs an answer to a question. Why spend twenty four years in the service, when idiots like this can use rank to ride rough-shot over more experienced officers?

"Of course, Sir. I'll get on to it straight away." He replies with a hint of sarcasm.

"Good man."

Not more than half an hour elapses when Bowen's solitude is interrupted. Hitchens pokes his head around the door. "Julia Spencer is here, outside your office, Sir, as well as her superior officer, Superintendent Ingrid Harvey. Who would you like to see first?"

Ingrid Harvey passes Hitchens, before he closes the door on his way out.

"Please sit, Harvey." Bowen directs, whilst scouring her file.

"If you don't mind, Sir, my rank is Superintendent and I would appreciate being addressed as such." She'd heard rumours of his brusque manner and is now witnessing it first-hand.

"What can you tell me about these unauthorized enquiries you permitted into the international data base?" Raising his face, Bowen looks directly into Ingrid's eyes.

"This is all news to me. I can't possibly be held responsible. It's impossible for me, or anyone else in a

similar position, to be permanently looking over the shoulders of my team. I trust them implicitly and if this indiscretion has happened, I'm sure it was done innocently with no possible ulterior motive." Ingrid smiles, but inwardly she curses Julia for her stupidity in not knowing her entry would be flagged up somewhere if not authorised.
"It's nothing to smile about, Harvey. This is..." Before continuing with his rebuke, Ingrid stands and confronts the Deputy Assistant Commissioner.
"I have told you already...if you can't or won't address me with my correct title, this meeting is over." A temper, rarely seen, erupts inside Ingrid as she stands firm, her cheeks flushing.
"Apologies, Ingrid. Please be reseated. Let's start again."
If only the boys and girls in her department could see her now, she thinks, her smile returning.
"I am attempting to put a file together concerning the murder of Jessica McGill. Last week Julia Spencer tapped into the data base to find her file...all I'm attempting to ascertain is why she did it?"
"As I have already said, I don't know. Why not ask her for yourself?"
"Thank you Ingrid. I will do just that. Oh...and by the way. I've made the decision to attach this incident into your file as a warning to your future behaviour. That will be all?" His hand gesture indicating her to leave, points to the door.
She stares at him as she gets to her feet. A second or two passes. No, she won't deliver a double broadside. She'll arrange her revenge more subtly.

Julia enters Bowen's office a minute after Ingrid's departure and stands fidgeting in front of the superior's desk.

"Sit." His words spit from a tight lipped mouth. Julia obeys.

"One question, Spencer. Why did you tap into the international data base without authorisation?"

Julia freezes. The first time she's been summoned to the higher floors fills her with apprehension.

"Come on, woman, speak up."

Close to tears, Julia is about to splutter an incoherent reply when a rap on the door, followed by its immediate opening takes Bowen by surprise. "Who the hell are you?" He barks across his office from where he sits.

"My name is Sergeant Hopkins and I'm here to advise Julia Spencer as her union representative."

"Get out of here, damn you." Bowen screams at the intruder. "Can't you see I'm busy?"

"No Sir, I will not leave. If you have anything to say to Miss Spencer, then it will be said in my presence." Remaining calm, Hopkins dares Bowen to overstep the line.

"Okay...okay. If this is how procedure works, then draw up a chair."

Julia's fear evaporates as her guardian angel sits close by.

"Now, let's get on with it. I'll ask you again, why did you search into the international data base without authorisation?" Intimidatingly, he leans forward towards Julia.

"I must stop you there, Sir. This appears to be an interrogation and warrants my colleague having legal representation. A lawyer with employment law knowledge should be present." Hopkins interrupts.

"For fucks sake man, all I'm trying to do is ask Spencer a question, as I'm quite sure she's capable of answering it." Bowen nears the end of his fuse and it's all too evident.

"I must advise you, Sir, to cease using expletives and to also refer to Miss Spencer with her title. It's common courtesy." Bowen might be six ranks above him, but Hopkins is enjoying himself. "Maybe, Sir, if I ask Julia the question. We might be able to proceed." Hopkins rubs his advantage in even further.

"Do it." Falling back into his chair in despair whilst simulating a *Noel Coward* like frustration, Bowen waves Hopkins to continue.

"Are you okay, Julia, how are you feeling?" Hopkins begins, purposely in a tone he knows will infuriate the Deputy Assistant Commissioner. She nods. "Okay... I guess." Hopkins continues. "Then let's begin. Are you able to answer the question that was posed?"

"Yes, I can." Julia responds, not directing her answer to Bowen but to Hopkins. "Last week I was asked by Debbie Glynn, our operations manager, to look up a file under the name of Jessica McGill. I didn't ask her why as she's a good friend and we have worked together for years, so assuming it was something to do with what she was working on, I obliged with the requested favour. It happens all the time. I found a file completely wiped clean, which is very unusual. I told her that and she took it from there. Nothing more."

"Thank you Julia. Let us know if you need any ongoing support" Hopkins rubs Julia's hand reassuringly

before directing his words to Bowen. “There, that wasn’t so bad, was it?” He mocks knowing there’ll be no response.
“No, thank you both. Would you mind leaving now? I need to make a report.”
In silence, Hopkins helps Julia to the door, chastising himself for not bringing a hidden recorder to the meeting. He could have had free lunches for a year with what could have been on it. He also made a point of phoning Ingrid to thank her for putting him wise to Julia’s situation and for making his day.

~O~

Confirming, Brighton came up with the same conclusion. An internal phone call and ten minutes later, Debbie Glynn’s file is spread out on Bowen’s desk. “Hello, Sir. It’s Bowen here. I have the information you require. May I bring it up?”

~O~

Bowen is not only confronted with the Deputy Commissioner, but also by the Commissioner himself when entering the office on the twentieth floor.
“Come in, Lewis and sit yourself down. What have you got for us?”
“Well, Sir. It appears the CID unit Operations Manager, one Debbie Glynn, has been asking for these files. I took the opportunity to study Glynn’s file and see that she was the assistant to one Clive Grainger, a Chief Inspector, before he retired four years ago.”

Bowen passes over the file to Commissioner Gordon's outstretched hand, ready to continue with his report. "Thanks, Lewis. That will be all, and Lewis, can you please ensure both Julia Spencer and Ingrid Harvey do NOT discuss your meeting with them to Debbie Glynn. I will speak directly with Glynn when appropriate. "
Biting his lip, Bowen turns to depart and is annoyed his input isn't required, knowing what was about to be discussed within these four walls will never reach his ears and was way above his pay-grade. If only he knew his capabilities had been sussed out by the promotions board and he will never proceed above his present rank. Regardless of who his great grandfather might have been, Bowen's years are numbered.
Sitting opposite his deputy, Commissioner Jack Gordon studies the file without a word passing between them. Moistening his lips, Gordon breaks the silence. "I know this Grainger fellow, even went into the bar he frequents, when I was down his way a few years ago before I got promoted. Left my card with the bar owner, if I'm not mistaken. Hope he's binned it or forgotten about my visit...no...this could work out quite nicely. I worked with Grainger on a number of cases and found him to be a very good copper. Someone who knows when to keep his mouth shut. He was a bit of a maverick, but that's what was good about him. He didn't need a partner as he relied on Glynn to do the dirty work. Yes...they made a bloody good team. Instead of having an internal enquiry, we'll put a cap on this hacking nonsense straight away, as it wasn't technically hacking. All connected had authorisation. It was just the name...Jessica McGill that brought up

a red flag. No...no more action is to be taken. I'll get Thames House in for a discussion on the matter. Resurface Grainger's file for me. If I know Grainger, and I believe I do, he's fishing around down there for answers, as he obviously knew Jessica. Hence, that's why he asked Glynn for help...to get the background on the woman. Should Thames House agree, and I have no doubt they will, Grainger can go places we can't. We'll feed Glynn all the relevant information we can without her getting wind of where it came from. She'll relay it back to Grainger and let's see where he goes with it. I believe Bowen is correct with his assumption, and so does *MI5,* about *IRA* involvement but this theory must remain within these four walls, as it must within Thames House." Gordon replaces his cup to its saucer. His deputy feels there's something more sinister than has already been said to come out of the Commissioner's mouth. "For some time now, both *MI5* and we here at the *Yard,* believe there is a mole working amongst us. For reasons I won't bore you with, since *Sinn Fein* became a legitimate political party with a handful of MP's, voted in on an *IRA* mandate, they appear to know what we're thinking before it even reaches the discussion stage. What with the odd non-secular murder becoming more frequent in Belfast, we're afraid we might be seeing a resurgence of the old troubles. Place Jessica McGill in the picture and one has to ask, how they knew she'd changed her name and where she lived under a witness protection order. I've seen her original file and believe me, putting her down is a big feather in their cap. Without anybody getting wind of what we are trying to instigate, we might be able to steer Grainger in the right direction and unearth our mole and God knows what else is scurrying around in the undergrowth. This matter doesn't leave this room or go down the ranks. If we keep this simple with only the two of us knowing plus a minimum of personnel at Thames House, there's a chance we can feed this infiltrator with anything we care to give him and he won't know the difference. Tell Bowen to cobble up anything believable about Jessica and hand it over to our Spanish friends when they meet. I believe they're going through the rudiments as we would do and might just want to wipe their hands of the whole caboodle."

Pushing back his chair, Gordon stands and walks thoughtfully over to a window. The Deputy Commissioner knows not to interrupt. Taking in the entire vista of London spread out before him, Gordon utters a few words, his deputy being unsure if they are directed to him, or if they are thoughts unintentionally spoken.

"We need a code word we can safely use without our mole friend knowing what we're up to." A minutes silence passes until he turns back to Andrew Brooks.

"It'll be OMIE." Gordon directs.

"OMIE...what does that stand for?" The curious Deputy enquires.

"Our Man in Estepona, of course."

CHAPTER 17

4.13pm. Monday 17th August 2015. Brighton Seafront.

I feel myself, quite unconsciously, comparing Brighton seafront with that of Estepona, whilst I stroll along its promenade heading for the *Palace Pier*, or whatever it's called nowadays. I know it's August and the height of summer, but the only thing I like about the place is the temperature, its way below that from where I took off this morning. Not that its coolness deters those spread out on the pebbles below, happily basking in what they believe is tannable sunshine. Okay, I can spot the odd 'lobster' of both sexes broiling satisfactorily on laid out towels, their stomachs appearing to be closest to the sun and reddening nicely, but there aren't any '*Chiringitos*' to get a beer or feast on freshly caught seafood. Nor does the sea appear to be inviting, though it's full of kids splashing about regardless of its temperature. No, I can't say I'd swap this for my little haven in Spain.

But I must stick out like a sore thumb, dressed in jacket, shirt, trousers, sensible brogues and a tan that's taken four years to nurture and impossible to copy with just a day under a considerate sun.

Ahead, I spot a pair of over-large parents and their candy-floss munching brood vacate a bench, so lengthen my strides before the space is devoured by other equally large backsides. I sit, remove a cigarette from its box and gaze out over the English Channel, with Jack Wakeling's words echoing in my mind. I have no doubt he was telling me nothing but the truth, but what he said gave me grave doubts I could proceed any further, after all, to anyone else's ears, what he said would be construed as just one gigantic conspiracy theory. I need more and something or somebody who can point me in its direction.

Alongside my cigarettes in an inside pocket, is my 'little black book', a piece of equipment I'd never be without when still in the job, now strangely feeling at home, even though it'd been forgotten about in the bottom of a cardboard box for years. Going directly to the last page, I bypass Jack's name, pondering on each handwritten individual for a few seconds, not wanting to miss someone who I'd forgotten and who could be another 'Jack Wakeling'. My finger stays pointing on a name for more time it'd spent on the others above. It's a long-shot, but hey, I've been gambling on also-rans since the morning I received Fred's phone call telling me about Jessica. I can afford to put my money on another outsider.

Well, at least the phone is ringing at the other end. I wait, not really knowing what to expect, when a female voice relieves the monotonous buzzing in my ear.

"Hello, Natalie Forbes speaking."

Natalie Forbes didn't register as the person inked into my notebook, well, Forbes didn't, but her Christian name certainly did. She must be wary as I didn't

respond immediately, attempting to put names into place.
"Oh...yes...good afternoon. My name is Clive Grainger and I was wondering if I have phoned the correct number. You see, I know it's been years since we last spoke, but it is Leonid Kuznetsov I would like to speak to, that is, if he still lives at that address?"
A long pause makes me believe the line will go dead any second, until a none-too-sure voice breaks the silence.
"Who are you and what do you want with my father?"
I thought I recognised the Christian name. "Natalie, you might remember me, but you were only a girl the last time we met. Didn't your father send you to Roedean, just outside of Brighton for some very posh education? I'm retired now, but I knew your father back in the late eighties and nineties." Better not mention I am an ex-copper, I quickly think. "And there's something that has cropped up in my life that your father might be able to help me with. Is he about?"
Again, a pause. "Yes." She finally answers, the tone of her voice audibly changed from official to accommodating. "I remember you, Mister Grainger, you used to come round and play chess with my father, not that I remember you ever winning though." She laughs for a second before settling back into seriousness. "I'm afraid my father is not at all well, he's getting old now, you see. He's bed ridden but comfortable."
"I'm sorry to hear that, Natalie, and for taking up your time. It's just I live abroad now and I'm only in the country for a day or so. I do appreciate this call is out

of the blue, but if your father would give me ten minutes of his time...who knows...he might even like reliving those bygone days and, by the way, call me Clive."

I pose the question and wait.

"Do you remember where we live?" She questions.

"Yes, in Hampstead. Are you still there?"

"Yes, Clive. Father loves this house and would never sell, so when he fell ill eighteen months ago, my husband and I moved in. It's much easier than traipsing half way across London to take care of him and my husband can easily get into the City for work in the mornings. But, I have to ask first if he wants to see you though, as he's getting a bit cantankerous at times and is funny towards some visitors, but I believe he'll be pleased to see you. Give me ten minutes to ask him, then call back."

As prescribed, I do precisely that and get the go ahead. Knowing absolutely nothing concerning railway timetables, I take a stab in the dark and suggest a time I might arrive.

~O~

With nothing to do with judgement and everything to do with luck, my arrival on Leonid's doorstep is an hour earlier than I expected due to jumping aboard the Victoria Station bound train just as it was about to pull out of Brighton.

I rattle the door knocker and wait no longer than a few seconds when I'm greeted by a woman appearing at first sight to be probably in her mid-thirties with shoulder length, brunette hair. I don't immediately recognise her, the last time we met being some twenty years ago when she was just fifteen or so. Not beautiful, but she's attractive in a way of exuding wealth. Of course she does. This is one borough of London where there's no place for the poor.

"Clive." She gushes, obviously recognising me as she extends a hand.

"Natalie." I smile, confirming her identity by bypassing her hand for a more conventional, Spanish style greeting. A left then right air kiss to her cheeks. She smiles showing a hint of embarrassment.

"Do come in, Clive. Father is quite excited to be meeting you again. Come this way to his room and I'll get some tea whilst you two get to know each other again after all this time."

As instructed, I follow and momentarily wait until Natalie knocks on his door and immediately enters. On the opposite side of the room, Leonid Kuznetsov, laying propped up in a massive bed, his broad, hairy chest visible from under a red satin dressing gown, beckons me with outstretched hands, a genuine smile creasing his face indicates he's pleased to see me.

"Clive...come in my boy. It's so good to see you." Leonid's voice roars, his familiar Russian accent as velvety as when we last talked. "Come and sit down here." He points to a chair next to his bed.

"Good to see you again, Leonid, after all these years." I return his greeting, genuinely sincere.

Natalie smiles and leaves the two of us alone.

"Now, what is all this Natalie tells me about you having a problem and you think I might be able to help you with it?" He grabs my hand with two of his and doesn't release it until I'm seated.

For the next ten minutes, I relate my story about Jessica and information gathered from my meeting with Jack Wakeling. The difficulty I'm experiencing, I tell him, is everything I've gathered so far is just theory. He nods his head approvingly when I say I was a good copper who in my time made a lot of assumptions to convict scrotes and career criminals. But this is vastly different. A case where the guilty are professional assassins, of that I am sure, but proof of such allegations are lodged deep in the bowels of secrecy. I need concrete, reliable evidence to add to what little I have accumulated.

"Well, Clive. That is one nasty tale. But, I'm not sure how you believe I can be of help."

Again, without proof, I assume he was undoubtedly trained by the *KGB* when he was an ideological communist card holder, trained to be able to pull out of nowhere a facial expression of absolute bewilderment. Leonid is good, but let me see how far I can cajole and poke the old rascal.

"Well, at the time the *Grand Hotel* was bombed in 1984, you were at the Russian embassy in your capacity as Charges d'Affaire." I wait for confirmation, as I'm guessing. He nods, so I'm on the right track. "You might need to correct me, Leonid, but during this time, if I'm not wrong, Russia and the West were still very much at each other's throats with both parties throwing threats at each other, but thankfully, it went no further than handbags at dawn. This being the case, and it's only an assumption of mine, I wager you lot inside the Russian embassy must have been lapping up this attempt on Thatcher's life. A Western leader, so nearly eliminated and the affair having nothing to do with your lot. I can just imagine the *KGB* and *Stasi* having a good laugh all huddled round a bottle of vodka, putting bets on who they thought might be responsible. With the likes of *Philby, Maclean, Burgess* and *Blunt* eventually sussed out in the fifties and sixties and all long gone, you can't tell me they were never replaced with another load of fresh faced, Oxbridge graduated luvvies, blackmailed or tempted by untold wealth to betray the very country who gave them such an education? You must have some idea what went on then." Leonid looks at me, not liking what he's hearing, but I turn the volume up by putting the onus on his conscience to unload information. "You and I are long retired. What harm can it do if you allow me a little snifter into your old world of espionage? I won't tell if you don't." I wait, giving Leonid time to weigh up if his allegiance to his fatherland remains as strong, or if it's time to let me into a secret or two. I have an ace of my own up my sleeve, one I don't want to play as it will seriously put our friendship in jeopardy, but if I can't get a response, I might have to use it.

"Clive...I don't understand a word you are talking about."

If Leonid notices I'm disappointed, he's not wrong. I don't want to, but there is no alternative. I play my ace.

"Do you remember the year 1996, a day in June when you phoned me at the *Yard,* asking for my help?

~O~

It was early in the previous year, when clearly there were other reasons responsible for my promotion to inspector, other than achieving an 'A' level in art, when a memo arrived on my desk one morning. It read I was to head a delegation of British police officers to compare our methods of law enforcement on the streets of London with those of Moscow's '*Militsija*', a bunch of uniformed ruffians, who passed off as policemen. Such a PR stunt, so the hierarchy above my rank believed, would be well received by the press and give the *Met* some much needed kudos, or as one prat of a part-time scout master superintendent put it, 'brownie points'. Surprisingly, none were vetted when allocated visas, though obviously all were hand picked and some, I do believe, weren't policemen at all, but members of a far more sinister organisation. Regardless of our differing methods of policing and their disbelief we didn't carry guns or provocatively whirl skull-crunching batons, the ten day extravaganza went surprisingly well. As a magnanimous gesture of their appreciation, the Russian Embassy in London threw a gala evening for all the British officers concerned. This is when and where I first met Leonid. Warned there might be an ulterior motive for this get together, by the said same part-time scout master, Leonid might have been prompted to befriend me by his superiors whose aim was to indoctrinate me into being their man at the *Yard*, be it by some foul means or another. But Leonid didn't come across as the archetypal trainer of espionage. Instead, we would meet and play chess, though, as Natalie reminded me, I can't remember ever beating him. Invites to his home to meet his wife and daughter became a monthly occurrence, not because I believed it to be my duty, but because we became good friends. Not unsurprisingly, a delegation comprising of middle ranking police officers were invited as a reciprocal gesture, to visit Moscow. Fortunately, I wasn't one of those chosen.

~O~

Leonid's facial expression changes. I feel he knows where I'm coming from. Eventually Leonid nods, as though accepting what I'm about to say, but needs confirmation from my own lips knowing this might cause the end of our special relationship. This emotionally charged moment is burst by Natalie entering the room, carrying a tray of tea.

"It's so nice to see you both together again. You must have so much to talk about. Are you staying for dinner, Clive? I would so enjoy you meeting my husband."

I'm put on the spot and see in Leonid's eyes I should decline. "Thanks Natalie, I would love to, but time isn't on my side. Maybe another time." I turn back to Leonid and see a look of gratitude. This is going to be worse than I thought.

We both trace Natalie's departure from the room. It is silent again. He knows exactly what I'm about to remind him of, but needs prompting.

"You phoned me to ask for a big favour. A favour that probably would have got me the sack, should it ever have come to light with my superiors. I was prepared to take that risk for you, a friend in dire need of my help." I look at Leonid, his eyes moisten. If there was any other way of getting him to speak I would have chosen it instead of putting him through this inquisition. "Greta, your wife, had just suffered a major heart attack and been rushed to *St Thomas's* hospital, but the news wasn't good. The doctors said very little, except she hadn't long and might die any moment. Understandably, you were distraught. You were sobbing and praying to God. A terrible moment for you. You asked if there was some way I could get Natalie to see her mother before she died."

Leonid bows his head so I can't see his face, but I don't have to. Tears drip off his chin, leaving darkening red wet spots on his satin dressing gown. This is not my finest hour, but I need to push my advantage home.

"Utilising my Brighton contacts and my rank, I sent a squad car to where Natalie was studying at *Roedean* and picked her up. With a motor cycle outrider as escort, Natalie arrived at *St Thomas's* within forty minutes. Ten minutes before Greta passed away. You had your wish that Natalie be at her bedside in the final moments of her life." I am about to continue when Leonid stops me.

"Clive...my boy...please. It is too painful. Yes, I remember what I said and my word today is as strong as it was then. I promised if I could repay you in any way, just ask. I suppose that time has arrived." His smile returns, albeit strained. "Ha...yes...you talk about the pre-Putin days." He shrugs his shoulders, a dead giveaway as to his feelings for his leader. "A time when the entire world hated us, but most of the hysteria was inspired by newspaper headlines and not what most governments thought. Russia was beginning to be brought into discussions on a secret level and I believed it wasn't bullshit. Thatcher hated us, but again it was promoted for the public eyes." He pauses, visually recollecting morsels from the past. "And what happened during the Falklands war? We off loaded plenty of stuff to her which Reagan knew, but kept to himself, deeming it might be misconstrued as taking sides, the arsehole. No, they were good times for me and my country until Yeltsin resigned in '99, leaving Putin in charge and how things have changed. Embassies around the globe were re-staffed with his cronies, kicking out the old brigade from day one. I swear he had it all well planned long before he took charge. There was no place for me in his reshuffle and, with Natalie growing up here in England, I had to make a choice. I believe I made the right one to stay in the UK. I am now a British citizen and so is my daughter. I have enough money and a lovely home, so why should I want to leave? Don't get me wrong, Putin is a very clever man and was nurtured to be where he is, but the old country is not the same anymore. Whether it's better or worse, I don't know." Dropping his eyes once again, Leonid goes into a remorseful moment, not surprising when taking in his extensive knowledge of old Russian Federation, or USSR as we in the west called it. "I have private records of my entire time at the embassy." He suddenly announces, his demeanour picking up. "If something happened all those years back connecting your Jessica with our inter-ambassadorial discussions, then it'll be written down. Over there." He points to a book stand. "Could you fetch the third volume to your left and bring it over to me. The row of files bound in red leather."

I do as directed and hand him the volume. I do not know what is ailing Leonid, illness-wise, but for a man in his late seventies, his ruddy complexion radiates health. Whether meeting me and being reminded of his previous undercover shenanigans has the effect of good medicine, I don't know, but he appears as perky as when I first got to know him. My sorrowful reminders of his wife have been placed back into the cupboard marked private, do not go there again.

Opening the thick volume, Leonid looks keen to continue, as though he's cocking his nose at the entire communist regime by allowing an outsider into the inner sanctum. "Where do you want me to start? What dates?"

I naturally begin with the Brighton *Grand Hotel* bombing. Nothing he tells me I didn't already know about the actual incident. It is when he ventures further, a month later, when my ears pick up.

"In November of that year, *MI5* chaired a meeting with all the homeland security units as well as *MI6*. They all knew who was responsible, but now they had names. The name of the actual bomber...one Patrick Magee. And they knew, near enough, where he was."

Leonid looks up from over his reading glasses and allows a smile. "And who do you think chaired the meeting?"

"Jane Florence Brewer or Jessica McGill as we know her now." I answer, a look of incredulity on my face.

"Correct. Now let's see what else is here." Speed reading each page, Leonid's fingers flick over pages at an alarming rate, sometimes flicking back for confirmation. Nearing the end of this volume, he suddenly stops, his body tightens as he lays it flat on his outstretched legs. If you were practiced enough, Leonid's eyes would give away his emotions. As they look into mine I detect they are deadly serious.

"You have told me about your friend, a Jack Wakeling if I'm not wrong? Well, he is correct with his recollections, but the missing piece of the puzzle is, who did Thatcher talk to on the phone when ordering three *IRA* activists to be assassinated? Do you need telling?" Leonid is as excited as much as I'm scared.

"Not Jessica again?"

"Correct." Leonid bursts out laughing. "She must have been quite a girl. Shame she was working on the wrong side." His laughter builds to a strength that if it continues, I'm getting afraid he might hurt himself. "This is good, Clive. I'm enjoying it. Now get me the other two volumes and let's see what I can uncover. There must be more."

Retrieving the one he finished, I replace it with one of the other two, laying the third on his bedclothes.

"This one goes back to the early seventies, when I first came over. There's pages and pages of what was happening in Northern Ireland." He commentates whilst reading. "But there doesn't appear to be anything..." Suddenly, in mid-sentence, he stops. A very eerie silence drops like a stone. He reads on. "This might be the reason why your Jessica was hounded the way she was and finally caught."

Leonid knows I'm hooked, but like any good story-teller, teases me to want to know more.

"Jessica was on special undercover operations in Belfast during 73 to 74. She worked as a barmaid in a pub on the Falls Road under the code name of Isabella. Very dangerous place to be in those days, especially if found out. For no reason, as my intelligence doesn't stretch that far, she was withdrawn and sent back to London." Leonid clams up again, digesting what he's reading. "Ah...this might be the reason...she was pregnant."

In my past life I'd heard many a story and seen atrocities no one should be put in a position to see, but this thunderbolt shook me to the core. What the hell have I unearthed? Warning, don't touch, danger signs taint each of Leonid's words

"Oh...it doesn't stop there." Leonid gushes, flicking through the last of his diaries, the one leading up to his retirement. "In 1988, the *SAS* foiled an attempt on Jessica's life, but your government and the press described it as an *IRA* attempt to bomb a parade in honour of the *Royal Anglican Regiment* in Gibraltar. That was just a smoke screen. In actual fact, the three operatives were just visiting the rock....playing sightseers if you like. A big mistake, as this put them on a British protectorate piece of land. No need for the Spanish to get involved. The *SAS* did what they are good at, rubbing them out in a matter of minutes. Two days later the *Guardia Civil* found another rented car of theirs with 130 pounds of *Semtex* and a *Kalashnikov* in the boot outside of Marbella, only some twenty miles away from the real target, Jessica's home. It was all nicely hushed up. She changed her name in the seventies, probably on advice from her superiors. We did it all the time with our agents."

It takes a minute or so for me to regather my composure. I knew she'd changed her name, but this only went to confirm everything else Leonid had related. "How on earth do you know all this?" I pose the question, knowing I shouldn't ask, but Leonid appears not to care anymore. Maybe coming in from the cold is the best medicine.

"When Philby and his cohorts were no longer on the payroll of Her Majesty's Secret Service and had run to safety." Leonid's laugh is becoming commonplace. "You don't think we shut up shop, do you? No...before the year was out, we placed another two inside your different organisations. Just like you have probably got one or two scattered around ours."

Neither of us have touched our tea. It's now cold.

"Does that mean we still have spies within homeland security and other agencies?"

With this nugget of intelligence, my place should be to still be employed within the *Yard* to hunt down and eliminate the perpetrators, but probably if I was still ensconced, would Leonid be so willing to spill the beans?

"Have you names of these people?" Asking is one thing, but getting answers is another.

"No Clive, I haven't. I would tell you if I knew, but I don't. My diaries only go up to 1999, the year Putin waved his magic wand over the entire Federation. That was sixteen years ago and the personnel must have changed since then. I was 'retired' on the spot, but they allowed me a good pension, even though I became a British citizen, which they allowed, probably thinking I might be of some use in the coming years. I have no axe to grind and what I did back then was for a country I loved. But times have changed. I've remained faithful for all this time, but you asked me a favour and I never go back on my word. You are a good friend, Clive, and I thank you from the bottom of my heart for what you did for Natalie. I only wish you be careful with what you have learnt. It could get you killed...and the culprits? Who could they be? Who knows? My side, your side? Be very careful, Clive."

Those eyes of his are confirming what he just said.

"There is just one thing I would like to know." I intend to ask him one last question, but Leonid holds his hand up, a signal he's offloading far more than he should.

"If it was, 'do I know who the father is', no I don't, and even if I did, for your safety I wouldn't tell you. But there is one question I would like to ask you, and that is, why would your government allow the Northern Ireland Office to share the same block of offices as *MI5* until 2013? It would seem to me they were asking for trouble with the 'enemy' just across the corridor. Would they ever allow The White House to share 10 Downing Street? No, I believe they wouldn't."

"You are kidding me."

"No Clive. It's common knowledge. I'm not telling you something you couldn't have found out for yourself. I just find it quite implausible."

~O~

It's gone nine when I find myself walking the pavements of Hampstead, having left Leonid's household on a better footing than when I entered. If there was a nicer man, regardless of his past, I have yet to meet him.
I should have phoned Debs before and suggested she remains in town. We could have met up and travelled back to Brighton together, but that was an oversight. My retired brain is no longer built to take in so much information or ponder on advice or how to utilise it. I'll phone now and maybe she'll meet me when I get down to Brighton later. I'll give it a go.

CHAPTER 18

7.28am. Monday August 17th. Brighton Station

Even if a drop of wine hadn't passed my lips during my Sunday spent being a domestic and horticultural Goddess, I'm sure Monday morning will arrive, just as they have all done in the past, with my brain suffering serious dehydration and I'm not wrong with my assumption...it's not only suffering, but I'm feeling physically sick. On this gloriously sunny morning, I need to be more prepared for the forthcoming, office orchestrated tsunami than any other I care to recall.

My face, like many of my other commuting comrades who reside by a beach, exhibits a look only too common when the sun shines at the weekend – a ferocious red that even bronzing powder can't disguise, leaving tell-tale white patches surrounding the eyes where sunglasses once sat. Like a panda bear, but in reverse. How I wish I hadn't shared that fifth bottle of wine when sitting at the *View* bar on Hove seafront with the gang. Seemingly a good idea at the time, I was desperate to blot out what lies ahead today, particularly what I'm going to say to Bronzey.

The train confidently leaves bang on time and I'm in my preferred seat. No annoying happy-clappy passengers next to me, which is a result. I flick through the *Metro,* nothing really readable or worthy of testing a dysfunctional brain. So I settle for the usual picture of Brighton Beach with the Brighton pier in the backdrop packed with South London day trippers under which the headline is splattered, “UK hotter than Barcelona”. Obviously short of news, or just plain journalistic laziness, a couple of Z list reality celebrities are caught canoodling on a yacht somewhere in the Caribbean...“Caught??” So, you wouldn't spot a boat full of paparazzi with long range lenses pulling up alongside, seriously, is this news? Well it is August, Houses of Parliament have broken up and most journalists are on holiday, so I guess this is the best we can expect until September.

My mind and thick head drifts back to the predicament I find myself in, all thanks to bloody Clive and his quest for the truth. I take my notebook and pen out of my handbag and write down the facts so far, as though in some cathartic way it will all make perfect sense.

Our Jessica’s murdered in Estepona.

Enter Clive’s “favour”!!

All records available to lesser mortals in the ranks appear to be wiped - why?

Phil cuts holiday short, attends funeral - on whose orders? - And why?

Martin O’Connell attends the same funeral - Why?

Phil introduces the same Martin O’Connell as Mark Connor at the barbeque - who is this bloke and why so particularly interested in Nick’s work in archive?

Julia connects my file request with the funeral order of service.

Bronzey, at the barbeque, recognises Martin O'Connell from the Neoface results and knows I've lied through my teeth about my reason behind the search.

No, I can't link any of this together, even when staring at it in print. I decide there is no other alternative but to come clean to Bronzey. Why? Because out of all those who profess to be my workmates and friends, he is probably the only one I trust in this delicate position. I might find myself out of a job by five o'clock this afternoon. No, I need an ally if I can persuade him to listen to my logic. Who knows, he might be able to do some digging into the Martin/ Mark scenario.

Clive hasn't so much as sent a text since our conversation on Saturday night - so much for his bloody guidance! Okay, so I petulantly cut him off, but it's still no excuse.

Yes, that's what I'll do - fess up - sod Clive.

The train judders to a halt again, between East Croydon and Clapham Junction station, throwing the poor souls standing in the aisle over each other, everyone in the carriage exuding that oh-too-familiar "what the fuck has happened now" expression. After 15 infuriating and stress inducing minutes, the guard announces that a signal box has overheated. It's been rectified, but we are now in a queue to get into Victoria and he sincerely apologises for any inconvenience that MAY have been caused - that fucking word again!

With blood boiling at *Network Rail*'s ineptitude at dealing with any type of weather that isn't grey, I email Baldrick and Ingrid stating I'll be late, explaining what's happened, and no, I don't know how long I'll be. I really don't need this today.

The train limps in at 9.23am. Judging a forced, ten minute stomp will just about get me into the morning huddle. I rethink, fuck it, I might just saunter. No, better not.

I get to the office just after 9.30.

“Morning Alan”

“Morning Deb’s, wow you’ve caught the sun”

No shit Sherlock - I want to respond, like I hadn’t spotted the Belisha beacon imitating my nose in the mirror this morning, but spare him my sarcastic tongue.

“Yes, lovely weather for once on the coast. Sat on the seafront yesterday afternoon and put sunblock everywhere except on my nose.” I can’t help it, but I have this uncanny notion of my irony going completely over his head.

“Factor 50 my wife always uses, you should do the same”

“Thanks, Alan, for the tanning tip, but I’m already late and you know what they’re like upstairs.” It is the only escape route I have, save for telling him to shut-the-fuck-up.

“Ha ha, get your drift, just show me your pass then”

I get through the doors just as Baldrick is instructing everyone to update their key objectives for the forthcoming week on the ever looming whiteboard.

Mine, I think, are quite simple - try not to get fired!!

I put the usual administrative piffle against my name, no one looks at it anyway. I could put anything down. Would be interesting if, say on Thursday, I write ‘solve international murder’ to test my theory.

I reach my desk, change out of trainers into shoe's and fire up the laptop. Two meeting requests one from Ingrid entitled 'Natter' in ten minutes time and the other, unsurprisingly, from Bronzey at 12.30 entitled 'catch up' - venue - usual chambers. I accept them both.

I wonder if I should try and call Clive before lunch. Better see Ingrid first via the coffee machine.

Ingrid's office is a far cry from her opulent home, despite her efforts to inject a little style with a few object d'art on her shelves but it's still stark and windowless however you dress it up. I'd far rather be out on the floor listening to the gossip than be stuck in here.

I walk straight in and sit in front of her desk

"Morning Ingrid, thanks again for the lovely barbeque, what time did it all wind up, much mess to clear up?"

"God Debs, we didn't get to bed till 2am. The last ones to leave were the neighbours and some of Steve's golfing chums. Someone found the brandy then the singing started. You should have heard it. These are professional, well-heeled adults of a certain age turned into drunk, wannabe Karaoke stars. The men were the worst of course, with Steve leading the charge with his favourite party piece of '*You've lost that loving feeling'*. You can imagine the racket can't you? I busied myself clearing the kitchen at that point with several large G&T's to shut out the noise. Julia got a bit pissed after you and Nick left, winding herself up over the woman Phil and Mark were talking to. I got her a taxi as a damage limitation exercise for her sake. Thanks again

for doing the ribs, as usual they went down a treat. You'll have to give me the recipe one day."
"Oh God, what is it with men and booze?" I attempt to keep her mind focused on her ability to be the socialising queen, rather than remind her of her rank, perish the thought. "Nick launches into Aretha Franklin's '*Say a little prayer'* when he's had a few, but lucky he was driving so we didn't have to suffer. I might let you into my culinary secret one day, it's all about the molasses, that's all I'll say for now. Yes, I texted Julia yesterday to make sure she got home okay. Well done for getting the taxi. It could have gotten into quite an ugly scene, couldn't it?"
"Oh definitely. Debs, can you do me a bit of a favour? Someone left a blue sports jacket in the hall. I've brought it in. There's a driver's license in the inside pocket, a Martin O'Connell. I don't recognise the name or the face, might not have the beard now, but still doesn't ring any bells. Steve's spoken to his friends and I asked around the neighbours, but it doesn't belong to any of them. So it must be a guest of someone from the office. Can you send an email round the troops so we can find a home for it? It's hanging over there on the coat stand. Take it with you...oh and we need to put some time aside to compile an update to the mission statement on the website. I'll put something in your calendar"
"Yep, no problem, what strategic message, or should I say bullshit, are we going to articulate this time?"
She gives me 'I'll pretend I didn't hear that' look, as I stand to go and get the jacket.

Just then her desk phone rings, she looks at the internal caller display. “Oh God, it’s that tosser upstairs...what does HE want? Better take it, catch you later” and waves me out.

I wander back to my desk and put the offending Jacket over the back of my chair, take out the drivers licence, remove the facial fuzz and there’s no doubt about it – okay, so how am I going to play this one?

I could:

Send a group email as instructed just describing the jacket and see if Mark/Martin collects it, or -

Go and find Mark/Martin and just hand it to him saying I thought I recognised him wearing it.

In each scenario he would guess I would have gone through the pockets for any ID clues, the first thing any normal person would do with lost property.

Well, as Ingrid or ‘she who must be obeyed’ has requested, I send an email. I think I’ll go with option A and copy Phil in, as he’s not on the team distribution list.

“Dear All

For those that attended Ingrid’s BBQ on Saturday.

A men’s sports jacket was left behind in the hallway, if you know who it belongs to, or have lost one yourself, please come and collect it from my desk.

Kind regards

Debs”

Well, let’s see what happens shall we.

Immediately, my in-box is a flurry of activity, predictable responses from the boys

‘What size is it?’

‘What colour is it?’

'Is it expensive, could flog it and split the money?'
Bunch of idiots!!
I spend the next hour or so sifting through more meaningful emails needing attention and catch up with the gossip from the weekend, only to suddenly think I hadn't yet heard from Julia today. I'll ring her.
"Hi, it's only me, thought I'd give you a call see how your Sunday was"
"Hello Debs, sorry can't talk now, got lots to catch up having been away, catch up soon"
She puts the phone down *'Sorry can't talk now'??* Now that's odd coming from her, she never says that, any excuse normally to have a chat, hope she's alright.
It's 12 noon here so 1pm in Spain, I'll go and have a smoke downstairs and call Clive, trusting the lazy bastard will have dragged himself out of bed. It galls me to do so, but I think I better tell him what I plan to say to Bronzey at lunch.
Outside, the rank, humid city air hits me, I can feel my nose reddening to a deeper shade as I light up.
I call Clive's number and immediately get *'The number you are calling is currently switched off, please try again later'* what is he playing at, switching his bloody phone off? I call it again in case it's a Spanish glitch - same monotone message.
Well bollocks to him, can't say I didn't try.
I head back in, grateful for the air conditioning.
As I approach my desk, I can see Mark/Martin walking towards it...oh lordy.
"Hey Debs, think you've got my jacket hanging there on your chair. Phil forwarded your email, Thanks so much."

"Don't thank me, Martin, thank Ingrid."

Shit...shit...shit, I just called him Martin. He knows I've rifled through his pockets. He responds with "I will - cheers." Picking up the jacket, he pats the inside pocket and fleetingly gives me a steely stare that bores right into my eyes, grins, then leaves the floor.

Now, add this to the brewing shit-storm that is about to descend on me.

Bronzey and I meet at the lift and walk in silence to *Balls Brothers.* At his usual table, he orders for both of us.

"So are you going to tell me what you're up to, Debs? That search has nothing to do with a favour for your friend, has it?"

"Well, it has, but not the friend or the circumstances I told you about "

Over our sandwiches, mine the stilton and bacon, his the Cumberland sausages and onion - the healthy options and a couple of large glasses of *Pinot Grigio*, I spew out everything from Clive's first phone call last Monday to Mark/Martin picking up his jacket half an hour or so earlier.

He wipes his moustache of residual *Merlot*, temples his fingers, clearly contemplating and digesting what I have just imparted to him.

"Fucking hell, Debs, a professional hit on a retired old lady with a history in the Yard. Phil and Martin just pop up at the funeral, internal records apparently wiped, this all stinks, but God, its juicy isn't it? Never met Clive, I was posted in Birmingham when he was here. Wish I had though, good old fashioned copper so I've heard, like a dog with a bone. Can understand why

he's looking for answers, once a copper always a copper, not many of us left about anymore. More's the pity." He pontificates, as though he's putting himself into the same bracket.
"I know, Bronzey, but I can't tie any of it together. There's obviously a probable link between all these events, but buggered if I know and as for Phil's involvement, again clueless."
"Hmm..." He mumbles whilst mulling it over. "I think we should surreptitiously try to dig into this Martin blokes background, what he's actually doing in our office and what this project, he's allegedly assisting Phil with, is all about, before we do anything else. I've got contacts who have contacts if you know what I mean. Some with the Northern Ireland affairs select committee boys. They may be able to get some intelligence on him and when I say 'WE' I actually mean 'ME'. I really don't think you should do anymore poking around for a while, Phil in particular - keep your head well and truly below the parapet, Debs, you're not paid enough to get involved or try to analyse whatever appears to be going on here. You're paid to deal with the team's administrative shite, specifically mine! *Sherlock Holmes* you are not - I am. This is right up my street. I'm fed up with low life drug dealers anyway - a big fat murder with internal shenanigans - lovely jubbly."
"One thing I can tell you as an absolute given." He continues. "Those records cannot just be wiped, it's that simple. They've been deliberately moved somewhere else in the ether. I'd say, someone is

covering up something big. So, what has Clive dug up so far in Spain, is *Interpol* involved?"

"That's the thing, I seriously don't know what he's bloody doing, who he's spoken to or what he's unearthed. As I said, the last time we spoke was Saturday night after the barbeque, he said nothing from his end. I tried to call just before we met earlier to update him, but his phone is switched off."

"Well, when you do speak to him, ask him - find out what he knows about Jessica, that's your role in our little investigatory partnership *Dr Watson.* Leave the snooping to me, come on let's have one for the road before we head back."

He orders another glass of *Merlot* for him and *Pinot Grigio* for me and gets the bill at the same time.

"I'll get this and you'll put it through expenses as an informant meeting, which technically it is." He chuckles.

He goes into the office first, leaving me outside having a smoke, with "You need to pack that up, you know" as his parting words.

"Whatever Bronzey."

I feel a wave of relief, as if a mountain has been lifted off my shoulders, having off-loaded all this crap on Bronzey. A problem shared is a problem halved and all that, although it's still a fucking problem, however you slice it up, but having him onside alleviates the depth of shite I could potentially find myself in.

Back at camp, I wander down the office to the kitchen area and coffee machine, noticing quite a few empty desks. Sam's there. "Where is everybody, Sam?"

"Dunno Nan, Bronzey was here, gone back out somewhere, Baldrick's in with Ingrid, Naomi's got a day off, that's all I know, glad you're here because this bleeding machine has run out milk again, can you sort it?"
"No, I can't - do I look like a bloody coffee machine engineer, I'll report it to Facilities, don't suppose you had the nous to do that? See that big, white thing, open the door and be amazed at what you'll see nestling on the top shelf – milk...Muppet. "
Luckily I take mine black. I grab my offensive mug and fill it with the dispensed brown sludge and a fast disappearing of a pair of *Speedos,* to go back to my desk.
Email from Julia:
'Fancy a drink after work? Sorry couldn't talk earlier, I'll meet you in Davy's at 5.15 - J'
Having already had 3 wines at lunch, I shouldn't really, but the thought of sitting on a packed train in this heat is too ghastly and *Davy's* does have air con. I respond saying yes but why not just meet downstairs in reception as normal.
'No - just meet me there - J'
'Ok then - D'
Well that's peculiar, maybe she's sneaking out early to do some shopping or something.
Better make a start on the confounded mission statement update. What was the last one, oh yes?
Treat everyone fairly.
Be open and honest.
Work in partnership... and
Change to improve.

Yeah, right!! Not a lot of that round here right now.

Davy's Wine Bar is rammed, obviously people have the same idea - avoid the rush hour heat and retreat to a cooling bar. Julia has managed to secure a table at the back. I wave and weave my way toward her.

Oh good, she's on the white wine today.

I pull out a chair. "Hi, what time did you get here to get a table, this place is heaving."

"Made the good sense to book it and left the office 4.45 to make sure."

"Oh well done, thought you might have done, given you've had a good swig of the wine already."

I top up her glass and pour one out for me, helping myself to the complimentary olives.

"So, anything to report after we left the barbeque, spoke to Ingrid this morning, it punched on to 2am apparently"

"You spoke to Ingrid this morning?" She says almost accusatory.

"Yes Julia, which part of 'I spoke to Ingrid this morning' didn't you get?'

"No need to be bloody sarcastic, Debs...what time did you speak to her?"

"What the fuck does it matter what time I spoke to her?"

"It does matter, what did she say to you?"

"Julia, what the hell are you on about. She just told me how the barbeque degenerated into a drunken song fest, ending at 2am, she got you a taxi and someone left their jacket behind, that's it."

"She said nothing else to you then?"

"No she didn't. Julia, you're beginning to get on my nerves with this questioning, spit whatever it is out. If you're wondering if she told me you were borderline battered, she did, but no change there, eh?"

We both take a large glug of wine.

After what seemed an eternity and two more mouthfuls, she finally speaks.

"I shouldn't be telling you this, really, but you're my mate and I just wanted to warn you - I got summoned upstairs this morning to Bowen's office."

"That complete, pompous, pooh-bar-fuck-wit, what on earth for?" I butt in.

She talks me through the meeting and how Ian Hopkins was her knight in shining armour. She also told me that Ingrid went in before her.

Fuck. How on earth did that get under the nose of the DA Comm office - something must have flagged up somewhere?

"So now you know why I didn't want to meet in reception, didn't want any of that lot seeing me with you, and why I was curious to know if Ingrid had said anything to you"

"Bowen called Ingrid when I was in her office, I assume it was him as she referred to him as 'that tosser upstairs', that's what it must have been for." I point out.

"Well, Ingrid gave me a bit of a wrist slap." She continues. "Not for doing favours but for being caught. She really hates that man, Bowen, you know - she did ask me if I knew why you wanted the information in the first place on Jessica McGill."

"What did you tell her?" My heart rate quickens.

"Exactly what you told me - you were just doing a favour for a friend. Are you going to tell me what's really going on, Debs?"
I think about this one, she's been a good mate, enough to stick her neck out by warning me when she shouldn't have, but her relationship with Phil and the risk of potential pillow talk - it's way too dangerous.
"To be honest with you, I genuinely haven't a clue what's going on."
"Aww Debs....come on, I've disobeyed direct orders here just talking to you about it." She confides, believing she might squeeze it out of me with another few vino blancos'.
"I know and I really appreciate it...I did a favour for a friend. That part is absolutely true. Let's just leave it at that."
"Who's the friend then? Don't give me that eulogy bullshit, I *Googled* her name and the article I found said she'd been MURDERED, for Christ sake."
She looks round, making sure she isn't being overheard. "And Phil goes to her funeral. What's that all about?" She whispers.
"I promise you I don't know. Look I can't tell you who asked me, come on, please just drop the bloody subject because I won't tell you no matter how pissed you think you'll get me."
She gives me a 'you've really hurt my feelings' expression, which I choose to ignore.
"So, no one from the Gods have spoken to you yet?" She asks.
"Nope nothing. I suppose, technically speaking I've done nothing wrong, other than trying to obtain what

appears to be sensitive data by slightly bending the rules. If asking you has put you in an awkward position, sorry about that bit. "

But she presents a very good point. If our Jessica's name search has appeared before the good and the great upstairs and now they know it was me who was enquiring, surely my backside would be hauled up there in a nano-second. Why haven't they? Very curious indeed.

We order another bottle as, bizarrely, it's cheaper to do so than 2 large glasses, certainly not what I should be doing on a school night. Mercifully she gives up with the interrogation and moves on to gas away about her and Phil, her favourite topic, how one day they'll be together properly...yardy...yardy...yar. She's completely and utterly deluded, but I let her ramble on.

We part company and I've just about got time to get to Victoria to pick up the 20.47 Littlehampton train to Hove.

I try to have a little snooze on the journey down, no, not happening, my brain is spinning too much wondering what the repercussions will be for me from the big cheeses. I should call Clive, but there's no point on the train, with all the tunnels, plus I hate people talking on their mobiles, anyway he's bound to be pissed in a bar somewhere in Estepona, probably Fred's.

21.40, the train pulls into Hove...I'm too bloody late to get the sole taxi, some other bastard has beaten me to it. Oh well, I'll walk down to Church Road enjoying the cool sea air, obviously have a cigarette and then get a bus along home.

Unfortunately, the bus stop is right opposite the *Seafield* pub and I can see quite a crowd through the frosted windows. My intake of wine should be sufficient and should just wait for a bus. There's one in 10 minutes - fuck it - another couple of glasses won't make any difference.

I cross the road and walk in.

Robbo moans that I haven't brought him the *Evening Standard* and presents me with a glass of what appears to be wine, but God knows where he's gets the stuff from - I've tasted more palatable disinfectant...not that I'm a connoisseur of that either.

I join Jane and the rest of the gang talking stuff and nonsense when my mobile throbs - Clive!

CHAPTER 19

9.40pm. Monday. August 17th 2015. Hove Station.

Jumping off the train before it finally stops at the platform became second nature when I was employed. And it's worked perfectly again to grab the single taxi waiting on the rank at Hove Station before the small swarm behind me disembark. I direct the driver to a place Debs has often talked about in Hove, the *Paris Wine Bar,* where she'd laughingly informed me they don't serve *Wetherspoon* expulsions, but offer an upmarket choice of beverages, especially cognac, and how I need one or more of those after the day I've had. The décor and lighting are subdued, making the place exude a welcoming atmosphere, whilst the restrained volume from a track off an *Ella Fitzgerald* album tastefully drifts unassumingly over the heads of a handful of customers, none of which pay the slightest attention to my arrival or hinder my approach to the bar.

"Good evening, sir. What can I get you?"

'Once a copper, always a copper' or how the saying goes, certainly applies to me and although I've been retired for four years or more, I'm still very much one at heart and can't resist weighing up first impressions of people. You see, I'm good at it and my sixth sense, if that's what you want to call it, persuaded me to join the force in the first place.

The barman is courteous and though he speaks fluent English, there's an accent there somewhere. Somewhere I can't pinpoint. He's good looking, dressed smartly in white shirt, black tie and waistcoat and has probably seen more than thirty odd summers. Obviously professional, but it's his wristwatch that troubles me. Unlike mine, his is the real McCoy, a *Rolex.* I begin to wonder if it was a mistake coming here, after all, if the barman can afford such expensive jewellery, how much is it going to cost me for a large *Remy*?

"Hi...yes...a large *Remy Martin*, please. No ice and if the coffee machine is still on, a café solo would be good." I reply, having not a clue to how much this small extravaganza is going to set me back.

"Certainly, sir. If you'd like to take a seat, I'll bring your drinks over." He acknowledges my order, but his accent still baffles me.

"I notice you have a garden. I need to make some calls, so I'll be out there."

"I must warn you, sir, the garden is about to close at ten."

"Why." I ask.

"Neighbours." A shrug of his shoulders and a one word answer are more than sufficient to satisfy my question.

"Okay." I smile at his response. "I'll only need a few minutes, anyway."

The rear garden is nicely set out, with tables and chairs under a creeper infested wooden pergola supporting see-through plastic sheeting as a roof, a forgivable flaw in the aesthetics, but a warning that fickle British summers can also bring downpours. The sumptuous wicker sofa and chairs are occupied, so I chose a vacant spot under an electric heater screwed into a beam above, a push of a red button bestowing five minutes of welcoming warmth. Withdrawing my mobile, I punch in Debbie's number.

~O~

"Where the fuck have you been all day? I've been trying to contact you." Debbie blasts down my ear before I can even greet her with a 'hello'. "I suppose you are in Fred's, getting pissed while I take all the flak back here."

I purposely leave a pause, which I know will seriously piss her off. "Hi Debs. Thought I'd buzz you to see how things are getting on." I smile, seeing in my mind the hackles on her neck bristling.

"How things are getting on, you arse? I'll be surprised if I have a job to go back to after the day I've had. Where are you, anyway?"

"I'm in Hove."

"WHAT."

"Yeah...I came over this morning. Had a few people I needed to meet, in Brighton and London. Just got off the train, so thought I'd give you a call. Where are you?"

"I'm in the *Seafield.* Where are you?"

"*Paris Wine Bar.*"

"Oh, bugger me, you're just over the road. Give me ten minutes and I'll be there. Get me a glass of their most expensive white wine your money can buy. You owe me large."

Our conversation abruptly ends as quickly as it began, coinciding with my amicable barman approaching with tray in hand.

"May I say, sir, with your tan you can't be from these parts or have you just returned from a long break in the sun?" Offering conversation, he places my order together with a fresh ashtray and the bill enclosed in a leather wallet, to accompany the miniature vase of paper roses already placed on the table.

I ignore answering his question by throwing in my own.

"What is the most expensive white wine you have?"

Eyeing me with suspicion, he tentatively replies. "A *Bonneau du Matray*. A delicate 2010 white *Burgundy* at £240 a bottle. Would you like me to put a bottle on ice for you sir?"

"I don't suppose you serve it by the glass?"

"No, sir. I'm afraid we don't." He replies unsurprisingly.

"How about an ordinary *Chablis*?"

"Yes, sir. I can do that." His smile is not one of sarcasm, but understanding.

I follow him inside, so as not to contravene the sound police, who hover behind drawn curtains counting down the minutes, similar to a curfew, when their desire for silence is obeyed and their viewing of an omnibus version of *Coronation Street* can be achieved with no hindrance from people outside enjoying themselves. The interior of the place is thinning out and makes my choice of an empty table easier, one situated at the rear and far enough away not to be in earshot of those savouring a late nightcap.

My new found friend returns with a single glass of Chablis and places it in front of a vacant stool, then thankfully departs back to his station without attempting to renew our conversation. The door swings open to reveal Debs, marching towards me with a look that doesn't say she's pleased to see me. She sits opposite and by her demeanour is counting to ten, obviously pre-arranged, gathering herself to quell her annoyance.

"Well, Clive. It's so good to see you." Sarcasm spills out from every syllable. "It would have been nice...no...respectful, had you phoned me to say you were over here." A silence ensues for a few seconds. "I wouldn't be surprised if I've just worked my last day at the firm after twenty seven years of service, and before you cut in saying I'm being dramatic, you have no idea of how much shit has hit the fan due to my digging into the life of your bloody Jessica McGill." Appearing to be satisfied she'd got it off her chest, Debs hoists herself onto her stool and picks up her glass. "A bloody *Chablis.*" She utters alarmingly, taking her first mouthful. "Couldn't you have got something more expensive, you cheap bastard."

I'm impressed she knows the difference. "Come on Debs. The wine is immaterial to what I found out today. I promise when this is over, I'll pay for an all-inclusive holiday down in Estepona."

I see a look in her eyes saying, in a way only Debs can, that she can't wait for the experience...yeah.

Over the following fifteen minutes, I give Debs a shortened version of my meetings with Jack and Leonid, purposely leaving the Russian's declaration to last, as it confirms my initial feeling that Jessica was not murdered by some botched burglary. She listens intently and by the time I've completed my summary, her glass is empty and is being suggestively pushed across the table in my direction. A not too subtle act of saying she wants a refill.

"That's all very good, Clive, but it doesn't get me out trouble, especially now Bronzey has picked up the scent of the trail and wants to get involved. He believes he's made out of the same mould that formed you, God forbid, by sniffing out something that isn't right. Something about doing real copper work. I tried putting him off, but he's insistent, even telling me to drop whatever I was doing for you and leave it to him."

I don't say a word, but this declaration of Bronzey's interest could seriously jeopardise my involvement, especially remembering Leonid's' account of foreign agents concealed in the workings of homeland security when he was involved and how the place is probably crawling with the buggers now. Debs continues, describing how Ingrid and Julia were hauled before a Deputy Assistant Commissioner, a certain Bowen and from what I can ascertain, a right plonker of a man, riding the rise of promotion due to a long forgotten ancestor who supposedly was the founder of the secret services. Both answered by declaring Debs was responsible for their innocent involvement into retrieving Jessica's file. It's always clever after the event, but how was I to know, just the merest bit of

interest into her background would flag up danger signals in Thames House and the *Yard.*
But this makes it all more interesting as both Lesley and Julia fingered Debs as the culprit. So why hasn't Debs been summoned to appear as a witness for her own defence?
"How far up the chain of command has this thing gone." I ask, as Debs turns towards the bar, silently pointing to her empty glass, believing this apologetic metaphor is understood to mean she wants a third helping of what she's already consumed.
"Oh...from what Julia says, it might go right to the top. To the Commissioner."
"And who would that be?"
"Commissioner Gordon." Debs pipes up, oblivious to the significance the name has with my past.
"That wouldn't be Jack Gordon by any chance?" I need confirmation.
"Yes...you remember him. In your day at the Yard, I think he was a Detective Chief Superintendent then."
Too many questions are being asked, but now I'm beginning to see a picture and if I'm correct with my assumptions, Debs not being called to face the music spells out just one possibility why she wasn't.
Gordon knows I retired to Estepona, because Fred told him so after giving him my name and description when going into Fred's bar all those years ago, before being promoted. He also knows Debs was my assistant, my right hand man, or woman, if you like. Seeing as he was my direct supervisor, he knew me well enough to know how I might react to Jessica's death, especially if she was a friend, I smelt a cover-up conspiracy of sorts.

He knew my methods to get an arrest and never brought me to book over some of my less conventional ways, if it meant a conviction. Yes, he knows me well and probably took the accolades of my successes to springboard himself up to his lofty position. I don't blame him.

"Clive...Clive." I hear Debs voice and feel her tugging my arm.

"Yes...er...sorry Debs. I was miles away." Coming out of my trance, I assure her I haven't had a stroke or something similar. "It's all coming together, Debs, but I'm sorry I can't tell what I'm thinking, as it might influence the way you react at work. I believe there are reasons why you haven't been reprimanded, but I must leave it at that. I'll tell you when the time is right, but now isn't that time."

"Oh...thank you for your trust." Debs at least lowers her voice as she confronts me. "There am I, putting my head on the line and all you can say is you can't or won't give me an explanation. Thank you very fucking much."

"I'm keeping you out of the firing line, Debs. If I'm right in my way of thinking, it might be dangerous if you know too much. Yes, I do trust you...very much, and I can't do this without your help. Saying that, I believe we might be getting some support from a very strange source."

Changing the subject completely and visibly bowing to the effects poured out from within a wine bottle, Debs poses her own question. "What train did you say you were on earlier?"

"The 8.20 out of Victoria...why?" I respond.

"I was on that train, but never saw you." She quizzes me with one of her stares. "I'm usually off that train like a bullet, as I know there might be just one taxi waiting at the rank outside the station, but instead, I saw some bastard get there before me. It was you, you bastard, who beat me to it, wasn't it? OH...thank you."

CHAPTER 20

8.14 am. Tuesday August 18th. 2015. Hove

I awake, but refuse the temptation to open my eyelids. Something is wrong as the comfort of a bed isn't at all recognisable from the position I'm lying in, nor is the lack of Spanish sunlight, which I've become reliant on to persuade me, hangover or sober, to remove my body from its overnight pit. When curiosity finally triumphs, my left eye becomes unstuck and I succumb to opening it. Not that it makes any difference as it's pitch black, except for a slither of light that draws my attention, emanating from a fissure in the drawn curtains. Where the hell am I? Re-closing my eye, I rack my memory for a clue amongst the infused cloud of confusion instigated by the night before. Slowly, nuggets of information slot into place. I'm in Debbie's flat.

It must have been long after midnight when we left the *Paris Wine Bar* the night before, and not the best of times to find a hotel. Vaguely, a discussion comes to mind where I found myself without a bed for the night, but true to form, even after our recent differences, Debs reluctantly offered me her sofa as an alternative. That's where I am and that's why I feel so uncomfortable.

Pushing my cover to one side, I'm wary of the effect chairs and table legs can have on toes when kicked in darkness, so diligently approach the sole clue of light as a reference point to begin my day. The vision of Aunt Jessie riding a pig, displayed on a photograph negative, isn't at hand to mask my vision, as blinding morning sunshine hits my face the second I pull the curtains apart, splashing the room with sudden light. Instantaneously, my head jerks away from the glare. I recognise Debbie's lounge from the previous night. Apart from my jacket and shoes, I'm fully dressed but with added creases down each leg that weren't there yesterday.

The kitchen is where I remember, beckoning me in to focus on the electric kettle. Under a jar of instant coffee (Debs knows my old habits and where I make for first every morning) a note juts out.

Morning arsehole. I'm off to work. Didn't have the heart to wake you even though your snoring from the other room kept me awake all effing night. Keep me in touch with what's going on. Debs

Glancing around, I see she's made her place very homely and comfortable, which only a woman's touch can achieve, unlike my apartment back in Spain, where a not too educated eye would plump for it belonging to a bloke. Endeavouring not to disrupt this vision, I return to the lounge with my resuscitating coffee mug in hand and plant my backside on the blanket I slept under the night before, turning to fluff-up Deb's cushions so as not to leave the place looking as if a herd of buffalo had decided to crash out.

What do I do next? I've pieced together parts of the jigsaw, thanks to Jack and Leonid, which when I started out on this private crusade, appeared to be no more than scattered fragments. Dropping into place, I believe I've cracked the reasons why the *IRA* were responsible for Jessica's death, but have no idea who the individuals responsible were. The last thing I want to do is advertise I'm pursuing the culprits. One person I'm not, though our privateering quests for justice are similar, is *Simon Wiesenthal,* the Nazi war crime hunter. Should my name crop up and become synonymous with this mission, it would be an act of suicide, much like putting myself in Jessica's position. No...my target will be the person who double-crossed her...someone who feels safe in his or her environment. Someone who must be trusted and, I'm sure, is still very much involved within the auspices of *MI5* or the *Yard.* Even though they didn't pull the trigger, they were just as responsible as if they had.

But where do I start? Of course, if I was still employed, I'd have the necessary clearance to scour every record and file of those working within those walls, even to some extent at *Thames House,* but I am not there anymore. Remembering Leonid's words, if the Russians have eyes and ears within these establishments today, after all the shenanigans undertaken *by Burgess, Maclean* and *Blunt,* who went undetected for years, then why shouldn't the *IRA* have similar operatives? So, we were led to believe *The Good Friday Agreement* put an end to hostilities in Northern Ireland, as testament by having two *Sinn Fein* (the political wing of the *IRA*) members of parliament would confirm. Though, when both refuse to take their seat at Westminster, their action might be a clue to their real feelings, when one considers the part they might have played concerning the murder of a prominent Conservative Member of Parliament in a car bomb under the Palace of Westminster. But splinter groups have resurfaced, who seemingly want to return to the old days. Their uncontrolled retaliations and willingness to commit sporadic murders on the streets of Belfast, herald a reminder that they have a long memory and still remain in business.

I have an idea and need to speak to Jack Wakeling again.

~O~

Finding myself, fifteen minutes later, on the seafront heading towards our arranged rendezvous, I can't help but admire the British constitution to lap up the sun on a beach where pebbles act as the most uncomfortable mattress. Even at this early hour, kids are bouncing in and out of the water, regardless of its temperature and seemingly oblivious to the pain of underfoot conditions. Having consecutive days of fine weather has made me forget the reason why I escaped these shores.

Jack suggested we meet at the same place as we met before, *The Queensbury Arms,* and as I turn up Regency Square and right into the mews, I see he has beaten me to it, standing outside, taking a few long drags on a shortening cigarette.

"Hi Jack." I greet my old friend as I approach.

"Hello Clive. What's this all about? I thought I'd seen the last of you after what I said. But I should have known better. You were never one to take warnings literally. Come on...it might be early, but I could still murder a pint."

We enter and are greeted as if we're old regulars. I order two pints of *Harveys* and watch Jack seat himself at the same table we occupied before.

"Now what's this all about, Clive?" Jack repeats his previous enquiry as I hand over his drink.

"Oh, just a few loose ends I need tidying up." I lie as I proceed to update him on what I learnt from Leonid, but the further I relate what he had written in his diaries, the more I see Jack fidgeting, knowing it is more than loose ends I need tidying up.

"Stop there, Clive." Jack holds his hand up as if it were a shield, meaning he doesn't want to hear another word. "If you go any further with this, Clive, you're going to find yourself in deep shit. I can't help you."

"I don't need physical help, just a name you might have who I can talk to. Who was around during the troubles and who might give me some information, like you did, as it happened so long ago?" Chancing my arm, his reaction isn't at all what I first thought it would be.

Jack doesn't say a word but picks up his glass and takes a large mouthful, his expression is one I remember from the past. He's thinking.

"Listen Clive. You're a pest, regurgitating all this crap from the past. Everybody else has forgotten about it and got on with their lives, but you, no, you want to drag it all up again."

Before he continues to give me all the reasons why I should drop it, I interrupt.

"Jack, I'm not interested in what happened all those years ago. What was done then stays in the past. It's the present I'm interested in. There's a mole somewhere in our security who is feeding classified information to the bad guys. That's who I'm after. This person was responsible for Jessica's death: might just as well have pulled the trigger. I know under all your bravado to warn me off, you feel the same or you wouldn't have made the copper everybody respects. Remember how you felt getting Thatcher out of the *Grand Hotel*, our Prime Minister, and then guarding her in the John Street nick. You're a copper at heart, Jack, and always will be." Nothing like a bit of flattery as I massage his ego a tad.

He looks at me and for a second or two and I am uncertain which way he'll fall. Another gulp of beer finishes his pint, before I've even started mine.

"I'll have another one please, Clive." He answers, pushing his empty glass towards me. But there's a semblance of a smile creasing his lips. "When you get back, we'll talk about it."

I look at Jack's eyes and know there's something he hasn't told me.

Returning from the bar with just the one pint, I don't say a word, allowing Jack time to ponder on the significance of what he is about to say. He's enjoying making me wait.

"You probably don't remember him, a detective inspector by the name of Seamus O'Hearn. I think he'd left Brighton nick before you joined. Anyway, we were a team before he was promoted. Seamus was a nice bloke, easy to get on with and was a good copper which, probably, along with a strong Belfast accent, were the reasons why he attracted the attention of *Special*

Branch. It was all done very secretively, but before they whisked him away up to London for training, we had a drink together and he told me all about what they had planned for him. Of course he could've refused, but this was right up his street, a covert mission to be placed right in the middle of Belfast, the city where he was born. Just like your Jessica before him, he was planted to be a spy, but his credentials were perfect for the job. I lost track of him after that and didn't hear from him for ages until about five years ago. Just like you did, out of the blue, I get this phone call saying he's in Brighton on holiday with his wife and grandchildren and would I like to have a drink for old time's sake. Of course he's retired, but we sit and talk about the old days with him recalling some of the antics we got up to. It's not until I bring up Ireland when he finally schtums up. Well, for a little while anyway. We'd put a good few beers down our necks when he starts talking about the troubles, all covert stuff with him talking from behind a shielded hand. He doesn't talk about his operation over there, but about all the shags he had. I must admit he made me laugh. You should talk to him."

This Seamus guy appears to be just the person who might be able to help, that is, if he's prepared to talk to me.

"Can I meet him?" I ask.

"He still lives in Belfast." Jack answers.

"Well, that's no problem. I'll pop over there."

"Oh, so he's going to open up and tell you all his little secrets, is he? Don't be fucking mad. If the other side got wind of what he did and who he was, I doubt he'd last long, even now after all these years."

Jack was right. Why would he talk to me? He doesn't know me from Adam.

"On the other hand, if I went with you he might just have a few answers that could come in useful." A mischievous look spreads across Jack's face. "He gave me his card, so I could call him and see if he'd meet with us."

"No Jack, I can't drag you into this. I don't know whose cage I'm rattling. Could be dangerous." Regrettably, I try to dissuade him, though the thought of speaking with Seamus is very tempting.

"Oh, Clive. It's unlike you to have lost the spirit of adventure. Come on, I don't know about you, but I'd love to get some excitement, a chance to relieve me of this boring existence my wife has squeezed me into, even if it's just for the day...come on. What do you say?"

From where I sit, I see Jack is up for it. He's perched on the edge of his seat just waiting for me to give the go-ahead. Now it's my turn to keep him waiting. I lift my glass and take a few, slow sips, purposely making him even more enthusiastic.

"Okay Jack, it's a deal. Call him to see if he'll play ball and if he's keen, I'll get the schedule of flights to Belfast off my mobile and book a couple of tickets. Suggest we meet at Brighton Station." Grudgingly, I give in to Jack's keenness, but I knew I eventually would.

"Don't be so paranoid. Nobody will raise an eyebrow to us spending a few hours over there." Jack attempts to admonish my fears.

"I hope you're right, Jack."

We part company, with me telling him I'll be in-touch later in the day concerning flights and what time we'll meet tomorrow to catch a train up to Gatwick Airport. I have no doubt when I phone Debbie, she'll give me a blast in my ear when I tell her what I'm up to, adapting her vernacular to drive home what she thinks of the idea. Still, no time like the present. I'll phone her now.

CHAPTER 21

Tuesday August 18th. Way…way too early!

There are no just words available to describe how utterly appalling I feel this morning.

Putting the obvious contributory excessive wine consumption aside, it's the sleep deprivation that has really tipped the scales. I cannot believe such noises can emanate from a single human concealed in another room. Jesus Christ, Clive's extreme snoring is the audible equivalent of *Darth Vader* choking on a wasp in the middle of a big kettle-drum. How could he not wake himself up, I really don't know? I try covering my head with my pillow. No good, can still hear it.

I'm consumed with the desire to get up and find a large heavy object. A frying pan would do. Then go into the lounge and calmly smack him round the head. Sadly, I decide against it.

I so totally get why he lives by himself. No self-respecting female could put up with THAT shit all night.

I continually watch the digital alarm tick over until 5.45. Finally, bearing the racket no longer, I tippy-toe to the kitchen to make a strong black coffee. Normally a tea person at home, but this morning is different after enduring a night of indescribable racket. I wonder why I haven't already had a visit from the 'noise abatement' people. I throw a couple of paracetamol down my throat, open the back door and head out to the garden for a cigarette.

Momentarily, I contemplate throwing a sickie today. What are the possibilities I could have been struck down by some debilitating, 24 hour, highly contagious virus – no, that just won't wash, particularly with Julia, having shown no symptoms whatsoever in *Davy's*. Reluctantly, I quietly steer to the bathroom.

Despite the shower, the hair-dryer and the radio, I note with interest and acute annoyance, that there is still no stirring from his slumber as I approach the front door at 7am. I'll leave the sod a note under the coffee jar.

For once, I'm eternally grateful for the drudgery of the train journey and today it's mercifully quiet.

I briefly try to mull over what Clive told me about his conversations with his Russian mate and Jack 'what's 'is name'. I don't recall all the details, as I think I zoned out with some of the historical references coupled with the late hour and wine intake, but what does stick out is that our Jessica changed her name in the 70's from Jane Constance Brewer, and he seems pretty convinced that someone from within the firm is connected to all this nonsense. I seriously think he could be getting in over his head with this crusade, but it won't stop him, I know that, he's so bloody stubborn. One thing is for sure, I'm going to keep my powder dry, as they say, for the next couple of days, tempting though, as should I start digging into the archives for one Jane Constance Brewer (JCB as I'll now refer, not to be confused with earth moving machinery, though I must admit, Jessica had put on a bit of weight over the years). But there again, it would be guaranteed career suicide, particularly with me on the radar of 'them upstairs'. No, just deal with admin and stationary crap. I will however update Bronzey. I know Clive isn't happy with me involving him, but what's done is done and irreversible. I firmly believe he's a trusted ally and I need to warn him to tread very carefully given that my antics have been flagged.

After two stops my eyelids grow heavy as my head lolls back on the headrest. I fall into a blissful snore free sleep for the remainder of the journey, aided by the absence on this fine morning of the conductor shrieking down the *Tannoy* announcing every station.

I'm rudely awoken with a start when the train judders to a halt at Victoria. I must have been in a deep one as when I open my eyes, I don't know if I'm going to or coming home from work!

I look at my watch, 8.41am, almost bang on time and certainly going to work. However, today I would have warmly welcomed a severe delay for an extended kip.

Walking to the "*Death Star*", with the morning London haze indicating it's going to be another hot and humid day, I ponder over the whole 'falling asleep on the train quandary', which has always perplexed me in my twenty five years commuting sentence. How can you fall into a deep, undisturbed sleep, on a journey lasting an hour, yet when I sit on a long-haul flight for twelve hours or more, there's not so much as a snatched doze until the final descent for landing? - Nope, I've never understood that. Perhaps when I'm fired, jailed or

exiled with time on my hands, I'll do a thesis and research the subject.
The good news is that I do have time to go to my favourite coffee shop for an industrial strength Americano and a bacon roll. The paracetamol seems to have kicked in. Just need the hit from the grease and caffeine to kick in to feel anywhere near human and face the day.
"Morning Alan, hold this bag a second whilst I get my pass."
"Debs, why don't you wear it around your neck, it'd be much easier?"
"I hate that look and I don't want to advertise that I work for this mob on a busy train."
"Fair point, you know I think your nose will peel before the weeks out."
"Thanks for that Alan - I'll make a note to put extra moisture lotion on. You can check the progress of the 'flake off' tomorrow. "
Honestly, he drives me mad sometimes with his banal chit chat. In fairness though, I'd be bored stupid doing his job and would welcome the chance of any conversation, no matter how irritating or trivial. I grab my coffee shop goody bag from him, show my pass and stroll to the lifts.
At my desk, I kick off my trainers, slip shoes on, fire up the laptop and then rather inelegantly tuck into my bacon roll, dripping brown sauce on my desk in the process, and sip my coffee.
No urgent emails, nothing from Ingrid other than a meeting request tomorrow at 10am to finalise the mission statement update on the web, Shit, I've

forgotten all about that. Unsurprisingly, given the revelations of the last sixteen hours. At least I've started the thing.

I check my desk phone - no messages.

All too quiet on the western front for my liking.

I think about Clive's insider theory and look around the office. It could be anybody. Could be the bloody cleaner for all I know. My money is on Mark/Martin. He's purporting to be someone else. Appears as a mourner in Spain, turns up at the barbeque and suddenly lurks around the building in Phil's shadow - yes all very suspicious indeed.

I spot Bronzey at his desk, clearly engrossed in something on his computer, his nose about an inch from the screen with his glasses in his hand. He so needs to get varifocal lenses, but he won't do it. "They're for old folk" he'd vainly respond. I stand up to try to catch his eye, a pointless exercise if ever there was one. I'll just go over there and indicate for him to follow me toward the kitchen area.

Thankfully, the morning refreshment rush and bundle is over and it's empty.

"Bronzey, we need to have a catch up, things have happened since yesterday"

"What things?"

"I can't tell you here, other than my sniffing around has reached the ears of the good and the great upstairs, but they don't know, I know they know. Look, let's nip out to the little cafe round the corner. I'll meet you in there at say 11.30 and you can also tell me what you were up to yesterday afternoon." I say with a raised eyebrow.

"The CAFE!! They don't serve *Merlot* there at 11.30. Can't we just do lunch as normal, Debs?"
"Honestly Bronzey, not today. If I so much as look at or smell another glass of wine at the moment I think I'll heave - had way too much yesterday - I'll explain - just be there and stop moaning".
Back at my desk, I take a good old fashioned A4 pad out of the drawer and start to try and put together a link chart using the simple circle and stick method. The team use this approach on certain cases normally on a big white or glass board display. The victim or key suspect(s) is centrally drawn and circled, all intelligence gathered, photo's, etc, are then posted on the board with a line to the central circle. Any subsequent connections, no matter how tenuous between the intelligence, are graphically illustrated with interlinking lines. It's supposed to be a visual aid so the team can see the whole picture and throw ideas and theories about. Often it works, with the obvious right there in front of you by putting all the links together. Other times, it just looks like a complicated map of the London underground system and gleans absolutely bugger all.
There is an on-line intelligence analysis program which I could use, but given my situation, the last thing I want is the IT Gestapo flagging that up, just in case I'm being monitored through the laptop. So pad and pen it is.
Our Jessica - murder victim (professional hit) is obviously the central circle - a line up for geographical location - Estepona - relevance? Probably nothing.

Next line - funeral - Phil and Mark/Martin in attendance. Why?
I continue with my various lines.
Our Jessica's role within the firm - huge question mark - note links to Northern Ireland.
My name search hits the naughty list - records wiped.
Mark/Martin. Who is he and what's his relationship with Phil - question mark.
Jessica's daughter with Phil and Mark/Martin at Ingrid's BBQ - What's her link?
Name change in 70's from JCB - why? Must refrain from smiling every time I refer to her as JCB.
Seconded undercover to Belfast as a barmaid - brought back when pregnant – father - question mark. Why was she there in the first place?
Guardia Civil - What are they doing - anything?
I suddenly realise it's 11.25. I pop my pad back in the drawer and lock it.
I get to the cafe just after Bronzey as I had a sneaky cigarette on the way. No doubt he'll tell me off for that. I remind myself that I must try one of those electronic vapour cigarettes. It's got to be better for you and cheaper, but I don't get the weird flavours though. Since when did any smoker choose cherry cigarettes as an option?
I join him at the table in the back and order a cup of tea. This is my favourite cafe, an Italian family run place. Best homemade sandwiches you can get and they have stoically survived the onslaught of the big corporate chains sprouting up on almost every corner in London.
"Okay, you go first Debs - what do you know?"

"Well firstly, my search requests have been flagged up with the bigwigs upstairs."

I recount last night's conversation in *Davy's* with Julia.

"So it's been twenty four hours. Ingrid has said nothing to you and you haven't been called to Bowen or indeed further up the ranks to explain what you were doing, and on whose behalf." He almost says as a statement to himself with his eyes to the ceiling.

"No, I told you, Julia and Ingrid were specifically instructed not to discuss their meeting with me. Luckily, Julia just can't help herself. The worst part is now I know that they know, I'm trying to act normally with it hanging over my head."

"Hmm, well they'll certainly be keeping an eye on you, I'd say. They could even know we're here in this cafe."

My eyes widen in horror.

"Hey, I'm only kidding - it's the 'why they haven't spoken to you yet' that puzzles me. How easy could it be to just call you into the office and question you? You're an Operations manager - hardly a flight risk."

We finish our respective tea and coffee and order another two cups. Thanks to Bronzey my paranoia level rises to Mach 3, Warp factor 9, as I suspiciously eye up everyone in the cafe.

I lower my voice. "Clive seems to think he has an idea why, but he's not sharing which, I can tell you, has seriously pissed me off."

"When did you speak to him?" His expression immediately changes from thought to interest.

"That's the other part of the update. When I got back to Hove last night, Clive called me and guess where he was?"

Bronzey shrugs his shoulders.

“Bloody Hove. So I met up with him in the wine bar. Now you understand my aversion to wine today as we sat in there for about 2 hours.”

“I have to say, I thought you looked a bit shabby this morning for a Tuesday.” He chuckles. “So what’s he doing over here? What did he have to say?”

“He met up with a couple of his old contacts - a retired copper in Brighton and a Russian chap in Hampstead, neither of which you would know incidentally. Anyway, without boring you with the historical details, the likes of which I’m a bit fuzzy about, the upshot is, he’s convinced this was a professional hit, possibly in retaliation to an order she may have given against the IRA back in the 80’s.“

He gives me a quizzical look.

“Yes I know - why take so long? I’ve asked that question myself. I don’t know.”

I briefly explain about the name change and her undercover secondment to Belfast in the 70’s.

“Here’s the good part and I have to say completely left field, even by Clive’s standards - he seems to think that someone or person’s here at the firm are connected somehow to the shooting of Jessica.”

“You mean he thinks there’s a mole?” He says almost incredulously.

“Yep, in a nutshell - it’s mad isn’t it? Personally, I think he’s read too many spy novels on his sun lounger, but there you have it, that’s the theory.”

“Well, that really is quite a bloody theory I have to say, Debs, but it poses some obvious questions starting with Mark/Martin.”

"That was the first thing I thought of and I've told Clive that you're going to dig into his background"
"And how did he react to that?"
"To be honest Bronzey, he wasn't a happy bunny with me involving you, but as I pointed out, you'd rumbled my porky pies at the barbeque and that left me no choice. It is what it is and reluctantly he accepts that."
"I would be equally wary if I was in his shoes." He continues "Well, on the subject of Mark/Martin, I met up with a pal of mine yesterday afternoon over in Blackfriars, the *Blackfriars* pub actually. Have you ever been in there?"
"Yes it's absolutely stunning, almost at the top of my list of London pubs of architectural interest! Come on carry on about your pal." My sarcasm goes unnoticed.
"Okay, his brother works for the Anglo-Irish Select Committee and has done so for about fifteen years and has agreed, on the old QT, to get as much information as he can on Martin O'Connell for me...so it's a start. It'll cost me in wine and ale, so brace yourself on the expenses front - I said this yesterday and I'll say it again, even more so now - keep your head down."
"Yes Bronzey, I know."
"When does Clive go back to Spain?"
"I have no idea, I left him snoring his head off on my settee this morning. God knows what he's up to today."
"You know what, I'd really like to meet him. Do you think he'd come up to town?"
"I doubt it. Wouldn't be his wisest move to be seen up here. Shame, as I actually think you two would really hit it off, particularly over a fine Merlot or two."

"Talking of which, Debs, it's nearly midday and I'm bored shitless of coffee. Let's grab a takeaway sandwich here and have a cheeky one for the office in the pub round the corner, only one I promise. The hair of the dog and all that rubbish will probably do you good anyway."

My will power is pathetic, but I can't feel any worse than I already do, so I agree just for the one.

We pop into the *Feathers,* a traditional looking pub but still part of a chain, sadly.

True to his word he orders just the one. I add soda to soften the blow to the system.

"So, if the *Blackfriars* is near the top of your list, what's your architecturally favourite pub then Debs?"

He snaps me out of my momentary trance thinking about all this mess.

"What? Sorry Bronzey, head in the clouds there for a moment."

He repeats the question.

"Ahh...this is a bit of a difficult one as there isn't a clear winner, but I'd say it's a toss-up between *The Princess Louise* in Holborn, and, although not as architecturally resplendent, *The Paul* off Borough High Street, even I have to duck to go in as it's so old and tiny, but I would also throw in *Gordon's Wine bar* by the Embankment, though technically speaking, doesn't count as it's not a pub. What about you? What would you choose?"

Poor Bronzey, he's still totally unaware I'm taking the piss out of him from a great height.

"Oh, there are far too many I've frequented over the years in my exhaustive research to give you an answer. I'll give it some thought and get back to you on that.

Have to admit you've got some good ones on your list. Come on, we better get off to camp."

Back at my desk, I eat my sandwich, check my emails, another one from Ingrid - "can you print off and collate the attached presentation x 24 for my senior management meeting - Thanks - Ingrid"

I wonder, what did her last slave die of!!!

I open the attachment. Just as I hit the print key to send the document to the printing monster, my mobile rings - deepest joy, it's Clive.

"Hi, Debs, its Clive."

"Yes I know that, remarkably my phone alerts me to the fact. Hey, let me call you back in two ticks, I'm at my desk and don't want to be overheard."

I walk down the corridor to the photocopying / printing room and call him back.

"Debs, how are you doing? Anything happening at your end?"

"Firstly Clive, can I just say you snore like a fucking pig. Jesus, how can YOU sleep through that? There are surgical procedures you know that can help. My recommendation would be immediate amputation from above the neck option."

"Come on, it couldn't have been that bad."

"I'll be the judge of that and trust me it was, anyway, it's all a bit quiet on the western front here, nothing from upstairs, nothing from Ingrid other than usual-work based stuff. Bronzey is doing a bit of digging with his contacts. He actually said he'd like to meet you. Can't think why! Anyhow, I told him you're unlikely to be in London any time soon. So...what have you been up to? Anything to report?"

"Where are you? What's that clattering noise in the background?"
"I'm in the copier room. Sorry, there's a print job running and I can't interrupt it."
"Well, I've just met up with Jack and we're planning to fly to Belfast tomorrow to meet an old colleague of his".
"WHAT the hell are you talking about going to Belfast?" I hiss incredulously down the phone
"Sorry, Debs, you'll have to speak up as I can't hear you above that noise."
"Ha...that's rich coming from you matey." I said. "Basically, why the fuck are you two going to Belfast tomorrow? Did you hear that?"
"Loud and clear...look, it could come to nothing but it's a lead worth following up, we think."
"Well, I think you're barking mad, Clive, for what my opinion's worth, which, to you, is clearly nothing. Do you know who this bloke is? Can you trust him?"
"I personally don't, but Jack does on both counts."
"Oh, so that's alright then, you just go on the say-so of an old codger, possibly rattle a few nasty cages and in doing so attract the wrong attention. Then guess what, you come back in a body bag. Go ahead, be my guest, knock yourself out. Heaven forbid, I stand in the way of you donning the international crime- stopper cape and flying off into the Irish sunset. Have you booked your flight yet? I suppose you want me to do it for you?" I spit down the phone.
"Have you quite finished ranting, Debs?"
I'm just about to blast him when he swamps any reply. "Look, I'm just meeting an old retired friend of Jack's who may hold some clue's and thanks for the very kind

offer, but I'll book them online. All I have to do is use my mobile, liaise with Jack to get his details and arrange a time to meet." His sarcasm insinuates he's learnt more than how to boil a kettle since he left the firm.

"Smell you with the technology! Bet you had to ask a small child to teach you that. Going from Gatwick - Does that mean you're hanging around Brighton & Hove tonight? If you are, for my sanity plus general well-being and for you to actually live to see the morning, I respectfully suggest you book yourself immediately into a B&B or hotel for the night."

"Don't worry, will do...oh, and by the way, putting my snoring aside, your sofa wins no comfort prizes either. Not too sure what I'm doing later. Give me a call when you finish work"

"You ungrateful shit. That's the last time you lay your head anywhere near my retro *G-Plan*. I'll call you when I'm done here - Ta ra."

I hang up. I can't believe, on the flimsiest of whims, he's going to start dipping his toe in what could be piranha infested waters. I might be used just as an office-bound 'intelligence moll', but surely therein holds a clue to what I might be good at. He definitely hasn't thought this one through with any sense of logic. Bloody typical.

I return my attention toward the printer and look forlornly at the paper mountain spewing out. Still ten copies to go. This has all the hallmarks of a long drawn out, boring day. Might as well just stand here and wait for it to finish.

"Ah, Debs, there you are. I was looking for you and thought you might be in here."
"Oh. Hi, Ingrid. If it's about the presentation packs, you can see I'm onto to it, although I think the beast might combust into flames any second. Luckily no paper jam yet, only a matter of time though, I'm sure."
"Oh, ye of little faith with our hardware."
"Too right I have no faith - this old mule of a machine is hardly state of the art. Nearly as old as me. You don't have to wrestle with the bloody thing on a daily basis, do you? I'm sure it's possessed by the ghosts of past employees." Not thinking, words just tumble out of my mouth. I wonder if it is Clive I'm thinking about?
"You got a fair point there, Debs, but no, that's not why I wanted to see you, but great and thanks that you've got it all this under control. Steve's got some last minute corporate event to attend to tonight in the City. The kids are having a sleep over, so I wondered if you fancy sharing a bottle of *Prosecco* after work in *Balls Bros*? I asked Julia but she has a Pilate's class at 7.30, so it would just be us two. What do you say - up for it?"
"Julia and a Pilates class? Oh, my God there's an image right there I don't want popping into my head. Alright, but it'll have to be a quick one though as an old mate of mine from out of town is in Hove later and I want to catch up. Shall we say 5.15 then? I'll pop these packs in your office when they're all done."
"Perfect, see you then and thanks again Debs." Turning on her ridiculously high heels, she heads back toward her office.

That's the last thing I want to do tonight, listening to her prattling on about the kids, Steve and recipes she's discovered in some bygone *Mrs Beaton* publication. No, I've come to a decision, I must try and look at her in a different light. After all, she can't be as daffy as she makes out, or how would she get into such a high profile position. But there again, I might be wrong. Did I mention earlier I was Clive's 'intelligence moll'? In the past years, just to spruce up her boring day, I've fed her some juicy bits of gossip from the floor in retaliation, but tonight there's no Julia for deflection. Unless of course, she wants to speak to me about her little visit to the Gods upstairs...hmm, I'll just play along - for once Clive has proved quite handy as an excuse to leave early.

Printing finally done and collated, hoorah! I gather the pile and go to dump it on her desk.

Heading back to mine, I can hear my internal phone going, I just get to it in time before it switches to voice-mail.

"Hello Debbie, this is Lorraine Brown, Commissioner Gordon's PA. Do you have a moment to come up to his office? He'd like a quick meeting with you?"

Oh shit!

"Erm, yes of course. What time?"

"Now, if that's convenient with you. Do you know where his office is?"

No time would be convenient for me.

"That's fine Lorraine, twentieth floor, isn't it?"

"Yes that's right. Turn right out of the lift, through the double doors and it's the first office on your left. I'll be outside."

Well, this is it then...show time. I scan around my desk and wonder if all my personal belongings will fit into just one box. I feel physically sick and cover my face with my hands. I so wish I hadn't had that wine and soda.

I press for the lift, dreading the doors sliding open to beckon me inside and raise me up to *Beelzebub's Cavern.* I feel myself shaking. Need to get a grip. Attempting to take deep breaths, my lungs refuse to cooperate. Ping...I reach the top floor. Instead of fire and brimstone greeting me, a plush carpeted corridor wheels away in each direction. On Lorraine's advice, I go through the double doors and spot who I assume she is, looking very much the original *Miss Moneypenny* to *James Bond.*

She greets me, knocks on his open door and announces me to someone I hope isn't the devil.

"Thank you, Lorraine. Could you close the door behind you?" He says without a trace of flames coming from his mouth.

He warmly shakes my hand. Good start. I knew him years ago when he was Clive's boss and seen him at conferences and in various publications, but he appears much larger now in the higher echelons of senior management. Maybe it's the uniform playing tricks with my memory.

"Please take a seat, Debbie."

Christian names, that's a good start. As ordered, I sit in a large, leather seat in front of his even larger mahogany desk, my hands dug deep in my lap, sweating. I cross my legs to stop the left one uncontrollably shaking - an annoying habit when I'm

absolutely terrified. Then he does something quite unexpected. He perches himself on the corner of the desk and imposingly looks down at me.
"Do you know why I've called you up here?"
I clear my throat. "I think I may have an inkling, Sir." I stutter.
"Well, the first thing I want to say is that you're not in any trouble, on the contrary actually. So please Debbie, try to relax."
Relax! Easy for him to say.
"I'll get straight to the point. You've been searching for data on the late Jessica McGill and if I'm not mistaken, this would have been at the request of Clive Grainger. Am I correct in my assumptions so far?"
Oh God, I can't lie to the Commissioner.
"Yes Sir. That would be correct."
"So, can you tell me exactly what Clive's relationship was with the deceased?"
"She was a friend of his, Sir, part of a close knit expat community down in Estepona."
"And Clive being Clive can't help himself and gets back in the saddle to conduct his own investigation and enquiries surrounding her murder. And what would naturally follow is he uses you as a resource to access intelligence from within."
"That's the sum of it, Sir." I respond, seriously wondering where this is going and have I just dropped Clive in a huge dung pile from a great height?
"Listen, Debbie, What I need from you is to brief me on everything you and Clive have unearthed to date, please don't worry, he will be protected by this office, as will you, more so with you as you're a valued

employee. It goes without saying that what you tell me will be treated as highly confidential and does not leave this room, do you understand?"
"Yes Sir."
"You're probably wondering what all this is about and why I've called you into my office? It is sufficient for me to say at this time, that this office is taking a keen interest in the developments of this case and what Clive hopes to achieve in Spain."
"Okay, Sir." I hear him, but apart from a lame response, I haven't a Scooby-doo where he's going with this, after all, he is the Commissioner of Police.
It seems the friendly, I'm on your side stuff has finished and it's back to business when he stands and moves round to the other side of his desk and sits in his chair, taking a pad and pen out of his drawer to obviously take notes.
I spend the next twenty minutes or so going through the sequence of events, beginning initially with Clive's first phone call asking for my help. I continue with my search results, the faces at the funeral and the barbeque, Clive's meetings with his old cronies, but specifically, I stick to the facts and purposely avoid Clive's theories. He's the top copper, he can work on his own damn theories. But, I must admit, it's all quite surreal seeing all those pips on his shoulders and ribboned endorsements on his chest, as he's scribbling away in an *Oxfam* note book.
My memory becomes void of anything else he might find interesting and he finally puts his pen down, leans back in his chair, puts his hands behind his head and looks me straight in the eye.

"Other than you and Clive, is anyone else privy to this investigation?"
Oh no...do I send Bronzey up-the-swanny?
I hesitate and he notices. If I say anything but the truth, he'll know and the trust he might have in me might just as well be thrown out of his office window, that is, of course, if the bloody thing opened this high up. Trust, what a bloody silly word in the year 2015 when, not a few miles down the Thames, in the City of London, the self-styled centre of the world's finance, nurtured by faceless grey suits, have been fined millions of pounds for contravening that very word. It's no good, I'm going to have to tell him straight.
"Well, Sir, I confided with Chief Inspector Bronze after he challenged me, when he realised I was lying regarding my motives for asking him to run the funeral photos through NEOFACE. I genuinely can't speak for Clive, with who he's spoken to, but you know what he's like. He has a habit of keeping critical information close to his chest until he's sufficiently processed it all, whilst keeping those he's talking to somewhat in the dark as to his motives."
"I would absolutely agree with your assessment concerning our friend in Spain. Without being able to speak to him, I'll assume it's just you three directly in the circle and now me, that are in the know. I'll speak directly with CI Bronze. Can I ask you for your personal opinion? Out of all of us, you know him best. What do you think Clive's next move is?"
I suddenly shudder with it abruptly dawning on me that I might be blabbing on to who Clive might be looking for. The culprit, responsible for murdering

Jessica? No, surely not. He notices me faltering, but what else can I say?

"As I have already said, Sir, he keeps everything very close to his chest and I can't really tell you much more, except, he's going to Belfast tomorrow with Jack to meet someone, and before you ask, no, I have no idea who with."

More scribbling ensues.

"My word, Debbie, he really has got the bit between his teeth. He hasn't changed, has he? Reacting just like he did when he was under my command. And don't think you'd be acting as an informer, Debbie, I expect you to discuss our little chat with Clive. In actual fact, I'm encouraging you to do so. But I do request, as an order actually, that other than Clive and CI Bronze, this meeting remains strictly confidential, do I have your word on that? Nobody must know."

"Yes Sir, you have my word."

"Good, now I want you to return to your desk and go about business as usual. I will be in touch, but if you hear anything you might think interests me, you call me immediately. Do you understand me, Debbie? Anything."

Adding to what he's said, as he gets up and heads toward the door. "Although we may have different agenda's, I believe both Clive and I are aiming for the same goal."

He shakes my hand again, before seeing me out and asks the fragrant Lorraine to call Bronzey up.

I stand in the lift shell-shocked, wondering what the fuck just happened in that room? Have I just spilled the beans to the bastard responsible for all this mayhem? But at best, I'm not in any trouble. I've not been fired. It almost sounded like he was taking me in his confidence. My gut tells me there's one a big cryptic message in there somewhere, but damned if I know. I'll tell Clive all about it later - maybe he can shed some light.

The lift doors open and there's Bronzey standing, waiting to exit.

"I've just been bloody summoned to..." I put my hand up to shush him.

"I know, I've just come from his office. It's okay Bronzey, trust me. When you get back down, let's nip out and compare notes".

The doors close and he just nods, he doesn't look at all happy.

Fifteen minutes pass and he returns back to the department and approaches my desk. "Come on, let's go and have a chat. I need a proper drink."

"Yes and I need a cigarette."

Back in *The Feathers* we sit at a table with a glass of wine each, I relay the conversation with the Commissioner.

"That was that...no bollocking and he'll be in touch. What the hell does 'he'll be in touch' mean? What did he say to you?"

"He basically made it crystal clear that I was to put a halt to any investigation into Martin O'Connell's background. That he would personally look into the matter and not to mention any of this to anyone as an order."

"Seriously Bronzey, what do you make of it all?"

"I don't know, Debs, I'm hoping that Gordon is one of the good guy's otherwise we could have just opened a huge can of worms for Clive and possibly put him in danger, so let's pray that's not the case. I think all we can do is follow orders, lie low and see what or if anything happens next. I'll call my mate up and tell him I don't need the favour, you just share what you were told with Clive. Let's see what his spin on it is."
"You're right - lie low, this is all getting a bit too confusing for my liking. On a positive note, at least we didn't get our backsides fired. Do you know what? I actually feel a weight has been lifted in that regard - lets drink to that, but do me a favour, on second thoughts keep in touch with your mate and get what he might know about O'Connell. We might need some bargaining shit to throw around, if it all goes pear-shaped."
Bronzey wasn't happy, but saw the benefits of such a suggestion.
Back in the office under the influence of a bottle of which Bronzey had already slipped in an expense docket, I focus on the mind numbingly dull task of starting to pull together the stats for the monthly divisional compliance reports. Back to what I'm officially paid for.
Balls Bros at 5.15 is beginning to fill up as I order the *Prosecco* and find an unoccupied table. I don't need to turn round as I can hear Ingrid's clip-clopping heels on the tiled floor approaching. She's the only woman I know that changes shoes to go home in, that are actually higher than the ones she wears in the office. Me, I'm in my trainers.

"Well done, Debs, I can do with this." Her enthusiasm is positively nauseating as the waitress pops the cork and pours into our glasses.

"Err...you're paying for this Ingrid, so you don't have to congratulate me"

"Ha ha, very funny, yes I know it's my treat. So how are things with you and Nick going? It's just, I can't help but notice you and CI Bronze have been spending a lot of time in each other's company lately, if you know what I mean."

"For fuck's sake, Ingrid, are you suggesting what I think you're suggesting, that Bronzey and I are conducting some sort of lurid affair in full view of the office?"

"Well, you two have been spotted going out or coming back into the office together quite regularly in the last few days."

"WHAT!!.......I can emphatically tell you that I'm not, this is hilarious - seriously, me and Bronzey! Give me a break. Lovely bloke and all that, but I just couldn't, please credit me with some taste - I so don't do moustaches. Yes, we pop out, I help him out with his expenses, which have been numerous of late, I can tell you. He in turn rewards me with wine - that's the full extent of it. Sorry to rain on your gossip parade."

"Well I did wonder, you can't blame me for that, can you Debs?"

"No I suppose not, I'd probably jump to the same conclusion and in answer to your original question, no I haven't seen Nick since the barbeque. I'm keeping him at arm's length at the moment with his notion of potentially ramping up our relationship, if his wife goes to France."

"Is he really serious about that...what will you do if he proposes a more permanent arrangement?"

"I honestly don't know. I'm quite happy with the current status-quo, which is why I'm avoiding any dialogue with him on the subject."

I refill our glasses while she starts blathering on about her dessert menu options for her forthcoming dinner party next weekend - Great!

"So, what do you think, should I go for the Pavlova or a Tiramisu?"

I couldn't give a rat's arse or a rolling doughnut what she decides to make, but I feign a modicum of interest.

"You know me, I'd just go to the supermarket and buy whatever they have on offer, sod all that faffing around trying to make it myself."

"I knew you'd say that, Debs, but my mother's coming round and she'll curl her lip up in disgust if it's not home made."

"Well go for the tiramisu then, it's easier that risking a flat meringue disaster."

"Yes, probably the better choice. Talking of my mother, you know what, she's actually requested to be my friend on *Facebook*, can you believe that? What on earth would you do in my shoes - accept it or ignore it?"

"Ooh...that's really a tough one. Luckily my mother is the furthest from the silver-surfer brigade, she won't even use a mobile let alone a computer. I certainly wouldn't want her following or to 'like' any of my posts. You're between a rock and a hard place here Ingrid, but

I think you're going to have to accept the request initially then maybe later, subtly de-friend her because she'll know if you ignore it."

"You're right, I guess, but it really doesn't sit well with me, dear Steve just laughs."

I look at my watch just gone six.

"Look Ingrid, really sorry, much as I'd love to sit here all evening debating your matriarchal and culinary challenges, but I've got to neck this drink and get the 18.17 Hove train home."

"Yes, of course, you go and I'll settle up, see you in the morning."

"Thanks Ingrid, yep, see you tomorrow as usual."

Outside, relieved that little tete-a-tete is over, I light a cigarette and quickly call Clive before heading for the train.

Come on, pick up you stupid bastard, please don't let it go to voice-mail.

"Hi Debs, what news?"

"Where are you, in a pub? Certainly sounds like it."

"Yes I'm in the *Pump House* in town with some old mates."

Good grief. Translate that into "I've been on the beer all day and getting slowly pissed!"

"Listen, I had the call from those up high this afternoon and I need to talk to you. I'm getting the 18.17 train to Hove, meet me in *The Paris* wine bar at 19.45. Don't get waylaid in any other hostelry en-route...pleeease."

"Aye, Aye Sir."

"Don't be a prat Clive, just be there...look I've got to go or I'll miss the bloody train, see you in a bit" I hang up.

I grab a copy of *The Evening Standard* and make my way to platform 17 where, fingers crossed, the train will be standing, in all its unwashed splendour.

Blimey, it's there alright, but only eight sodding carriages and each one absolutely heaving, with only three minutes to departure, I just press the nearest door button and squeeze my way on board, ignoring the tut-tutting of those already packed in like sardines, wallowing in sweat instead of the usual tomato or oil conserve. No chance of reading the paper now with my face pressed against some blokes clammy shirt, this is going to be a deeply unpleasant experience, not a candidate for the *'Great British Train Journey's'* TV series - seriously, cattle have stricter travelling rights than commuters. The conductor apologises yet again and announces that due to overcrowding, first class compartments are now declassified - as if he's doing us all a huge favour - like anyone takes any notice anyway of first class restrictions when there's short formation - idiot! He'd better stay in his little cubby-hole or risk his ticket machine being shoved where the sun doesn't shine.

Eventually, I get to Hove, having had to stand all the way, enduring two whacks round the head by ignorant prats swinging their rucksacks ala *Quasimodo* style, oblivious to having a large lump on their back and we're fifteen minutes late.

I text Clive...'On my way. F***ing train late again and crammed, get a wine in pronto.'

CHAPTER 22

12.48pm. Tuesday. 18th August 2015. Commissioner Gordon's Office.

"Hello, Lorraine, I hope you haven't anything booked for lunch as I need you to work through. Can you get Striker at *Thames House* on the line?" Gordon orders, knowing full well, after eavesdropping an earlier exchange on the phone, she'd arranged to meet her husband for lunch. Something to do with an anniversary. Too bad, he thinks. There are more important issues on the table. Like his job, for example.

In the last hour, an office manager and a Chief Inspector had passed through his office with both relating the same story. Freely displaying a nervous, fidgeting demeanour, he knew Debbie Glynn told it how she saw it without embellishments. There was no reason to lie, as she appeared as if she was crapping herself during the entire duration of her first visit to the 'top floor'. What she said about face recognition at Jessica's funeral must be hard evidence that O'Connell and Deputy Commissioner Blunt were there, but why and on whose orders? Not his. Chief Inspector Bronze confirmed her diagnosis, even snooping around the

Northern Ireland office, on his own whim, to ascertain O'Connell's credentials.

For good reason, Shelly McGill, was in attendance at the funeral, but how come they appeared to know each other like old friends, especially at the barbeque, as Glynn wasn't backward at pointing out? What's their connection? More worryingly, who gave O'Connell permission to snoop around his department and who issued the regulation security passes? It certainly wasn't me, the Commissioner thought. Indulging himself in even deeper thoughts, a buzzing monitor awakens reality, indicating an incoming call from *Thames House.*

"Good afternoon Commissioner." The dulcet tone of the Director General of *MI5*'s voice resounds in Gordon's ear. Disregarding a courteous response, Gordon gets straight to the point.

"Now I want some straight answers to straight questions, so do you want to do this over the phone or do you want to come over here?"

A pause of some five seconds elapse before Paul Striker responds.

"Well Commissioner, it all depends on what you want to ask." He didn't get to his lofty position by not being able to play verbal chess, playing his audio partner to find weak points in his opponent's attack.

"Listen here, Striker. It has come to my attention that someone, and it must be one of your boys, has been snooping around here in my domain. I don't know what he expects to find nor do I like the fact he's been given a guided tour by a Deputy Commissioner, who I might say, is not from my division. Now either we talk about it on the phone or you get over here, because their instructions could have only been ordered from your office."

It is a gamble and he knew of the possible repercussions, but Gordon is willing to give it a throw of the dice. Only going on information gleaned from Glynn and Grainger's curiosity, it was Chief Inspector Bronze's involvement, chasing up O'Connell's file that gave Gordon cause to believe orders could have only come from *Thames House*, but why wasn't he at least informed there were possible shenanigans happening under his very nose. There's never been any love shown or lost from either department, but courtesy he believed, still reigns.

Even if he was way off course with his assumptions, Striker wouldn't advise him to reconsider his position, allowing, no, even encouraging Gordon to dig an even bigger hole for himself, but if this escalated into inter-department warfare, this whole covert operation could fall flat on its face, ruining any chance of nailing the culprit, and this could rebound and have serious consequences for the head of *MI5*, and he knew it.

"We can't discuss this over the phone and I can't get over to you, for reasons which will become clear when we meet. And I don't want you traipsing over here for the same reasons, so choose somewhere neutral." Striker responds, allowing nothing to be gleaned from the verbal contents of their conversation or the tempo of his voice.

The line goes silent for a few seconds before Gordon interrupts the vocal stalemate. "Do you know the *Serpentine Sackler Gallery* in Kensington Gardens?

They have a restaurant in the place. I'll even buy you a glass of wine. Say, in half an hour?"

"You wouldn't be in uniform, would you?" Striker throws in a question, a smile on his face knowing Gordon should understand his comment. Though disguised in meaning, his words obviously spell out to the Commissioner that he is speaking to a superior officer, a non-wearing uniform position.

Gordon understood the rhetoric as soon as the words hit his ear, but dismisses them. "Yes, I am in uniform, for God's sake man, because I'm the Commissioner of police, but what has that got to do with undermining my authority?"

Daring to disobey office policy, because he knew he could, Striker flicks the ash off the end of his cigar into an ashtray. "Disguise it with a raincoat and ditch the hat. I don't want some trigger happy journalist aiming their camera at us having a cosy drink together. Believe me, Gordon, this is important business and the last thing I need is a picture of us on the front page of the *Daily Mirror.*"

~O~

The restaurant is busy, but Gordon is the first of the two to arrive and secures a table by a window. An ideal position to spot any unwanted observers looking their way with telephoto lens in hand. He orders a bottle of *Sancerre* and waits.

Within ten minutes, Striker joins him, an inconspicuous individual in his fifties, clad in the obligatory grey suit, but by its quality obviously bespoke tailored. Standing about five feet ten, he resembles not a man of extreme power, but one more comfortable educating the fifth form of an inner city comprehensive school.

"Now you might be used to all this cloak and dagger nonsense, but it's totally alien to me." Gordon greets his opposite number without a welcoming handshake, coming straight to the point.

No sooner than his backside has time to hit the wicker seat of his chair, Striker mimics Gordon's lack of niceties, usually appropriate at this time, by not wasting time with formalities. "What I am about to say is for your ears only."

Before Striker continues, Gordon interrupts with his own brand of disparaging humour. "Oh, I believed the saying goes something like 'it is for your eyes only'. Sorry, seen too many *James Bond* films." A smile, this time, spreads across his face and not Striker's.

"Whatever." An immediate put down flies across the table. "Look, I'm not here to take part in imbecilic small talk. We have reliable information that there is an undesirable working inside your establishment. Not knowing who it is, we, of course, needed to be discreet, everybody is a suspect and sorry to say, Commissioner, that included you." Striker expects a rumbling volcano to erupt, but, thankfully, Gordon chose this place and raised voices would only attract attention.

"Do you seriously believe I could be a spy?" Gordon spits his reply in a venomous voice, no louder than a whisper.

"Everybody had to be put in the hat until we whittled the suspects down. No Gordon, you're no longer one of those under surveillance." Enjoying defeating his opponent's bluster, Striker infuriates the Commissioner even further by stopping in mid-sentence to sample Gordon's choice of beverage. Not the best is his verdict. "That was why you weren't informed of this exercise which, by the way, came direct to us from the Home Secretary."

"Is there someone in particular under scrutiny?" Gordon responds, not expecting an answer, as getting one out of Striker is similar to opening an oyster with a toothpick.

"Can't tell you, Jack."

Gordon inwardly smiles when the head of *MI5* calls him by his Christian name. What else has he up his sleeve? He wonders what he's not telling him.

"Well, Paul..." Omitting titles, Gordon throws back his own brand of disrespect. "I believe you've made a complete pig's ear of all this and your covert operation isn't as covert as you once thought."

Striker peers at Gordon over the rim of his wineglass, his act of taking a mouthful stops in mid-flow. Now he ponders, should there be a look of surprise, or should he nonchalantly suggest he's talking nonsense? Neither is forthcoming. He'll prompt and then just listen.

"You obviously have something to say on this matter." Dangling, what he hopes is a carrot, Striker replaces the glass back to his lips, accepting the Commissioner might have a snippet that might have escaped his ears.

"What you appear to have seriously overlooked is the common factor of being a copper. Now I can't talk for you lot over in *MI5*, as you're mostly made up of ex-military types from all the services, with some even reaching a high level of command. No, I'm talking about the fact that once you have retired from being a copper, you never lose the art of what first attracted you to the force. Of course, you will not have experienced this as you came into security direct from the army."

Striker is just about to correct Gordon's assessment of his career, but now has proof the Commissioner hasn't done his homework concerning his personal file.

Feeling it prudent to allow him the sense of clawing back some of the ground he verbally lost, Gordon, mistakenly, feels better, believing what he is about to say, might get right up Striker's nose.

"Something that happened miles away from here in a different country prompted one of my ex-officers to poke his copper's nose into something he should have left well alone, but he didn't. That's what separates us from you lot...our noses. And from that little acorn, it has grown, whereby there are three of us who know we are dealing with an infiltrator inside my division, without the need for your two henchmen fumbling about. In less than two weeks, we have unearthed a murder, which was in fact an assassination and leading on from that, my little team believe and have proof, that the crime was instigated by the new face of the *IRA*, perpetrated care of information leaked from our files. So, thank you for your supposed help, but I believe my department can wheedle out our spy without it." Speaking as though he'd been on top of this situation for weeks, instead of fumbling his way

into a quagmire of subterfuge only in the past hour, Gordon displays a certain satisfaction.
It takes a short period for Striker to digest and consider what he's just been informed. "I would consider it a favour if you would pass on your file containing all the pertinent facts to my office, Jack."
"Well, Paul, therein lies the problem. As we are dealing with something so explosive within home security, we purposely don't have a file that can be read by someone who shouldn't be reading it. We do everything on a need to know basis, orally, with no paper trail. So Paul, my small team might be just as good or better than your lot...as there's one thing we treasure...we trust each other. Now, can you put your hand on your heart and say the same. If my team are correct with their assumption concerning the *IRA* connection...didn't you share your department with the Northern Irish Office up until a few years ago?" The Commissioner's sardonic smirk is evident.
"You are taking this way above your pay level, Commissioner. This is a Homeland Security dilemma and comes under the auspices of my department, not yours." Appearing to have lost a modicum of his authority, Paul cuts him off before threats to promotion and lack of pension rights enter the conversation.
"Director General." Gordon intercedes, emphasising Striker's title. "This all began with an English national being murdered in Spain. My man down there, who we code named 'OMIE', knew the deceased personally and probed deeper without the aid of the Spanish police who are now content, after being in discussion with my department, to believe it is an unsolved murder.

Nothing more. But due to fine police work by 'OMIE', we have unearthed the true identity of the victim, a retired director of your organization, living under a changed identity, who was heavily involved with the Northern Ireland problem in the seventies and eighties. We also know the three *IRA* terrorists killed in Gibraltar by the *SAS* were sanctioned to make the hit, but unfortunately for them, they unwisely ventured onto British sovereign land, purely as sightseers. After *The Good Friday Agreement,* interest in our girl in Spain faded, but as time has passed, the emerging, younger personnel have renewed their interest...keen to take back Northern Ireland and settle scores for their forefathers. Hence, the assassination of Jessica McGill or as she was Christened...Jane Constance Brewer.

"Well Commissioner, you have been busy. You have bypassed a few small facts, but in all, yes...you appear to know the nuts and bolts of the problem we are faced with. And it's not a *New Scotland Yard* problem. Let's be honest with each other, you are the police, we are protectors of home security. There is a big difference. You solve anything up to murder, we go from there to resist terrorists planting bombs on our homeland to murder hundreds. So can we work together on this? Who is 'OMIE'?"

Striker finishes the wine and is in the process of attracting a pretty young waitress's eye, who, if she knew what was going through his mind, could have him arrested for sexual harassment.

"That, Director General, I'm afraid I can't tell you. And working together...I'm not too sure it would be a healthy and worthwhile liaison. Get O'Connell and

Blunt out of my building and take advice, do not attempt to access my people. If you do, it might fuck it up for us all."

Striker turns abruptly to face Gordon, his mind diverted from ordering another bottle. "Don't threaten, Gordon. You're treading on very thin ice and can be relieved of your duties with just one phone call to the right person."

"It's no threat...just a fact."

CHAPTER 23

7.30pm. Tuesday 18th August 2015. Paris Wine Bar. Hove.

Strange, isn't it, that whilst having a drink with old workmates, you realise when they are out of uniform and their closeted, regimental environment, you have little or nothing in common with them. I made my excuses and left half a dozen of my old comrades twenty minutes ago in *The Pump House,* escaping the inevitable intoxicated mayhem before it got into full swing, the type of disorder that if they weren't ex-coppers, the management would have called the law ages ago to get them turfed out.

I'm early for my meeting with Debs, but am immediately recognised by the barman sporting the real-McCoy *Rolex*, when sidling up to the bar.

"Good to see you again, sir. What are you having? Maybe I can tempt you with a bottle of *Bonneau du Matray.*" His humour isn't missed.

"No, an expresso for me and a large *Remy*, thanks." I smile, liking his memory of the last time I was here. "And a large glass of *Chablis* for my guest."

"Of course, sir. Will you be in the garden? I'll bring your order out."

He interests me, as I still can't place his accent.

"Tell me, what part of the world do you hail from? I've been trying to work it out, but, I must admit, I can't nail it."

"I'm from Bosnia and I'm called Elvis. Yes, it's true, my name is Elvis, but it's quite a common name from where I come from."

Who am I to argue, but I wish I'd been born with that handle. It might have been a possibility had one of England's winning team in the sixties been named Elvis, when my mother might have given in to my father's wishes, but no...I'm Clive. Can you imagine the respect I'd get flashing a warrant card with Elvis Grainger? Much raunchier. Or even standing in the witness box when the usher asks me to identify myself. I can just imagine the impact on the faces squatting up on the bench under their coiffured wigs and 'million' pound wage packets, those who privately wish they could reinstate the death penalty by signing away someone's life with an exaggerated signature beginning with a Julian, Vivian or even a Titus. Yes, I've been in the witness box before these same high court judges whose parents must have consulted 'The Eton School Book of Christian Names' before the little, pompous bastard crept out of his mother's womb.

I squat at the same table under the overhead heater and don't have to wait long for Debs to appear, giving the impression the same wasp had flown into her mouth, but this time, she'd spat it out with venom. She's ready.

"You'll never guess what happened to me today?" Her enthusiasm clearly rekindled, enough to sidestep a mocking answer, she bursts forth, but in a mindfully, muted tone. "Old man Commissioner Gordon had me in his office. I don't know what's happening, but you and I appear to be flavour of the month. My job is safe and, if I'm not wrong, could go after his job." She laughs, obvious relief spreading throughout her diminutive body.

She grabs her wine glass and swills back more than a demure lady would do at a 'ladies who do lunch' soiree. I wait until her fluster and bustle subside.

"Tell me. What did he have to say?" It's a question I pose, hopeful of an actual transcript of the conversation rather than faint memories.

"He knows what you're up to and my involvement to furnish you with Jessica's files, as well as Bronzey's involvement with trying to find out who this O'Connell bloke is. Also he was a bit perturbed that you're going to Belfast tomorrow. Wanted to know why."

"Oh, Debs...why did you have to tell him all that? If there is an insider giving the wrong people information, the fewer who know my whereabouts, the better. Who knows? Old Gordon might just be the informer I'm after and you've told him everything what I'm up to." Debs doesn't need a magnifying glass to see I'm not happy.

"Look...you haven't been in the position I've been for the last week or so. I was cornered and we're not dealing with some petty corporate treachery here, this is fucking serious stuff. If we can't trust the Commissioner, then who the fuck can we? The last thing he said to me was, if I should need help, don't hesitate to contact him. Now does that sound like someone who we can't trust?" She's flustered and I've just ruined her day.

"Is there anyone else who knows of my involvement?" I probe.

"No...as far as I can figure out, just the ones you know about, but I'm really getting worried about your safety. Even Gordon expressed his concerns. Without knowing it, I think you're getting close to whoever is responsible and I think they know it too." Her concern is sweet, but doesn't deter her from ordering another round from a passing Elvis.

"Maybe we'll know more tomorrow when I meet Jack's mate in Belfast. Now, are you absolutely sure only the four of us know where I'm off to? There was nobody earwigging our telephone conversations?" I ask, knowing this could have serious repercussions.

"I'm certain, Clive...that I am sure of."

I look at her and fear, in her innocence, she might be wrong.

CHAPTER 24

10.23am. Wednesday 19th August 2015. Gatwick Airport.

It's probably not the wisest time in the year to arrive at an airport, but hopefully the crowds departing on their holidays are more likely to be going to departure gates in the opposite direction to where Jack and I are heading. Though I suspect Belfast has all the trappings of a western, modern city, I doubt it's on the top of the list of where families decide to spend their summer vacations.

I spoke to Jack last night and got the go-ahead to purchase the tickets on-line, but when I asked if he had told Seamus of our true intention for this visit, Jack fudged his reply, not entirely convincing me that this might be a wasted and expensive journey. His theory of 'let's get over there and see what happens', might have convinced a DCI years ago, when we were in the force, to chase down a possible lead, but the two of us are retired without the luxury of having this little junket paid for by signing one of Debbie's expense dockets. No, it's coming out of my pocket as, after all, Jack's doing me a big favour and I can't really expect him to pay for his own ticket.

"Now tell me, Jack, what did Seamus really say to you? Does he know something or does he see this as a get-together with an old friend and an excuse to get pissed?" I ask, seated beside a window in a *Ryan Air* Boeing 737 waiting for take-off.

"No, Clive, he'll be fine once we get a few pints down him."

Contrasting with my body being lifted into the air inside a glorified cigar tube by two powerful turbines, I can't shake off this sinking feeling that I'm wasting my time and money. And it doesn't improve when I attract an attendant for two gin and tonics and am asked for sixteen pounds for the privilege of drinking out of a plastic beaker with not even a slice of lemon. No, I must get rid of this lethargy creeping into my day and stop comparing how far the same amount of euros would go to quench my thirst in Fred's bar. It might only be an hour and twenty minute flight, but I wonder if it's short enough to dissuade Jack from asking for refills.

"Where are we meeting Seamus?" I ask as we touch down.

"Oh...he says just hang around and wait for him outside the terminal, so he can pick us up and then drive into town. Saves him using the car-park." Jack answers stopping himself finishing the sentence with 'the mean bastard'.

With only two other planes parked on the apron at *George Best City Airport* and seemingly their cargo has already passed through customs and immigration, Jack and I breeze through the formalities, heading straight for the exit. It's a sign of the times we live in when armed *Guardia* officers scrutinise everybody with suspicion, but I don't mind their eye-balling as it's reassuring to see such diligence. Sunshine, with a touch of heat, greets our exodus from the terminal and couldn't come a moment too soon for Jack to light up and take a deep pull, overcoming his nicotine craving. I follow suit with one of my own cigarettes.

"Fill me in a bit more about Seamus. When did he retire?" I ask, suggesting to Jack we move away from the dribble of human traffic shuffling through the funnel-like entrance/exit, to where a line of trollies are parked outside a glazed facia, running the entire length of the terminal.

"Oh...I don't really know. He is a few years older than..."

Before Jack completes his answer, a plate glass section behind us, one of four stacked from floor to where the protective canopy juts out, shatters with a sound so disorientating, we both instinctively dive to the ground.

"What the fuck..." Screams Jack, grabbing my arm for support.

"Are you okay?" I shout back, but all I see in Jack's eyes is utter confusion; probably the same state as what Jack sees in mine.

Everything indescribably slows down and goes deathly silent; simulating a *David Attenborough* wild life documentary, without his commentary, where a camera reels off a million frames a second to capture every flexible sinew of a chasing lioness after its prey. I see hi-viz jackets scattering like chased gazelles, but all imitating the speed of the chaser. But nobody, apart from Jack and I, or so it seems, appears to have noticed a gaping hole not a few yards from where we stand, measuring some two metres by two, where once a plate glass window was fixed.

In a fraction of a second, my bewildered state dissolves, leaving me witnessing disorganized bedlam whilst cowering down, a protective arm round Jack. Sound is restored to my ears as shouting and screaming erupts, giving me no hint of a clue from what direction this mayhem originated. A carpet of a trillion shards of glass are scattered across the walkway.

"Jack. Are you okay?" I repeat, shouting even though Jack is close, by my side.

"Yes mate. I'm fine." He responds, but I feel his body shaking.

There are people emerging like headless chickens, all undoubtedly trained for such emergencies, but when the time comes, there's no reasoning to how individuals react. A copper dressed in black, aping some *Jedi* warrior in protective armour, sprints to where we remain crouched, his automatic rifle clutched to his chest, but nobody is prepared for what happens next.

A second plate glass pane, right next to the first, explodes in similar fashion.

Shielding our position, our *Star Wars* hero kneels, much like the stance of a tin-soldier I had as a kid when playing war games, his eye fixed to a telescopic sight, focusing, not on the airport but out into the distance across the Sydenham By-Pass, the main artery out of Belfast, to trees and fields beyond.

"Get into the terminal building, now." He screams and repeats it with even more ferocity.

This is not the time to ask questions. Grabbing Jack, I would very much like to sprint off, but my speed is governed by Jack.

Above the crescendo of turmoil left outside, we stop in the middle of the concourse, Jack's heavy breathing giving me a good hint he'd run out of steam. His face appears ashen white, looking not too good as he bends at the waist, his hands clasping his knees, his mouth sucking in air.

For the third time I repeat my question. "Are you okay?"

Jack looks up from his bent position and gives me a grimacy smile. "Yes mate. What the fuck was that all about?"

"I think some bastard has just taken a couple of pot-shots at us."

If ever the spoken word can straighten an ageing body, my last sentence does the trick.

"What the fuck. Are you telling me we were the fucking target?" Jack's eyes are wide and he seems to have forgotten about the state of his lungs.

"Well, tell me if there was anyone else standing anywhere near where we stood? Those windows just didn't explode by themselves. High velocity bullets created that mess." My voice has no volume, but is loud enough for Jack to hear.

"Fuck me, Clive. Who the fuck is trying to kill us?" Jack swivels on his axis to eye all corners of the building, believing he might pick out the culprit.

"That's just it, Jack. I don't know if they were trying to rub us out or if that was just a warning. Now, get Seamus on your mobile and see where he is. If he

doesn't pick up, then he has a few questions to answer."
Shaken, Jack retrieves his mobile from an inside pocket and punches a few buttons before putting the contraption to his ear. A few seconds elapse.
"Seamus, where the fuck are you?" Jack's voice, though low, probably sounds like a scream at the other end.
There's a pause when Jack, for my benefit, voices what he's being told. There's been a major accident on the Belfast road and he's been held up. Probably won't be here for another half an hour. I tap Jack on his shoulder to get his attention.
"Tell Seamus we've called off the meeting and are going back to Gatwick. Don't tell him what has just happened. Let him work it out for himself when he hears it later on the news. Apologise and say we'll meet up to have a drink some other time. If he is an astute operator, as you say he is, he'll understand the ramifications of all this."
Repeating to Seamus what I just said, Jack puts his mobile back in his pocket. "What do we do now?" His eyes are asking the same question.
"We're catching the next plane out of here, regardless of where it's going." I advise, looking at an illuminated overhead flight information board for any clues.
"Why, Clive? We're safe inside this place with all the security." Jack reasons well, but hasn't digested what will undoubtedly happen in a very short time.
"We're getting out of here before this becomes a crime scene and everybody, as witnesses, will be locked in to wait their turn to be interrogated. Well, I don't want to

be around when that happens, especially as I believe those two shots were meant to attract our attention and no-one else's."

Looking over Jack's shoulder I see what I'm looking for. Not believing my luck, an *easyJet* flight to Malaga is blinking its 'last call' message to board and will be closing shortly.

Running up to the flight desk, I leave Jack to make his own, not too hasty way over.

"Your flight to Malaga. Is there time to buy two tickets and get aboard?" I burst out my needs to a cheery looking face, who obviously appears totally unaware of what has just happened.

"You have left it late, sir, but due to a delay of ten minutes, I can fit you in if you hurry. May I take your names and passports?"

I look at Jack and give him a confident smile, but his face is solemn, even apologetic.

"I can't gallivant round the world like you, Clive. I've a wife at home who'll already be wondering where I am. I'll wait and get the one I'm booked onto later this afternoon. Don't worry about me. I'll be fine. If it comes to it, I'll give 'em any old bollocks they want to hear. Go on, you be off, but keep me informed with what happens. Good luck, mate." He puts an arm around my shoulders as a signal he's fine with the arrangement.

"It looks as though I'll be travelling alone, so just the one ticket, please?" I return my attention to the girl, decked out in the orange budget airlines livery.

Sucking in a lungful of free oxygen when she mentions the price, I hand over my debit card and passport, thinking this seemingly futile expedition has grown into a nightmare and is costing me a fortune.

"I'll just phone the gate to say you're on your way, but please be quick. They won't wait forever." She instructs, her smile never leaving her red lips.

I turn and embrace Jack for a second, but enough time to show gratitude. A last nod in his direction is greeted by the same before I run towards passport control, customs and the prescribed departure gate number.

~0~

Squeezed into row 14, seat A, on the 14.55 *easyJet* flight EZ6755 to Malaga, the aircraft's undercarriage releases its connection with the runway at near enough the same time as the proverbial manure begins to be distributed by an overzealous muck sprayer, down below on terra firma in the concourse of the Belfast airport.

Being on board, out of harm's way, gives me time to analyse what just happened at the airport. It was too much of a coincidence and I don't believe in them when it comes down to nearly losing my life from a shot released by the resurgence of the *IRA,* who might have mistaken me for someone else, not the same someone who might cause them trouble. No, those shots were definitely fired for my benefit, whether they missed on purpose just to frighten me off, or they were just bad marksmen, they sure did the trick. Not realising in my amateurish way that I'm getting close to disrupting their network, today's events evidently were a sign that

I'm certainly on the right track. But who put them onto me?

CHAPTER 25

7.14pm. Wednesday 19th August 2015. Tiffany's Bar (Fred's place) Estepona.

It's as though I've never been away when I enter Fred's bar. He's standing in his usual place by the *Amstel* beer dispenser, behind the pump washing a glass, with Teresa and Lawrence squatting on stools on the other side with Gus and Fiona making up the party. Behind them on banquette seating, that defies all logic how it supports anything other than a fly, Mac and Jackie are in semi-intoxicated discussion with a piss taking couple called Colin and Emma, admirably backed up by my mates from the Isle of Man, Pete and Sandra. No everything is normal, just how I left it.

"Hi Fred." I announce my arrival from the door.

Everybody turns to greet me in differing tones of welcome. Even Dutch Walter, all six feet six inches of him, manages to escape the swirling propellers of the ceiling fan situated no more than a cigarette papers width above his head to wave a greeting. Yes, I'm home.

"Clive...I need a word." A voice from behind the bar alerts me to Fred's intention that he wants to speak in private. Ollie's request for a half gets the response we've all grown to accept as the norm, 'fuck off, I'll be a few moments'.

Once outside, I relate, not in detail, but sufficient to whet his appetite, what happened in the UK, leaving out Belfast. If he knew about that, it would be all over town in minutes and probably back to the *Seafield's* landlord, Robbo, in Hove, within four minutes. No, there are certain times when he needs to know as little as possible.

I love this place just because there doesn't appear to be many pretentious arses pretending to be anything but themselves and that includes my Spanish buddies, and there are a few, who are content to leave me making a prat out of myself when attempting my version of an Andalusian conversation. I'm not good, but I know after four years I should be better.

I attempt to make small talk in the language I was taught from a baby with those in the bar who probably have downed a few more than me, but my mind won't allow me the privilege to relax. Was I nearly replicating Jessica's demise only hours before, with a bullet in my head? How did my travel plans get into the wrong hands? One thing is for certain, whoever is responsible has a close proximity to Debs, could even be in her office. So it narrows the search and is worrying.

On my way back to my apartment, I call into Fergusons/Andy's place for a nightcap and can't believe it's gone midnight when I finally arrive back home, the temperature unaltered since I left a couple of days ago, still hovering uncomfortably high in the 30's. I'm back in the town where it all began, Jessica's murder, and nine days of a seemingly personal crusade have passed where I've unearthed plenty of information, been shot at, but am no nearer to achieving a result, other than what I unearthed on the first day. I must be missing something but my copper's nose keeps telling me I'm not a million miles away from nailing the bastards. There are certain irregularities, but who is there to ask? Debbie has been brilliant and says she trusts Commissioner Gordon. Should I do the same? I don't know. But all this can wait until tomorrow. I'm totally and utterly whacked and need sleep, lots of it and I couldn't care a rats arse if the temperature reaches 40 degrees, I know as soon as my head touches the pillow, I'll be off in the land of nod.

CHAPTER 26

8.04am. Thursday 20th August. 2015. New Scotland Yard.

"Good morning Lorraine. Could you see if Chief Inspector Bronze is available? If he is, send a message for him to come up and see me. Thanks." Commissioner Gordon replaces the handset into its cradle, conscious of her off-handedness. Must be something to do with yesterday's debacle over her luncheon arrangement. Life's a bitch, he thinks and returns his attention to his *Oxfam* note book, a strange object he keeps under lock and key, knowing the scribbled data on the pages inside could be priceless. Striker would pull his hair out if he knew this is the file he so much wanted to put his hands on.

A solitary figure in an elaborate office, he attempts to put himself into Grainger's shoes...what might he be thinking to do next? He didn't even know where Grainger was or have the remotest idea how to contact him. But would that be in his remit concerning his 'police code of conduct'? Knowing Grainger, as his superior officer before he retired, Gordon knew his qualities, particularly the way his unusual brain had the ability to get results when all others floundered. He also knew Grainger trusted nobody. That will be his biggest problem. Will he trust Commissioner Gordon?

Just as his lips are about to welcome his first cup of coffee, his internal connection to Lorraine buzzes. "Yes Lorraine, what is it?"
"Sir, Director General Striker is on line one."
"Yes Paul, what can I do for you?" Feeling confident after yesterday's meeting, his day begins to crumble when he hears what's relayed into his ear.
"I don't know if this has any connection with you, Gordon, but our friends in Belfast appear to have taken a pot shot at somebody who'd just flown in from Gatwick yesterday lunchtime. Now, we are going through the passenger lists to see if we can identify that person, but as yet, have little to go on. What is interesting though, a passenger on that flight re-boarded an *easyJet* flight to Malaga twenty minutes later. Strange behaviour, don't you think? By the time we'd worked all that out, it was too late for the Spanish police to apprehend him at their end. He'd gone and disappeared into the ether. Does a Clive Grainger ring any bells with you? You could save us time if you know something about this? If not, sorry to have troubled you...Gordon...are you still there?"
The Commissioner knew Grainger was going to Belfast, but conveniently omitted to inform Striker, just as well he thought.
"Yes, I'm still here. Bloody contraption sometimes goes dead on me, sorry, er...in answer to your question, no, I can't help you on that matter."
Withholding evidence is one thing, but when you're the Commissioner of Police, the connotations of such an act, if found out, could be calamitous. He knows the

gloves are off and the time for prompt action is about to start.

“Lorraine, now I want you to do this discreetly and not allow yourself to be seen doing this by those on the floors below, contact Debbie Glynn and get her up here as soon as possible.”

“I'll do that, sir. Quite simple really.” Lorraine still hadn't forgiven the Commissioner for scuppering her anniversary lunch date with her husband, innocently unknowing the importance of such a request, her voice shows she isn't happy. “I'll simply text her on her private mobile; that is if she hasn't changed it. We have that information on all personnel working in the building...oh, just a sec...Chief Inspector Bronze has just walked into the office. Do you want to see him now?”

CHAPTER 27

8.26am. Thursday 20th August. Commissioner Gordon's office.

"Sit down Bronze. We have a big problem and it seems to be getting worse. Yesterday, at Belfast airport, Grainger was shot at. Thankfully he's okay and using his wits, immediately boarded a flight to Spain before security got their hands on the witnesses. Hopefully Glynn will be joining us shortly, but before she arrives, I want to know what you found out about O'Connell. I know I told you to leave it, but if you're half the copper I think you are, you'd have done it anyway. I hope I'm right?"

"Yes, you're correct in your assumption, Sir." Even a seasoned copper in the same mould as Bronzey sweats when he feels the weight of the hierarchy bearing down. "Regardless of your order, sir, both Glynn and I thought it prudent to proceed as it might prove to be a bit of insurance should things go wrong..." Bronzey is cut off in mid-sentence.

"Yes, yes, yes...I fully understand, but what did you find out?"

"Well, sir. It's very interesting. O'Connell was part of the Northern Ireland office, actually working at *Thames House*, when seconded into *MI5* some three years ago after the Irish moved out. By all accounts, when a

young lad, he had been an instrumental henchman within the *Ulster Volunteer Force.* When the *Good Friday* peace talks began, he was moved over to their political wing, the *Progressive Unionist Party*, not in the position of a diplomat, but purely to protect those who might still be targets of the *IRA*. It appears he became good at his job. When peace was reinstated, because of his knowledge of the *IRA*, he was brought over to London to liaise with *MI5*, they believed it was a ticking time bomb and only a matter of time before it erupted again. The rest is pretty much mundane stuff. He looks like he's genuine." Feeling a tad more relaxed than when he entered, Bronze sits back in his chair, confident there would be no recriminations at his disobeying an order.
"Thank you DCI Bronze. Good work."
Bzzzzzz..."Yes Lorraine."
"Debbie Glynn is here. Shall I send her in?"

~0~

"Well, you two. I find myself in a very precarious position. I lied to MI5, not once but twice, the second time being this morning when I found out from them that Grainger was shot at in Belfast." Before he continues, Debbie collapses in her chair, the words 'Oh my God no' gasping from her mouth.
"Quick, Bronze. Get her a glass of water." Gordon orders, leaping from his chair in support of Bronze's attempt to stop Debbie sliding to the floor.
"I knew that bastard was heading for trouble. I told him so many times to be careful. Jesus, is he hurt,

please don't tell me he's...dead?" Debbie looks at Gordon from her slouched position to confirm her worst fears.

"No Debs, he's fine and managed to escape back to Spain before the whole airport was shut down."

"What about his friend Jack who was with him. Is he okay?"

"Yes, he's also fine, the gunmen missed them both. But this is precisely why I sent for you. I wanted to take a back seat in all this, but now it's too serious and I'm heavily involved. I need to speak to Grainger and you are my only way to get in touch with him. I'm sorry to say this Debs, but it looks like someone clearly knew he was on that flight before informing the boys in Belfast. And it could be from here in this office. Why? I don't know." Leaning by Debbie's chair, Gordon hands her a glass of water.

Visibly shaking and in barely a whisper, she utters: "Holy fucking shit." Gordon and Bronze nearly trip over their own feet at Debbie's involuntary exclamation, ditching her normally cultured office phraseology. "There could be someone in the downstairs departments that knew Clive's plans, thanks to me."

CHAPTER 28

9.20am. Thursday 20th August. Commissioner Gordon's office.

I just sit there with my head reeling and guts somersaulting from the runaway train of emotions that have just smacked me from all directions in the space of 5 minutes - shock, fear, panic, relief, anger the list goes on, all the time with two sets of eyes boring down on me from what seems a great height - I can't think straight - Clive...SHOT at.

I deliberately hadn't contacted Clive yesterday, knowing he had this madcap rendezvous in Belfast. I spent an unremarkable hassle free day in the office, number crunching for Ingrid's report, enjoyed a *Pizza Express* free wine offer at lunch, catching up on boyfriend gossip with Naomi & Emma, yes, all was quiet and blissfully normal on the office administrative western front.

As Clive and I had parted company outside the *Paris Wine bar* the night before -

"Don't worry, Debs, it's just a meeting...everything'll be fine"...he'd said.

"Look, I'll call you if there's anything significant to report", he'd said.

REALLY! Well, which part of "I've been shot at" doesn't he think to be sodding significant? Just wait till I see him, on one hand I'd like give him a big hug with relief he's okay and unharmed, but on the other hand, I'd like to punch his bloody lights out.

More importantly, which sickens me to the pit of my stomach, is, if my very left field theory is to be confirmed, it could be entirely my fault he got shot at in the first place and could have been killed, as could have Jack, God, it just doesn't bear thinking about, and as for his fleeing back to Estepona - how's that going to protect him from whoever took a pot shot at him in Belfast, not doing the same down there? What's he going to do? Have there been armed guards posted outside *Fred's* bar and at either end of his sun lounger? I don't think so.

Bronzey and Commissioner Gordon snap me out of the maelstrom of thoughts whirring round my brain.

"Debs, are you alright?" Bronzey asks genuinely concerned.

"Yeah...sorry, was just in a bit of a state of shock there, thanks for the water, though I could have done with something slightly stronger, I know - way too early in the day, even by my shabby standards."

Bronzey looks relieved as I appear to be returning back to my normal self.

"She doesn't seriously mean that Sir." He suddenly says to the Commissioner, trying to defend me.

"No, she's absolutely right Bronze, I have a bottle of good brandy in that cabinet for such occasions...I don't believe in all that sugary weak tea nonsense... Debbie would you like a drop?"

"No Sir, honestly I'm fine, thank you all the same, I'll wait till lunchtime".

Bronzey shoots me another one of his looks, okay, not the most PC thing to say in front of the Commissioner, but hey, I'm sure he has had the odd tipple over lunch. He sits back at his desk.

"Alright Debs...you prefer that to Debbie? So what did you mean when you said just then about someone in this building may have been privy to Clive's plan?"

"Sir, Debs is fine...I do prefer that actually. Well, firstly can I just ask, before I share my thoughts with you, are we all assuming that news of Clive's intended trip was leaked from here in the office, or is it not entirely possible that Clive or his friend Jack could have said something to the wrong person themselves?"

"You have a valid point, Debs, and one that, yes, I have considered, personally I think it's unlikely, but will get further clarification when we've spoken with Clive. For the sake of argument, and unless proved otherwise, right now we keep the focus on the leak coming from within this factory's walls".

God, my hunch is so incredibly flaky that even *Kellogg's* wouldn't be interested, I have absolutely no shred of proof and there's, seemingly, no connection to Clive and his investigation whatsoever, but I could put a completely innocent senior officer in the frame - once again I assume my oh-too-familiar position of being between a huge rock and a very hard place.

Shit, shit, shit.

"Alright, Sir, other than you and Bronze, I told no-one of Clive's meeting, that I will swear to." I look at four eyes piercing mine and know they have to be told.

"On Tuesday when Clive called to update me, approximately 10 minutes before Lorraine called me up here to see you, I was sat at my desk, I didn't want to be overheard so I hung up and called him back from the printing/photocopying room. I had to do a print run anyway. When the call ended I turned back to the printer to collect the output and a senior officer was standing there in the doorway waiting speak to me. Now, I genuinely have no idea how long they were there for, nor do I know if they heard any bit of the conversation."

"Who was he, Debs?" Opening up his ever present notepad, Gordon smelt the waft of a significant piece of incriminating evidence about to reach his ears.

"He's a she, Sir...my superintendent Ingrid, and all she wanted was to ask me was if I was available for a quick drink after work. I can't believe she would have anything to do with any of this. It's all so very tenuous, but I've racked my brain and have to say that it's the only possible singular occasion where I could potentially have been overheard talking to Clive about the trip."

Silence fell in the office for what seemed an age while he made a few notes, Bronzey's jaw seemed to have just fallen to the floor looking at me wide eyed in disbelief as the Commissioner scribbled. I just shrugged at him.

"So did you go out for that drink Tuesday after work with her?" He asks.

"Yes, Sir, we went to *Balls Bros,* as we often do, and shared a bottle of *Prosecco.*"

"Just the two of you?"

"Yes, Julia from HR was invited but she had an exercise class so couldn't make it."

"And what did you both talk about? Did she ask you any probing questions at all?"
This is turning into a bloody interrogation. He'll get the tape recorder out next. The more this goes on, the more absurd it seems to me she overheard anything.
"No Sir, not at all, she subtly asked if Bronzey and I were anything other than work colleagues as we'd been spotted out together on numerous occasions."
At that, Bronzey nearly chokes on his water.
The Commissioner raises one of his eyebrows and almost smiles looking at the both of us. If the situation wasn't so serious it would be hilarious, with Bronzey and I sitting like naughty children in front of the Commissioner denying an office fling.
"No, don't worry Sir, we are absolutely not and I told her that, making some excuse about helping Bronzey with his expenses management. She continued to waffle on about the forthcoming dinner party she was planning with her mother and what would be the best dessert option. Then she asked my advice on Facebook etiquette, about accepting someone as a friend when you don't really want to. Look, it was complete stuff and nonsense, absolutely nothing out of the ordinary. I did wonder, though, whether she would use the opportunity to unofficially query me over the Jessica McGill search, which I know she knows about, but she didn't. I then left her to pay the bill so I could catch my train to meet Clive in Hove."
"Did you tell her you were meeting Clive?"
"No Sir, I said to her earlier at the printer that I could only join her for a quick drink as I'd arranged to meet a friend visiting from out of town back in Hove and left

it at that. She didn't probe as to who - I really do think we're barking up the wrong tree here."
He leaned back in his chair and looked up toward the ceiling.
"Yes, we could be and there's a huge 'why would she?' out there, but until I get clarification from Clive, Ingrid appears to be the only individual outside our little circle of trust who could have known what he was up to, all hinging, of course, on whether she did indeed overhear you in the first place." The Commissioner replies, though it's just possible he's thinking out loud.
"Now I need you to get hold of Clive and ask him to call me on this secure number - I want to speak to him, the sooner the better."
He writes a number on the back of a business card and passes it to me.
"I'll speak to him alright. There's the small matter of him being shot at and buggering off back to Spain and not telling anyone, to be discussed."
"Don't envy Clive that conversation, I can just picture him holding the phone at arm's length, whilst you eloquently rip his head off."
Gordon chuckles to himself then seriously addresses both me and Bronzey.
"Did either of you two see Ingrid yesterday?"
"Actually no, Sir, but that's not unusual, I had my head down most of the day, she could have been in her office, I just didn't see her."
Bronzey chipped in - "No, Sir, I was out in the morning and like Debs says, didn't see her in the afternoon."

He stands up and slowly walks around his office as Bronzey and I just watch him wondering what's going through his head.
"Hmm, interesting..." He quietly says to himself, more pacing, but stops finally and perches on the corner of his desk looking directly at me.
"You're quite chummy with Ingrid, aren't you Debs? What do you know about her personally, her private life, her family?"
"I wouldn't exactly use the term 'chummy' Sir, we chat for sure, normally she instigates it. I pay lip service of course, because she's the boss. Her private life? I don't know much, there's her husband Steve - nice enough chap, works in the city on the board of an Insurance company and he plays golf a lot, two young daughters, a mother, never heard her talk about any siblings. She lost her father a couple of months back, big old house in Hertfordshire, she likes to bake things and enjoys a G&T, that's about it I'm afraid." I reply.
"I want you to dig and find out as much as you can, very subtly of course, you are going to be my eyes and ears down there on the floor and that also goes for you Bronze. Keep everything peeled and come back to me with any information, no matter how trivial you may think it is - is that clearly understood you two?"
"Yes sir." We both say in unison.
"Thank you - you can both go now." He gestures towards the door and we are promptly dismissed.
We politely nod at Lorraine and make our way through the doors to the lift.
"Bronzey, this is doing my head in, what the fuck is happening around here? What started as a simple

name search has now spiralled completely out of control, I don't get what his nibs upstairs thinks we can possible 'dig up'." I say using the air quotes sign in the lift as we travel down to our floor.
"We've still got an unsolved murder in Spain, laughing boy gets shot in Belfast airport and now the preposterous suggestion that someone here has tipped off someone there to stop Clive sniffing about - it's mental - it can't be Ingrid, it's ridiculous. Come on, think about it Bronzey, she frets over a bloody meringue, her budget numbers, the mission statement and then, heaven forbid, she might even assist in the odd criminal case. What possible motive would she have to be involved in any of this shit?" I continue with my rant.
The lift doors open and Bronzey takes me to one side before we go on the floor.
"Just ring Clive. See what he has to say and try to stop over analysing. Okay? Leave that to me."
"Alright Bronzey, I'll call him, what are you doing at lunch?"
"Nothing so far, let's re-convene at 12.30 see you downstairs."
At that, we both go our separate ways to our desks.
I hadn't even logged on earlier when I got Loraine's call to hot foot it upstairs. I fire up the laptop, barely concentrating, check emails, usual crap, though two are from Ingrid, the first, a meeting request for 10am to run through the budget, obviously I'd missed that, the second reads..."Where ARE you? I need to see you in my office."

Bollocks - I can't go in there right now, I need to make that call first.

I grab my handbag and just as I'm about to make a dash for the lift, Ingrid approaches with a face like a slapped arse.

"You didn't accept my meeting request, nor have you come by my office. I checked with Steve (Baldrick) he said he briefly saw you come in this morning then you disappeared. When I send a request, I expect you to have the courtesy of responding either way. Where have you been? No one knows where you were." She tersely spits the words in my general direction.

"Look, sorry Ingrid, I've only just seen my emails, I...I..." Shit...think on your toes. Where the hell would you have gone?

"I had to go downstairs and help Nick find replacement film for his antiquated microfiche reader as he has no access to the online stationary catalogue. The machine being so old, it took a while to find."

God that was pathetic, but I think she bought it.

"Well you're here now, I have a conference call in 5 minutes for half an hour, be in my office at 11.30, if you can possibly spare the time and drag yourself away from matters of stationery."

"Yes of course, Ingrid, it would be my absolute pleasure" I respond with the sincerest smile I can muster, two can play the sarcastic game.

She glares at me - "Just make sure you do Debs." With that, she struts back to her cave.

I can see Bronzey peering over his monitor at me, I give the little finger & thumb phone sign and point downstairs.

Seeing her like that, perfectly normal behaviour, her going into officious bitch 'I'm the boss around here' mode, makes this notion that she had anything to do with Clive and Jack being shot at, all the more ridiculous.

I quickly text Nick.

'If Ingrid asks you if I was with you first thing this morning, just say yes you wanted microfiche film - thanks hun xx'.

I go downstairs and head out of the building, passing Alan on the way.

"You need to pack up that smoking Debs, but if you're passing the coffee shop can you pick me up one of those cappuccino frappe things, I'm roasting down here, the air con's packed up again."

"So there are advantages to my ciggie breaks then, alright I'll pick one up for you, get on to the maintenance guys about the air con."

"I have, Debs, but they said its low priority, actually, when you get back, could you do me a favour and call them, say something like one of the bigwigs complained how hot it was, they might listen and do something about it."

I need this like a hole in the head. "Okay Alan, as it's you, I'll see what I can do."

Outside the office, the smoking den is empty, I light a cigarette and dial Clive's number. Its midday in Estepona.

He picks up on the third ring.

"Ahh, Debs, I was just about to call you" I can tell when he's defensive and lying through his teeth.

"Were you really...well how spooky is that? Was it to tell me that, yes, you both enjoyed a pleasant flight to Belfast, yes, the onboard refreshments were to your satisfaction and yes you got fucking shot at in the airport?"

"Sorry, Debs, I really was going to call you today. I literally only managed to jump on a flight to Malaga before they would have shut the terminal. It was a long day and a mad one, as you can imagine".

"Can I remind you of your parting words to me - 'I'll call you if anything significant happens' - what, may I ask, in your world is the definition of the word SIGNIFICANT, as it clearly bloody differs from mine?"

"Alright, alright, Debs, I'll take the rollicking - now please stop with the shouty-shouty swearing at me. I'm fine by the way, bit shaken, thank you so much for asking and for your heartfelt concern."

Sarcastic bastard. I take a deep breath and a drag of my cigarette - he's right, screeching down the phone won't do any good, other than me just venting, notwithstanding I'm paying for this call.

"Look, I'm sorry Clive, I lashed out, it's just you really scared me, I was almost sick with worry and panic when I heard, which was incidentally in the office of my new best friend - the Commissioner. Think I'm now on his Christmas card list. I got called up as soon as I got to my desk this morning, Bronzey was already in there. Seriously though - how are you? It must have been terrifying."

"It wasn't the greatest airport experience I've ever had, but I'm fine now, just need to find out who and why someone or other wants to rattle my cage so much. How did Gordon know what happened?"

"I have absolutely no idea, but he wants you to call him on his secure line as soon as you can. I've got the number here...you got a pen? Or shall I message it to you?"

"No, don't text it, I'll write it down, hang on let me get a piece of paper...right, fire away"

I read out the number to him.

"There's something else, Clive..." I hesitate, oh God now I've got to drop the bombshell.

I look around making sure no one else is in earshot.

"Come on what is it, Debs, spit it out?"

"Okay, but please don't go ballistic, here's the thing. Gordon is convinced there was a leak somehow from this office or his peripheral departments, as to your movements concerning Belfast, assuming that is, that neither you or Jack dropped the proverbial bollock and let slip your plans. When I finished speaking to you on Tuesday from the printing room, Ingrid was waiting to talk to me, well, ask me to join her for a quick drink after work actually. I don't know how long she'd been there, I don't know if she heard anything and if she did, I can't see how she could possibly fit into any of this anyway. I told Gordon and Bronzey, expressed my views at how ludicrous the suggestion of her involvement was, and now, if you please, Gordon wants me to start poking around into her personal life. Fuck knows how I'm supposed to do that, then report back to him with any findings, this is madness."

The silence is deafening on the other end of the phone.

"Clive, are you still there? Don't give me the silent treatment, in fact now I implore you to go ballistic, at least I can deal with that...Clive?"
Eventually he sighs, then speaks in that crushing 'I'm so disappointed in you' pissed off tone that makes me want to crawl under the nearest rock.
"I asked you, Debs, if other than the four of us, did anyone else know of my involvement and plans - and you said no."
"Yes correct - to the best of my knowledge no one else did bloody know and as far as I'm concerned, the fact that Ingrid may, and I stress the word may, have overheard some bit of my conversation with you doesn't necessarily make her the spy in the camp you all seem to be so fixated on. Look, I didn't tell you because I didn't think it was relevant and I still don't for the record, but it's out there. Now I've fessed up to Gordon about the slimmest possibility I could have been overheard in the first place."
"So now you're defending her?"
I can tell he's in a right strop and I'm so heading the same way - this conversation is not going to end well, I feel it in my waters.
"I'm not defending her, Clive, I just don't believe she could have anything to do with this, I know the woman, you don't, I can't see any remote connection. We all agree someone clearly knew that you were going to Belfast and contacted some bad boys over there to scare you off this investigation of yours. With you and Gordon having bees in your bonnets that the mole is here in this building, I just don't think it's fair to try to pin it at Ingrid's door without a single shred of proof,

other than it was just me pointing the not-too-sure accusing finger. It smacks of desperately clutching at straws. The reality here is that you're clearly in danger, as much in Estepona as bloody Belfast, snipers can get on planes, you know. What really worries me is the focus from upstairs maybe shifting in the wrong direction and will hit a brick wall, all the time you're still a sitting duck until you drop this crusade."

His phone demeanour thankfully changes.

"Debs, I hear you and I didn't mean to snap, but I agree with Gordon, just see what you can find. Yes, of course this could lead to a dead end but let's eliminate her as soon as possible, facts are facts, whether you like it or not. Right at this moment she's the only person who may have known my movements. Now what about the Mark/Martin character...what did Bronzey find out?"

Ooh I hate it when he's right.

"Yes, I suppose you've got a point, I just don't like it one little bit and if I'm honest, I like even less the thought that you being shot at could unwittingly be my fault. I believe Mark/Martin is legit from what Bronzey briefly said, but I haven't really had a chance to catch up properly with him."

"Don't beat yourself up, Debs, just do as Gordon says, start digging...have you seen or spoken to her since yesterday?"

"I saw her on the floor just now before I came outside to call you, she wants me to go to her office at 11.30 about the budget, didn't see her all day yesterday. So...what's going on down there...? Anything?"

"Nothing that I know of at the moment, hey, I only got back yesterday. Look, I know you feel bad about all of this and it certainly could be getting a bit too close to home for your liking, but I want you to behave as normally as you can, be your usual acerbic self in the office. I'm sure you won't find that too difficult, now will you? And whilst you're going about your business, think and start to dig."

"Well, thanks for those pearls of wisdom, Clive, I will endeavour to do my utmost. One nagging thought that has just occurred to me, though, if someone's willing to take a warning pot shot at you, what's stopping them doing likewise to me, eh? Have you thought about that?"

"Now you're getting downright paranoid, Debs, stop even thinking like that. I'm the one they want to scare off, now you just be calm, be a good girl and go back in the building as if nothing's happened, let me know how your meeting with Ingrid goes. Call me back when you're at lunch, if you've anything to report."

Patronising bastard.

"Fine." I respond, knowing that ending a conversation with that particular word or the phrase 'yeah whatever' really irks him, and hang up - ooh another paranoid induced thought - could my phone be tapped? No that's ridiculous - he's right - stop it.

I saunter via *Starbucks* for 2 cappuccino frappes to take back to the office.

11 days ago, all was quite tranquil in my life, 11 days ago no-one was murdered, 11 days ago I'd never been hauled in front of the Commissioner, 11 days ago no one was shot at, 11 days ago the boss was just the boss and 11 days ago I didn't fear for Clive's, or my, life!

I hand Alan his frappe whilst yet again he insists I show him my pass - seriously!
Back at my desk, I have an idea as to how to snoop on Ingrid if I've really got to do it.
I ring Julia.
"Julia, its Debs, how was your Pilates class the other night?"
"It's great, Debs, felt positively invigorated, you should come along one evening, you'd love it, did you have a drink with Ingrid, she seemed quite desperate that someone should?"
"I'd rather eat my own entrails than go to a bloody pilates class, you should know that. Yes, I took one for the team and went, only for a while though, quick question for you..."
She butts in "Oh no...Debs don't ask me to look up anything dodgy again."
"No, no, no, nothing like that, don't worry...do you happen to know Ingrid's maiden name?"
"Weird question, Debs, why don't you ask her yourself? But I do, as it happens, we had a conversation once about the palaver she went through when she got married, of having a different surname on her birth certificate to that on her passport. She adopted her stepfathers name for an easy life when her Mum remarried, years ago when she was a kid. It's Simpson, why'd you want to know?"
"It's a *Facebook* thing she was talking about the other night, I thought I'd go and have a peek."
"Why don't you just friend her?"
"I don't think I can and I really don't want to either, can you imagine, there's me with the usual suspects

enjoying a Sunday afternoon drink on the seafront or in the pub, honestly, some of my friends are obsessed with posting anything from what they eat to who they're with - I come in Monday morning not feeling entirely chipper and get that look from her as she's seen what I've been up to - I so don't think so."
"Yeah, she's the boss, I get that - fancy a drink this week after work?"
"Okay, I'll give you a shout - maybe tomorrow if you're not out doing samba or pole dancing lessons. Is this all for Phil's benefit at the Christmas party?"
"Fuck off Debs, you can be such a nasty piece of work sometimes...see you tomorrow."
"Ha ha...cheers Julia."
Right, quick call to Jon - head of maintenance
"Jon...Debs here, do me a favour, can you get one of your boys to look at the air con in reception, I was up with Commissioner Gordon earlier and he mentioned how hot it was down there, not great if we have visitors who have to sit there for any time."
"Oh shit, I'll get them onto it, it's normally just Alan that moans, but thanks for the heads up."
"Thanks Jon, appreciate it mate" Job done.
I get yet another copy of the updated budget pack and head to Ingrid's office.
Her door's ajar, I lightly knock and she invites me in to sit. "Right Debs, we need to nail these budget figures."
"I worked on the seasonalisation most of yesterday, as it happens." I drop the pack on her desk. "Here they are, but as I said before, it doesn't matter how we pretty them up, the end result is an 8% cut across the board.

I would have discussed with you before preparing the pack, but you weren't around that I could see."
"Touché, Debs - not that it's any of your business, I was actually working from home yesterday."
'Shirking' from home more like.
"What? Waiting indoors for your *Ocado* deliveryman from *Waitrose* to arrive with the nosh to feed your weekend guests?"
"Don't be so bloody cheeky, I had some work to do that couldn't really be done in the office, come on let's go through and finally sign these numbers off - deadline's tomorrow."
At that, we spend the next twenty minutes or so finalising the report. I'm looking for any unusual signs or questions from her, but there are none forthcoming. No, she's acting perfectly normal, confirming what I think regarding her involvement, but what was the pressing work that she couldn't do in the office I wonder?
Back at my desk, got half an hour before meeting Bronzey for lunch.
I get my *iPad* out of my bag, open it up and tap the Facebook app, ignoring the predictable drivel on my newsfeed involving cute looking pets doing odd things, people 'checking in' to bars, pubs, restaurants, various annoying drunk selfies, friends putting 30+ photos of holiday cocktails and beaches, posts involving inspirational motivational messages for you to share and receive love and world peace - what a load of old bollocks!
I tap on the search banner and key in Ingrid's maiden name - let's see what comes up.

Most married women sign up to Facebook using their maiden name, just in case someone they may have gone to school/uni with or may have snogged at the 6th form disco, want to connect with them.

The search throws up many with the same name from around the world, but the second Ingrid Simpson looks to be favourite, the profile photo looks like her, albeit an old one, so she looks younger, even glamorous - 'lives in' Hertfordshire.

Right, open the page, tap on 'about' - yes definitely our Ingrid. Tap on 'photo's' - the usual collection of the kids at varying stages of age, holiday snaps, Steve and hers' anniversaries, Christmas day table and tree etc., etc., etc..

Tap on 'friends' - bless her, she hasn't got many in Facebook terms - 56.

I scroll down them all, chuckle when I see Margaret Simpson, she obviously caved it and accepted her mother's friend request.

Whoa, stop the fucking clock - what's this? There is the unmistakable face of Shelly McGill.

I stare at the screen, how the fuck can those two be *Facebook* buddies?

I tap on Shelly's 'about' 'page. She hasn't put much on, other than she lives in London, nothing about work, same as Ingrid. 'Relationships' - 'It's complicated' why do people put that? It smacks of either you're in relationship you hate, just about to get dumped or having an affair, either way why would you want to share that with the masses? Her photos equally don't glean much. Will look a little closer at them later.

I look up her 'friends' certainly more than Ingrid's, but recognise no one, again this needs to be scrutinised later.

So there is a connection, but what is it? Okay, so she was at Ingrid's barbeque hanging around Mark/Martin and Phil, but in what capacity? - I just haven't a bloody clue.

I need to run this by Bronzey and Clive.

Jesus, this could change everything or it could be nothing, too much of a coincidence though, methinks.

12.25pm, best go and meet Bronzey downstairs before he gets the hump.

Alan, in a heightened state of excitement rushes up to me as I pass through the security barrier and almost hugs me - "They're fixing it this afternoon, Jon called me - thanks so much Debs."

"No probs, I'll remind you of this next time I leave my pass at home, Alan."

Bronzey and I walk in silence to *Balls Bros.* Once at his usual table, he orders a white for me and a red for him, not bothering to look at the menu, 2 sandwiches and a bowl of honey mustard cocktail sausages.

"Well...that was one hell of a start to the morning Debs, wasn't it? What did Clive have to say when you spoke to him?"

"You first Bronzey, what did you find out about Mark/Martin?"

He recounted his conversation with Gordon on what he'd unearthed before I arrived.

"So, he's not really a suspect then, working alongside Phil?" I say.

"Looks that way, come on what news from Clive?"

Our wine turned up, I so need this.
I ran through the gist of the call with him plus my uneventful meeting with Ingrid.
"Bronzey, I think I may have made a very loose connection between Ingrid and the case."
"Really??" He wipes his moustache of Merlot and looks at me intently.
"I had an idea, and searched Facebook for Ingrid, a long shot I know, but I found her under her maiden name and one of her 'friends' is Shelly McGill."
"Jesus Christ - how on earth did their paths cross? What else did you find?" - He looks genuinely stunned.
"Beats me and not a lot so far, I literally only just discovered the link between the two of them about 10 minutes ago."
"So you haven't told Clive or Gordon yet?"
We simultaneously drink more wine as our sandwiches are brought to the table, not that I'm remotely hungry.
"No, obviously not, Bronzey, given I spotted it 10 minutes ago as I said, but I think I should call Clive first, he's met Shelly a couple times in Spain and may know more about her background, would you agree?"
"Good idea, why don't you go outside and do it now, I'll order us a couple more glasses."
"Okay - let's see what he says."
Outside, I go round the corner, off the main pavement and out of the way of the hordes of people rushing about in their lunch hour.
2pm in Estepona, dial Clive
Hoorah, he picks up on the first ring.
"Hi, Debs, how'd it go with Ingrid?"

“I’ll tell you in a minute, I’m just out with Bronzey, Have you called Gordon yet?” I reply
“No, was about to actually, come on what’s happened?”
“Right, the meeting with Ingrid was completely unremarkable, a genuine budget discussion, nothing suspicious to report whatsoever. Now listen, I’ve been doing a bit of digging as you all requested and have just found on Facebook a connection between your gal Shelly and Ingrid, they’re friends on it.”
“Debs what exactly does that mean?”
“Fucking hell, Clive, you seriously do live in a different era, I really would have thought you’d have a sliver of social media knowledge, evidently not. Bottom line is that they somehow know each other.”
“You sure you know that for a fact, Debs?’
“Yes, it’s out there on bloody *Facebook*, I did a search using Ingrid’s maiden name to see whether she was on there in the first place, and, if she was, could I find anything of interest in her personal life.
“So, what happens is, one of them has to invite the other to connect and be a ‘friend’ and the other has to accept the request. That’s how it works. Do you understand that Clive?”
“No, not entirely, but I’ll bow to your superior expertise on the matter. I just want the facts, don’t try to confuse me with how you came by them on these sites. This is really interesting, well done Debs good work, I’m presuming you have no idea how these two are acquainted?”
“High praise indeed coming from you matey, thanks! No, not a clue, I only discovered the link about half an hour ago, Bronzey and I both agreed I should call you

first. I think I need to poke around some more to see what I can find, if anything, before throwing the cat among the pigeon's taking it upstairs, what do you reckon?"

"If something turns up I'd prefer you didn't take it to Gordon, but first allow me to digest the evidence. Then I'll decide what to do with it. In the meantime I'll give Gordon a ring, see what he wants. You and Bronzey carry on sleuthing over the net and enjoy your lunch. Keep in touch."

"Cheers, Clive, by the way Bronzey is about as clued up as you are on the social media front. So, the whole of this sleuthing thing will be down to little ole me then, won't it? Okay, talk to you soon. You just go on enjoying your sunbed."

I return to Bronzey and, true to form, he's ordered and there's another large glass of Pinot Grigio waiting on the table.

"Well...what did Clive have to say?" He asks

"He's going to make that call to Gordon, he suggests we, or more specifically I, dig around some more on this Shelly link before we go anywhere with it."

"Sounds like a plan, Debs, lets drink to that."

CHAPTER 29

2.15pm. (Spanish time) Thursday 20th August. Paco's Chiringito, Estepona Beach.

Sitting at a table on a wooden planked patio connected to the busy *Chiringito,* under an oversized white umbrella, infested with logos advertising *Cruzcampo* lager, is probably not the ideal location to make the call to Gordon, but as I got the call from Debs only minutes before, I'm not shifting my sweating torso back out into the sun to relocate somewhere more private. Nonchalantly peering over my shoulder to those sitting in close proximity, it appears English is not their mother tongue...so no...I'm not moving. I'll take the gamble they're not interested in what I have to say anyway.

A napkin, wedged under an ashtray, displays Gordon's scribbled number, but I need time to digest how I want this conversation to proceed. For all I know, I might be speaking to the very culprit I'm attempting to dislodge. This is going to be delicate, to say the least. Trust, what a strange word. In one sense, faith and conviction come readily to mind, but the literal meaning can also describe a consortium or cartel, exactly how I would describe the *IRA*. Though I believe I know this man well, it's been four years since I had any dealings with him and during such a period, who knows where his allegiance might have wandered. Easy money, especially when closing in on retirement, can cloud judgement and persuade even the most loyal to jump ship. I need to be ready...I'm ready.

Punching in the number, I put the mobile to my ear and wait. Strangely, I feel my heart-rate quicken. Very unlike me. On the other end, a landline ring tone repeats itself three times before a voice breaks the monotony.

"Commissioner Gordon...who is this I'm talking to?"

"Afternoon Commissioner...it's Clive Grainger. You wish to speak to me." I return his serve, putting him in the prime position to begin the match.

"Clive, good of you to get in touch. Debbie has obviously spoken to you. From conversations I've had with her and DCI Bronze, I'm now more in the picture on what you've been finding out down there in Spain and here in the UK. I must admit that I was sceptical with your initial theories, but coincidences of this nature don't happen and with you being targeted in Belfast, well, it has convinced me there is every possibility we have an informer amongst us here at the *Yard* or at *Thames House*."

I listen intently to him talking like a copper, not relaxed, being too businesslike and all in the same space of time it took for a milky-white newcomer to the sun to dash past me, marking his trail by offloading large droplets of water in every direction, believing it to be all very hilarious having only seconds before been fully submerged in the Mediterranean.

"Oh...thank you...you arse." I shout, leaving the stranger in no doubt as to how I consider his generosity.
"Sorry...what was that Clive...are you thanking me...or...?"
"No Commissioner. Not you...I was giving some other idiot a piece of my mind." Oh shit, that didn't come out right.
"Well..." He replies, but I'm not entirely convinced he's happy with my flippant analogy. "As I was saying, I believe we should work together to wheedle out this mole. And please believe me, you have my word that anything that is said shall be deemed to be secret and only shared between the four of us. But I believe it's important that we meet as soon as possible to thrash out what we should do next. Can we do that, Clive?"
I'm not liking this one bit. Now he wants to see me and a meeting doesn't really go along with my plans. If I'm to believe his integrity, and that's a big 'if', should there be a whiff of his cooperation reaching the wrong ears, all my delving into his murky world could spell real danger for those on my side. I'm not worried about me, I can look after myself and that goes for Gordon and Bronzey. They face threats in some form or another every day. It's part of their job. No, it's Debbie who I worry about, especially now. Whoever is responsible has additional evidence that she's an integral part of this investigation. Take her out of the equation and I'm sunk and they must know it.
"Clive...are you still on the line?"
"Sorry, Commissioner...I...er...yes, I'm pondering on your suggestion and I don't think it's such a bright

idea. Look, allow me to work on this my way and if we talk in future, I'll figure a way of getting in touch. Oh...and by the way. Just on the off-chance, did you happen to talk to anyone concerning my trip to Belfast."

Gordon sat in silence for a second or two before remembering, but he was loathed to admit the fact he surreptitiously checked Grainger's flight times and who might be his travelling companion. "I did phone Gatwick to find out what flight you were on."

"No, Commissioner...you wanted the name of who I was with."

I press the end-of-call button leaving him hanging on to my last word. Maybe I've just severed my best link for information, but I need to be certain when I receive it, it hasn't been fiddled about with to purposely lead me down another garden path. God, am I getting paranoid?

I press Debs' recall number and wait, at least what I'm going to ask her might keep the Commissioner on my side after I just royally snubbed him, that is, of course, if he's Kosher.

"Hi Debs. Look, can you do me a big favour? I've just spoken to Gordon and I'm not entirely convinced he's happy with the way the conversation went. It might have gone better." I can see her cringe as she pictures the consequences that what I said might have on her personal future within the *Yard*. "Could you go to *Tesco* and buy a cheap, pay-as-you-go mobile and put twenty five quid's worth of time on it, then send me its number. Don't worry, I'll reimburse you. It is imperative that nobody witnesses you handing it over to Gordon, so no direct contact. Also, don't put it in the post, as a parcel will be security checked before it arrives on his desk. Debs, this is very important. I know I can trust you to find a way of getting it to him. The next time I speak to Gordon, I don't want it to be on a landline or on his own personal mobile."

"Bloody hell, Clive, you don't trust anybody. I hope you're not putting me into that category?" Debs' response is exactly what I expect.

"No girl, you are the only one I DO trust. Will you do that for me?"

~0~

I know I annoyed and rattled the Commissioner's cage, but that was my intention. I don't want to make friends or solve other people's problems. Camouflaged behind a uniform, displaying an array of pips, insignia and ribbons of bravery to bolster all the pomp and circumstance attributed to his rank of office, Gordon knows the buck will finally stop at his door, regardless of the outcome, and I don't intend to be his stool pigeon should it all go belly up. No, he can help, but only on my terms.

I place the mobile back onto the table, next to my empty glass and attempt to attract attention for a refill. It's nearing lunchtime and *Paco's* is filling up, but I'm content sitting alone in a space which could cater for four, despite getting obvious stares from one of the sisters who owns the place to move to a smaller table. Okay, I get her drift, but why doesn't she just get me another beer instead of making me feel I've just killed her pet cat?

My attention is distracted as I wave and get a return blown kiss from Mette, a rather scrumptious Danish lady artist, who has found a vacant table a little way off from mine to sit with her friends. It seems to surreptitiously slide up to you and is a devil of a job to shake off, this feeling of pure laziness, whereby, when anything is thrown at you, your first reaction is to duck and consider the consequences tomorrow. I could very easy be enveloped and sink into the little rascal's arms, forgetting the last two weeks and go back to a mundane, stress-free existence. What am I thinking about?

The murder, or should I say assassination, of a high powered, ex-deputy director of *MI5*, has ruffled but few feathers outside the town limits of Estepona. Had it occurred in central London, all hell would have broken loose, with the strong arm of the entire workings of *New Scotland Yard* put on red alert. I've been shot at in Belfast and still it appears these separate but connected crimes are considered sufficiently inconsequential to merit deep investigation by supposedly the UK's finest detectives. Only Commissioner Gordon, in his figurehead-like position, appears to be taking me seriously, but what if he's part of the problem? I would have thought *MI5* would be seeking answers and it would be unforgivable if they weren't. Surely they'd been liaising with Gordon, but why hasn't either of them let me know? There must be a clue to follow, no matter how flimsy, concerning culprits and reasons why this atrocious episode

unfolded here in Estepona. For fuck's sake, won't somebody tell me? I feel I'm attempting to climb a hill with my feet firmly encased in buckets of custard.
I know the players in this game and also have proof of who Jessica was and why she fell to a terrorist's bullet. I am also sure, well 99% sure, that there is a spy somewhere in *Thames House* or at the *Yard.* My money is on the *Yard,* though yet again I have no proof. Damn you Gordon. You know so much more, but you're keeping it away from the person who could put it to good use...me. He's offered to talk, but should I listen to a version he wants me to act upon? I want facts and I can do without being his personal accomplice just to cover his incompetent backside.
Should I try and contact the Director of Homeland Security himself at *Thames House*? It can't be that difficult to get a number with my contacts. It would certainly ruffle a few more feathers. Why not? I've got nothing better to do today than drink beer on a beautiful, sandy beach, surrounded by a bevy of flimsily attired females all disrobing to the tune my old mate in the sky...the sun, is playing. Nothing will probably come of it, but I'll give it a go.

~0~

"Hi Debs. Sorry to disturb your lunch. Is Bronzey still with you?" I ask, knowing full well he is.
"Why do you ask?"
She's putting up an early fireguard, I can tell.
"Oh...he might have a telephone number I'm looking for, also a name." I make my reply sound as

nonchalant as my acting career allows, meaning, I know she'll smell a rat.

"Oh...and who might that person be?"

She's mimicking me with a dollop of her usual sarcasm. "The guvnor of *MI5.* Why do you ask? I don't suppose you have it hanging around do you?" I respond keeping to the script.

"Well, lardy-arse, I'll consult my psychic power and see if I've logged it under 'Names and numbers an arsehole might be asking for in future'."

I can see her now whispering to Bronzey with a hand over the mobile, asking him if he has it.

"If you intend to get up his nose, then by all means call him guvnor, but his rightful title is Director General Paul Striker. Have you a pen somewhere shoved down your *Speedos* to take down his number?"

The time has long gone since when I was first introduced to one of her *Pinot Grigio* enhanced responses and judging by this one, I would say she's through three glasses and working on her fourth. Impressed by her lack of using any word which might offend a vicar's ear, I do as directed and get a pen from Anna, a waitress, before scribbling down the number on a napkin.

"Thanks for that, Debs. I'll just try and squeeze the pen back into its hidey-hole, but there doesn't seem to be a lot of room down there, even for such a small object." My teasing opens the floodgates to be countered.

"Urck...that's a disgusting mental image, Clive, now fuck off."

Yes, I thought it was too good to last as her line goes dead.

CHAPTER 30

4.28pm. Thursday 20th August. Clive's Apartment, Estepona.

What I'm about to do next would be the worst action a serving police officer could take, going over the head of his commanding officer, but I've been a long-time departed subordinate, unshackled from procedure or governed by any such-like protocol. No, Commissioner Gordon, you're still on my radar and if anybody is going to scupper my plans for a future of peace and contentment, it isn't going to be you. An assortment of nagging doubts continually pop in and out of my brain, but the one which continues to rise to the top could be the result of the culprit's first mistake.

MI5, with all their professional wisdom, had no idea of my involvement, until my name must have been bandied about after they checked the passenger list of the plane that had just landed in Belfast, only to find I was aboard another, heading in the direction of Malaga, twenty minutes later. It wouldn't take the mercurial investigative powers of *Sherlock Holmes,* just basic police work to decipher I might have been the guy responsible for causing a major disturbance in a public place. So, calculating two and two must be four, if *MI5* only knew of my existence after such an ordeal and not before, I can safely assume the mole couldn't have got his/her information regarding my Irish trip from *Thames House.* Which tells me, I'm correct to assume my target must be housed up in the *Yard.* And if this is the case, only a handful knew of my plans to visit Belfast. I'm narrowing down the suspects, but it's the all-important proof which, for the moment, escapes me on how I'm going to get it.

Should Debs be successful in getting the mobile phone to Gordon, without attracting attention, at least it's a start. My trust must ultimately fall on the Director General of *MI5.* The fact our paths have never crossed is a plus, as he doesn't know me, though he's probably flicked through my file by now. And I doubt if he's shown his hand by mentioning me to Gordon, but even if he did, I doubt he'd get much out of the old bugger. Knowing the Commissioner, if he was the bad guy, he'd want to bury me away from prying eyes, but if he turned out to be straight, he'd want me for himself, to claim all the plaudits when I solve the case. No, I'm going to enjoy this verbal jousting match, because if I'm to be successful, that's what it's going to be.

I sit on my terrace with a cold beer and a packet of *Superkings* at the ready, whilst I punch in the numbers. Very efficient, only one ringtone before I hear a female voice telling me I'm through to *Thames House* and her name is Janet. Very business-like, but friendly, not what I expect. In the marble-halls of homeland security, I anticipated being greeted by a Miss Fanny Double-barrelled-residing-in-Hampshire sounding surname.

"Good Afternoon Janet. My name is Clive Grainger, you might want to make a note of that. I would like to be put through to Paul Striker, the Director General. Thank you."

"I'm afraid, Mister Grainger, all calls to the Director General have to go through his office. Stay on the line, I'll put you through. Good-day."

All very business-like and I like her professionalism.

"Good Afternoon, Sir, I understand you would like to be put through to the Director General?" Oh why do they keep giving him this cumbersome title to reinforce his importance?

"Yes." I answer, swallowing an initial reaction to voice my hate for pumped up pomposity. "I would very much appreciate you putting me through, thank you." I put the ball back into his court. This, I feel, is not going to be straight forward.

"If you would give me your name, I'll see if he is free."

You have my name already...oh, I see your game. Trying to put a trace on to see where this call originates from and probably recording it. Okay, I'll play along.

"It's Grainger...Clive Grainger, but you already know that. If the Director General knows I'm on the line, I believe he'd want a word with me. So please, just put me through." Oh, you confident bastard, I say to myself.

The line goes quiet for a few seconds and I can't believe it when the silence is broken by a few chords of *Vivaldi's Four Seasons* before a voice abruptly replaces a high pitched violin solo.

"Mister Grainger. How good of you to get in touch. I was wondering if we would ever get to talk. You have been a busy boy down there in Estepona, haven't you?"

"Look, you haven't introduced yourself, so I take it I'm talking to Striker. And please realise, Paul, I'll give you as much respect as you give me, so let's cut this sarcastic crap. I'm not part of your set-up, nor am I with the *Yard* anymore, so we talk on a level playing field with none of this cap doffing rubbish. Agreed?" I feel better getting it off my chest before the conversation continues, that is, if he allows it.

"Good, I like frankness and I feel I can work with someone of your past experience. As I said, I'm pleased you got in touch, as you have probably worked it out by now, we have serious issues with homeland security in the shape of a mole within our midst. I take it you've talked to Gordon?" I listen and he's saying the right words to relieve me of any doubt that this is a man I might be able to trust. He is the Director General of MI5, for God's sake.

"Yes, I have, but forgive me when I say, although he's protecting a uniform and a position, I'm afraid he is still very much on my radar as a possible culprit. You might say, I don't believe I'm on his Christmas card list at present." I might have just said something I'd regret in future, but let's hear the response. He laughs. A good sign.

"Yes Clive, I know what you mean about dear old Gordon, but I think you can be sure he's not who we are after. No, his heart is in the right place, but sometimes I wonder if it's situated up his arse." It's my turn to laugh before he continues. "Just to confirm privacy, you're on a mobile, phoning from Spain and I can confirm my line is also clean, so feel free to talk."

Just as I thought, they're attempting to track me, but I basically begin at the beginning, reciting what I gleaned from Fred on that fateful day, followed by my meeting with Leonid, though I don't give a name to this source of information. I'm probably telling him stuff he already knows, the *Grand Hotel* bombing and the wiping out of three *IRA* terrorists in retaliation. The shooting of three more of their associates in Gibraltar, disguised in the press as an attempt to bomb a regimental parade, rather than letting it be known their orders were to assassinate Jessica. And my unease with having an Irish poacher turned gamekeeper snooping around the *Yard* with a Deputy Commissioner acting as a chaperone. A nagging disbelief, though everything conveniently points to her having some sort of involvement, that an unassuming Superintendent who's more concerned with the quality of barbequed spare ribs, can seriously be in the frame. The daughter of the deceased who went out of her way to put me off the scent, not to mention her apparent friendship with the said chaperone and his mate, who for some reason turned up at Jessica's funeral. But I say, just to endorse the distance I've travelled with this investigation, "you should know all about Shelly McGill, as she works in your department". A further ten minutes pass while I finally finish my monologue with the episode in Belfast, though I do point out, if they wanted me dead, I'm sure my brains would have been splattered across the walkway, instead of a million shards of tempered glass. I wait for a response. "Look Clive, I won't bullshit you. What you just told me is very interesting and we knew most of it, but not all. Look, I need to put a face to your voice. I'm catching the seven o'clock flight out of Gatwick to Gibraltar tomorrow morning. This is too important and delicate to drag on. We need to catch the culprit quickly. Will you pick me up from the airport? I promise I won't have a sniper waiting outside for your arrival." Striker laughs, but it doesn't register with my humour. I wonder if he's ever been shot at.

"If you think it's necessary, of course I'll be there, but don't expect a limousine or anything like it. Remember I'm a poor, retired copper."

"Oh, save me the sob story. I've seen your pension pot and a single bloke can have a very nice retirement on what you get, not to mention the healthy inducement to get you off the payroll early." There's humour in his voice, but he's just let it slip, he's been through my file with a fine tooth comb.

"I'll pick you up at ten thirty, Spanish time. See you tomorrow. But how will I recognise you?"

"Don't worry about that." His humour evaporates. "I'll recognise you."

Of course he will. I bet he has my mug shot in front of him as we speak.

CHAPTER 31

10.43am. Friday 21st August 2015. Gibraltar International Airport.

Believing I was in good time, as the *easyJet* flight from Gatwick hardly ever arrives on schedule, there was no need to put the accelerator to the floor of my 'antique', little Japanese four seater, a car smothered in fine sand blown over from the Sahara, visual proof that I don't use it that often. A quick swish with the rear and front wipers give me sufficient vision, but, to emphasise my timekeeping misjudgement, I mistakenly take the scenic route down to Gibraltar, rather than go via the motorway, arriving at the Spanish/Gibraltar border where there are no hold-ups with either set of custom officials and I easily locate a parking space on the airport's concourse.

That was the good part.

Now, as I unravel myself from behind the steering wheel...horror...I can see, from the side of the terminal building, the orange tail-fin of an *easyJet*. The fucking thing has got in early. Oh shit. I twist round and scan the exit for someone who I have no idea what he looks like. There are people emerging dressed in an array of attire, wheeling all sizes of luggage, but my eyes settle on one figure who's staring at me.

His tie is loose with the top two buttons of his shirt undone. Both sleeves are rolled up to elbows and his jacket is flung over a right shoulder, obviously not dressed for the weather. I don't know what image I expect to see from this character, *'M'* of *MI6*, but this one certainly doesn't resemble *Judi Dench* or *Ralph Fiennes*.

My shorts, vest and flip-flops are in stark contrast to his clothing as I stride purposely towards him, my right hand pointing to my watch, as if to say...well, I don't really know what I mean, but, by hunching my shoulders, I hope he's getting some sort of message.

"Mister Striker, I presume." I greet my guest with an outstretched hand. Thankfully, he reciprocates.

"Mister Grainger...good of you to make it, at last."

He's not a happy bunny. I am about to offer excuses, but then again, why?

"Look, we seem to have got off on the wrong foot, so why don't I drive you to a nice little place up the coast where we can get a drink and hopefully some privacy. And to bypass all the formality, it would be better if I call you Paul." Now I am stretching his patience, but I forget, he possesses a sense of humour.

"Only if I can call you Clive."

I smile and in turn, notice he does likewise. The ice is broken.

~0~

Inside my little jalopy, the heat soars, but with the windows down and sunroof open, a sense of normality is restored as I head northward, retracing the coastal route I made going south only fifteen minutes earlier.

"I haven't been to this part of the world for years." Striker breaks the silence. "With Misses Striker choosing the Caribbean every year for our holidays, I'd forgotten how beautiful it is down here."

I glance to my side and see him with a faint smile on his face, his eyes closed and his nose pointing up, breathing in fresh, uncontaminated air. He's enjoying the experience and if I'm not mistaken with my initial assessment, he's just a normal bloke.

We reach our destination some ten miles up the coast at a place called Chambao, Sotogrande, where I park the car.

"It's only a short walk to the beach club, but with the way you're dressed, it might appear longer and you'll certainly need a beer when we get there." I mention looking back to him following along a narrow line of duck-boards leading to the upmarket *Chiringito*. He in turn stares back at me, as if to say, are you doing this on purpose?

We settle at a table, under a large umbrella, and fortunately, though still high season, there are only a few other customers. Perfect surroundings to have our little chat.

"This is a nice place, Clive, good choice." He says, taking in the vista, his eyes unaware of my copper's nose weighing up the person and his personality.

I must not forget he has one big advantage over me and that is, he's seen my file and knows everything about me, whereas, I know absolutely nothing about him. I would say he's about my age and medium height, with

a good head of un-greying hair and the persona more of a school teacher rather than a grade one civil servant.
“Right, where do you want to start?” I initiate the conversation on why he is here.
“I’m interested to discover how you know about the *Grand Hotel* bombing and the consequences of what followed.” His voice is low, but sufficient for me to pick up every syllable. “It would have been before your time in the force and I do believe it hasn’t been documented in print in such fine detail as you related to me...so how do you know?”
Nonchalantly, as he empties half the glass of ice chilled *San Miguel,* my attention is confused for a second regarding the importance and secrecy on how I obtained this information. Oh, he’s good and it’s easy to underestimate the power he holds, bequeathed to him by the present Home Secretary of Her Majesties Government.
“Look Paul, I was a good copper.” How many times do I have to keep convincing people of that fact? “And worked under high ranking officers, some of which shouldn’t have been given the privilege. Yes, I didn’t always go by the book, but I got results by knowing the right people to ask, when the hierarchy within the force might consider them the wrong people. I’m not apologising for the way I did things, so if this is an interrogation about how I get my information, I’m afraid you’ll be disappointed.”
“No, Clive, I’m not interrogating you, it’s just what you told me is so hush hush, I’m fascinated to know how you got to know...nothing more. And then, maybe, we

can put our heads together to try and wheedle out our mole, because I believe you are more informed than my lot back at *Thames House*. That is why I'm here."

He's not stupid and allows me time to think. Eventually, and I know I've thought this through on many occasions, I reason it's time I trusted someone, and who better than the Director General of *MI5*. I relate the entire story but leave out names, though it probably wouldn't be too hard to trace a person if you have the resources of Striker's office to look into the names of the 'chargé d'affaires' in London's Russian Embassy during the period I quoted.

"How did your friend know all this?" Striker is eagerly inquisitive, shifting his weight so that he now sits on the front edge of his chair, not daring to miss a spoken word.

"Because they had spies within your fabled organisation. When you got rid of *Burgess, MacClean* and the others, they just shipped in some fresh faces whilst you were all slapping each other on the back, saying it could never happen again and how clever you were in uncovering their network. Well, you are so wrong. How do I know? Because my dear old friend kept diaries during his entire tenure within the embassy. He thought, in some way, his secret written word might act as an insurance policy for a safe life in the UK. He knew he couldn't return to Russia, because the old country, the place he was born in, wasn't there anymore. Putin's revolution put paid to that. He was happy to live here with a loving wife and bring up his daughter in a western regime. I believe he's been proved right for thinking in such a manner."

"Are you telling me, there might be some of his boys' active in my department?"
"You're saying 'might', I'm saying I'm bloody sure there are, but that's another problem for you to work out after we've solved this one."
Slowly relaxing back into his chair, I take the opportunity to order two more lagers. Well, that little outburst took him by surprise. I suppress a need to smile, then add. "And just for my own peace of mind, who ordered the placement of Blunt and his Irish tail-gunner into the *Yard*? Was it you?"
I'm beginning to understand, Striker's smile means nothing, except beware of it when he consents to show it. A chosen person with absolute power, dangerous, beware.
"Yes...you're correct. We have known of an infiltrator for quite some time and after doing extensive searches within *Thames House,* we are convinced the culprit resides in the *Yard.* I sent Blunt and O'Connell in under cover. Not very good were they, as their concealment appears to have been blown. Never mind, it'll keep our mystery person on their toes and might dissuade them from doing too much damage, that's if we can't wheedle them out in time. When Gordon was informed of an imposter within his realm, he wasn't too pleased." A loud burst of laughter replaces his smile but also attracts glances from nearby sun-worshippers. Not the wisest impromptu action delivered from the Director General of homeland security. Their returned smiles indicate they're joining in with his humour, but might have second thoughts of displaying such joviality if they knew what was

tickling Striker. He lowers his voice and shuffles his backside closer.

"The Gibraltar shootings? Did he also tell you about that episode?" He whispers, realising his previous mistake.

"Yep…in fine detail and don't ask. No, you can't meet him."

Recognising my smile and deciphering its meaning, Striker holds up his hands, as if in mock surrender.

On his arrival, I wasn't expecting to see him dressed for a vacation, but a woollen, pinstripe suit might have been replaced by a pair of chinos and a cotton jacket, something more in keeping with the temperature and surroundings, after all, he is the head of homeland intelligence and should have known what to expect down here in the fiery month of August. Maybe this is his chosen uniform, what he feels comfortable wearing, it certainly wasn't designed to camouflage his arrival, more like making him stick out like a sore thumb. If he purported to be viewed as a businessman, one would expect a brief case of some description, but he carried nothing. No, he possesses confidence, a man fully aware of his importance, but, as I've discovered over the years, such characters are usually are devoid of basic common-sense. Lacking this quality highlights his discomfiture, with sweat discolouring his shirt as he reaches for his jacket, folded over an adjacent chair. From an inside pocket, his fingers rummage around and extract something hidden in his palm. Sitting back in his chair, he keeps his fist clenched. He doesn't smoke, so it's not a packet of cigarettes, nor is it a recording device, though I wouldn't be surprised if he had a tiny gizmo placed somewhere on his body recording every spoken word. Obviously not intending to stay the night, as not even a tube of toothpaste would fit in his hand, no, what he held was intriguing and he purposely prolonged his pleasure in not divulging what he held. If this was his intention, he certainly holds my interest and he knows it. I hope he's not playing games with me. His eyes follow the direction where mine are looking.

"You're wondering what I'm holding?" Again, that smile.

"You could say that." I say, knowing it wouldn't take a soothsayer to read my mind.

Opening his hand, an unmarked memory stick lays in his palm.

"A present from me to you. It appears, you know more about what's going on inside my department than I do, so, not to keep you in the dark any longer and to give you a helping hand, inside this little beauty are files appertaining to the entire workforce of *New Scotland Yard* and that includes Gordon. If I'd known what I know now, I'd have probably attached those within *Thames House* as well." Now he's laughing again. This Director General has one weird sense of humour.

"You mean to say, everybody within the *Yard* is on this thing?"

If he's picking up from my facial expression that I'm shocked, then he's right.

"All the way down to the cleaners." His smile broadens. "Of course, I don't have to tell you, it is for your eyes only. The information in there, if it got into the wrong hands, could be catastrophic to homeland security, so no showing it to your Russian friend. I trust you won't allow it get into those hands? When all this is over, I might ask for it back, but you could always copy it, so what's the use. But you never know..." He doesn't finish the sentence and leaves me wondering what he means.

"This is precisely what I've been after since the day Jessica was murdered. Is her original file on there? If it is, then the answer to all this will have something to do with her past."

"Yes, I thought you might like the unabridged version. My boys have been through it with a magnifying glass and can't spot any irregularities, but a fresh pair of eyes can't do any harm. I totally agree with your analysis concerning the involvement with the IRA, but proving it and arresting those involved is another thing. With the political climate between Northern Ireland and the UK in something of a content state, we don't want our relationship slipping back thirty years to the old days. So, Clive, give me one hundred percent proof and then leave the rest up to me. So, that's my business done with. Oh, and by the way, the thing's useless unless you know the password. I chose one word I thought you wouldn't forget...Gordon." His laugh is beginning to get annoying, but, I must admit, also infectious. "Let's order some lunch and allow me time to relax here in the sun for an hour or two before you give me a lift back to the airport."

"Sure, good idea. I suppose it'll all be going on your expense account, paid by the taxpayer?" It's my turn to smile.

"Damn right it will, but just one last favour I ask...you have the memory stick and all I ask is a tiny peek at those diaries...any chance?"
"No." We both laugh.

CHAPTER 32

8.47pm. Friday 21st August. 2015. Clive Grainger's Apartment.

Arriving back home, with Striker's little gift fitting snugly inside my pocket, I beeline for the fridge and extract a bottle of chilled *San Miguel*. Darkness has already descended and the best place to be on a sweaty evening is on my terrace, especially if it's graced by a cooling breeze. Positioning the bottle alongside cigarettes, lighter and ashtray on the glass topped table, I draw up a chair and place my precious memory stick alongside my laptop. Swivelling from the waist to flick on the light, I feel my heart-rate quicken again, a good sign. With sufficient illumination, I insert the thing into its rightful USB port. My heart goes up another notch. Locating the 'on' button, I punch in my own unforgettable password, one Debbie had bestowed upon me years before saying I'd never forget it, 'wanker'... and wait.

The manufacturer and layout of my laptop are foreign to me and am dreading the possibility of having to phone Debs for instructions on how to get the thing to work. She'll want to know where I got the memory stick from, who gave it to me and everything else that I can't tell her. Oh please, let it be easy.

Suddenly the screen glares back into my face and is ready for action. A square box on the left corner suggests I fill it in with a password. This isn't so hard, so far. I type in the letters spelling G.O.R.D.O.N and wait. Bingo...there will be no need to phone Debs. Some introductory rubbish flashes up, asking me to understand the official secrets act, followed by some other useless paraphernalia designed to keep some faceless civil servant in a job. Aaah...another box appears asking for a title. I punch in Jessica's real name and immediately there's her entire history on the screen, just waiting to be scrolled down until I get to the juicy parts. I have an awful amount of reading to do. Thank you Director General Striker, you've made my life a lot easier.

Bloody marvellous. I light a cigarette and start to delve into her shady past, a past a lot of people don't want me to see. Ten minutes into my research, my throat is sending me messages, I'm thirsty again. On the way to rectify my yearning, I make a detour and pick up a pen and pad. Only by putting them down on paper will I be able to recall places, times and names that might need cross-referencing with the suspects, that is, when and if I get to them.

Oh, Jessica, you were a naughty girl, I say to myself with a smile permanently spread across my face, but this has nothing to do with what I'm after. I scroll down and make the occasional note. If Leonid hadn't already told me, what I'm reading would be spell-binding, but now, I speed read, impatient to find a clue. Regrettably, there's nothing in her file I didn't already know. Disappointment.

Right, let's go on to the main protagonists in this game. Firstly, and in some peoples mind the favourite, Ingrid's file fills in the space left by Jessica's. Oh, I bet she would go stark, staring ballistic if she knew what I was up to. I'm like a kid in a toyshop. Scroll down...nothing of interest yet, but she's worth a few quid going by her bank statements. How did Striker get hold of those? Still, it appears her old man earns a fortune in the City. Good luck. No, I'm leaning towards Debs' analysis of the situation. She appears clean. This is going to be a long job. I've only gone through two files and it's taken nearly two hours. I soldier on. It's four in the morning, the twelfth day after they found Jessica's body floating in her pool, when I finally decide to call it day. If it's anything like what I've just been through, tomorrow is going to be a long twenty four hours. But hey, if nothing else comes of this poking around, I'll certainly have some ammunition to go into the business of blackmail. I can't wait to fire-up Debs' file. No, she certainly wouldn't be pleased if she knew. Best not to say a word.

~0~

I awake on the morning of the Saturday, 22nd August, twelve days after Jessica's demise and feel, amazingly, quite refreshed. Having only six hours sleep and a lack of alcohol from the previous day, seemingly ten minutes of clean living must have done me some good. Do I detect a slight decrease in temperature, I don't know, but it's not laying on me like a heavy blanket as it has for the past three months or more. My daily ritual doesn't change, moth-eaten robe, coffee, cigarettes, terrace, and adding to the list, my new toy...the laptop.

If I'm to believe Striker, there's the complete employment and personnel file of every *New Scotland Yard* employee, as well as our Jessica's stashed away inside this magical machine, far too many to commence my search by beginning with surnames starting with the letter 'A'. No, if my senses haven't deserted me, there are possibly only six individuals who readily come to mind requiring scrutiny. I hope my logic is well founded, otherwise I could be here for weeks.

My dear, old heart quickens as Jack Gordon's credentials flash up. Oh, wouldn't he be pissed off, to put it mildly, if he got wind of what I'm up to?

I'm in good spirits when my mobile shakes to a theme I'm beginning to get bored of. Make a note. Must change ringtone...theme to *Psycho* might be an apt choice. I look at the caller's name. I have a sinking feeling, but try to disguise my voice when responding.

"Hello, Natalie, it's good to hear from you." I stop any further conversation to allow her to speak. She takes a long pause and when finally she speaks, her voice is shaky.

"Clive...it's good to hear your voice. I'm so sorry to inform you, but my father, Leonid, passed away last night."

My head drops as if my neck is broken. My grief-ridden sigh must be audible down the line. Neither one of us speak. She is probably sobbing and my throat contracts feeling the urge to do likewise.

I hear her emotional voice crackle in my ear. I cannot temper natural emotions any longer. Tears flood down my cheek.

"Clive...are you there? I know it must be a great shock to you, as it was obvious you were very fond of my father and he was with you." There is a further long pause. I cannot speak.

"The reason why I'm phoning is because," Natalie stutters, distraught, but stoically continues. "I was with him when he died and he made me promise, his last words, that I get in touch with you." It is getting tougher for her. "He said it is extremely important." Again, a pause. "He wrote a letter to you before he became incapacitated. He knew he didn't have long. It's in a sealed envelope, along with his diaries he wants you to have. He said he has no use for them anymore, but if you found anything, he trusted you would put it to good use. He also emphasised, and I can endorse his anxiety when he said it, that you might be in danger."

Silence falls on the conversation like a dead weight. Natalie is giving me time to reflect on what she just said, but a year wouldn't be sufficient to digest the gravity of the situation. One thing I learnt when Leonid was in good health, if he suggested something, you listened.

"Would it be possible for you to come over and pick up the diaries and letter? I'm afraid I'm too distraught to do even basic housework, but it would be good to see you again."

"Natalie, I can't do that. I'm nigh on two thousand miles away in Spain. What I will do, is send over a very

trusted colleague, someone I would trust my life with to collect them." I might have gone over the edge a tad there, but Debs is the closest person to Hampstead who I undoubtedly have faith in. "Please Natalie, call me on this number and tell me when the funeral is to take place. I will try, with all my heart, to be there."
"News travels fast when such a dignitary passes away. You might not want to meet some of those who will undoubtedly turn up." She warns, but in such a soft whisper, the danger of its meaning wafts over my head.
"If you could do me the courtesy of remaining at home on Monday, I'll send round a person called Debbie Glynn. It might be advisable if you ask her for identification, as you never know who might turn up, after all Natalie, those diaries could have dynamite printed between the pages in the wrong hands."
"I understand. Yes, I'll be here. I have nowhere else to go. My heart is broken."
I feel the knot return to my epiglottis.

~0~

I end the call and inadvertently slouch back into my wicker chair. I awoke feeling excited, anticipating the revelations I might stumble upon within the laptop, but my euphoria has been shattered by this tragic news. I truly did like the old boy.
Extraordinary things can happen when in a remorseful mood. A brain resurrects joyous and humorous times, but seems to conveniently eradicate those which were not too good when remembering the deceased.

Shit...Clive, get yourself together. This is serious and I have no time to get into self-indulgent melancholy.
Grabbing my mobile, I punch in Debbie's number. Looking at my watch, I subtract an hour and figure out she might be still in bed after one of her 'Okay, I'll have a cheeky one' enhanced Friday night with like-minded friends.
"And what can I be so pleased about to receive a call from you on this bright, sunny, Saturday morning?" She answers, obviously she remembered to take her anti-sarcastic pill before retiring the night before, but it didn't work.
"Did I wake you, sorry if I did?"
"No, I've been up a while. Decided to give my liver a long overdue holiday last night by catching up with the omnibus edition of *Corri.* Like fuck I was. No, you bloody-well woke me for God's sake...hang on whilst I just go into the garden... right what do you want now? I had a shit day yesterday and you'll never guess why. The..."
Before she rattles off with a tirade of abuse directed solely at *Southern Rail*, I cut her short. "Look, things are happening fast and I don't want you to question my motives. I need you to get over to Hampstead and pick up a parcel on Monday morning. You'll be met by Natalie, Leonid's daughter, Leonid passed away last night. I told her to ask you for your ID." I continue by giving her the address.
I'm not listening to her objections that come into my ear attached to diatribe of euphemisms. Only when she's exhausted her thesaurus of words beginning with

the letter 'f', does she realise the futility of it all and offers her condolences, knowing I was very fond of him.
"Listen Debs, thanks...but this is serious. I wouldn't ask if there was someone else." I purposely leave out the fact she could be in danger. "Have you found a way to get the mobile to Gordon yet?"
"Okay, of course I'll do it. As for the mobile, I've got it with me and will text you the number, No...I haven't got it to Gordon yet, I only got the thing yesterday, but I think I might have the answer. Alan, the doorman, owes me a big favour after I got his air-conditioning fixed, so I'm counting on him to do the business."
"Could you do it first thing Monday?" I ask, weighing up the options of what she should do first.
"Well...yes, sure. Why?"
"You have to trust me on this, Debs. Use all your undoubted charm to get this Alan to do the job, because he might be your only chance." Debs attempts to break in, but I counteract her highly charged vocal disapproval. "Listen. This is no joke." There's silence on the other end of the line. I believe she's finally getting the gist of what I'm attempting to put over to her without me having to spell it out.
"I didn't say it was a joke, Clive, okay. After I've persuaded Alan, what do you want me to do next?" Her voice is level and tempered. Debs is back on my side.
"Go to Hampstead. Pick up the parcel. Then get the first plane out of Gatwick heading for either Malaga or Gibraltar. I know this is a big ask, but don't worry about the office for the time being, I'll get it all smoothed out with Gordon when the dust dies down. Believe me, Debs, this is very important."

CHAPTER 33

9.10am. Saturday 22nd August, The Garden of Debbie Glynn's Apartment.

Clive hangs up and I need to sit. I commandeer my garden bench with an unintentional scowl reminiscent of a disgruntled bag-lady, this has the effect of scattering the previous occupants...seagulls – I know you're a protected species, but you're in my space, so piss off. I reach for my cigarettes. The complete incompetence of the Sussex rail infrastructure blighting my daily commuting activities, pale into insignificance compared to what Clive has just dropped into my lap from a great height.

What the bleeding hell is going on here? What is he up to? Why do I have to go to Estepona when he can so come to London, surely that would be easier... questions...questions...questions - oh, it's doing my head in. I calm down slightly after a blast of nicotine.

I make myself a cup of tea, shit, a gut-feeling tells me this is a very, very bad idea, but I'm just going to have to go along with this hair-brained demand for my indulgence. He must have his reasons for me going over to Spain to deliver this package, rather than picking it up himself. Afraid to be shot at again is a good enough reason for not coming to the UK, I suppose, but what about me? Could I not be the target of some nutter taking a pot shot? I dismiss the thought, grab my iPad and have a look at flights. Now where did I put my bloody passport?

There's availability on the *easyJet* 16.40 to Gibraltar from Gatwick, so when am I coming back? That wasn't even mentioned...the next day? No way, I'm just the delivery girl, but I think I deserve a little beach time for my trouble whilst he digests whatever the parcel yields - let's make the return flight Thursday. It's £254 return, Jesus that's expensive, well, Clive's paying for it and that's not even checking any luggage in.

The logistical timing seems do-able. First thing on Monday, get Alan to do the business getting the phone to Gordon, which shouldn't be too difficult. I've put it in a sealed jiffy bag with a note inside that just says *'From Clive. Keep this handy and don't tell anybody you have it. Will be in touch shortly.'* He needs to understand to get it to Gordon sharpish and without anyone seeing him do it.

Next, schlep over to Hampstead, pick up this parcel, go back to Victoria and pick up a train to Gatwick, making sure I get there by 3.30 at the latest.

Oh God, and what, precisely, am I supposed to say to folk in the office?

Big wave 'Bye everyone, sort your own expenses out, I'm off to the Costa del Sol' whilst humming to the classic 70's blockbuster *'Viva Espana'* – No, can't see that happening!

All very good up to now, but Clive saying he'll square it with Gordon when the dust settles; the dust hasn't even taken off, yet let alone had time to come to rest. No, he's not the one who's got to go in there and make some plausible excuse. I'll try and extinguish it from my mind over the weekend and do what I normally do, and that is absolutely nothing, that is, if lifting a glass doesn't contravene the laws concerning the same category.

Just then, I have that light bulb switching on in my head moment; it's obvious, don't go into the office itself at all, just reception to see Alan, then email Baldrick and Ingrid today or tomorrow with some tissue of lies about why I need four days off at such short notice, luckily I have enough holiday entitlement to do so. After all, twenty-seven years of working in this kharzi, it's my turn to take the piss.

What I can't put off, is what I'm going to take to wear! I open my wardrobe, as if some divine inspiration is going to come forth, and both practically and efficiently pack what I require for a short break. No, this is going to have to be a random selection given the time restraints. For blokes it's easy - shorts, t- shirts, shirt, trousers. Do I take a sun dress, evening wear, beach wear - I haven't got a clue, and what about shoes, how many pairs excluding flip flops? This is the stuff of a female nightmare - one of everything should cover most bases, but there's not enough room, actually, forget evening wear, can't see Clive partaking in fine dining, certainly not with me anyway and if I leave toiletries out - I'm going to Spain for God's sake, not some third world country. They, as does *Gatwick* airport, have shops. Weighing it up, I could just about do it.

Packing loosely completed, flight booked, checked in and boarding pass downloaded onto my phone, good, all that's left now is to check the route to Natalie's

address in Hampstead and to send Baldrick and Ingrid the email, both can wait till tomorrow. For now, all I have to do is a bit of housework and washing, then meet up with Jane for a spot of lunch in The Lanes.
I text Clive giving him Gordon's mobile number and details of the flight, demanding he pick me up.

CHAPTER 34

10.32am. (Spanish time). Saturday 22nd August. Clive Grainger's Apartment.

Passing out of Hendon training college all those years in the past, the general consensus in every recruits mind was to get on the streets and immediately rid the world of the scum who profited by the misery of law abiding citizens. A beautiful, naïve notion of one's own self-belief and ability, ingredients personified by the likes of *Batman* and *Spiderman,* allowing them to flourish. Yes, we all believed we could make a difference in this crazy world, but none, when so young, were blessed with patience. This quality was reserved as a given right within the higher echelons of the force, meaning promotion made you lazy. But I was one of the few who, when given the opportunity to climb the ladder of promotion, retained the belief I had on my first day on the street. A few close associates in the past have acknowledged I have a few virtues, but their kindly assessment was probably diagnosed after a skin-full. When sober, none of them would merit putting patience amongst my greatest assets. No, even the card game of the same name drives me up the wall. So, having to wait for Debs to arrive on Monday evening with her 'parcel', has prompted my nerves to tingle and fingers to uncontrollably tap any surface they find, which can be a bloody nuisance for anyone on the receiving end.

As a measure to control this so-called flaw in my character, and noticed early in my career by some supercilious arsehole of a superintendent, I was ordered to embrace yoga, but the vigours of attempting to tie a reluctant body in knots, lasted as long as it took me to smoke a cigarette outside the gym in pouring rain in some dingy alleyway.

No, I must look on the positive side and view this situation in a different light. I'm convinced I'm a fag-paper's width away from nailing these bastards. In my possession, I have Striker's memory stick which in any investigation, even if I were still connected to the Yard, would be considered gold-dust, so why do I feel two days of inactivity is being wasted?

The culprits are going nowhere and if I'm to believe their arrogance, they know an ongoing investigation is taking place, but feel so entrenched and trusted within the organisation, they feel their identities will remain secret. Ah...this could be their undoing.

I sit on my terrace going over what my brain is telling me and ponder on what I've just thought...could this be their undoing? When the element of confidence is so high, what is the only flaw in their thoughts that could knock the big-headed bastards off their perch...why, a mistake, of course. I have an idea. Adapting a similar scenario to the first, that could so easily have resulted in my death, I'll call it the 'Belfast Project'. Allowing it to be known that I possess vital information to hand over would be signing my own death warrant, if the culprits ever got wind of it, but if

I can polish up the idea, then it's worth thinking about. The only trouble is, and it still remains the big question, who is the spy?

I guess I'll just have to wait for Monday and do what Striker and Gordon are doing right now, probably down the club quaffing with their inner circle of friends and not caring a damn about what is on their weekday agenda. It's the weekend and I'll do precisely the same, take myself back to when Jessica sat at a table with a glass in her hand, denouncing my theories concerning the rights of man, giggling at a suggestion *The House of Lords* should be demolished and rebuking me robustly for suggesting revolution is just around the corner. Oh, how I wish I could turn the clock back to times when I didn't have a care in the world and blood was still pumping around Jessica's ample body.

I have no idea what Leonid, bless him, was up to, or what he wrote on his deathbed, but knowing the old rascal, it won't be a negative load of nonsense. The heat is building, but thankfully, it's lost its furnace-like ferocity. I've forgotten what it's like to be here in the winter, weather-wise, but when it arrives, I'll embrace it. My dream intensifies to when all this will be just a memory, where my life goes back to how I remember. Roll on Monday.

CHAPTER 35

7.29am. Monday 24th August 2015. On The Way to London.

I couldn't look more out of place on the 7.29 if I tried, in linen cropped trousers, short sleeved shirt and newly acquired *Birkenstock* shoes. It's my turn to receive the death stare from my commuting comrades this morning, having taken up more than the allotted individual space with my bag on the overhead luggage rack. I'll allow them their morning sulk, as it's obvious I'm not going into work but away somewhere nice, just to really piss them all off - if only they knew what I was really doing.

I sit in my favourite seat, ignoring them. I review the email I sent to Ingrid and Baldrick yesterday along the lines that my boiler has sprung a huge leak, going downstairs; can't get an engineer until Thursday; my water turned off; I've had to stay with friends; will take the time off as a holiday, but will respond to email, really sorry, etc. etc. What an absolute crock of shite - will they buy it?

I text Bronzey and ask him to meet me in the cafe round the corner from the office at 9.30.

The route to Hampstead doesn't look too onerous, two tubes and about a 15 minute walk.

I ignore the train conductors' apologetic drivel about the delay due to overrunning engineering works in the Balham area, actually it's quite handy it's late today, as I don't want to go into reception during the 9am rush and draw attention to myself dressed like I'm on the Benidorm express and wheeling a case behind me. I just hope this delay doesn't have a knock on effect when I'm trying to get the train to the airport.

I walk into the pleasant, now sufficiently air-conditioned, building and greet Alan. Before even asking, I show him my pass.

"Hey Debs, you going on holiday?"

"Morning Alan, yes, I've got to go away for a few days."

"What are you doing in the office then?"

"Never mind that, look, I need a big favour from you. Shouldn't take you long, but if you don't want to help me, that's fine. I can always make another call to the maintenance boys saying reception is now too cold, if you get my drift."

"Oh God, please don't do that Debs, what do you need?"

I reach into my bag and retrieve the package.

"This needs to be given to Commissioner Gordon straight away. Don't worry, it's not an explosive." I give him one of my doleful smiles before reiterating Clive's demand for secrecy with a 'if you don't do this I'll have your bollocks dangling off a knitting needle' look on my face. He gets my gist as I hand it over.

"Why don't you just take it upstairs to him yourself?"

"There are good reasons why I can't, Alan, one, I'm dressed like this and two, I'm not going in the office. I haven't got the time to explain. That's why I want you to do me this small favour. Ring Lorraine and tell her you need to do a routine check of the master security swipe card access to his office suite or something like that. Is he up there now?" I ask and get a positive nod in return.

"This all very cloak and dagger stuff Debs, I don't know if I like it. What if Lorraine says no?"

"She won't, not to you. This is really important - will you do it?"

He takes a deep breath. "Okay, I'll get onto it now whilst it's quiet down here."

I'm just about to thank him, when he needlessly adds. "You're late again, Debs, were the trains delayed?"

I summon every sinew from my minute frame not to reach over and floor him, which I guess, would scupper him doing me this favour. Instead, I smile obediently. "Alan you're a star, I won't forget this. Thank you, and by the way, Alan, you haven't seen me this morning."

He reluctantly nods as I hand over my business card and tell him to text me when the mission has been successful.

First job done.

I walk back out of the office and along to the cafe, securing a table at the back. I order coffees.

Bang on time Bronzey walks in and doesn't spot me, I wave at him. His face is a picture seeing me all holiday clothed up.

"What the..."

I stop him in mid flow.

"Just sit down Bronzey, look, I have to go to Spain this afternoon."

Our coffee arrives.

I carry on before he has a chance to speak.

"You need to cover for me for a few days. I've sent Baldrick & Ingrid a tissue of lies in an email that I have a boiler leak going downstairs, the engineer can't come out for a few days, no water, have to stay with friends, taking days leave, you get the gist."

"You live in the basement, Debs, you have no 'downstairs."

"Hmm, yeah, good point, well spotted - you know that, but they don't. Oh, for fucks sake Bronzey, stop nit-picking, don't make this more difficult than it is."

"Okay, Debs, I'll cover, but are you going to tell me what's going on?"

"I don't really know myself. I have to take a parcel down to Clive, so please, be a mate, just watch my back, Gordon doesn't know I'm going."

"Just promise me, Debs, you'll be careful."

"I will, don't worry."

Bless him. As he leaves I reach up from my diminutive height to his normally out-of-reach cheek and plant a kiss on it. At that point, brushing aside embarrassment from both parties, I finish my coffee and head to Victoria tube station.

Oh my God, I might moan about *Southern Rail*, but descending into the underground station and getting a tube in August exceeds any human endurance challenge. It's got be 50 bloody degrees down here. It's a sweat box and I don't sweat generally, but it's pouring off me and by the smell in the carriage, so is everyone else, I'm almost gagging. I can't image doing this every day, this is truly the worst form of travel in any heat. An Indian tuk-tuk going through the middle of a Delhi market at midday would be more acceptable to the nostrils. I get off at Euston and take the Northern line to Hampstead, please Lord, let it be slightly more sufferable than the Victoria line. Of course it's not - how silly of me to even think that would be the case, way too much to ask for, evidently.

I've read somewhere that in the summer months, the deeper the tube lines, the temperature often breaks what is illegal to transport cattle - well just stick an udder on me and call me Ermintrude!"

I eventually emerge in daylight at Hampstead, stand for a moment flapping my blouse to get some airflow moving around the heat affected parts and have a cigarette whilst looking up my *Google* map GPS route to Natalie's house.

Arriving in a very leafy neighbourhood, I find the opulent residence at 11.15. I ring the bell. No more than a minute later, Natalie, I assume, opens the door. I announce myself and show my driving license. Bless her, she looks like hell and I don't really know what to say. 'Sorry for your loss' is way too naff in the real world, but easy for script writers of American police dramas.

I just say limply "I'm really sorry, Natalie, about your father. I lost mine and know what you're going through."

I'm invited into the hall.

"Thanks Debbie, his last wishes were that Clive gets these documents and puts them to good use. You will do that, won't you? Make sure he reads the letter...these were my father's last words."

She hands me a large carrier bag containing the wrapped up parcel.

"I'm flying down to Spain this afternoon to give them to him, hence the attire and case. Don't worry, I know he'll honour your father's wishes. I wish there was more I could say to you. Please take care and I'm sure Clive will be in touch soon."

"I know he will." A single tear rolls down her cheek as she hands me the package.

"Make sure some good comes out of whatever is in there." She adds.

"Clive will do all he can - Thank you Natalie and again I'm so sorry."

"Tell Clive to take care of himself. My father would want him safe, I know what a maverick he can be sometimes and you also take care - thank you for doing this for my Dad."

At that, I leave and she closes the door behind me.

Jeez, I feel wretched. She's going through hell and there she is, a woman who doesn't know me from Adam, selflessly telling me to look after myself.

I walk back to Hampstead tube station and before I brace myself to go into the bowels of hell again, I call Clive.

He picks up.

"Debs how are you getting on?"

"Clive, you best not be lounging on the beach, else I'll kill you myself when I get there. This morning, let me tell you, I've lied through my teeth at the office. Ducked & dived not to be spotted, persuaded Alan to do his bit...he will by the way, but it took a bit of vocal arm wrestling. I met Bronzey and he's going to cover my backside, but he's not happy. I've endured the worst tube journey of my life - multiples thereof I might add, and have just picked up the parcel from Natalie - it's bloody huge, you didn't tell me that. I'm going to have to rethink luggage arrangements now. I'm booked on the flight that gets into Gibraltar at 9.30pm. Your time. Did you get my text? Did you not think to respond, can it be that difficult? You had better pick me up as I'm not getting a taxi unless you pay for it. That will be in addition to the flight, additional charge to put my meagre case in the hold plus the cost of buying a rucksack to carry these papers on the plane. When I get there, you and I are going to have a little old chat about all the shit that I find myself getting deeply immersed in, as it appears to be in aid of the 'Clive Grainger couldn't care a fuck if I'm shot at again' fund and I'm not signing up to that.

"Great Debs, call me when you get to Gatwick from the gate."

He hangs up!

Absolute classic response. It was always the same, when I do all the running around like a headless chicken and give him a bit of a verbal lashing as a result, I get the "great...give me a call". This time though, I bet he's swinging from his frigging sun bed - even more infuriating - what an absolute arse he can be.

I endure the two subterranean, slow-cooking torpedoes back to Victoria, then, outside the station, I check my phone.

Two missed calls, one from Ingrid, one from Baldrick - shit!

Call Ingrid back - "Debs, what's this about a leak?"

"Really sorry, Ingrid, but as I said in the email, my boiler is pissing into downstairs, so I had to arrange someone to come round to fix it and the waters off, so I can't stay here. I'll be back in Friday when hopefully all of this is fixed."

"No Problem, Debs, sounds like you have your hands full there. I've sent you a couple of emails on the numbers, if you could have a look over the next few days. Good luck with the leak...I'll let Baldrick know as well."

"Cheers Ingrid, yep, I'll look at the numbers and of course I'll check and respond to any other emails."

Oh bugger, I hate lying, but needs must when the devil shows his face and it seems to have worked perfectly. This also goes some way towards confirming my theory that our Ingrid has nothing to do with any of these conspiracy theories. Surely, if I'm wrong, she would have quizzed me much deeper and wouldn't take that lame leak excuse so readily for me disappearing for a few days. Note to self - remind Clive of this.

Text from Alan *"Package delivered."* Good, that's one thing out of the way.

I've got loads of time to get to *Gatwick*, so I need to buy a rucksack. I find a luggage type shop round the corner from the station, £35 for quite a good one, add to Clive's bill.

I put the parcel in, and ditch the carrier bag and head back to the station via *M&S* for a sandwich.

Unsurprisingly, the next *Southern* train to *Gatwick* has been cancelled due to the aforementioned troubles at Balham.

Sod it, I board the next *Gatwick Express* train which technically my ticket doesn't actually cover, but hey, I'll wing it. The train leaves on time, I have a civilised and comfortable seat and guess what, it sails through Balham, no problem. It makes my blood boil that one train franchise can grind to a screeching halt whilst another has no problem on the same piece of track. Stop it, enough moaning - I'm heading for 3 days in the sun.

After what seems an eternity explaining at the *easyJet* counter, that, no, my ticket didn't include hold luggage, but now I want to check one in and yes I'll pay the additional £27 for the privilege, (add to Clive's bill). I pass through security, buy some toiletries and head to the bar with half an hour to kill before going to the gate. I order a wine and sit at a table, people watching. At any airport it's the greatest way of passing the time, particularly the outfits; shiny gold shoes with matching gold bags; blokes on a stag holiday barely standing; couples arguing before they've even got on a plane - love it.

I call Clive.

"Hey, Debs where are you?"

"I'm at *Gatwick.* The package got to Gordon okay and the papers went through security no problem and are in my hand luggage with me. I'm just having a glass of wine as you would no doubt predict - going to the gate in 10 minutes, all looks on time. You're going to pick me up, right? "

"Yes of course I'll pick you up. Can you get me some *Superkings* when you get to Gib?"

"What?? So now I'm your cigarette mule? I'll be getting some for me only, that being the law matey. Okay, if I can blag it, I'll try - see you at the other end. I seriously don't know why I'm fucking doing this."
"Because you know it's the right thing to do and makes sense if we're going to get to the bottom of this."
"Yeah...whatever Clive."
"You know you love all this really, come on, it beats stationery orders. I'll see you in Gib."
"I so do not love all this intrigue. Please let me return to my mundane, stress free existence of post-it notes and biro orders that I've been trained for twenty-seven years to do with absolute perfection."
I hang up.
I saunter to the gate and board the plane, settling in for the two and bit hour flight.
It's been a long day and I relax for the first time, read my book and enjoy a miniature bottle of *easyJet's* finest vintage and a minute bag of crisps.
We land on time and true to form having picked up my case, I manage to blag a carton of cigarettes for both of us at duty free. He better pay for this as well.
It's 9pm and it feels like an oven opening in front me as I walk out of the terminal.

CHAPTER 36

9.00pm. Monday 24th August. 2015. Outside Gibraltar International Airport.

Learning from past mistakes concerning Striker's flight, I've parked up early. I can just imagine the look on Debs' 'boat race' if she appeared out of the terminal and found no sign of me. Over the weekend I've taken a leaf out of the Superintendent's book on yoga and relaxed a tad, not twisting my body to resemble some boy-scouts attempt at tying a sheep-shank, but released the tension whilst sipping a superior *Rioja.* So, the thought of hiding myself from her view when she exits and witnessing her boil to a point of explosion, is very tempting.

Minutes pass, as passengers from the flight begin to emerge from the terminal, the automatic doors constantly swishing open and closing. While camouflaged behind a large family group, I get my first glimpse of Debs. My first thought is that it's a Nepalese sherpa. Bent forward from the waist to compensate the load she's carrying on her back, she also hauls baggage, the size of which is big enough to contain his entire family and pet llama. Balancing the entire visual effect, in her other hand is a bulging carrier bag which, I hope, contains my duty frees, that swings in unison with her short strides. I should take a picture of Debs' impersonation of a circus act and pin it to my fridge for when I wake with a hangover and need a laugh, but then a thought hits me, just how long does she think she's staying?

Appearing as if it's all too much for a little person and is about to crumble, she halts her progress on the forecourt and looks pleadingly around for evidence of my arrival. Yes, I've seen that happy look on her face on many occasions and know what it means. She's spitting blood.

"Hi Debs." I call out as I approach.

"Give me a fucking hand, you bastard." Debs has no intention to disguise her mood.

"Oh, what happened to hello Clive, good to see you and all that sort of thing?"

"Shut up and just get this thing off my back." She resigns herself to just standing there until I relieve her of the weight.

"Oh, I don't know, Debs. We'll wait around for a bit to see if there's a film director coming through. You're a natural for the part of *Quasimodo.*" I see my humour is completely lost.

Easing the backpack off, I take the weight and feel she wasn't exaggerating.

"Bloody hell, Debs, what have you got in here?"

"Leonid's sodding diaries, that's what." Her mood isn't improving.

~0~

The journey back to Estepona is blissfully quiet as, on leaving La Linea, she happily falls asleep, bless her, she's exhausted.

"Debs, come on, wake up. We're home. Here, you take the keys and open up whilst I grab your bags." I offer in my best *Sir Galahad* fashion.

"Oh, you can be such a plonker." At last, I see a smile crease her face.

Dumping her bags at the door of her bedroom, I separate the one holding my interest and carry it to the terrace.

"The kitchen is there. Grab yourself a drink out of the fridge and I'll have a lager, cheers." I call out whilst undoing the buckles and flaps of the backpack. "Where's the letter Natalie gave you?"

"It's inside the cover of volume one." Debs calls out whilst revealing a bottle of *Pinot Grigio* from its hiding place amongst other suitably cheap bottles of wine.

Retrieving the volumes, each the size of a thick encyclopaedia, I flip open the suggested edition to find Leonid's letter. A subconscious acceleration of my heartbeat coincides with ripping the thing open. Oh, I've been waiting for this moment for nigh on three days.

I begin to read as Debs appears, holding two glasses, and settles herself down on the wicker sofa. "Nice place you have here, Clive. What did you say the rent is?"

I don't reply and keep reading. The first few paragraphs spell out Leonid's worst fears, that he doesn't expect to live much longer. The cancer has spread and the doctor has given him only days. He then goes on to explain why he wrote the diaries in

English, not in his mother tongue, as he believed if anybody sneaked a look whilst at the embassy, they might not be as astute with the foreign language as he was. A proud Russian, but didn't apologise for keeping an eye open to cover his back; I did the same at the Yard, adapting my own form of hieroglyphics before retiring, which even baffled Debbie.

I sit and ponder whether Leonid truly believed all the crap orchestrated by the bigshots, which originated from behind the Iron Curtain. My eyes soak in every word knowing it must have been a physical effort to put his thoughts down on paper. His handwriting is perfect but shows signs of trauma. Oh, why didn't he use a word processor or some other contraption?

Turning to page two, Debs is muttering on about something, but my concentration is focused. My pulse quickens when he writes about Jessica and the night she received orders from the Prime Minister to remove three known IRA operatives. God, his spies must have been everywhere. Leonid confirms, once again, the order was carried out by Special Branch, but on that night or should I say early morning, the 12th October, 1984, there were two more murders of attributed *IRA* sympathisers. The problem he faced is not being able to identify, from the five names, the three individuals who turned out to be Thatcher's target. He has written a list of all five and as much information about each he obviously could muster at that time, but it is scant and doesn't say a great deal.

But what he wrote on the third page excites my copper's nose. By a process of elimination, he suggests I go through all my suspects, though the list might just get longer if nothing turns up, and determine if there are similarities in any of their bloodlines with the list of defunct terrorists who perished on that night in Northern Ireland. Of course, he goes on to say it might be difficult, no, impossible, to get this type of information. Poor Leonid, he knew nothing of my present from Striker. It should all be in there, somewhere. It just needs finding.

I read the entire letter once again, just to be sure I hadn't missed a vital word or clue. I finally lift my eyes from the written word and see Debs smoking a cigarette, completely oblivious to the fact that I may have the ammunition at hand to nail the bastards responsible.

"What's he say?" Debs questions, but probably not expecting an answer.

"Oh, this and that." I mumble.

"Bloody typical. I put my twenty-seven years of employment on the line, blackmail Alan the doorman, trudge over to Hampstead in a converted *Aga* cooker, jump aboard a plane at the last moment and all you have to say is 'this and that'. You have no idea about social niceties, have you Clive?"

She's right, of course, but how do I tell her she might be in as much danger as myself. I'm sure she wouldn't be too happy, but, for the time being, she needn't know. She goes quiet and I feel a mood is resurfacing.

"It's not easy for me to juggle what I know with what you would like to know. If that makes sense. It won't be long now and then the whole story will explode. I'm truly grateful for all that you have done for me, Debs, and I couldn't have got this far without your help." My words appear to appease her.

She smiles and hunches her shoulders as if to say, 'well, fuck you,' but unusually for Debs, she doesn't actually say it.

"Why don't you finish off that bottle and hop off to bed? You look knackered and there's the sun and sea just waiting for you tomorrow. I'm going to be working most, if not all of the night with what I've gleaned from Leonid." I stop there and give Debs one of my own impish grins as I remove my laptop from its case.

"What's that?" Debs interest soars from total lethargy to mild curiosity.

"Oh, I'm not the Philistine you thought I was. I do happen to own machines invented in the twenty first century, like my mobile and this little beauty. Add to this a small present given to me from our lord and master, the Director General of *MI5*, and we have here a device to finally break the secrecy of the bastards we're after."

"It's just a laptop, Clive. Not such a big deal." Her enthusiasm wanes.

"Yes, but you don't know what's inside...do you...no, you don't. I have a complete profile of everybody working at *New Scotland Yard* at my fingertips." My keenness is all too visible.

"Am I in that thing?" She questions, her enthusiasm beginning to fester.

"Yes...you are." I reluctantly respond knowing what to expect.

"Let me have a look." Long gone is her apathy. Now standing by my side, her mood is unmistakable and is eager to open her file.
"Sorry, girl. No can do. If you saw anything inside my magical box, I'd have to kill you." I laugh, but Debs isn't in unison with my humour.
"You bastard."
I expected a stronger retort as she turns and heads for her room, a loud slam of the door indicating I'll be unlikely to see her again until the morning. She's not happy.

~0~

Leaving only the one terrace light on, I switch off all inside illumination and sit at the table supporting my laptop. Looking at my watch, it's just coming up to eleven at night and the town below has quietened. Though my thermometer displays it's 29 degrees, a soft breeze deadens the humidity. Looking out to the Mediterranean, the dark mass is only broken by the moons reflection, a soothing sight if ever I saw one, and one that I'll never tire of, but if I'm correct with my assumption, I have the mechanics at hand to bring these people to justice, causing more than a few storm clouds to descend over their lives.
On a sheet of A4, I scribble down the five names outlined in Leonid's letter in big letters before firing up the laptop. The thing springs to life and I begin what I know will be a laborious task. Bypassing all the paraphernalia concerning job title, pension rights, promotion etc, etc, I concentrate on their parents and

offspring, checking each to see if they are connected in any way to my five names.

Hours drag by and my eyes feel heavy. I'm bushed. My watch indicates it's just after 5.30 in the morning as I empty the remnants of what's left in a lager glass, down my throat. Steady, go back and read that again. Blurred vision retraces the summary on one individual. There, in black print, is a name matching that of the third down on my list. My senses tingle, as if being stimulated by a shot of caffeine and a hit of nicotine, as I would describe my style of Spanish breakfast. I'm wide awake.

Leonid, you old son of a gun. You figured this out for yourself, but didn't want to tell me due to pointless persistent allegiance to some past, ridiculous theology. Instead, you give clues to piece all this together. I forgive you.

But what is the connection to Jessica? What reason was there to assassinate her? There, Clive, I tell myself, is your next assignment. Put the two together and you've solved the puzzle.

I need information, the type of which doesn't come from the mouths of Director Generals or Commissioners, no, they only have access to what I want in the form of hearsay or written reports. No use to me. What I require is knowledge from street level, eyes and ears who lived and breathed during the time when this egg was impregnated. My time piece indicates only fifteen minutes of progression since I last checked. Too early to start dialling contacts for favours. No, patience is definitely not one of my virtues. I'll just have to wait. Setting my alarm clock for nine, I try to close my eyes, but the factory inside my brain, spewing scenarios, refuses to knock off and permit sleep.

A vision of complete beauty saunters past my sunbed. She's topless and radiating a smile, so broad, it can only be for my benefit. Slithering down next to where I lay, she inserts a finger into her mouth and salivates round it with an elongated tongue before slowly, oh so slowly, removing it from red lips and beckons me. Oh shit, what is that fucking awful noise? Rattling on my bedside table, the alarm clock screeches me out from my dream.

Sitting bolt upright, my head swims for a second, not quite understanding fiction from reality. My right hand swings in an arc and connects with the offender, knocking the feet off the object, but more importantly, silencing the bloody thing.

Sliding out of bed, I'm still clothed in what I wore yesterday, but ablutions can wait. All, it appears, is peaceful on the other side of Debbie's door, so I'll leave her be. Kettle switched on with a Super King waiting to be lit. I'm ready for a long day.

~0~

The sun is where it usually is, moving slowly across the sky, but the intense, unforgiving heat, has mercifully abated. Set out like a military manoeuvre, I place a note pad and pen alongside a new packet of cigarettes, a lighter and coffee cup accompanying the laptop, and most important, my mobile and little black book. The terrace table is prepared to see some action.

9.30am here, 8.30 back in the UK. Time to go into combat mode.

My ear recognises his phone is ringing and by the fourth pulse, a voice interrupts the pattern.

"Hello…Jack Wakeling speaking."

"Hi Jack…its Clive…Clive Grainger. Good morning old fella." I purposely sound chirpy to try and deflect any notions he might have of why I'm phoning….some hope.

"What do you want, Clive? For fuck's sake, it's 8.30 in the morning." His brusque words give me a clue into his state of mind.

"I want you to do me a small favour." Before the words have left my mouth, he nigh cuts me off with a Gatling–gun-like volley of abuse.

"After our little escapade in Belfast, you want me to do you a favour? Go fuck yourself, Clive."

"Steady Jack. Apart from the bullet-thing, we had a laugh and a few pints. We both got out in one piece. Didn't it rekindle old feelings? Come on. In a sick sort of way, you must have enjoyed the mayhem and intrigue." My words are carefully choreographed to stir an old coppers memory bank of past exploits.

"Well…apart from having to hang around the terminal until they were happy I had nothing to do with the fucking shooting…yeah…it was a good day out." Jack admits in a normal voice, even with a tad of nostalgia in there somewhere.

"There you go." I confirm it wasn't all bad, though at the time, we both shat ourselves.

"If this favour means something similar…forget it." A quite acceptable request resonates in my ear.

"Nothing like it, Jack. All I would like you to do is phone your old mate Seamus O'Hearn in Belfast and ask him a few, innocent questions. No danger. You don't even have to leave home to do it."

"Innocent questions, my arse. If they are coming from you...innocent questions?" Jack knows me too well.

"Listen, Jack...Seamus was in Belfast in the early years and knows far more than I can get hold of in any folder, whether it be from *MI5* or *Special Branch* or any other fucking organisation. He was a man on the street, hearing all the banter. I just want you to ask him a simple question. That's all." I leave him to reply after whetting his appetite.

A short silence ensues before a cough and splutter indicate he's about to give his decision.

"What do you want me to ask?"

Yippee...Jack is on my side once more.

"I want you to ask if he knows a Patrick O'Hare. His name has cropped up in my investigation and it's essential I get to know who he was. Can you get a background on him, you know, if he was married, how he financed himself, whether he had kids, that sort of thing? I would be forever in your debt." Trying not to over guild the lily, I pose the question for Jack to digest.

"Shouldn't be too hard if Seamus knows this character. I'll have a cup of tea and think about how I'll get him round to spilling the beans, that's if he knows where the tin opener is." Jack laughs, a good sign. "Remember, this is going on your phone bill and not mine, so, call me back in an hour. By that time I'll have what you want or nothing at all."

Replacing the mobile back on the glass topped table, I take a gulp of coffee. It's cold. I hear movement in the bathroom. Debs is up.
"Fancy a coffee, Debs." I call out.
"Cheers. I'll be out in a jiffy." A muffled reply resonates amongst the sounds of a flushed toilet.
Placing two mugs next to the laptop, I retake my seat in preparation for how I'll explain the reasons behind what I've asked her to do, after all, she's the one I trust and has done most of the donkey work, or sherpa work as I'll rename it.
"Morning." Dressed as though ready for the beach, Debs saunters into the sunlight. "What a beautiful day."
"Yeh, it's better now than a few days ago. You would have come back here from the beach resembling an over-done lobster if you attempted to lie in the sun for more than half an hour."
"So, taking that as a yardstick, how would you describe your colouring...a delicate shade of Chernobyl?" Her snakelike tongue flicks out, delivering another barbed reply.
"Funny...so funny." Is the only miserable reply I can muster so early.
"Well, laughing boy, what is this all about? You've kept so much to yourself; I feel as though I'm a mushroom, kept in the dark and fed shit. What's with this present Striker gave you? Are you two having an affair, cause it's the only reason I can figure why he should do you such a favour. You know, a Blunt, Burgess and McClean thing, them all being up each other's arse."
I laugh at her reasoning, but notice she's not.

"Debbie, put that tongue of yours away, have a ciggy and listen to what I have to say."

For an hour I relate everything to her, leaving nothing out. On occasions she attempts to interrupt, but I raise my voice and she gets the hint to stay quiet. I finish with the conversation I've just had with Jack Wakeling.

"There, you know everything I know...the lot...happy now?"

Her mouth isn't smiling but her eyes give her away, she's ecstatic. "Thank you. Now, that wasn't hard was it?"

"One thing I must add though, I got you over here on false pretences, not that I didn't need Leonid's diaries and his letter immediately, they are very important, it's just I had to get you out of the firing line. I believe you are in danger and the furthest I could get you away from the office, the better, until I've sorted all this out. Don't worry, it won't take long."

She remains silent, a dangerous sign in any woman's demeanour, as I have learnt to my cost in the past. She stands and takes my coffee mug.

"Another mugful?"

"Please." I reply, totally flummoxed to what she's up to.

"Good...whilst I'm waiting for the kettle to boil, you can reimburse me for this lot...I'll accept euros if you haven't got pounds to hand."

A piece of paper is thrust in front of me, itemising everything she's paid out for, including my cigarettes from duty free. I look up and see her grinning face. Good old Debbie, she's back in the fold and worth every penny.

~0~

The last thing I see of Debs is when she disappears out of the door with a beach bag slung over her shoulder. "Bye...see you later." Are the last words I hear before the door slams shut. Debs has a lot of foibles, but one thing she isn't and that's stupid. She knows I have to be alone for what is about to happen.

Picking up the mobile, I re-call Jack and wait, fingers crossed, to hear what he has to say, if anything.

"Hi Jack, its Clive."

"Clive, have you a pen and paper handy?"

Just these few words confirm he has something to say that I need to hear. I answer in the affirmative.

"Good. Yes, Seamus knew of Patrick O'Hare. Not personally, but enough. Though he was on the radar with the Brits, nothing could be proved concerning his involvement with the IRA. He was clever and disguised himself well, as a pub landlord of a joint in the Falls Road area of Belfast. The Golden something or another, Seamus couldn't remember its name, but it was a hotbed of activity in those days. O'Hare was married and had a kid, but there were stories going around he had a bit on the side and got her up the duff. As to money, he had his hands in his own till so was never short of a few bob. What Seamus thought weird was the fact O'Hare got taken out on the morning of the 12th October, 1984, the same day as four others got their comeuppance. I just said it was a coincidence and knew nothing about it. Is it helpful, Clive?"

I thank Jack and promise to get back to the UK and have that drink before cutting the line. No sooner have I put the mobile down, I sprint into the lounge and rifle through Leonid's diaries, trying to recollect which one he read from, outlining with accuracy, Jessica's undercover operation in Belfast in the seventies. My fingers can't keep up with the speed my brain is working, flicking through pages of unrelated material until I get to the date I'm searching for. The twelfth of October shows something going on in some other part of the world, but totally unrelated. But following on from there, a few days later, subsequent leafs report O'Hare's death, as it probably only came to light if there was a Russian infiltrator writing about the events days after they happened.

I thumb backwards, possibly as much as ten years or more, to where Leonid read me the account of Jessica's undercover involvement. It takes time, but finally her name shines out from the written text. Bingo...Jessica worked at a pub called the Golden Harp...thanks Seamus...owned by one Patrick O'Hare. Could it be O'Hare was the father of her unborn child, Shelly? The probable reason why she was hauled back to England and given protection under a different identity. It's all beginning to make logical sense. Jessica gave the order for three *IRA* terrorists to be assassinated on the Prime Minister's command, a decade after she left the *Golden Harp*. Whether she was privy to the names of those who were to be on the receiving end, is open to conjecture, but one thing is certain, her actions killed the father of her child. And if Seamus is correct with his recollections, there is another, older sibling. And I know who it is. Someone who obviously, somehow, got hold of the same information I'm reading and wanted complete and utter revenge for the death of their father.

CHAPTER 37

11.08am. Tuesday 24th August 2015. Clive Grainger's Terrace.

Here we go, finally putting the coffin nail into some nasty people's freedom by solving a case that I believed, when I started out fifteen days ago, was an impossible task. With only Debbie's help and an inkling of ideas and some unconventional police work, I've uncovered the main protagonist and hopefully, some of the followers.

But this is the delicate part, not fucking up what I've already established.

"Hi...Commissioner Gordon...it's Clive Grainger." I speak before Gordon has the opportunity to respond.

"Of course it's you, Grainger. Who else would it be on a *Tesco* phone you got to me under some ridiculous cloak and dagger scheme?"

He's not happy, a tinge of his coppers nose may have been sliced off, but overall, he might come out of this with some kind of glowing recommendation, even though he's been left in the dark for most of this investigation.

"Are you alone in the office?" I ask for confirmation before continuing. "Do you check your land phone lines to confirm they haven't been bugged?"

"What a strange question to ask. Yes, I have them done by a private company once a week."
"Don't tell me they come round on the same day to check your office?" I dread the answer, but it will only confirm the person's guilt.
"Yes, every Thursday morning, at ten thirty...why do you ask?"
I can't give him an answer, as his persona would surely change if confronted by the culprit. I need the Commissioner to be himself without giving anything away. Not telling him, guarantees to me he'll be as much in the dark as he was before my call to him.
"Look, I'm going to phone you on the landline, but don't react as if we've just spoken on the mobile. Pretend you haven't heard from me since our last call. Got it? Don't ask any more questions, please. This shall all become apparent in a day or so. It is imperative this does not go any further than just the two of us. Do you understand, Commissioner?" I throw in his title just to polish his already inflated ego.
I disconnect and redial Striker's number at *Thames House.* It's answered near enough immediately.
"Clive, good of you to call." Oh, he is a smooth operator.
"Paul, how are you?" I replicate the nonsense.
"What can I do for you?" Coming straight to the point, that's a positive.
"I know who the culprit is and can prove it with a little bit of your assistance."
The line is silent, then a voice tells me he's all ears.
"I need you to bug a mobile phone for me. Is that possible?" I begin.

"Clive, we are capable of doing anything and I mean anything and in the majority of cases, don't have to ask permission. Bugging a mobile doesn't create a problem. We do it every day. Who does the mobile belong to and the number, please." His monotone voice makes the hairs on the back of my neck stand to attention. I'm glad he's on my side.
"Aah....there might be a problem with the number. I don't know it." I might have scuppered my chances.
"No problem, just a bit more work to bend someone's arm to get the number. The name will do but if it is a cheap throw away job, just tell me the building and the boys will do the rest to listen to everything coming out of the place on a mobile phone." That bloody laugh again. One day I'll understand his sense of humour.
"Is that possible? 'Big Brother'...eeeh? When can this be enforced?"
"Give me an hour, then call back to confirm. Now tell me everything."
I wish I'd made a recording of what I'm about to say, as once I've related the entire workings of the case, when needing to repeat it, it wouldn't seem to be such a drag. Like before when updating Debbie, I fill in the Director General with the entire repertoire, but leave out the culprit's identity, though he'll probably guess with the information I unloaded.
"So, the memory stick wasn't such a bad idea." His turn to speak happens twelve minutes after I began my well-rehearsed monologue.
"Yes, to some extent, but there were many other important factors." I tease him, knowing he'll take the bait.

"And pray, what would those be." He's bitten.
"For starters...Leonid Petrushev's diaries." I wait for what I know is coming.
"You have them. Oh, my God. Do you relia..."
Before he finishes the sentence, I butt in. "No, Paul, you can't see them. They are in my safe hands and not yours. I trust you, Paul, but handing you this stick of dynamite, you might be foolish enough to light the fucking fuse." It's my time to laugh. "Now, here's what I'm going to do."
I inform Striker how this drama will be played out and when he's listening to his own bugging machine and gets confirmation I am correct with my assessment, he can round up a few more suspects and give me a large slap on the back. His laugh does annoy me.
When I'm told the listeners at *GCHQ* are prepared with their bag of tricks and are waiting for me to start the ball rolling, I reconnect to Gordon's mobile.
"I'm just about to phone you on your landline, so don't question what I have to say, go along with it."
Disconnecting, I punch in Gordon's office phone.
"Hello, Commissioner Gordon speaking...who am I talking to?" He's direct, as I would expect, giving nothing away that he's just spoken to me on his *Tesco* special.
"Hello Commissioner Gordon...its Clive Grainger. Look, I hope this line is safe, because what I have to say is very important and not for the wrong ears. I have unearthed your spy. I'm coming over and will be staying in London at the Kensington Regency Hotel from Wednesday afternoon, hopefully seeing you on Thursday morning. So be ready."

"That is great news, Clive. I'll get the troops sorted to round up these bastards. Thursday morning, you say." Gordon is playing his part a little bit too enthusiastically.
"Are you sure your line is safe." I question, knowing what the answer will be.
"Yes, entirely safe. I have it checked every week."
I know you do, so does the person who's listening in on your call. That's why the bugs are removed before the check and replaced after the all clear. How bloody stupid to keep to a rigid timetable...you idiot.
"Very well, Commissioner. See you Thursday morning."
I nervously disconnect. I would look such an idiot if Debs were here, she would undoubtedly have a far fruitier vocabulary to describe my actions if she believed I was wrong with my assumptions, putting some innocent individual's liberty at stake.
This is beginning to become a habit. I call Striker.
"Phone calls made. Now it's up to you to hear the conversation that, if I'm right, is being made about now."
"Hold on Clive. I've an open line to GCHQ. Yes, you should have been a clairvoyant, they are speaking as we speak, confirming your conversation with Gordon. Sorry to have ever doubted your ability....oh yes, there was a time I thought you were a bit of a wanker, but since that time, I've reserved that accolade for our Commissioner instead." His laugh is really getting on my nerves.
"How do you want to play this?" I speak only when humility is restored...and he calls me the wanker?

"Well, the trap is sprung. So we'll wait until Wednesday, the day you're supposed to be arriving. Probably go the whole hog by having a lookalike double of yourself getting on a plane in Gibraltar... just in case they are keeping tabs on you. Then stake out the Regency with our lads so they can arrest or eliminate the boys sent to your room to permanently silence you. Whatever is their preference. The best part we'll leave to last when we confront our Irish sympathiser over at the *Yard.* Gordon isn't going to like having his thunder stolen from under his feet, but bollocks to him. Good Job, Clive. I'll be in touch. Needless to say...you won't read about this in the newspaper. Oh...and by the way, any chance of having a quick glance at Leonid's diaries."

"No Paul...I've already told you. They are locked away in a very safe place. Nobody knows where they are, except me...sorry." I lie, as they are sitting on the table, not four feet away from where I'm standing.

CHAPTER 38

1.37pm. Tuesday 25th August 2015. Paco's Chiringito, Estepona beach.

I make an effort, though it would be easier to just stay where I am on the terrace, but having invaded the fridge and swallowed the entire contents of cold booze, I give in to a nagging voice in my head choosing the pleasure of just doing nothing instead and make my way down to join Debs on Paco's beach.

I spot her before she spots me and, good girl, hasn't succumbed to going topless. I'm sure it wasn't Debs in my dream. No, positively not.

"Hi Debs." I call out before reaching her sunbed, having encountered Steven, the beach boy, on my way in to order a round of drinks. Yes, I know what her ladyship's favourite tipple is. I've bought it enough times.

"Hi Clive. How did it all go?"

Sitting up, I can't help noticing that during the short time she's been on the beach, the sun must have been stronger than I first thought. Lobster would be unfair. Let's say cooked prawn.

"All settled. The plan's in action as I speak. It's in the hands of MI5 and they could go and arrest the culprit right now. They have the evidence, but the greedy sods want the lot, the entire shooting party on who probably pulled the trigger on dear Jessica. Sorry about the metaphor, but somehow it seems apt. Striker's lot will probably use them in the future as some bargaining tool to get concessions when something ugly raises its head. You know, something *Sin Fein* might not normally agree to." I nonchalantly whisper, taking care I'm not being overheard.

Steven interrupts and places the glasses in each of our hands. Now if I thought I was impatient, Debbie's appearance resembles a red balloon just before bursting.

"Are you going to fucking-well tell me, or am I going to shove that kid's spade up your arse. Tell me who sanctioned this murder mystery, you bastard."

Those within close attendance turn and are rightly not amused with Debs' eruption and her use of the odd expletive. Only one conclusion could be taken from their obvious disapproval and that was they probably aren't Spanish. I begin to laugh, which only makes matters worse and I get a clip round the back of my head for my troubles.

Holding my hands up in mock submission, I think I've left her in suspense for too long, but to hear the culprit's name, she'd have to wait a little longer.

"I can't tell you yet…sorry Debbie…the culprits' are still at large and haven't yet been apprehended. If something should go wrong, they'd be on the loose to cause all sorts of mayhem. But believe me, they won't be on the loose for long. What I will do, though, is tell you how, with your help, we wheedled out the bastard."

I look at Debs and believe it's only right she knows how she was an integral part of this investigation. Without her, I wouldn't have got this far. I continue with as much information as I dare.

"With Striker's memory stick and Leonid's diaries, I unearthed a bloodline connecting the suspect with one Patrick O'Hare. Now, this is the person who is central to this investigation. He once owned a pub in the Falls Road area of Belfast when it was a hotbed of activity, but could never be tied down or associated with being a high roller within the *IRA*. He was on the radar for ages, so it was decided to get nearer to him by planting an undercover spy. Unfortunately, it was our Jessica who was chosen. She was a young woman then and, having seen a photo of her, she was quite a looker. But who said 'The best laid plans of mice and men'? It didn't work out. Our lovely old Jessica fell for O'Hare's charm and became pregnant with his child, even though he was married with an offspring. When news of her condition reached London, she was withdrawn for her safety...where six months later, she gave birth to a daughter, Shelly. Some ten years after that, Jessica had risen through the ranks of the department to become the Deputy Director...very high powered job and a worthwhile target for any terrorist. She deserved to get the position within the agency, she was extremely proficient in the role, but hadn't counted on getting that phone call from Margaret Thatcher one fateful night all those years ago. Reacting to the Prime Minister's order, Jessica, instigated the assassination of three high ranking *IRA* operatives in revenge for what they did at *The Grand Hotel* in Brighton. Unbeknown to Jessica, one of the three happened to be Patrick O'Hare, the father of her own child. Now, I have no evidence she knew the names of the targets at the time, believing them to have been picked at random, but I'm sure she later got to know and had to live with the fact. With the advent of '*The Good Friday*' agreement, most of the *IRA* old-school, who'd been slammed behind bars, were released, and sane peaceful reasoning resumed north and south of the Irish border. Believing it to be prudent, and with the timing right, Jessica was pensioned off, given a new identity and placed under a protection order...this is when she came to Spain believing all her troubles were behind her...with the emergence of a new splinter group of the *IRA*, old wounds opened and retribution was in their eyes." Debs remained utterly silent as I continued.

"Years before, a sleeper had been installed inside *Scotland Yard*...not for any specific purpose, but just because they had the means to do so. By some fluke, Jessica's file must have come into the possession of this person. It wouldn't have taken an Einstein, if you were the offspring of Patrick O'Hare, to work out Jessica ordered his assassination, where she now lived and what she was calling herself. With revenge as the sole reason, wheels were put in motion to get rid of her. Somehow, this person got through security checks, even though their file was scrupulously checked. They'd done an incredible job to disguise the mole's past and buried it in a maze. Being in the department and, with training, it was easy to bug Gordon's phone, and knowing the ritual of having his office swept every Thursday, all that was needed was to remove the offending little buggers and, when it was clear, replace them until the following week. Easy. Having Jessica's files to hand, the resurgent thugs of the IRA were informed about this operative from a bygone age, the very one who had acted on orders to have her father killed...and the rest, I'm afraid, is history. Simple retribution. Now let's party. I wouldn't advise going back to work just yet...or ever, if you feel like it. Why not take early retirement and stay down here. With what's coming to you, you can easily afford it. Who knows? A new life."

CHAPTER 39

8.26 am. Wednesday 25th August. The Kensington Regency Hotel. The Manager's Office.

"It's good of you to see me at such short notice and at such an early hour." Striker begins, knowing what he is about to inform the hotel manager, Perry Evans, might result in it having an adverse effect on his nervous system. Catering college and business diplomas didn't prepare a perfunctory, simple administrator, that such a thriving hotel, nestling in the heart of London, was about to be taken over by Homeland Security which, just so happens, to include members of the elite regiment, the *SAS*.

"I'm not going to pretend this is just a run-of-the-mill operation...the people we are dealing with are terrorists and murder without thinking about the consequences. So, you understand the seriousness of the situation."

Striker might have attained the top rung of his chosen profession, but he certainly didn't get there by using charisma to dilute his verbal description of what to expect in the next twenty four hours. Evans positively froze, picturing his, once tranquil, catering haven transformed into a war strewn battlefield, but his vision only worsens when Striker continues.

"It is highly likely there might be gunfire, but if there is an altercation, it'll be limited to a small area...well away

from your other guests. I have studied a plan of the layout of your hotel and have allocated a room on the third floor, half way along the corridor where our man will be booked into to alleviate this possible problem. The target will board a plane shortly and, on landing will take a taxi to arrive at your hotel at approximately three o'clock. We are in no doubt he is being tracked all the way. I want six of my operatives, kitted out in your hotel livery, three as floor waiters and the other three as reception staff. When we hear our man is ten minutes away, I need your staff to vacate the reception, leaving just one to take care of business. It is imperative the area appears to be running as normal."
It wouldn't take the finest of Scotland Yard's detectives to ascertain the effect of Striker's words on the hotel manager. Sitting bolt upright, displaying an ashen face, Evans fidgets nervously, wanting to ask questions, but is unable to voice a single word.
"It is also imperative your staff know nothing of what is going on. Explain to them it is your companies' policy to replace staff, at a moments' notice, should there be an emergency and that this is just an exercise to ascertain how smoothly it can be achieved. I'll leave the actual wording to you."
Five minutes later, in an adjoining office, Striker stands before a group of over a dozen individuals, all attired in a range of summer outfits available on any high-street, with a few braving shorts. The sole giveaway to their involvement, is that each is armed to the teeth with an assortment of lethal firearms. Remove these deadly weapons and there would be nothing in their appearance to suggest they possess a

licence to kill. If asked by an untrained eye to guess their profession, it might be easy to suggest manual workers of some kind, with the odd one or two being on the 'dole'.

Allowing the group to settle, Striker outlines the timing of the operation is imperative. As to the arrest of the fugitives, whether they surrender their arms or prove to be more troublesome, this is left open and will be decided by a split second decision by individuals within his force when the time dictates. Being a separate operation, the apprehension of a spy within *Scotland Yard* to near enough coincide with this action, isn't mentioned. But one thing is instilled into each of the operatives; at no time can the terrorists be given the opportunity to warn the 'mole' that they have walked into a trap. Should there be resistance, then the *'Primark'* brigade will alleviate the problem by doing what they do best. Getting nods from each, Striker knows his troops understand the gravity of the situation. The meeting ends.

~0~

3,07pm. Wednesday. 25th August. The Kensington Regency Hotel security room

Inside a darkened room, just after three in the afternoon, the emitting glare from eight screens illuminate three faces staring at the images being transmitted. In an age when surveillance is dominated by cameras, every entrance, from the front door to the fire exits, each corridor and underground carpark and even up on the roof, is covered by the magical eye.

What once would take a security guard an hour to patrol, just one operator now has the equipment to scan the entire hotel in seconds.

Directing operations, Striker sits in the middle, Major 'John' Thomas of the *SAS* to his left with the operator to his right - a young man in his twenties glued to the action as though he's some kid with a computer game. All twelve operatives are at their rightful position, a few behind the reception desk, others in hotel livery pretending to be waiters, whilst a number just pose as guests. All are ready.

"*Gatwick* airport taxi approaching" Striker hears through his earpiece.

There is silence. Everybody knows to keep the airways clear.

"Target approaching hotel entrance." Heartbeats quicken.

From his vantage point, Striker identifies Clive Grainger's stand-in on screen, an overnight bag at hand, greeted by the concierge before having the large glass door opened to afford easy access from the outside pavement to the comfort inside. Looking at the image, Striker smiles, the similarity between the real target and this doppelgänger is quite extraordinary. It would take a sharp pair of eyes to ascertain the difference.

They follow his progress to the reception, where he's attended to by the real receptionist. Though there is a conversation being held between the two, all is silent in the small room. Forms are signed and he picks up his room card...nothing out of the ordinary. Casually 'Grainger' approaches the elevators and waits. What can only be described as an American tourist appears from the bar and heads in the same direction.

"I've got him." A voice from G1 crackles in Striker's earpiece.

'Grainger' allows the Yank to enter first before the doors automatically begin closing. From the stairwell, suddenly a figure appears sprinting towards the ever decreasing gap. It is too late to stop him before the doors squeeze together.

"What's wrong with the camera inside the elevator...there's nothing coming on screen." Striker hears himself ask, watching illuminated red figures indicating which floor the lift is bypassing.

They stop on the third floor. From inside the small room, eyes are glued on the screens covering the corridor. From each end, operatives in all modes of dress can be seen sprinting towards the elevator, hand guns held at arms' length.

They wait in silence, each aiming their chosen weapon at the satin finished, stainless steel doors. They begin to slide open.

'Grainger' is standing at the back, still holding his cabin bag, whilst the Yank hovers over a collapsed figure, a Heckler & Koch pistol trained at his head should it move.

"One down." G6 instructs control, as he confirms what he's just said by seeing the effect of what a well-placed boot has on the corpse.

"There's bound to be more." Striker throws the line that he knows is being heard by every operative.

Whilst the euphoria of the exercise is clearly affecting Striker, Major Thomas is calmly directing operations,

knowing exactly the quality of the personnel under his command.
"G2...one apprehended in the underground carpark."
"G9...one down in the north stairwell. Threat neutralised."
Moments later, a further voice breaks the airways. "G7...one apprehended, the driver, parked in Addison Road."
Not more than two minutes later, Striker hears the words confirming the mission's success. "Hotel...all clear."
"Now." Striker rubs his hands in anticipation of what will happen next, "Let's go and get the real culprit."
Within minutes, three unmarked Ford Transits pull-up, in line, adjacent to one of the hotel's fire exits in Kingham Close. With military precision, two filled body bags are dispensed in the front vehicle, whilst each prisoner, their faces shielded by black bags covering their heads, their hands shackled behind their backs, are dumped unceremoniously into separate wagons. Each is accompanied by three operatives. Within ten minutes, there isn't a trace of what had just happened. The hotel is back into the routine of what it does best...entertaining guests.
"Right Major." Striker turns to the brains behind the operation. "If you and a couple of your associates would accompany me to *Scotland Yard,* we have some unfinished business to take care of."

~0~

Twenty minutes after leaving the Kensington Regency, two unmarked, black Jaguar saloons park directly outside the front doors of *Scotland Yard*, only for an unsuspecting traffic warden, a woman in her fifties, to receive the full force of what she can do with her ticket. Delivered in a Scottish accent by a sinewy, forty-odd year old individual resembling a Glasgow Celtic supporter, whose official uniform once upon-a-time displayed three stripes before joining the elite regiment, she took heed and did the wisest thing by pretending she never noticed the illegally parked vehicle. Forgetting the dire situation which he'd soon encounter, he smiles before following the others, dressed in Bermuda shorts complimenting a fake 'Hard Rock Cafe' T-shirt.

Debbie's un-favourite security doorman, Alan, doesn't stand a chance to stop the sudden intrusion into his domain. His complaining falls on deaf ears, when an operative is stationed at his post to stop his probable next movement...the pressing of the panic button.

In silence, four individuals with the same intent, travel up to the top floor, three of them armed. Allowing the door to slide fully open, they wait for a few seconds, but all appears to be as it should be...tranquil, without a hint of what is about to happen. Their swift action at the *Regency* went to plan, timed to perfection to thwart word filtering through to Commissioner Jack Gordon's office. The Director General of *MI5* is beginning to enjoy this escapade which has turned a very ordinary day into a one he will relish and remember.

Whilst foot soldiers in offices below are out putting their life on the line to solve some of the most heinous crimes, the plush, top-floor corridor is deserted, but for the soft shuffle of four sets of footsteps cushioned by deep carpet. Positioned each side of a door advertising the occupant's rank, the underdressed sergeant and fellow corporal take their place, ready to be first to take the target by complete surprise. Weapons are drawn and are coordinated by the Major's silent finger movement counting down three seconds before they burst in.

No need to break the door down, just a turning of a handle releases the two armed professionals, their pistols raised in readiness for what they might encounter on the other side. Screamed orders mortify Lorraine as though she has turned into a pillar of marble. Whilst muzzles are trained on the Commissioner's secretary, the Major, followed by Striker, bypass the traumatised secretary and burst into Gordon's office.

Caught in mid-rise from behind his desk, the disbelieving look on his face is one Striker will cherish.

"What the fuck is going on?" Gordon hollers, finally retrieving his senses.

"Calm down Commissioner." Smiling slightly but in a calm, condescending voice, which only aggravates Gordon's hatred of the man further, Striker indicates for him to sit down.

"Commissioner Gordon." Striker begins, completely at ease compared to his adversary standing bolt upright on the other side of his desk, seemingly unable to bend his knees to sit. "We have come to arrest the 'mole' who has been working here for years under your very nose and you had no idea who it was. Major Thomas, will you do the honours and arrest the suspect."

Savouring the moment, Striker glances over his shoulder to his associate before refocusing his fixed smirk on Gordon, daring him to wipe it off his face. If there weren't any witnesses, he might have got his wish.

Dressed, not as casually as the others, but at least covering his legs with jeans, the Major turns and retraces his route back to the outside office. If there is such a thing as a thunderous silence, then this effect shrouds Gordon's office. Whilst Striker and Gordon stare at each other, they hear Thomas punctuate the silence with words every criminal dreads when the law finally catches up with them.

"Lorraine Brown nee O'Hare....you are under arrest for the murder of Jessica McGill, contrary to common law and further, under suspicion of a breach of the Official Secrets Act. You have the right to remain silent..."

Whilst the indictment and caution hangs heavy in the air, Lorraine's face shows nothing as her hands are being cuffed behind her back.

"There you go Commissioner. You can get back to work now, safe in the knowledge your domain is clear from prying ears." Striker can't help but sink the dagger in even deeper, smirking at Gordon's anger, but also loving his embarrassment.

"One day, Striker..." Gordon allows the sentence to remain unfinished, certain that Striker understands its meaning.

"I look forward to it." Striker hurls his reaction to the threat over his shoulder, as the heavily restrained Lorraine is marched out.

CHAPTER 40

9.24am. 20th September. Clive Grainger's Terrace, Estepona.

It's been over a month since I heard of the arrests back in the UK and though two were dealt with in a fashion where they required the assistance from an undertaker, my conscience is clear and I'm pleased I was instrumental in nailing the killers of our Jessica. Yes, she put herself in danger, but that was the nature of her job, doing it in a fashion that few outside her 'circle' would have the stomach or guts to see through, the ordering of three IRA terrorists deaths as a fine example.

No, I miss Jessica, but she leaves fond memories.

My dear old friend is still climbing in the morning sky, but has lost its sting, radiating a temperature much more forgiving than the past couple of months. My black robe is showing even worse signs of wear, but thankfully it's not now having to soak up sweat. And to accompany me on this most peaceful of mornings, I have my cigarettes, my favourite mug containing coffee and mobile, just in case someone out there remembers me.

Debbie flew back and continues her daily trips in a 'cattle-wagon' up to the smoke, being treated like a hero on her first day back. The job vacancy left behind by Lorraine...well, there was never any doubt who would fill it...yes, Gordon couldn't really chose anyone but our Debbie. With a large pay-rise and inflated holiday benefits, I'll probably see her happy little face down here before too long, almost a certainty, should Gordon lose his tolerance for colourful vernacular.

Lorraine remains under lock and key, as do her associates and, as Striker predicted, nothing reached the prying ears or eyes of the media.

Yes, I'm nicely relaxed and as some of my friends have pointed out, I appear much happier with the world. I don't know why, but I brought out all three of Leonid's diaries, which are now sitting on the terrace table. I knew at some time I'd get myself buried into their contents and today appears to be a good time to start. For no particular reason, I choose the last volume, the one dating from 1990 until the day Leonid retired. What puzzles me, is the reason why Leonid should bestow this treasure upon me, as they must contain data which, at the time of writing, must have been top-secret as to the workings of Soviet Russia. Okay, there can't be any repercussions for Leonid...he's dead, but was there an ulterior motive for them to fall into my hands. Similar to Lorraine, was Leonid nudging me in a particular direction? Was he playing games from the grave? Is there something in one of these volumes he couldn't tell me about, something he knew I should know, but couldn't divulge for fear of being considered an informer...he knew me well and knew one day the temptation to go through them would finally take over. Well Leonid, you've got your wish.

Something really strange happened two weeks ago and the way I'm thinking now, might just be connected to the incident. Living six floors up, throughout the summer, unless it's raining and that hasn't happened in months, I leave my terrace doors open. I'm on nodding terms with both my neighbours and can't see either of them scaling from their terrace onto mine, as they're both in their seventies, but that is what I believe happened. Someone entered my flat from the terrace, but didn't take anything.

How did I know...well, for one, you might already have read that I have a copper's nose. That morning, I'd just showered and as usual in the summer, to alleviate the risk of covering the bathroom floor with talcum powder, I retreated to the terrace, knowing if the wind doesn't blow it away, rain, when it eventually falls, will. It's a trick I learnt from an old fisherman, that a few shakes under the armpits helps to deaden sweat, but invariably, I sometimes leave a trail.

When I returned that evening, I poured a beer, stripped off my T-shirt and ventured out into the open, only to be stopped in my tracks by a footprint of a trainer, hardly visible, but definitely imprinted in the few speckles of talc. It wasn't mine as I don't wear that type of footwear and I'm usually barefoot when traipsing around my apartment. I immediately scoured the apartment for anything missing, but everything was in place, but I could tell, someone had been mooching around my wardrobe. I thought whoever it was might have been disturbed and did a quick departure as nothing, that I could ascertain, was missing. I quickly forgot about the incident, but now,

I'm wondering if what I have on my lap is what they were after.
But it's all coming back to me. That particular day, I put the volumes in the boot of my car, intending to go to the beach and do some reading. Was that what they were after?
Now, with this little episode on my mind, I can't wait to get started. Even more so now, believing the incident could quite well have been connected to these volumes.

CHAPTER 41

10.14am. 20th September. Clive's Grainger's Terrace. Estepona.

I'm in for the long haul, so have plenty of ammunition readily at hand, cigarettes and beer. I open the embossed cover and immediately recognise Leonid's writing. For a Russian, his understanding of the English language is impeccable, and to make it visibly impressive, he used pen and ink...no second rate *Biro* for our Leonid.

I start to read, noting the dates above each entry. 1991 Boris Yeltsin is elected as President, yep...I remember, but Leonid's scurrilous remarks concerning their new leader might have been frowned upon from certain sectors of the Russian embassy. The dissolution of the Soviet Union after a military coup might interest historians the way Leonid describes it, but I thumb past most of it. He goes on to chastise the government for allowing his beloved country to sink into depression, where up to fifty per-cent of the population are heading into poverty, with even more dying through alcohol related deaths. All very interesting, but though Yeltsin is depicted as an un-principled oaf for his involvement and willingness to go to 'war' with Chechnya, his own people, it's not what I'm after.

I need a break and stop off at the toilet before grabbing a beer. I settle down again and begin from where I left off. 1996 and a surprise. There is my name, the senior officer in charge of a Russian delegation visiting London to compare policing methods. I smile and remember it well. The first time I met Leonid. I skip over a few insignificant things which happen in the first few months of that year, then turn a page to be reminded of the British police's turn to visit Moscow. How diligent was Leonid, even to be bothered with such nonsense, but I glance down the list of twelve officers who took part.

S.H.I.T...the fourth name down is Paul Striker.

Why did I assume he came from an army background, it must have been something someone said, and I just didn't question it. Obviously, he must have been a copper, but not in the Metropolitan Police...must have come from up north or somewhere insignificant. I read on. On the third day of their visit, they are taken to a large building in the heart of Moscow and are greeted by no other than Vladimir Putin and if my eyes aren't playing tricks, before he became President, it appears he was a big noise within the foreign intelligence service...in other words, a spy. Oh Leonid, you naughty boy. You knew I would eventually find it. What is more incriminating, Striker appears to have been singled out for a more in-depth 'tour', and if I can read between the lines of what Leonid means without spelling it out, he was recruited there and then.

I have my reason for knowing where my intruder came from and why he visited. Very few knew of my acquisition of Leonid's diaries; Debbie, probably

Bronzey, Gordon and Striker, and I never suspected or smelt a rat when the last mentioned kept pestering me for a look at the diaries.
Oh, this is going to rock the very foundations of British Government, let alone the stability of our own secret service, as well as MI6. What do I do? Well, to start the ball rolling, knowing how much Commissioner Gordon can't stand the man, I believe a phone call to his office is where I'll begin. Knowing it's not bugged this time, I'll just sit back and from a safe distance, sitting behind *Ray Bans* in the sun, watch the fun begin as everything unravels and the downfall of a very arrogant, civil servant starts to materialise. I'll drink to that.
Thanks Leonid.

Other books by David Spear and published by Old Treacle Press

Salvation

A toxic friendship, murderous revenge, the horror of the battlefield; Hobbs and Church may change the course of history but will their friendship survive the ultimate betrayal.

1915. Bewildered and proud, Matt Hobbs, watched as his two brothers' marched away, headed for the front lines. Three years later, his brothers lying buried in an unmarked grave on the Somme, Hobbs emerges from army training a cool, precise sniper. He is ready to kill, ready for revenge.

A strange, misfit major, begins to exert control and friendship mutates into a force for evil.

David Spear has produced a thrilling, detailed novel exposing the underlying malevolence of some of the men who went to war. This page turner takes the reader from battlefield to racecourse then back to the front lines, peering through the curtains of the racing elite, exposing prejudice, snobbery, and the forces of good and evil. Damaged souls, betrayal and malice ooze through this novel.